WATER OVER STONES

WATER OVER STONES

A Novel

BERNARDO ATXAGA

Translated from the Spanish by
Margaret Jull Costa and Thomas Bunstead

Graywolf Press

This publication is made possible, in part, by the voters of Minnesota through a
Minnesota State Arts Board Operating Support grant, thanks to a legislative appro-
priation from the arts and cultural heritage fund. Significant support has also been
provided by the McKnight Foundation, the Lannan Foundation, the Amazon
Literary Partnership, and other generous contributions from foundations, cor-
porations, and individuals. To these organizations and individuals we offer our
heartfelt thanks.

AC/E
ACCIÓN CULTURAL
ESPAÑOLA

This book was supported by a grant from
Acción Cultural Española (AC/E).

Published by Graywolf Press
212 Third Avenue North, Suite 485
Minneapolis, MN 55401

www.graywolfpress.org

Published in the United States of America

ISBN 978-1-64445-095-6 (paperback)
ISBN 978-1-64445-183-0 (ebook)

2 4 6 8 9 7 5 3 1
First Graywolf Printing, 2022

Library of Congress Control Number: 2021945933

Cover design: Kyle G. Hunter

Cover art: clu / DigitalVision Vectors / Getty images (boars); Daniele D'onofrio /
EyeEm / Getty images (hand)

Il était un petit navire . . .
(Once there was a little boat . . .)

1972

1

Elías was fourteen when he arrived in Ugarte one afternoon in late summer. He was going to spend some time living with his uncle, the owner of a bakery that supplied bread to the surrounding towns and villages. The next day, August 27, a Sunday, he found a block of wood in the workshop opposite the house and set about making a boat with his Swiss Army knife.

"You'll find it easier with these, Elías," said his uncle, placing a saw, hammer and chisel on the workbench that occupied the centre of the workshop.

The boy nodded his thanks and got straight to work. He spent all morning and afternoon shaping and hollowing out the wood, not once going up to the bakery which stood barely a hundred metres away along the hill track.

On the Monday morning, at breakfast, his uncle said casually:

"Come up and see how we make the bread, Elías. Come up, and you can help with putting the bread in the baskets when it's fresh out of the oven or with loading the baskets into the Chevrolet. Everyone who works for us is from around here, they're all good people, especially one guy who I know you're really going to like: Donato. Know what we call Donato?"

He waited, but the boy showed no intention of answering.

"The Gitane Blonde we call him, like the cigarettes, or Blondie for short. He's great fun, plus he plays the accordion."

At this, the boy smiled.

Come supper that same day, August 28, his uncle again tried to get the boy to speak:

"You remember *my* name, don't you?" Adding a little too light-heartedly: "Come on, what's my name?"

The boy should have answered "Miguel", but once again he only nodded. After supper, his uncle insisted he go along to the bakery.

"I hardly notice the smell of the bread now, but for you, it'll be your first time – you're going to love it. Plus, it's summer: it's so warm, you can go for a dip in the canal. Trust me, that cool water, you can't beat it."

Again, there was nothing but a nod of the head from the boy, and as soon as he could, he went back out to the workshop to continue making his toy boat. The bulb over the workbench was bright enough for him to work there at night. The only problem were the moths and nocturnal insects, which came swirling up around him like flurries of mud-flecked snow.

It had been a week – first, at home with his mother, and now in his uncle's house – since Elías had uttered a word. A little more than a week, in fact, given that he had stopped speaking while away in the south of France on an intensive language course, at a college called Beau-Frêne in the city of Pau. It was there that the miracle had occurred, the opposite miracle to that attributed to *Notre-Dame de l'Immaculée-Conception* in Lourdes, the college's patron saint: the student, who had arrived talking quite normally, had lost the power of speech.

After three days in Ugarte the boat was finished, and he carved an "E" for Elías on one side with his Swiss Army knife. However, when he tried to remove a slightly raised knot at the back with gouge and hammer, the whole thing cracked. Miguel saw this on his way back for lunch at midday when he called in at the workshop with one of the men from the bakery.

"You should have used a harder kind of wood, not cherry wood," he told the boy. "Try some ash. You'll find a whole load of felled ash further up the canal. Donato isn't in today, it's his day off, but go with him tomorrow and he'll help you pick out a better piece."

"I can show him where if you like," said the employee standing beside Elías' uncle. His blue denim shirt was covered in flour.

"No," said Miguel. "Youngsters with youngsters. Donato's a good kid, he should go with him."

"What do you think of that?" The man gave an exaggerated frown. "I'm only fifty-five, and yet everyone at the bakery calls me Greybeard. Donato gets called Blondie and I get called Greybeard."

Elías smiled.

"A blonde gypsy and an OAP; you see the kind of people who work for me?"

It was no use. The boy was not going to talk.

"Joking aside, Donato will show you where the ash has been stacked. As well as the best places for swimming in the canal," Miguel said, before turning and heading off to the kitchen on the ground floor of the house, a few steps away from the workshop.

Ignoring his uncle's advice, Elías went to the canal that same day for some new wood, dragging an ash branch back down the path on his own. Miguel's hopes were therefore frustrated: he thought Donato's company was sure to induce his nephew to speak, even if only a word, and that many more would then follow, with, ultimately, a return to normality. Elías was back in the workshop at nightfall, hollowing out the new block of wood on the workbench, apparently quite content, occasionally whistling the tune to a French nursery rhyme: "*Il était un petit navire qui n'avait ja- ja- jamais navigué. Ohé! Ohé!*" As he whistled, it seemed as though the moths and insects swarming around the lightbulb were moving in time to the tune.

Elías' mother rang her brother Miguel every day to ask after the boy, and August 29 was no different. He tried to sound upbeat:

"He seems fine, really into making that little boat of his. He tried cherry wood to begin with, but it cracked, which was a shame because he'd already carved his initial on one side with his knife. Now he's trying with a bit of ash, and that's going much better."

This, however, was not what his sister wanted to know. Miguel could sense, at the other end of the line, that she was waiting. In the end he had to tell her the truth:

9

"Still not a word. But I'm sure he'll start talking as soon as he settles in."

It was better, he thought, not to go into detail, and he did not mention that the boy avoided having lunch with him and the bakery staff, or the fact that he even failed to acknowledge Marta, the kind, friendly woman who cooked for them all.

He could sense his sister holding back her tears.

"It must be a strain for you, Miguel, I'm sorry. If Elías goes on like this, I'll close the restaurant and take him somewhere, wherever he needs to go."

His sister was a widow. She had a restaurant on the coast, and her takings during the summer season sometimes saw her through the whole rest of the year.

"Don't even think about it. Your place is at the restaurant. There's lots of us here, and he'll end up talking to one or other of us, you'll see."

Rather than being a strain, Elías' presence simply made Miguel uncomfortable at times, especially when they sat facing one another at supper. That day, after speaking with his sister on the telephone, Miguel made an exception and took two trays into the room beside the kitchen, one with leftovers from lunch for himself and the other with olives, ham, cheese and pâté for his nephew. He turned on the television, and they watched the roundup of the day's action at the Munich Olympics. The star that night was a Japanese gymnast called Sawao Kato.

"He's a kool kat, don't you think?" joked Miguel during the parallel bars.

When Kato concluded his routine, landing back on the ground, Elías gave a thumbs-up and applauded.

While preparing the meal for the bakery staff, Marta stepped out of the kitchen to check if the boy was still in the workshop with his wood and his tools. As she did so various thoughts came into her head, memories of other strange people she had known in her life, like Antonio, the engineer at the mine where her husband had worked, and whom, because he was a Frenchman, everyone called Antuán and who never went anywhere without his dogs, apparently the most important thing in his life; or like that girl she had been at school with who spent every second of every day laughing, often not just laughing but roaring with laughter, almost to the point where she would be gasping for air; or like Lucía, her one-time best friend, who had only ever been attracted to bad boys. She wondered whether Miguel's nephew would be similar; whether it was normal to spend the entire day making that boat, for goodness' sake, his silence broken only by the occasional bit of whistling, the same song over and over, refusing to go anywhere near anyone or say a word, not to Miguel, not to her, not to any of the staff. And he had no interest in going up to the bakery, even though it was right there on the doorstep, and that was strange too, because boys usually loved nosing around in all the bags of flour and the bread baskets, and that, of course, went for her twins as well, who never needed any excuse to stop by.

Elías had been at his uncle's for four days when Marta went to the workshop with a bowl of soup for him, and to introduce herself properly:

"I'm Marta, and I'm a very important person in this house because I do all the cooking. Now, what's your name? Your uncle told me, but I've forgotten."

She was doing this at Miguel's bidding: he had asked her to talk to him like that and ask the boy straight out what his name was.

The boy just pointed to the "E" he had carved on the side of the broken boat.

A couple of hours later, with the thermometer showing 24°C, Marta went over to the workshop again, this time with a glass of lemonade.

"So," she said, "aren't you going to tell me your name? If you don't, I won't know what to call you."

The boy drained the glass, then bent over the workbench again to carry on with his task.

11

Marta went back to the kitchen feeling worried, and she struggled to concentrate as she prepared the staff meal of hake in cream sauce, potatoes and peas. She thought about her boys, the twins Martín and Luis, and she simply could not understand Elías' behaviour, for the twins – who at twelve and a half were a little younger than Elías – were both such chatterboxes, especially Luis. She did not know whether or not Elías had been taken to see a doctor. Given a comment Miguel had once made, she thought perhaps he had, but it seemed to have done no good. No illness or injury was preventing the boy from talking.

The more she turned the matter over in her mind, the more unsettling it became. She knew about the boy's father dying, and that his mother ran the family business single-handed, a restaurant that left her no time for anything else, including paying proper attention to her son. Marta tried to put herself in the woman's shoes, asking herself how she would react if one of her boys suddenly stopped talking.

At home that night, as she heated up the dinner for her husband and the twins – the hake, potatoes and peas she had brought back from the bakery – she continued to brood over it but said nothing until the twins had gone out to play in the square and she and her husband were seated in the wicker easy chairs on the terrace. There before her, in all its vastness, was the night sky, the half-moon in one corner and the stars way above; all around, the lights from the kitchens and living rooms in the village shone like yellow and blue rectangles in the darkness.

"It's quite a thing, isn't it, Julián? To stop talking so suddenly, just like that. And he's such a good-looking boy, too."

Her husband nodded as he lit a cigar. On summer nights when they went out on the terrace, he always smoked a Monterrey.

There was just a breath of wind, a light breeze that carried the village's night sounds, all of them faint apart from the shrieking of the children playing in the square. It was a night for talking, but Marta was tired. She always was after six hours spent cooking for the bakery staff, then tidying everything away ready for the next day, working nonstop from ten until four, and the tension she felt at the presence of Miguel's nephew only added to that tiredness. It was so awkward, having someone right there in the workshop, a stone's throw from the kitchen, someone who could talk but who refused to.

Gradually, as it grew later, the things Marta was saying to her husband – "It seems they get a lot of foreigners at his mother's restaurant, that's why he was away studying French", "apparently he *did* go to Lourdes, but that was on a college excursion before he stopped speaking" – began to falter, to come apart, until she could only enunciate single, separate words: "France", "danger", "illness", "obsession", "not normal" . . . And she had the impression not so much of speaking these words as of having them sail out of her mouth and away into the vastness of the night – what a wondrous thing she found that vastness to be, the way it dropped its great calm upon the world, truly wondrous, and how *necessary* that calm was, that peace, because there were so many problems in the world, and you were unlikely ever to go to bed without something on your mind, without some conundrum, some painful memory, without suffering of one sort or another.

"It's quite a thing, isn't it, Julián?" she said again. "Losing the ability to talk, just like that, all of a sudden . . ." And again her words leaped away into the vast and peaceful night, accompanied by the smoke from her husband's cigar.

She, however, did not feel at peace. She felt at peace when setting the trays of food neatly in the middle of the table, or crying over some sad event, or, more than anything, when something that had been puzzling her finally became clear; whereas, if the food trays were not neatly lined up on the table, if the tears failed to come or the explanation to the problem remained out of reach, worry would trickle down into the farthest reaches of her soul. Which was what was happening now. She had not breathed easy since the boy had arrived at Miguel's.

"It'll work itself out, woman," said her husband.

Julián enjoyed talking too, but while he took his time over his cigar, concentrating solely on the ashtray and on stopping the ash from blowing into his eyes, he preferred to let Marta talk.

From the terrace they could still hear the shouting of the children in the square, not dissimilar to the cries of the swifts a few hours earlier as they wove through the air above the village at sunset. This was summer: children out in the open air, swifts hunting for mosquitos, the serene murmur of the men outside the bars, and the southerly wind, the stars, the half-moon. All of this was summer, and life seemed easier, less fraught with danger, as though the year had come into equilibrium and a thin piece of cloth rested over the village like the blanket with which a mother covers her baby, protecting all the people and all the lives gathered there. Luis, Martín and the rest of the children were off playing together, peaceful and happy in the square; the man next to her with his cigar was peaceful and happy too; but Marta was on the outside, at the mercy of the elements, unprotected. Elías' arrival had reminded her that the most unexpected things, the strangest things, could become reality, and made her think that Martín and Luis could suffer the very same fate as Elías, or indeed any other misfortune, Luis in particular, who was the wilder of the pair.

"Miguel is really into his hunting," said her husband, stubbing the cigar out in the ashtray and getting up. He wanted to go inside and watch television.

She took no notice of the comment. Another worry had just assailed her: she had told the twins about Elías and they, Luis especially, had been desperate to go and meet him. "You know how much we like Miguel's bakery. We'll go tomorrow and help him with his boat." It was too late now to make them change tack, and as for how Elías would react, she dreaded to think of it. His mutism did not appear to be contagious, unlike meningitis or chicken pox. It was silly to think that. But it would have been better not to have said anything to the boys and let them go on playing in the square as usual, with their shouting and their whooping, just as they were tonight.

"What do you mean, Miguel's really into his hunting?" she said. "What's that got to do with anything? It's Greybeard and Eliseo who are the hunters, not so much Miguel."

Eliseo was the third employee at the bakery, after the Gitane Blonde and Greybeard. He delivered the bread in the Chevrolet truck.

"If they go out in the hills and let the boy have a go with the shotgun, maybe that'll have an effect on him and get him talking again."

Julián was standing in the kitchen doorway, ready to go inside. Marta shook her head.

"What nonsense."

The thermometer, hanging from a hook on the terrace wall, stood at 22°C. Not so terribly hot, but sweat beaded her brow nonetheless.

"I wouldn't let some child with mental issues get his hands on a shotgun!"

She regretted saying this as soon as the words were out of her mouth. She needed to get a hold of herself, watch what she said. Elías had stopped speaking, but other than that he was a normal child, albeit more serious than any of the other children in the village.

"It reminds me of a delivery guy who worked at the company," said Julián. "He never used to talk. But then one day he was in a car accident and got the fright of his life. And after that, what do you know, the guy starts talking nonstop. Constantly telling jokes. Couldn't get him to shut up."

The voices from the square had grown quieter now. People were starting to turn out their lights. The night was very silent. Again, Marta shook her head.

"I really don't know what you mean."

"Nothing, it doesn't matter."

Julián waved his hand and made as if to go inside. He wanted to watch the Munich Olympics roundup.

"Aren't you coming? There's a great gymnast from Japan, Sawao Kato he's called. You'll like him."

Marta did not want to go inside.

Luis and Martín went to Miguel's the next morning. Looking out at them from the kitchen, Marta felt relieved. From the look of things inside the workshop, the twins and Elías were getting on fine. She watched Elías nodding or shaking his head, showing them the boat he was making from the piece of ash wood, and she saw the twins going back and forth, or else bent over the workbench with the gouge or some other tool in their hand; everything seemed to be going well.

Before it got to midday, she saw her boys leave the workshop and head for the bakery.

"Where are you off to?" she called from the kitchen window.

"To get some more wood," Luis and Martín responded in unison, like they were one single person. "We want to make boats too."

She was used to this, and normally she would not have batted an eyelid at the twins doing everything the same, giving the same answer with the very same words. But it affected her now in a particular way, awakening an old anxiety – one that when the twins were three or four had prompted her to seek medical advice. "Marta," the paediatrician had said, "twins aren't like other children." Then, half in jest: "You might as well get used to it." Time had shown that there was nothing out of the ordinary or bad about the boys' behaviour, but the arrival of Elías had stirred up the sediment of concern and anxiety that was always there, somewhere deep inside her.

She shook her head and began preparing lunch. To start, potato salad with hardboiled egg and generous amounts of lettuce, the way Miguel liked it. And for the main course, tuna with sautéed onions. But the twins were not great fish eaters, and perhaps

16

Elías was the same. She would grill them a pork fillet with some chips on the side.

When the men from the bakery arrived for lunch, Miguel put a hand on her shoulder and thanked her for bringing the twins.

"It'll do my nephew the world of good, them being around. They're clearly having a great time together."

Marta showed him the dish with the potato salad – "With hardboiled egg and lots of lettuce," she said, "the way you like it" – and put it on the table in front of Donato.

"Donato, you're still my assistant, right? You serve the salad while I go and get the cider."

In summer, Marta left the drinks to cool in the river near the house; it branched off from the canal there before running down to the village.

"I need to marry a cook like you, Marta," said Greybeard when he tried the salad.

Donato, without looking up from his food, shot back:

"Now's your chance, Marta! Quick, leave your husband, here's the man for you. A once in a lifetime opportunity."

"I'm past anybody loving me," said Greybeard. "But things are hardly looking much better for you, Donato. Twenty-three years young, and have we once seen you with a lady friend?"

Donato, the Gitane Blonde, spent his days off playing the accordion in the other nearby villages, where he was a popular figure. On Sundays and public holidays, the girls from the village would go out walking and stop by the bakery for brioche buns, and they would blush whenever he made a joke. He was good-looking, with blue eyes and blond, curly hair. But Greybeard had a point. Donato had never been seen with a girl.

The other member of staff at the table, Eliseo, gave a laugh, as did Miguel. Greybeard went on:

"Whereas, unless I'm much mistaken, Eliseo here has got something going on. A year ago, he'd drive off in the Chevrolet and need four hours, four and a half max, to do the deliveries. Nowadays it's five hours, or five and a half, sometimes six. Just you wait and see, soon enough I'm going to be down one hunting buddy."

Eliseo was a man of few words and responded as laconically as ever:

"A year ago I had five hundred deliveries to do. Now it's almost a thousand. Women have nothing to do with it."

Their working day started very early, before sunrise, and sitting down to have lunch together was always a moment to relax. They were all fit and strong, and with the temperature outside reaching 24°C or 25°C, it was a pleasure to sit in the shade of the kitchen and enjoy the food and the cool cider.

The banter continued unabated as they started in on the main course of tuna, especially after the second bottle of cider had been opened, and Marta was aware how happy she felt in this company, almost as happy as she was at home. Perhaps at home the happiness was greater, because being there meant being with the twins and they were the most important thing in the world to her, but there was no getting around it: working at Miguel's was a significant factor in her happiness, especially on days like this.

She went into the pantry at the rear of the kitchen to get the dessert: chocolate and vanilla ice cream. Suddenly, as though the white light inside the fridge had dispelled any doubts, she confessed to herself: "Yes, I am happier here than at home." But she immediately banished the thought and, returning to the kitchen, put the ice cream down in front of Eliseo.

"You serve, will you?"

"Marta," said Donato, "wasn't I supposed to be your assistant?"

"That's right, which is why you're getting the bowls and spoons. I'm going to finish the boys' lunch now."

Marta had put the chips in the oven so they would be nice and crisp, and just as she sprinkled the salt on them and put the pork fillets in the griddle pan, the twins appeared, asking if lunch was ready. Beyond them, standing in the sun beside the workshop, Elías was waiting, saw in hand, apparently not wanting to take a break. Marta said:

18

"These twins of mine can smell chips a hundred metres away."

Miguel went through to the back and brought out a couple of lunch boxes.

"Why don't you take your lunch down to the canal?" he said, speaking loudly enough for Elías to hear. "It's cooler there."

The twins simultaneously turned to look in the direction of the workshop. Elías nodded.

After eating together, everyone from the bakery usually went home and Miguel went upstairs to rest. But that day, after the boys set off for the canal, nobody got up from the table. Greybeard wanted to know what was going on, why Elías had come back from France early, and why he wouldn't speak, whether it was some illness.

"Come and sit with us, Marta," said Miguel.

"I'll just do the coffee," she said.

Donato got up.

"No," he said. "Your assistant, the Gitane Blonde, can do the coffee."

"Fine by me."

She took off the hairnet she wore for cooking and shook out her shoulder-length hair. "You look like a young girl with your hair like that, Marta," said Donato, taking his seat again after putting the coffee pot down on the table.

Miguel smiled at this and, folding his arms, began explaining the situation. There was nothing wrong with his nephew's vocal cords, or with his head, though he needed to have some more tests to examine the innermost part of his brain. The doctors had tried to get him to tell them if something had happened at Beau-Frêne, the college in France, and had asked his mother for the version of events given by the management there, but all to no avail.

"They said Elías fell out with one of the teachers and threw a stone at him, and that was the reason he was sent home early."

"I doubt you can learn much French if you're mute!" said Greybeard. "But what made him stop speaking? That's what we need to find out. Everything else, stones being thrown or not, is irrelevant."

They all agreed.

"It's the teachers you need to speak to," said Donato, "they must have an idea. Some teachers, and I don't say all of them, but some are real pigs, and they can do a lot of damage. Right here in the village there was one, a real, real pig, I don't know if you remember, we used to call him The Teeth. He very nearly stopped me getting my school certificate. Throwing stones at a teacher? I can promise you there were plenty of kids who would have happily shot The Teeth."

"We'll go and find him if you like," said Greybeard. "You can use my shotgun. First we need to know if you've got the balls."

Donato lit a cigarette and blew the smoke at Greybeard.

"Oh, I've got the balls, there's none bigger."

Everyone laughed. Then Miguel said to Marta:

"He *looks* like an angel, with that nice curly hair of his, but don't be fooled."

On September 1 the twins went up to Miguel's very early, even before Marta, and as soon as they got there, along with Elías, they began working on the pieces of ash in the workshop. The piece Luis had chosen was wide and short; Martín's longer and not so green. When Marta arrived she found them immersed in their work, each with his own gouge, saw and hammer.

"Did you bring those from home?" she asked, pointing to the tools.

"Miguel let us borrow them," said the twins.

Elías gave a confirmatory nod.

"I can't wait to see your boats when they're finished," said Marta. "They're going to be great."

Luis was throwing himself into the task, taking out great chunks with a large gouge; Martín was being more cautious, working away with a small gouge; Elías was using a saw. His piece of wood, at almost a metre long, was the largest. He had already hollowed it out and was working on evening up the sides.

All the bakery staff took a break at eleven, and it was Donato's job to collect the basket of food Marta usually made up for their mid-morning snack. That day, as he was about to enter Miguel's house, he heard someone whistling in the workshop. He went inside and asked:

"Who's that whistling?"

"Elías!" said the twins.

Donato crouched down and brought his ear level with the boy's mouth.

"Now then, what was that song? I don't know it. And if the Gitane Blonde doesn't know a song, that means it isn't from around here."

Elías bowed his head.

"Don't worry, no problem," said Donato.

He went over to Luis, took his gouge and hammer and knocked three small shavings from the piece he was working on.

"The trick is to go really easy with the hammer, and just nudge the gouge along. Not one big whack. You need to be strong for fighting, but not when you're doing this. Take it from me."

He was sweating, and his blond curls stuck to his forehead. He turned to Elías again:

"You did good throwing a stone at that teacher. I'd have done the same."

He went over to him and kissed him on the cheek.

Marta leaned her head out of the kitchen window.

"You're going to be late, assistant. Get this basket up to them before the cider starts getting warm."

At midday it was Miguel who dropped by the workshop. The boys were still hard at work. Elías was making a rowboat, wide at the back and tapering to a point at the front. Martín's was long and narrow like a canoe. Luis' was more like a barge.

"I can give you some paint if you like," he said. "The boats won't last a second if you don't paint them."

"Great!" exclaimed the twins.

Miguel beckoned to them to follow him and led them over to the garage. There were five tins of paint on a shelf, each a different colour: the first one was white; the second, red; the third, green; the fourth, black; the fifth, yellow.

"Which one do you want, Elías? What colour are you going to paint your boat?"

The boy pointed to the third tin along, the green one.

"Nice," said Miguel. "Nicer than black, that's for sure."

The twins, both at once, pointed to the red tin.

"If Luis wants that one, I'll have the white," said Martín.

Miguel rummaged in a cardboard box and came up with three paintbrushes, one for each of the boys. He then showed them a plastic bottle.

"Pay attention. This is turps."

He took another bottle down from the shelf. It had no cap and was empty.

"Put a little turps in this bottle, and when you're done, use it to clean the brushes. Not water."

The three boys took the tins of paint and the brushes. Elías took the turpentine as well, and Martín the empty bottle.

Back in the workshop, they moved the tools to one side and made a start on painting the boats. The green tin stood beside Elías' rowboat, the white by Martín's canoe, the red by Luis' little barge. They put the turpentine and the empty bottle down in one corner.

Marta appeared, casting an eye over proceedings.

"Good, you've put the turps on the floor. Be careful with that stuff."

"We know!" said the twins.

"When are you thinking of having lunch? It's two o'clock! The men have finished already."

"Later, later!"

The twins were sweating. There was not a breath of wind and it was more than 20°C in the shade. The bakery staff approached, chatting among themselves. All except Eliseo had a cigarette in hand.

"Why don't you flip the boats over and put them on the floor?" said Miguel. "You'll find it easier that way."

Donato, cigarette between his lips, picked Elías' boat up with his fingertips so as not to get paint on himself.

"You grab that side," he said to the boy.

Between the two of them, they turned it over and lowered it onto the floor. Martín followed suit with his canoe, before helping his brother do the same with the barge.

"You'll definitely paint them better like that," said Greybeard. "And with this heat, they'll be dry in no time."

Eliseo agreed.

"So, when's the regatta?" he asked.

"Tomorrow!" exclaimed the twins.

Before going back out, Donato turned to Elías again:

"You have to teach me the song you were whistling this morning. You'd be doing me a favour. Everyone loves it when an accordionist plays a new song at the dance."

"I can teach you the words," said Miguel. "I know them well."

On the way back up to the bakery, Miguel told Donato about his time in Pau, where he had gone to learn how to be a baker. A priest from the church he attended had invited him to join the Beau-Frêne choir, and he had agreed, partly because he liked singing, but more because it was a way of meeting people. It was there that he had learned the song, just as Elías had twenty years later; it had been on Miguel's recommendation that Elías had gone on the French course. Miguel now gave a little rendition: "*Il était un petit navire qui n'avait ja- ja-jamais navigué. Ohé! Ohé!*"

"Things haven't changed much there," he said. "The same repertoire."

They were at the bakery door. Miguel placed a hand on Donato's arm.

"Keep going with the boy, keep asking about the song. But say you want him to sing it, not whistle it. Maybe if he starts singing, talking will follow."

Greybeard and Eliseo caught up with them.

"Good thinking," said Greybeard. "The name escapes me,

but there was an artist with a bad stammer who could still sing better than anyone alive."

Miguel and Donato looked at him.

"It seems singing's easier than talking," added Greybeard.

"Why don't we take him out hunting?" asked Eliseo. "If we start shooting with him right close by, maybe he'll get a fright and it'll shock him into speaking. In my village there was a story about that happening to someone once."

Miguel looked doubtful:

"Marta said her husband had the same idea, but I'm not convinced. I heard a similar story when I was growing up, but the other way around. About a cat jumping out at a guy one night, and him developing a stammer because of it."

"People have pretty vivid imaginations in these old villages," said Greybeard.

Donato grabbed Eliseo by the shoulder:

"In Castilian villages as well though, right? I don't just mean yours, of course. I mean in general."

Eliseo was from Castile; he had been a shepherd there before coming to Ugarte. Donato and he had done their military service together.

A southerly wind, 23°C. Up above the terrace, the night in all its splendour, the stars and the moon, and in the square the swift-like shouting and shrieking of the children; but the beauty arrayed before her left Marta cold, and the longer the conversation with her husband went on, the worse she felt. She had given him a gabbled account of the boys painting their boats and not getting around to eating until 5 p.m. because of it. Luis had painted his red, Martín had painted his white, and Miguel's nephew had chosen green. The boy still had not said a word, but all the signs were that he was having a good time with the twins.

"He's not dangerous in any way, at least he doesn't seem to be," she concluded. "I don't know what happened in France, him throwing that stone at a teacher, or whoever it was, but all the time he's been at Miguel's he's seemed very well behaved."

Her husband glanced at his Monterrey.

"Give him time," he said.

The thread of smoke from the cigar rose and then instantly dispersed, as though wafted away by an invisible hand.

"It's such a warm wind tonight," he said. "The paint on those little boats of theirs will be dry in no time."

"Exactly!" said Marta. "And tomorrow morning they're going down to the canal for a regatta. Just the thought of it puts me on edge."

The river that ran down from the hills had been diverted two hundred metres or so above the bakery into a canal; from there the water curved off between trees, reeds and rocks, before continuing straight ahead and then splitting in two: to the right, it formed a narrow channel that ran underneath the bakery itself, while to the left, the larger watercourse carried on for a further forty metres before cascading over a rocky edge.

That final stretch was what Marta had in her mind's eye. This was why she was worried. If the boys failed to stop the boats at just the right moment, at the point where the canal forked, they would keep on sailing downstream, and Luis, the most reckless of the three, might then jump in and try to fish them out, and . . . Were there walls, or any kind of a dam, before it came to the waterfall? She could not remember. This was the first thing to establish; she would ask Miguel. Until she knew, she would not let the boys go anywhere near the canal. She would tell them in no uncertain terms when they got back from the square: the next day they would go with her to the bakery and not run off the second they got out of bed, as they had that morning. Also, a few extra hours would allow the paint on the boats to dry a little more.

"It was the men's 100 metres final today," said her husband. "Valeri Borzov won. Gold medal."

"Julián, go and watch television."

In the end, they both moved inside. He went into the living

room and turned the television on. She took her pack of L&Ms and a lighter from a drawer in the kitchen and sat down again out on the terrace. She was an occasional smoker. Ten or so cigarettes a week.

Now that she was alone on the terrace, the night and the sky seemed vaster than ever; the stars further away; the moon, also far away, although still very large. And there were no children in the village square now, or if there were, their games did not involve the usual shrieks and raised voices. That silence was what troubled her most, making her sense of solitude all the more acute. It was a new solitude, or, at least, a kind she had not felt in a long time. Similar, perhaps, to what she had experienced when she was a few years older than the twins were now, in the days when she and Lucía used to go to dances in the neighbouring villages. They would dance, and then there would be nobody to walk her home. Lucía would have someone, but she would not. Lucía always fell in with some bad boy or other, because she was the more intrepid one, unlike cowardly Marta, saying no to all the boys whether good or bad, and always therefore ending up going home alone, hurrying all the way.

She lit the cigarette and watched the smoke rise. In spite of the lack of a breeze, it vanished immediately. Thoughts came into her mind, a trickle of thoughts, as faint and insubstantial as the cigarette smoke. She was thirty-eight. Fifteen of those years she had spent married to Julián. She had two sons, both born on the same day, first Martín and then Luis, or so she had been told. There were other things in her life, but what were they? Of all the thoughts, this was the most insubstantial, the most unanswerable. Her memory only presented her with ordinary experiences, not brightly coloured boats, but unremarkable boats plying their usual routes. Lucía came to mind again. They used to sit together at school, at a double desk, and had stayed friends for years afterwards. Now Lucía was dead. She had just one memento of her friend, a beautiful headscarf Lucía had brought her from Italy.

She cast around for the ashtray, but it was not on the chair.

She let the ash drop onto the terrace floor. Sooner or later the wind would come and sweep it away, so why worry.

A thought appeared among these memories. Julián had not batted an eyelid when she said how the boys' boatmaking meant she had not returned home almost an hour and a half later than usual. Instantly, another thought: since she had been working at Miguel's house, she had only noticed her husband being suspicious at the very start, and then just one other time, when he found out that Donato, the Gitane Blonde, was working there. "Donato doesn't seem to have much time for women," she had told him. "He jokes around with the ones who go and flirt with him, and it never goes any further." She had played that wrong, she told herself now. Lucía used to say, in their dancing days, that it was always a good idea to have a dummy boyfriend, a pretend mate to arouse the jealousy of the boys you were actually interested in. But, lest she forget, Lucía was dead. Hers was hardly a lead to follow.

Sliding her foot along the terrace floor, it met with the ashtray, and Marta stubbed out her cigarette. She had made a decision: from the following day she would start getting home later than usual – 5.30, 5.45, 6.00, 6.30 – and see what happened. The idea excited her. It was something new, an unknown boat sailing down the river of her life.

She went straight to bed. Before falling asleep, she returned to the thought with which she had started the evening. She must talk to Miguel about how dangerous the canal was. If anything happened to one of the children, she'd never recover.

Elías and Luis walked from the workshop to the bakery with their boats, the red barge and the green rowboat, on their shoulders; Martín carried his, the small white canoe, under one arm. Miguel was waiting for them when they got there.

"Leave the boats on the ground and come with me."

The boys put them down on one side of the path, parallel to one another as if they were on a jetty, and they followed Miguel inside the bakery until they came to a bolted door.

"Now, be careful!"

He opened the door, and the four of them went through and found themselves on a platform, where the roar of a waterfall filled the air.

"See what it's like?" he said, stepping forward to where there was a wooden handrail.

He motioned to the place where the canal came to an abrupt end. There was no proper wall there, only a loose assortment of rocks in a line. After that, the water fell some ten metres down into a pool at the bottom.

"There used to be a dam there, but it burst last winter and now the water just goes straight over the edge," Miguel explained. "If you're ever planning on a swim, you go to the upper part of the canal, right, don't even think about doing it near the bakery. The current on the final stretch is really strong, there's no way you'll be able to stop yourselves, you'll just get swept along."

He motioned to the left, to the waterfall. The three boys nodded. It did not seem to be the same water to left and right, upstream and downstream. Roaring and splashing, it fed away into a stream that ran around Miguel's house and the workshop, before continuing its course alongside the road. Stream and road alike then descended to the village a kilometre further on.

Donato appeared behind them, grabbed Luis by the arms and propelled him some twenty centimetres closer to the edge. Luis let out a cry, as did Martín.

"What's the matter? Are you boys scared?" Donato was wearing a vest and his arms were white with flour.

"Donato will show you the dos and don'ts of being by the canal," said Miguel, going back into the bakery and waiting for them before he shut the door.

The three boys went out onto the path, Luis and Martín dashing over to where the boats were. Donato picked up Elías' boat.

"I'll carry it for you, but in return you have to teach me the words to that French song."

"How's he supposed to do that if he doesn't talk?" said Luis.

"He can whistle it," Martín offered at once.

Donato shook his head.

"No, I need the lyrics. At the fiestas, I like to sing just as much as I like to play the accordion."

Elías said nothing. There was not even his usual smile.

They walked to the point where the canal forked. There was not so much as a murmur there and the water appeared to be flowing placidly. But this apparent calm was deceptive, as Donato showed when he threw in a twig. In under a second or two, it had travelled more than a metre. The current was strong. Added to which, it drifted away to the left, towards the incline and not towards the section that flowed under the bakery. Donato pointed to the twig. Away it went to the left. Another five seconds and it was lost from sight.

Next to the canal wall, to one side of the path, three sticks lay on the ground. Donato picked one up and showed them how long it was. Easily long enough to reach the far side of the canal.

"When your boats get to this point, or a little bit before, use your stick to steer them over to this side, so they go towards the bakery. Just a nudge. You don't need to do much."

Luis and Martín both picked up their sticks. Elías held out his hand for Donato to give him the one he was holding and the green rowboat.

Donato did not do so immediately.

"We need to go upstream," he said, "it's a bit of a way still. This little rowboat certainly isn't light. You don't want me to carry it?"

Elías shook his head.

"I'll help him," said Martín.

With his boat, the white canoe, under his arm, he took one side of Elías' rowboat. Donato picked up the two boys' sticks and started walking upstream.

The canal had a set of stone steps at the place where, after a bend, it flowed straight along to the bakery. There was a break in the concrete wall and the steps descended into the water. Donato used one of the sticks to mark a line on the ground.

"You'll start the first race from here," he said.

"What happens if our boat sinks?" Martín asked.

"Then you'll just have to make another one."

Luis threw back his head and laughed, before dropping his boat into the water. It sank a little, but immediately bobbed back up to the surface. A small red barge afloat on the current.

The canal wall was built flush with the path; the water was a metre or so below. With the utmost care Martín, lying on his front on the ground and reaching down as far as he could, placed his white canoe on the water. It tilted slightly, apparently heavier on one side, but even so it overtook the other boat in seconds. The white canoe moved along far better than Luis' red barge.

"It'll go even faster if you put some stones in to balance it," Donato said.

Elías got down on the ground as well, shimmying forward until half his body was hanging over the edge. The green rowboat set off looking ungainly, the prow pointing backwards, as if it wanted to go in the opposite direction. Elías hurried to pick up his stick to set it right.

"And they're off!" cried Donato.

Martín's canoe got there first, despite bumping into the wall in the final stretch and filling up with water; next came Elías' rowboat; and last, Luis' barge. There were no problems at the fork in the canal. They needed only to tap the prows with their sticks to bring them to the safer side.

They took the boats out of the water and left them by the bakery door.

"When are you going to teach me that song, Elías?" Donato asked. "It's nearly fiesta time in one of the barrios, and it'd be great if I could play it there."

Elías smiled at him. Then, picking up his rowboat and his stick, he turned and headed back up the path to start another race. Luis and Martín ran after him.

*

September 3 was a lovely day, and the night even more so: 20°C, a light southerly wind, and the moon hanging full in a completely clear sky. Sitting out on the terrace, Marta filled Julián in on the day's events. The main news was of a visit from Miguel's sister, Elías' mother.

"She seemed like a very decent woman. She really didn't get much time with her son, though, you know how crazy the boys are about their boat races, but I think it eased her mind to see him in such good spirits. When she was giving me a hand in the kitchen she talked about the state he'd been in when he got back from France. How he shut himself in his room, wouldn't open the door, and how she could hear him crying when she went to work at the restaurant. She said it was doing him good being here. A very decent woman, like I say. She offered to help making the bechamel sauce, but I wouldn't let her, her clothes were far too nice. Later on, when we were having dessert – an apple tart she herself brought – she thanked us all for our efforts in helping the boy recover."

Julián was smoking his nightly Monterrey and, every now and then, gave his glass of whisky a shake, tinkling the ice cubes. He held it out for her to have a sip.

"You know I prefer rum. Would you be a sweetie and bring me a glass?" she said, and then, as he went into the kitchen: "And the L&Ms too!"

As usual there were the echoes of the children playing in the square, though that did not include Luis and Martín, as they were staying over at Miguel's with Elías that night.

Julián returned to the terrace, waiting for her to light her cigarette before handing her the glass of rum. Marta took a sip.

"I love Negrita rum," she said.

A pot hung from the terrace railing with soil in it but no plants. Marta put her glass there so that she could more comfortably smoke her cigarette.

"The boys are so enjoying the boat racing," she said. "It is actually a lovely sight, the three boats bobbing down the canal

31

together. To begin with Martín kept winning, but then Donato weighted the boats to make them more balanced. Luis told me he's won three times, Martín five times, and Miguel's nephew twice."

The sound of her own voice bored her; she felt no need to talk about these things, but at the same time found it impossible to stop.

"Racing's always a fine thing," said Julián. "I'm going in shortly to watch whatever's happened in Munich today."

Marta went on:

"At least there's no chance of the boys going anywhere near the waterfall. When the boats get to a point where the canal forks, they use sticks to steer them over to the section that goes towards the bakery. I won't say it doesn't frighten me anymore, because the danger's still there. But the boys have been told they're not to even think about getting in the water in that part of the canal."

On going up to the canal that morning to see the boats, Marta had run into Greybeard, who was examining some scratches on the bark of an ash tree. "A boar," he said. "It'll have been using it as a scratching post. I'm going to say to Eliseo and Miguel that we ought to bring the shotguns up to the bakery. They'll be easy enough to hunt. They can't stand being thirsty – they're like humans in that way – and they come to the canal in search of water." To which Marta had said: "I'll have to see if I can find a good recipe for boar stew." The joke immediately struck her as silly, and she wondered what the boar would do if it encountered the boys. She had heard they were generally unlikely to attack, but could be dangerous if provoked. And when it came to her twins, provoking was what they did best.

Julián swirled his whisky around in the glass. The ice cubes tinkled more quietly now that they had begun to melt.

"What did Donato do to balance the boats?" he asked.

"He used stones. He added a piece of wood to Martín's too, because it kept veering off to one side. Now it goes in a straight line."

From the terrace, everything seemed quite motionless. The

32

moon embedded in the dark sky like a battered coin; the windows of the houses in the village like framed paintings. All was quiet in the square. The cigar and the cigarette butt lay in the ashtray. "I'm going to watch the Olympics roundup," said Julián, looking at the clock. "It was the 3,000 metres quarter-finals today. Keino's the favourite."

"Hurrah for Keino!" Marta raised her glass and drank it down in one.

She lit her second cigarette as soon as he was gone and began thinking about the fact that she had come back from the bakery an hour and a half later than usual, at 6 p.m., and the previous day at 5.30 p.m., and that Julián had not even asked why. She decided to wear a miniskirt to work the next day. The mere thought of it gave her goosebumps.

Marta was still awake when Julián joined her in bed.

"Marta, where in France was it the boy went?"

"Pau," she said, not opening her eyes.

"I don't mean that. I mean what kind of college was it?"

"Why?" She had no desire to open her eyes.

"Do you know or not?"

He turned on the light. He had a sports magazine with him.

"There's an article here about a guy called Julianovich, an ex-footballer. He talks about the punishments he was given in college. Maybe something similar happened to the boy. If he threw a stone at a teacher, there must be a reason."

"It was a college run by monks. Miguel said it was a good place. He knows it. He sang in the choir there when he was in Pau learning to be a baker."

Julián put the magazine down on the bedside table and turned off the light.

"I wouldn't be surprised if what happened to Julianovich happened to him. They're sadists, those monks."

"Who won the 3,000 metres?" Marta said, opening her eyes.

"It was just the classifying round today. Keino got the best time."

33

"Hurrah for Keino, hurrah for Negrita rum!"

"You seem very happy tonight," Julián said, putting a hand on her belly. She brushed it away.

"I'm happy because I'm going to wear my miniskirt tomorrow. I've barely worn it all summer, I'm looking forward to it."

"What for? To impress the Gitane Blonde?"

"That too," she said, turning onto her side with her back to him.

Into her thoughts came the image of the canal as she had seen it that afternoon: the water slipping quietly between trees, reeds and rocks, and, suddenly, the three boats appearing – red, white, green – all being swept downstream. It seemed to her that she could feel the cool of the place, and then sleep overcame her.

On September 4 the three boys took their boats further up the canal than they had previously, to the part where the ash trees grew, and, after a discussion between the twins over the number of stones the boats should each have to ballast them, they leaned over the edge and let the current take the small crafts. The green rowboat instantly surged into the lead and was some ten metres ahead of the white canoe and the red barge before it had gone halfway around the curve. Suddenly, something caused the rowboat to veer off and smash into the wall. There was some tossing and turbulence in the water. Luis and Martín ran to see what was happening.

"A boar!" they cried. Elías started making noises, as if he were calling to someone, but making no sense at all.

There was a boar in the canal, only its head above the water. It looked at the boys and twisted about, first towards the path, as if to attack them, then over to the other side, trying to scale the wall. But the metre drop was more than it could manage. It tried over and over again, but always ended up falling back and slapping the water with its front legs, as though afraid of going under. After each failed attempt, it would wait twenty seconds or so before trying once more.

Rowboat, canoe and barge were lost from sight downstream. Luis picked up a stick and held it out to the boar. Elías grabbed hold of him.

"I just want to put it in its mouth," protested Luis, "so that it bites it."

Elías shook his head, telling him not to. Martín picked up a stick as well, but only to point with:

"Its hooves are bleeding," he said.

It was true. The boar's wet bristly fur looked completely black, but red blotches were visible between the clefts in its front hooves.

The boar thrashed about for a moment, as if trying to dive under the water, then paddled some five metres further on. The boys moved back a couple of metres.

"It gave me such a fright!" said Luis, again holding up his stick.

The boar scrabbled at the canal wall. For the first time they heard it grunt, making a grating, snoring sound more like that of a pig.

"It won't be able to get up that side either," said Martín.

"That side, or anywhere else. It's going to drown," said his brother definitively.

Now the boar was kicking its back legs, trying to keep above water, creating waves all around it. It was no use. Slowly, stopping at intervals to try and get up the wall again, it went drifting downstream.

"It's running out of strength," said Luis. "The current's too much for it."

Bending down over the water, he prodded the creature in the side with the stick. The boar spun round with a grunt, showing its tusks as if it was about to go for him. Water splashed the boys' faces.

Elías threw Luis to the ground and took the stick from him. He started wailing, making a noise that sounded like "Eeee!" The veins on his neck bulged, and he looked a completely different boy.

"Elías is right! Leave it alone!" said Martín, shaking his fist at his brother.

Luis ran off in the direction of the bakery. Elías went after him, but stopped a little further on, by the stone steps where the straight section of the canal began. Martín was there in a flash.

"You're right, Elías! The boar could get out here!"

The two boys started beating the water on the far side with their sticks, trying to drive the boar towards the steps. Elías kept up his cry of "Eeee!" while Martín was talking to the animal:

"Over to this side! To the steps! You can get out here!"

The boar did not change tack. When it came level with the boys, it started trying to scrabble up the side, and for a few seconds managed to get the top third of its body out of the water and rest its snout on the edge, only to slip back in once more.

"This side! Up the steps!" Martín repeated.

The boar stopped still against the side. Its hooves were covered in blood.

"It doesn't understand!" Martín said, dropping his stick.

Elías picked the stick up and handed it back to him. Then, running a few metres upstream, he jumped into the water.

"Watch out!" shrieked Martín. "It's going to bite you!"

Elías climbed out of the canal on the opposite side. He wanted to shout, but he was panting, short of breath. The boar's head was very close to him now: ears, head, eyes, snout, tusks, tongue, the roof of its mouth. The animal was panting too. There was blood down its front legs, and the hooves and the clefts between its toes were completely red. Elías pressed the stick against its neck, pushing it in the direction of the stone steps. They were right there, three metres or so away.

"Get out over here!" yelled Martín.

He moved back from the steps to leave the way clear, but the boar threw itself into the water and swam on for another five metres.

"It's useless!" Martín said, again dropping his stick.

He was crying. The boar carried on drifting downstream, no longer stopping but letting the current take it, and growing ever closer to the bakery and the waterfall, where it would be impossible to get out.

Elías jumped in the water again, then climbed out using the steps.

"We tried," said Martín.

They ran to catch up with the boar, then slowed to a walk, keeping pace with it. As they went along, Elías wrung out the water from his clothes.

They had been shouting, beside themselves, for several minutes, and now that they were quiet they became aware not only of the silence but of everything around them. They were in this familiar place, with familiar people nearby. The bakery was a stone's throw away, and beyond that by the stream was Miguel's house, with, directly opposite, the workshop, and inside the workshop the bench with the tools, the saws, the gouges, the hammers.

"What about the boats? My canoe?" said Martín, pulling up.

Ignoring him, Elías carried on walking along the canalside, watching the boar. The animal was being dragged downstream like a sack. Soon it would come to the place where the dam used to be and go hurtling over the edge.

They heard voices. Everyone from the bakery came running up the path. Luis and Donato in front, Greybeard and Eliseo just behind with their shotguns, followed shortly by Miguel and Marta. They stopped where the canal forked.

"There! There!" cried Luis.

"I don't see it," said Greybeard, coming past him, gripping the shotgun in both hands.

"There, where the boys are," said Eliseo calmly, pointing to the spot where Elías and Martín were standing. "Shoot if you want. He's yours."

The boar became aware of their presence and started paddling furiously about, now this way, now that.

"I see it!" said Greybeard, swearing loudly. He raised the gun to his shoulder and fired.

"You missed. Want me to have a go?" Eliseo laughed coolly, enjoying the moment. His shotgun looked very sophisticated.

Between the butt and the two barrels it had a silver inlay with an engraving of a hare.

"It's mine, Eliseo!" bawled Greybeard, uttering another string of curses as he raised his shotgun again.

Elías ran over and threw himself at Greybeard, knocking him to the ground. The shotgun fell and bounced a couple of metres away.

Elías' cry of "Eeee!" drowned out any noise Greybeard might have been making. For a moment he ran out of breath, then started up again: "Eeee! Eeee!" Finally, with all the veins on his neck seemingly close to bursting, he spoke the words: "Don't shoot!" He scrambled to pick up the shotgun. Donato intervened and, throwing his arms around Elías, snatched the weapon from him.

They could hear the boar grunting. It was paddling from one side of the canal to the other, while still being carried downstream. Elías kept on shouting, over and over: "No! No! No!"

"Easy, easy," said Donato.

Greybeard got up off the ground.

"Have we all lost our minds, or what . . .!"

Miguel put his finger to his lips and said to Donato:

"Quick, go and get the bread paddles from the bakery." Then, to Elías: "Why do you want to rescue the boar?"

"I don't know."

"That isn't a reason."

Elías started to cry.

"Because its hooves are all bloody!"

Marta went over to them.

"He's talking!" Miguel told her.

Where the canal forked, there was a wire mesh to stop leaves from getting through to the section that led under the bakery. Miguel went and pulled it off its hooks, clearing the way. Greybeard took it from him and went and sat on a boulder by the path, all the time keeping his eye on the boar. The animal wanted to get away, and was trying to swim upstream, but it lacked the strength to go against the current.

Donato and Eliseo appeared on the other side of the canal, Donato with a bread paddle and Eliseo with his shotgun. Luis followed behind with a metal bucket in one hand and a hammer in the other.

First Miguel and Marta, then Martín and Elías, started throwing stones at the boar, to force it to swim onwards. When it was a metre short of where the canal forked, Donato thrust the wooden paddle into the water. The boar thrashed about when it felt something touching its belly. Eliseo pointed the shotgun into the air and fired.

"Go for it, Luis!" said Donato, at which the boy started banging the bucket with the hammer.

Eliseo fired another shot in the air. Terrified, the boar swerved away from them and into the section that led under the bakery. At that point, it suddenly grew calmer, as though it knew where it was now, and carried on paddling in the direction of the bakery. It resembled a very shaggy pig.

Marta had taken up a position by the bakery door.

"I've opened it!" she said.

"Over here!" shouted Miguel. "That's where it'll get out!"

The noise was deafening. Luis went on hammering on the bucket. Donato was shouting at the top of his voice. Eliseo fired a third shot.

At last, the boar came running out of the bakery and, for a moment, headed down the slope towards Miguel's house. Then, changing tack, it disappeared into the undergrowth.

2

The Collège Beau-Frêne was on the outskirts of Pau, set in extensive, leafy grounds, with horse chestnuts and poplars predominant among the hundreds of trees. It had its own sports facilities, with football and rugby pitches, basketball and tennis courts, a pelota court and various athletics tracks.

The grounds were open to the public. In the mornings, before classes began, there would always be one athletics group or another using the facilities, and later on, when the students went outside at break time, the summer camp girls would appear, youngsters from across France who went around in groups under the watchful eye of their chaperones. In the afternoons and evenings, it was the turn of people out for a stroll, mostly people of a certain age.

Elías arrived at Beau-Frêne on August 1 for an intensive French course and at break the following day, a Wednesday, walked with his fellow students down to the basketball court and the football pitch. These, however, were not sports he liked, basketball even less than football, and he preferred to stay on the sidelines watching the other boys play. The same happened the next day. Then, on the third day, August 4, a Friday, feeling more used to the place and a little less lonely than he had when he waved goodbye to his mother, he decided to leave the others at the basketball court and go for a walk in the grounds. The breaks at Beau-Frêne were an hour long, and there was still plenty of time.

He had only gone a few steps when one of the students playing basketball called out to him:

"*Billage*! Don't go! Come and play with us!"

The use of that name, *Billage*, pulled him up short. During the introductions on the first day he had stood at the front of the class and said that he was from the Basque Country, just over the border, from a "*village*", and he had used the French word, but pronounced it as if it were Spanish, with a *b* instead of a *v*. Ever since then, a number of the other students, especially those from Madrid and other big cities, had been calling him *Billage*, cruelly mimicking his Spanish pronunciation. Though annoyed, he ended up going over to the court.

"It's only natural that he should avoid us," said the boy, putting on a friendly face. "After all, we never asked if he wanted to join in."

Elías knew none of this was sincere. The boy who had called him back was José Carlos. He was taking the same French course and had been constantly trying to get a rise out of Elías. When Elías stepped onto the court, José Carlos went and stood in front of him, dribbling the ball:

"Try to get it off me, *Billage!*"

He was very good, passing the ball between and around his legs as he dribbled. His friends said he was in the Real Madrid youth basketball team, and he himself had said as much during his introduction on the first day. He had wavy hair with a side parting.

Elías tried to get the ball off him, but without success.

"What's the matter, *Billage?* Don't they play basketball in those mountains of yours?"

He laughed, and the others laughed too. Some of the summer camp girls were looking on, and they applauded. Elías turned and went to leave the court.

"Catch!" he heard someone shout.

He turned around, but not in time to hold out his hands, and the ball hit him right in the stomach. He doubled over in pain.

José Carlos winked at the other boys and gave an exaggerated bow.

"Sorry, *petite fleur*. I thought you mountain folk were tougher than that."

Elías remained doubled over until the pain began to subside; then, straightening up, he marched over to José Carlos, ready for a fight. But another of the students from the course, a skinny boy, went and stood between them, facing José Carlos.

"*Le ruban!*" he said, holding out a red ribbon.

It was forbidden to speak anything but French while at Beau-Frêne, and it was down to the students themselves to enforce the policy. Whoever had *le ruban* at the end of the day was grounded for the weekend.

At first, José Carlos refused to take it, and went on spitting insults in Spanish.

"*Le ruban!*" repeated the skinny boy.

"Don't give me that!" said José Carlos, turning to look at the summer camp girls. "I've got a party to go to tomorrow. I'm not going to be stuck here kicking my heels."

The skinny boy put the ribbon in José Carlos' pocket.

"You know where you have to put it," he said, tapping him on the chest. "Here!" He had a superb French accent.

On Saturday, August 5 – 20°C, sun and cloud – it was not yet 10 a.m. by the time the grounds of Beau-Frêne began filling up with visitors, many of them disabled or sick people who, judging by the images of the Virgin Mary sewn on their clothes, were using it as a break in their journey to the shrine at Lourdes. Elías went for a walk in the grounds, before deciding to go back to the college library to look over his notes from the week and continue with the translations the choirmaster had set them the previous day. He had almost a week to do the translations, the next rehearsals were not until the coming Friday, but the words were neither easy to understand nor easy to translate so that they actually sounded good.

The young choirmaster, Pascal, who also taught French Culture, was blind, and made his way along the corridors and up and down the stairs with the aid of a white stick. Elías had taken a real liking to him, because the choirmaster was kind and funny, and Elías wanted to show that he was good and honest by working alone on the translation, rather than imitating the other students, with one of them doing the translation and the others simply copying it out, since there was no way a blind man would be able to tell their handwriting apart.

There were two songs, one traditional, "*Il était un petit navire*", and the other modern and very popular in France: "*Tous les garçons et les filles*" by Françoise Hardy. It would not be that difficult with the help of a dictionary. His French was not as good as that of the skinny boy who had given José Carlos *le ruban*, but it was passable.

"*Il était un petit navire qui n'avait ja- ja- jamais navigué. Ohé! Ohé!*" This part was easy, and, besides, he knew it already, because his uncle Miguel often sang it at family celebrations. He wrote the translation below the first line: "Once there was a little boat that had never been to sea. He-hey! He-hey!" The second line was: "*Ohé, ohé, matelot, matelot, navigue sur les flots*". He looked up *flots* in the dictionary. It could mean two things: "a large quantity" and "waves". He did not have to think twice, and immediately wrote out his translation: "He-hey, he-hey, sailor, sailor, sailing on the waves".

It was a spacious library, with fifty or so double desks flanked by bookshelves and cabinets with glass doors on both sides. A rectangular blackboard covered almost the entire wall at the front, and there was a harmonium on a raised dais by the window. The phrase copied out by Pascal the previous day was still on the blackboard, the handwriting surprisingly good for someone who could not see: "*Le sort tomba sur le plus jeune*". This was another line from the song. The song described a small boat setting out on a long voyage across the Mediterranean, and how, after a number of weeks, the crew ran out of provisions. The starving sailors decided to eat one of the crew. They drew lots, and the "chosen one" was the youngest among them, little more than a boy. Pascal had said: "Doubtless the sailors rigged the drawing of lots, thinking he'd be the tenderest to eat." He enjoyed making the students laugh with comments like this.

The college warden stuck his head around the door. He looked to be about sixty, with completely white, gelled-back hair. He glanced around the library before addressing Elías:

"What are you doing in here? You ought to be out playing sport or having a look around the city. It's Saturday."

Elías did not move from his desk. The warden went over to him. His hair gave off a faintly mentholated smell.

"What's your favourite sport?" he said.

He had ugly, glittering green eyes. Elías could not compare them to Pascal's, because the dark glasses the teacher usually wore meant you could not see what colour his eyes were, but in Elías' mind they were light brown.

Elías shrugged.

"Pelota, but I haven't seen anybody playing it here."

The warden shut Elías's exercise book and gestured to him to get up. His clothes smelled of wax. Mass was held daily at the college, and it was one of his tasks to assist the priest.

"Come with me. There's a racket and a ball I can let you have."

"But I need to study!" Elías protested. "I want to make sure I pass."

It was true. He knew the month's course was expensive. He had heard his uncle Miguel saying as much to his mother.

The warden patted his cheek.

"I'm sure you'll pass. You're a good student."

Again, he motioned to Elías to get up, then went back over to the door.

"Come along, boy."

At midday the grounds of Beau-Frêne were deserted except for a group of five nuns standing near a flower bed and who appeared to have been left behind by the Lourdes bus. The emptiness meant that the two sounds on the tennis court, Elías hitting the ball and the ball then hitting the wall, could be heard clearly from a distance. With no choice but to play by himself, he hit the ball alternately with the racket in his right and left hand. He was bored and decided he would take himself back to the library.

Then he saw the skinny boy. He was walking towards the court and had a racket of his own.

"Why don't we both play?" he said, going onto the court.

Elías looked at the other boy's racket. It was not like the one the warden had given him.

"It's a Dunlop," the boy explained. "My parents gave it to me as a present."

"Everyone here seems to be rolling in it."

"So now I'm just another rich kid am I?"

"No . . . well, yes."

They both laughed.

"Elías, isn't it? That was what you said at the introductions."

"Well, I'm definitely not *Billage*. What's your name? I don't remember."

"Makes sense. I always sit at the back. That's a privilege we veterans enjoy – it's my second year here. Anyway, it isn't much of a name, not compared with yours at least. I'm Mateo."

He held out a hand, and they shook.

They did not play for long. Within ten minutes they were sitting in the shade of the pelota wall, Mateo smoking a cigarette.

"Gitanes," he said, showing him the packet. It was blue and bore the image of a dancing gypsy woman. "Do you like this place?" he added. Elías looked doubtful. "Something sinister about it, I think. See what I mean? Such enormous grounds, and only five nuns in the whole place."

"And soon not even a single nun," Elías said, for, at that moment, the five brown-robed figures began moving off into the distance.

They both laughed again.

No lunch was served at Beau-Frêne on Saturdays, and the students, whether they chose to go into the city or to stay and use the sports facilities, were given a lunch bag.

"Why don't we have a picnic? If you like, we can see if Miky wants to join us."

Elías could not remember who Miky was.

"He sits at the back, like me. He's crazy. He smokes cannabis, and he's always broke. That's why he's stuck here today."

"Why?"

"Because of the red ribbon. Didn't you know? People buy and sell *le ruban*. José Carlos gave Miky fifty francs to take it off him. That guy, he's the pits. Throwing the ball at you like that. If you'd hit him, though, you'd have got it in the neck, not him."

They failed to find Miky, and, in the end, it was just the two of them taking their lunch bags and finding a grassy spot in the grounds to sit down.

"He's probably gone into town. He'll have run out of cannabis."

"But . . . he'll be expelled if they catch him."

"Hardly. On the welcome day, they love going on about all the strict rules, but generally nobody gets expelled. Plus, Miky's father is some high-up politician in Madrid. A deputy minister, I think."

"What strange families you rich kids come from!" Elías said.

If he had added up every single surprise he had ever had in his life, it would not have equalled the astonishment he felt during this conversation with Mateo.

They ate, fell asleep on the grass, and at around 4 p.m. went inside to the library to work on Pascal's translations.

"You really like singing, don't you?" Mateo asked. "You're good at it. Not me. Know what Pascal said to me the other day? 'Since you're sitting at the back, why don't you make the most of it and keep quiet.'"

"Pascal likes making jokes."

He pointed to the phrase on the blackboard, "*Le sort tomba sur le plus jeune*", and reminded Mateo of the teacher's comment about the sailors surely having played a trick so that they could eat the tenderest member of the crew.

They sat in the same places they had occupied during the previous day's rehearsal, Elías in the front row and Mateo at the back. They opened their desk lids and took out their exercise books and pens.

Mateo sang the words: "*Il était un petit navire qui n'avait ja-ja- jamais navigué. Ohé! Ohé! Ohé, ohé, matelot, matelot, navigue sur les flots.*" He made a horrible job of it, intentionally singing out of tune.

"How did you translate it?" he asked afterwards, when Elías had stopped laughing.

"'Once there was a little boat that had never been to sea. He-hey! He-hey! He-hey, he-hey, sailor, sailor, sailing on the waves.'"

"Good, almost the same as mine: 'Once there was a little boat that had never been to sea. Olé, olé! Olé, olé, sailor, sailor, sailing on the waves.'" He read in his loudest voice, going up an extra notch for the *olé's*. "It's more Spanish that way, don't you think?"

They both laughed again, then went back to their translations. The song talked about how, after the youngest crew member had drawn the short straw, the sailors did not carry out the fatal sentence straight away, but entertained themselves discussing how they were going to eat him, whether fried or in a stew, and what kind of sauce they should put on him. Meanwhile, the young sailor begged the Virgin Mary to forgive their sins, as well as spare him from being eaten. Mary then worked a miracle: thousands of small fish jumped out of the sea and into the boat, the sailors ate them fried, and the boy was saved.

Mateo went over to the blackboard and underlined with a piece of chalk the phrase Pascal had written out: "*Le sort tomba sur le plus jeune*".

"Now, what do you think of my translation?" he said, and he started writing: "If we just change 'le sort' to 'la soeur' we get 'the nun' . . . Voilà!"

On the blackboard it now read, in large letters: "The nun fell upon the youngest one".

Seeing Elías' disapproving look, however, he immediately rubbed it out.

"You're right," he said. "They'd all start laughing, that lowlife José Carlos more than anyone. Pascal wouldn't like it one bit."

Mateo opened the window next to the blackboard and lit a cigarette.

"Are you done with the translation?" Elías asked.

"My mother's French; it's easy for me. They only send me here because it's a long way from Madrid."

He leaned out of the window to exhale the smoke.

"One thing, Elías," he said, breaking the silence. "I'm really pleased that my parents sent me here this year. It's meant that you and I got to meet."

Then, flicking the cigarette out of the window, he went over to Elías.

"Sorry," he said, and kissed him on the cheek.

He made as if to return to his desk at the back, but almost immediately turned and said:

"What about a spot of tourism tomorrow? I could show you around Pau if you like. I know it quite well."

"Okay," said Elías, and carried on with his translation.

After taking the bus into the centre, they walked up to the castle and sat on a stone bench on the esplanade. It was a dull, over-cast day, but from that vantage point you could see for several kilometres around: just below them, the River Gave and one of its many bridges; beyond that, light green fields and dark green woods; and further off still, the Pyrenees. Rising highest among the mountain peaks was a craggy pile whose summit twisted away to one side.

"Pic d'Anie," said Mateo. "It looks like an animal's horn from here."

He took out his Gitanes and lit one.

"I always smoke dark tobacco. Know why? Because if I smoked blonde tobacco, I'd end up getting into cannabis. That's what happened to Miky, and look at him now, always on the scrounge. Obviously, he can't ask for money at home. They'd guess what he wanted it for. Have you ever tried it?"

Elías gave a half smile:

48

"In the village where I live there aren't any drugs. Nor at my school either, I think."

Mateo told him what it was like to smoke cannabis. The one time he tried it, he had become ravenously hungry and hysterical with laughter. Miky, too, laughed at more or less anything when he was smoking. It seemed none of the other students shared that vice. Most of them were your usual kind of boy, with the exception of the basketball player, nasty José Carlos, and one or two others besides. There was nothing particularly unusual about any of the teachers either – apart from Pascal, although he was unusual in a positive sense. He was the best teacher at the whole college, not just among those who taught French Culture.

"What I like most about Beau-Frêne are the Friday choir rehearsals," said Elías.

Mateo stubbed his cigarette out on the ground.

"You've got a good singing voice. Have you ever thought of becoming a singer?"

Elías laughed. Then they both fell silent.

Pau seemed a peaceful city that Sunday, sleepy even, with the roads virtually empty and the Pic d'Anie rising statue-like into the sky. The only activity was on the river. There were people in kayaks, paddling smoothly up and down as though out for a stroll.

"Fancy going round the castle?" asked Mateo. "They've got a cradle made out of a turtle shell. Apparently the king who was born here lay in it as a baby. I don't know, I saw it last year and it seemed like just another gimmick. The usual stuff they make up for tourists."

Elías pursed his lips. He was not especially interested.

"How about we go down to the castle park and have a walk?" suggested Mateo.

"We've already got the grounds at Beau-Frêne, we hardly need more of the same."

"You're quite right! Around the city then? What about a nice cake?"

"Sure. Good idea."

They walked down the castle hill and took the street dedicated to Henry IV of France – he of the supposed turtle-shell cradle. Fifteen minutes later they were in the old part of town.

Mateo stopped outside a wooden door.

"Pâtisserie Artigarrède," he said. "I came here all the time last year. I put on two kilos in a month."

He went to go inside, but the door would not budge.

"It's closed!"

He looked around, unsure what to do. But only for a moment.

"There's another one nearby, Pâtisserie Bouzon. Let's see if it's open."

It was not, and they finally ended up at an ice cream stall on a café terrace. Mateo, taking out his money to show that he was buying, read the flavours from the blackboard: "*Vanille, fraise, chocolat, pistache, banane, café . . .*"

"*Vanille!*" said Elías.

Mateo hugged him.

"You're such a *Billage*! People from villages always go for vanilla."

They went down to the river and watched the kayaks from the bridge.

"What do your parents do?" Mateo asked.

"We've got a restaurant. My mother and father used to run it together, but now it's just my mother. My father died."

"A long time ago?"

"When I was eight."

"Do you remember what he was like?"

"A bit. We've got a photo of him at home, in the living room. What about you, Mateo, what do your parents do?"

"They're both architects. Always working."

There was still light in the sky, but on the river it had grown dark. There were only a few kayaks on the water now. They decided to head back.

They began to climb once more, towards the old part of town. When they passed the town hall, Elías noticed the clock on the front of the building. It was almost 7 p.m.

"It's time to go," he said. "We have to be back by eight."

"Don't worry. We'll make it. And if not, we slip the warden ten francs, and everything'll be fine."

Elías looked confused. Mateo put an arm around his shoulder.

"What an adorable *Billage* you are, Elías. Get with it: José Carlos does it every single day. He's got some squeeze in Pau and never gets back before ten at night. Haven't you noticed? He's never there when we line up for lights out."

Elías had not noticed.

"Well, he isn't . . . He gets back at ten, slips the warden ten francs, and off he goes." Mateo laughed. "Let's get the bus. Got to save those centimes!"

The Friday rehearsals on August 11 began with Pascal going over to the harmonium and playing the opening notes of "*Il-était . . .*", and the students bursting enthusiastically into song, almost shouting the words: "*. . .un petit navire qui n'avait ja- ja- jamais navigué. Ohé! Ohé! Ohé, ohé, matelot, matelot, navigue sur les flots. Ohé, ohé . . .!*" Pascal raised his white stick for them to stop and turned his head from side to side as though he were able to see.

"Who's going to begin reading his translation?" he asked.

"Me!" said José Carlos, before anyone else had a chance to answer.

"José Carlos?" asked Pascal.

"Yes, it's me." He stood up and started to read. "Once there was a little boat that had never been to sea. He-hey! He-hey! He-hey, he-hey, sailor, sailor, sailing on the rubber rings. He-hey, he-hey . . ."

Laughter broke out.

"Read it again, please," said Pascal.

Disconcerted, José Carlos looked around. Five or six of his fellow students were laughing surreptitiously.

"Go ahead," said Pascal, shaking his stick. The tip of it flexed like that of a cane.

This time José Carlos rushed his reading: "Once there was a little boat that had never been to sea. He-hey! He-hey! He-hey, he-hey, sailor, sailor, sailing on the rubber rings. He-hey, he-hey . . ."

"José Carlos, what have you done for the following line? '*Regardant la mer entière, il vit des flots-flots-flots de tous côtés.*' 'Looking out to sea, he saw rubber rings, rubber rings, rubber rings all around.' Is that how you've translated it, José Carlos?"

Most of the students were now making no effort to hide their laughter. Somebody whispered, "Wave!"

"I know *flot* is 'wave'. I just forgot."

"Let's move on to the Françoise Hardy now, José Carlos," said Pascal. "'*Tous les garçons et les filles de mon âge se promènent dans la rue deux par deux. Tous les garçons et les filles de mon âge savent bien ce que c'est d'être heureux . . .*'"

"It says the boys and girls go out walking together . . ." José Carlos stopped. "I'm sorry, I haven't had time to do the translation."

Pascal struck the ground with his stick. One of the other boys stood up:

"'All the boys and girls my age walk down the street in pairs. All the boys and girls my age know that they are happy.'"

"Not bad," said Pascal, pointing to the back of the classroom. "Can you do any better, Mateo?"

"I'd change the ending and put, 'they know what it is to be happy.'"

Pascal nodded, and repeated the phrase, emphasising the final words:

"'*Tous les garçons et les filles de mon âge savent bien ce que c'est d'être heureux.*'"

"Sir," said Mateo, "can I ask a question that has nothing to do with translation and nothing to do with French?"

Gripping the white stick with both hands, Pascal clasped it to his body.

"You will find no better moment to formulate your question, Mateo."

"Sir, what would you say happiness is?"

The students burst out laughing, but immediately went quiet when they saw that Pascal had raised his stick.

"'*Heureux qui, comme Ulysse, a fait un beau voyage,*'" he recited, once the room was silent.

Some of the students joined in with the last couple of words. It was the beginning of a poem they had been looking at in their French Culture classes. Pascal turned his head in the direction of Mateo's desk.

"As the poem says, the secret of happiness lies in going on a long journey, like Ulysses. Do you agree?"

"Yes, sir."

"Well, you shouldn't. You seem much happier to me than last year. And you haven't had enough time to go on a long journey like Ulysses. From which it is to be deduced that, when it comes to the question of happiness, other factors are at play."

"Okay," said Mateo. "I see what you mean."

The rehearsal in the library was supposed to carry on until 5 p.m. but ended half an hour early that day. The college had organised a trip to Lourdes on the Sunday, and the headmaster wanted to give a short preparatory talk on the Virgin Mary appearing to the young country girl Bernadette Soubirous.

The headmaster, who was around fifty, was an extremely thin man, with a long, thin nose and sunken eyes. He was noticeably frail and, having come in and greeted the students, he slumped down in the armchair that Pascal brought over for him. His voice when he started to speak sounded faint:

"One day, in the winter of 1858, a girl called Bernadette Soubirous was out collecting firewood near to the village where she lived, along with her sister and a friend. They had to cross a river to get to the cave where the firewood was kept. At one point she fell behind to take off her espadrilles, and at that moment she heard something, a rustling. She looked around and saw the figure of a beautiful lady dressed in a white tunic with a blue girdle. There was a yellow rose on each of her feet. The lady told her that she was the Virgin Mary, '*qué soï era immaculado councepcioū . . .*'"

After the rehearsal with Pascal, the students struggled to concentrate on the headmaster's talk, and his opening remarks barely registered. Then, however, as he repeated the Virgin Mary's words in an Occitan accent, "*qué soï era immaculado councepcioū . . .*", his voice broke, and suddenly they were all paying attention. With barely contained emotion, he started describing the healing of the sick:

"Close to three million Christians make the journey to Lourdes each year, and some of them, only some, but nonetheless thousands of people, thousands of sick people, bathe in its waters. And some of them, only some, but nonetheless dozens and possibly hundreds of people, make a complete recovery. It is a quite extraordinary thing, and very, very holy. Pascal would like to go into the grotto and emerge with his eyes filled with light. As for me, would that I could come out cured of my cancer. But we cannot ask everything of the Lord. Not all of us are chosen. And despite all, whatever the circumstances, we must continue to love the Lord."

The students were silent. Pascal listened, head tilted back. The headmaster said nothing for a few moments. Then, in conclusion:

"I say all of this to you so that on Sunday you will behave in a respectful manner. It is a holy place you are going to. I wish what happened to Bernadette might happen to every one of you. After seeing the Lady that first day, all Bernadette wanted in the world was to go back to the cave. She felt sure she would be given a rose like the ones she had seen on Our Lady's feet. And Our Lady heard her. On another of her apparitions, she gave her a lovely yellow rose."

The headmaster closed his eyes.

"Remember what I have told you. In Lourdes, you must behave with respect and kindness."

Pascal helped him out of the armchair, and, as he left the room, the students got to their feet.

On Sunday, August 13, Mateo and Elías sat together on the bus that was to take them to Lourdes. They were both wearing grey-and-yellow peaked caps in the style of Confederate soldiers from the American Civil War, and throughout the journey, the other students kept coming up to ask about them. Mateo gave the same answer every time:

"I've got an American uncle, and his grandfather's grandfather fought under General Lee in the war against Lincoln. He sent them to me from Cincinnati."

In fact, they had bought them the previous day at a department store in Pau. Elías would have liked to tell the truth and put an end to the incessant questions, but Mateo insisted, and the aisle became ever busier with the students going back and forth. First, with them wanting to know where the caps were from, then because they were keen to hear Mateo repeat his joke.

The warden, who was sitting at the front, got up. He had been put in charge of the group for the excursion.

"I'm making a note of the name of anyone who doesn't sit down this instant, and when we get back I'll give the list to the headmaster."

Mateo leaned close to Elías in the seat.

"Did you see the way the head looked the other day when he gave us the talk? He had death written all over him."

Rugged mountains passed by outside the window, with no sign of villages or farms, and a succession of alternating greens unfolded under a wide, blue sky. At intervals, they saw the occasional flock of sheep or herd of cows on the banks of the river. Inside the bus, the hum of the engine merged with the students' chatter. Elías looked out at the landscape, tears in his eyes.

"What's the matter?" asked Mateo.

It was a few seconds before Elías could speak.

"In a way I'm happy, because when my father died I was only eight and I can't remember his face. It would have been like the headmaster's is. My father had cancer as well."

Mateo squeezed his arm.

"I told you that I go to a Jesuit college in Madrid, didn't I? Well, one time, someone in my class asked the religious studies teacher what our family and friends who died before us would look like if we met them in heaven, if they would be the same as they were when they were young, or if they'd look older, or the way they looked just before they died, and the teacher said they would look radiant, resplendent, and that we didn't need to worry about it. So I said: 'What about if we go to hell and meet one of our family there? I don't imagine they'd be radiant and resplendent then. People always say there's nothing uglier than the devil. Everyone will be ugly in hell.'"

Elías gave a timid laugh.

"You're ugly too, Mateo." This came from José Carlos, who had come and sat in the seat behind them. "And you think you're cleverer than everyone. You'd better watch out!"

Ignoring him, Mateo went on with his story:

"And the teacher said, 'Just be good, and make sure you get to heaven. That way you won't have any problems.'"

"Dickhead!" exclaimed José Carlos, reaching over and grabbing the cap from Mateo's head.

"*Le ruban!*" Mateo said in a theatrical squeal. "*Le ruban pour José Carlos!*" The ribbon rule did not apply on Sundays, and even less on an excursion, but, out of pure reflex, everyone turned to look. Quick as a flash, Elías swivelled round in his seat and grabbed Mateo's cap back.

"Temper, temper, *Billage!*" sneered José Carlos. "And we all thought you were a dainty little flower!"

The warden turned and stood up.

"That's enough, the lot of you! We're coming into Lourdes."

Small, slate-roofed buildings passed by outside the window

now, the majority of them hotels. The warden blew on the microphone a couple of times to check that it was working. As he proceeded to give the instructions for the day, there was more of a spark to his voice than they were used to, and in contrast to his usual dark work clothes, he was dressed rather elegantly, in cream-coloured trousers and a navy-blue blazer.

"We're going to the sanctuary car park, and from there we'll walk to the grotto where the Virgin Mary appeared. Then, at midday, we'll hear Mass at the basilica. At one o'clock, we'll all eat lunch down by the river. Don't forget your picnic bags. After lunch, you've got free time until six. At six, everyone is to meet back at the car park. No latecomers. If you're late you won't be allowed out next weekend."

A hundred or so pilgrims were waiting reverentially on the benches outside the grotto entrance. Elías and Mateo lined up behind them, next to the space reserved for wheelchairs. A priest went through the Lourdes story, in terms similar to those the headmaster had used in his library talk, but without the emotion.

"I think I know why José Carlos was rude to you," Elías said to Mateo in a half-whisper.

Mateo started singing in a low voice: "'*Il était un petit navire qui n'avait ja- ja- jamais navigué. Ohé! Ohé! Ohé, ohé, matelot, matelot, navigue sur les flots. Ohé, ohé . . .!*' Yes," he said, "the miracle of the rubber rings was entirely my doing, and with no help from the Virgin either."

The warden, who was standing next to the priest, motioned that they should uncover their heads and be quiet. They took off their caps.

"Do you actually want to see the grotto?" whispered Mateo. "If not, we could hit the shops. There's much more in Lourdes than there is in that department store in Pau."

Elías raised two fingers to say they could do both. Mateo was about to return to the subject of José Carlos and the rubber rings, but, seeing Elías' expression, he stopped. Elías had a faraway look in his eye.

When the priest finished his speech, they all filed into the grotto and Mateo lost sight of Elías in the darkness. When he next saw him, near the mouth of the grotto, he was dipping his fingers in the water that ran down between the rocks and dabbing his face. Mateo tried to get his friend's attention, but Elías signalled to him to wait, before going over to a corner in which a large number of candles were burning.

Mateo went outside to wait for him. Suddenly someone tried to knock the cap off his head, but he grabbed hold of it just in time. José Carlos and Miky were standing right behind him.

"Put it on if you like, but don't get your hopes up," said José Carlos, almost shouting. "You're just as ugly with it as without."

A pilgrim, a young woman, put a finger to her lips and gestured to them to go away. Mateo followed José Carlos and Miky.

"Don't you touch my cap again, José Carlos. There's no way I'm letting you do it three times."

Miky turned to face him. He looked furious.

"Actually, it was me. What, think you're untouchable, do you? We aren't allowed to have a little fun with you, but you can piss us off all you like. That was a mean trick you played on José Carlos."

"He'll get what's coming, don't you worry – he'll get what's coming," said José Carlos, again in a loud voice.

Once more the young pilgrim woman shooed them away, this time with an "*Allez! Allez!*"

José Carlos and Miky went over to the group that had formed around the warden. Mateo stayed where he was. Elías left the candle-lit corner and came over to him.

"Such a devotee," said Mateo, looking at an effigy of the Virgin set in a niche above the grotto. "I had no idea!" Her white robe and blue girdle were visible, but not her feet, so there was no way of knowing if they were adorned with yellow roses.

Elías took Mateo by the arm and led him over to the others in the group. On the way to the basilica, they passed some invalids being wheeled on stretchers to the grotto.

"So," said Mateo, "with the translation the other day, Miky said he hadn't had time to do his, and could he use mine, and I guessed José Carlos would be using it as well, so I copied it out myself, with one small change: '*Matelot, matelot, navigue sur les flots*'. 'Sailor, sailor, sailing on the rubber rings' . . ."

He waited for Elías to laugh, but he did not.

"Do you think I shouldn't have done that?"

Elías shrugged. As on the bus, his eyes were moist with tears.

"My father was brought here when he was ill. I would imagine he too was pushed along like that on one of those stretchers."

Mateo put an arm around his shoulder.

"Sorry, Elías! Here I am babbling away, when you're feeling really sad."

Elías wiped away his tears with one hand.

"I'm fine."

Mateo patted him on the back.

"After lunch, we'll go shopping. Don't try and tell me you didn't have a good time at the department store yesterday."

"That's me, *Billage* through and through."

In the shop, Elías stopped to have a look at a pocketknife. It was dark red with a white cross set inside a white shield. It was open, with all the various implements on show: scissors, corkscrew, file, tin opener and two knives, a long one and a short one.

"They use them in the Swiss Army," explained Mateo, and asked the man in the shop if he could pick it up.

Elías spent some time playing with the different implements, occasionally enquiring about how to use one or the other. Finally, he asked how much it was. Seventy-five new francs.

"It's an incredible gadget, isn't it?" said Mateo.

"Yes, very expensive though."

Seeing what the problem was, the man brought out a knife with a single blade and an image of the Virgin Mary set into the handle. It was cheap, less than ten francs. Elías said he would think about it.

It was a street exclusively of souvenir shops. Mateo stopped outside one and picked up a snow globe with a miniature Lourdes shrine inside it. He went to show it to Elías, but Elías was moving on to the next shop.

Tiny flakes of snow swirled around the shrine as he shook the globe. And as if this had opened his eyes, Mateo suddenly understood that Elías had no need of mementos from Lourdes, neither needed nor wanted them, for the simple reason that his father had gone there in the hope of being cured and had left frustrated, or, worse still, having had his final hopes dashed. Just like the headmaster at the college, perhaps, or Pascal. Mateo put the snow globe back in its place and caught up with Elías.

"I didn't buy anything," he said. "What I am going to do is buy a silk scarf from that department store in Pau. I think my mother would like that."

Elías gave him a thumbs up.

"Good idea. I will as well."

The street was starting to fill up with people. Mateo stopped outside a shop selling soaps and bath salts.

"We're being spied on. José Carlos and Miky have been following us for the last half an hour. Here's what we'll do, Elías . . ."

He explained his plan. The two of them would go into the shop together; then, as soon as they came back out, they would split up, and meet up again in a quarter of an hour at the top of the street.

Elías could not see why they had to split up.

"If they're looking for a fight, we're better off sticking together, aren't we?"

Mateo shot him a scornful look.

"Fight? Those two? I know them, and they know me. I taught the two of them a lesson last summer they won't have forgotten."

Elías did not know what he meant.

"So anyway, let's get one over on them," said Mateo. "Give

them a little run around. And we ought to take off the caps. They'll have a harder time finding us among all these people."

Elías looked at his watch. It was nearly five o'clock.

"What time are we supposed to be back at the car park?"

"Six. We'll go along the river; we'll be back in plenty of time." With that, Mateo went one way down the street, Elías the other.

On the bus journey back to Beau-Frêne, things grew increasingly boisterous. The boys were shouting more than talking, constantly swapping seats and going up to Elías and Mateo to ask them, yet again, where they had got their grey-and-yellow caps. "I was sent them from Missouri," said Mateo. And if someone picked him up on this and reminded him that earlier he had said Cincinnati and not Missouri, he would add:

"Have you any idea just how many of my ancestors fought with General Lee? Seventeen! Some were from Cincinnati, others were from Missouri and Texas, some from Virginia . . . It's hardly surprising I get them mixed up."

Finally, after another three or four repetitions of the joke, he went to the front of the bus and asked the warden to turn on the microphone.

"Let's see what you've got to say for yourself now," said the warden. "All your clowning around is wearing pretty thin."

Mateo blew on the microphone several times to check that it was working.

"That'll do," said the warden, as Mateo blew on it for the fifth time. All of the boys had fallen quiet.

"I am pleased to announce that, should you go to the second floor of the Pau department store, specifically the jeans section, you will find grey-and-yellow caps just like these."

Some of the students clapped.

"However," he went on, "this particular department store has no wish to take sides, and, in the same section selling Confederate caps, you'll also find those worn by Lincoln's soldiers, the blue ones, a sight uglier to my mind. But of course, it makes sense for me not to like them. Eighty-four of my ancestors fought on the side of General Lee. Eighty-four, possibly more, it's difficult to know exactly."

The applause grew louder.

"Given the circumstances, and in memory of my ancestors, I now invite you to join me in a rendition of the Confederate anthem." And he began to hum the tune.

"That's it, ever the troublemaker," said the warden.

The boys all knew the anthem from films they had seen, and the bus filled with an enthusiastic chorus of voices.

"Thank you, all of you, for this small homage to my ancestors. You will soon be receiving, at your home addresses, a diploma from the Ku Klux Klan."

"That'll do. Back to your seat," ordered the warden.

"I am going to sit down now, friends," Mateo said. "But first, one final request. We are all going to sing the song that our dear teacher Pascal has taught us. You know, the one with the sailor sailing along on the rubber rings."

There was laughter from all the seats. The warden snatched the microphone from him. The boys in the back seats started bellowing out "*Il était un petit navire . . .*"

The clamour gradually subsided as the journey went on, as though the mood inside the bus were keeping step with the landscape outside, where the river flowed ever more placidly, the mountains grew less wild, the brightness in the sky became less intense, and the clouds, with their honey-coloured haloes, softened. After "*Il était un petit navire . . .*", the students moved on to Françoise Hardy's "*Tous les garçons et les filles*", and after that the noise died down. The only sound was the hum of the engine. Many of the students fell asleep in their seats.

Elías gazed out of the window. Every now and then a wooden shack appeared on the riverbank with a row of kayaks outside. They were approaching Pau.

"How about we swap caps?" said Mateo, removing Elías' from

his head before he had time to answer. Mateo had his own cap in his hand, tightly folded up. "I'll have yours, and you'll have mine."

"What's this?" said Elías, taking the cap. Unfolding it, he found a Swiss Army knife inside.

"For you," said Mateo.

There was a sharp intake of breath from Elías. He held the knife with the palm of his hand flat, as if it were a collection plate. They hugged, and for a few seconds, their bodies remained clasped in a tight embrace.

The suburbs of Pau came into sight, with their elegant riverside houses. Elías had now opened up all of the knife's tools. It was amazing that such a small device could contain so many different implements.

"Now I get the thing about the spies," he said. "You wanted to be on your own so you could go and buy the knife, that's why you said José Carlos and Miky were following us."

"What makes you think that? I'm not completely sure they were following us, but I saw them lurking about in the . . ."

He was interrupted by the warden standing next to them in the aisle, staring down at the knife.

"That isn't stolen, is it?"

Mateo took a receipt out of his pocket and showed it to him.

"Just as well."

The warden returned to the front of the bus and picked up the microphone.

"We're nearly back at Beau-Frêne. Nobody leave anything on the bus."

Elías closed the knife up.

"Honestly," said Mateo, "I wouldn't be surprised if they had been following us, or if they went and told the warden about me stealing the knife. When I bought it, I thought I'd put on a little show for them, and so I came running out of the shop."

Elías gave him a little shove.

"Honestly, Mateo!"

During supper, they tried out the scissors, the knives, the file and the tin opener, as well as the corkscrew – going into the kitchen and asking the cook to let them open a bottle of wine.

"What a shame a day like today has to end!" said Elías as they left the dining hall.

They had half an hour before bedtime, and the pair went to the pelota court and sat down on the ground, their backs against the wall. It was dark now, but the sky was a summer sky, clear and full of stars. Mateo lit a cigarette.

"Want one?" he said, holding out the Gitanes.

Elías said no. He edged closer to Mateo, leaning against him, and they stayed like that until the Beau-Frêne bells rang out. It was time to go inside.

"Well, I feel just the same. I wish today wouldn't end either!" said Mateo, and they remained there a minute or two longer, until the bells chimed for a second time.

The students all slept on the top floor of the college, in a long, corridor-like dormitory. The beds were set out in one row, a couple of metres apart. Elías' bed was the first one as you entered; Mateo's was the twelfth along.

Most of the boys fell asleep instantly, tired out after the long day's excursion. Mateo waited until all was quiet. He then got up and padded over to Elías' bed, slipping in between the sheets.

"It's me, Mateo."

"What about the warden?" said Elías, his body stiffening.

Being night-watchman was another of the warden's duties. His room was just outside the door, not far from Elías' bed, with only a partition wall between them.

"Can't you hear him snoring?"

Elías strained to listen.

"Loud and clear."

They were wearing nothing but their underpants, and each could feel the warmth of the other's body.

"You smell of cigarettes," Elías said, giggling.

Mateo kissed him on the neck.

*

64

In the days following the excursion, Elías and Mateo found the daily routine hard to bear. The mornings and afternoons dragged, and they found it impossible to muster any interest in the classes – including French Culture with Pascal – and even more so in the sporting activities and all the energy the other students put into them. They were not, however, unhappy. They lived in a state of dazed rapture, awaiting the night. After lights out, when Mateo picked his way through the cave-like darkness to Elías' bed, all the heaviness of the day, indeed of their whole lives up until then, melted away. There occurred between them the very thing the headmaster had described in his account of Bernadette Soubirous: how the girl, after her first awestruck sighting of the lady in the white robe and blue girdle, had wanted only one thing, to go back to the cave, and how she had dreamed of being given one of the yellow roses she had seen on the Virgin's feet – a desire that nourished her soul and helped her rise above the poverty in which she lived. These nocturnal meetings were Elías' and Mateo's yellow rose.

On Monday, August 14, as on the previous night, the two of them were lying side by side, keeping very still, with Mateo kissing Elías' neck. On Tuesday, August 15, it was Elías who started kissing Mateo, and for the first time they began caressing each other's chest and belly. The next night, Wednesday, August 16, they each removed their underpants. On Thursday, August 17, no sooner had Mateo climbed in next to Elías than they heard a noise at the door, and saw a figure standing by the bed. A moment later, a torch was being shone in their eyes.

"Get out of there at once."

It was the warden. No shouting, no harsh words, just that blunt order. Mateo sat up in the bed.

"It's all my fault."

"I can believe it," said the warden. He was wearing a pair of off-white pyjamas that stood out in the darkness. They could not really see his face.

A commotion broke out around them.

"Poofters!" exclaimed two voices in unison. "There they are! A pair of poofters!"

Mateo shouted even louder:

"And there *they* are, José Carlos and Miky, a pair of snitches!"

"Silence!" boomed the warden.

Mateo whispered to Elías:

"I'll get my own back on him in Madrid. I know where Real Madrid do their training . . ."

Somebody turned on the lights. All of the students, either half out of their beds or standing up, were staring at them.

The warden grabbed Mateo by the arm.

"Get your things and come with me."

"Faggot!" yelled José Carlos.

"Snitch!" yelled Mateo even more shrilly.

The warden lost patience:

"Back in bed, the lot of you! Lights out!"

Somebody turned out the lights, but Mateo protested. He needed to be able to see in order to pack his suitcase. Torch in hand, the warden accompanied him to his bed and used the master key to open his locker.

On Friday, August 18, Mateo did not appear at the morning lessons. In the afternoon, during choir rehearsal, Pascal spoke to Elías.

"Mateo is on his way home," he said, sitting down next to him. He was not a big man, and easily fitted in behind the desk. "He's been driven to Biarritz, and he'll catch a plane there."

Pascal put a copy of that day's song between them on the desk, and began to sing in a soft voice: "'*Heureux qui comme Ulysse a fait un beau voyage* . . .' It's Georges Brassens, a variation on the Du Bellay sonnet we were working on. Look, read it."

Elías was crying.

Pascal went on softly singing: "'*Heureux qui comme Ulysse a fait un beau voyage. Heureux qui comme Ulysse a vu cent paysages. Et puis a retrouvé après maintes traversées le pays des vertes années . . .*'"

It was noisy in the library. José Carlos said loudly:

"He can't sing, sir. He's too sad."

Pascal got up and brandished his white stick.

"*Voilà la porte!*"

José Carlos stood up, arms raised.

"What's wrong? He is sad, isn't he? Am I lying?"

Pascal pointed his stick at the door.

"*La porte!*"

José Carlos left the library, hands in his pockets. Pascal went over to the harmonium and played the song's opening phrase, once, and then several more times.

It took them the best part of an hour to get the hang of the melody.

"Have the translation ready by next Friday," said Pascal at the end, before adding: "Could you translate the first line for us right now, Elías? '*Heureux qui comme Ulysse a fait un beau voyage.*'"

Elías wiped away his tears with his sleeve.

"Happy is he who, like Ulysses, has made a long journey."

Pascal raised his face to the ceiling.

"'Fortunate' would be more exact than happy, but not bad." He pointed to the library door. "My office is just there, the next door along, as you know. If you need to talk to me, just knock. I'm always there."

On Saturday, August 19, Elías went up to the library straight after breakfast to work on the translation Pascal had set them. He finished the second line – "*Heureux qui comme Ulysse a vu cent paysages*": "Fortunate is he who, like Ulysses, has seen a hundred landscapes" – and moved on to the next one: "*et puis a retrouvé après maintes traversées le pays des vertes années.*" This was harder, and he needed to use the dictionary. After confirming that "*traversée*" meant "crossing" or "voyage" he looked up "*maintes*", a word he did not know. At the top of the list of definitions was "*maintes fois*", meaning "often" or "frequently"; but "numerous" struck him as a better fit. He wrote in his exercise book: "And who then, after numerous voyages, has returned to the land of his youth." It felt overly long when he read it again, and the meaning not quite right. Pascal would not like it, he thought. The beginning of the second verse also seemed far from easy: *"Par un petit matin d'été, quand le soleil vous chante au coeur."* He understood each of the words, but not the overall meaning. He didn't feel like continuing just then, and decided to come back to it later on; after all, he still had nearly a whole week before the next rehearsal.

There was the sound of footsteps outside the door, so faint that on any other afternoon they would have been inaudible; but it was Saturday, all of the students had gone into Pau, most of the staff would be resting in their rooms, and there was not a sound to be heard anywhere. Elías looked at the door. It was opening very slowly. Then it suddenly seemed to come to life, swinging open and shut in an instant. The warden was inside the library. He walked over to Elías, one careful step after another.

"Yes, you're a good boy. All the others go off to bars and discotheques, but you'd rather be here, studying."

His face was red, as if he had been in the sun. He stopped in front of Elías.

"What are you up to?"

Leaning closer, he picked up the exercise book. Then he saw the Swiss Army knife on the desk, which Elías had placed in the groove meant for pencils and pens.

"Ah, the Lourdes knife!"

The warden was so close now that his head and Elías' were touching.

"The one who gave this to you was a bad boy, and he certainly doesn't deserve you feeling sad about him."

He started to pant, as though he were suddenly short of breath.

"And he taught you nasty things. But maybe you like them. Is that it? Did you like it?"

He reached out for the knife, but Elías got there first. The warden tittered.

"Don't worry, I'm not going to take it off you. I don't want anything of wicked little Mateo's. It's you I want."

Reaching down to Elías' waist, he thrust his hand down the front of the boy's trousers. Elías escaped the warden's hand by jumping out of his seat. He tried to open the long blade on the Swiss Army knife, but failed, and got the corkscrew out instead. A second later, he stabbed the warden with it, first in the arm and then in the collarbone, near his throat.

On any other day, the warden's screams would have been heard throughout the college; in the silence of that Saturday afternoon, they seemed fit to crack the walls. The warden tried to run over to the door but stumbled and fell flat on his face. Elías headed in the opposite direction, toward the back wall of the library.

Pascal appeared in the doorway, tapping the floor with his stick.

"What's going on in here?"

The warden, whimpering, was trying to get up.

"I need a doctor! This boy has just tried to kill me!"

"Can you walk?"

"I . . . I think so."

"Well, go down to the headmaster's office and phone from there."

The warden left.

Pascal patted Elías' exercise book, which lay open on his desk.

"Elías, where are you?"

There was no answer.

"Elías, tell me where you are before anybody else gets here! I'm your friend!"

From the back of the room there came a groan, a rasping sob, leading Pascal to where the boy was cowering.

"Elías, what happened?"

The only answer was more sobbing. Pascal repeated the question twice more but received no response.

"You can't talk now, but it's okay. You'll tell me when you can."

The sobbing grew louder.

"Listen, Elías. I can imagine what happened. Not every single detail, but I know. It's okay."

Elías buried his face in Pascal's chest and burst into tears.

The headmaster's office was on the ground floor, not far from the warden's lodge on the corridor that led to the games room. Its spartan interior featured a wooden desk, three chairs and two metal filing cabinets. The only ornament was a figurine of the Virgin of Lourdes on a plinth, placed so that the light from the window fell on it.

The table was cluttered with papers and folders, and the headmaster, inviting Pascal and Elías to sit, opened one of the folders. He fixed his gaze on Elías.

"Pascal tells me you're an intelligent boy. He himself is an intelligent man. And I, too, am intelligent. So we're going to resolve this matter between the three of us."

His voice sounded just as feeble as it had the day he gave the talk in the library. But it was a Sunday – August 20 – and the college was even emptier than it had been on the Saturday, so that even the faintest noises could be heard, down to the buzzing of the flies against the windowpane.

"Yes, of course we will," said Pascal, leaning his white stick against the table.

"Pascal has told me," the headmaster continued, "that you're unable to speak, or that you don't want to speak, but I would be very grateful if you would respond to the things I say with a nod or a shake of the head. All right? Will you do that?"

Elías nodded.

"When I was a young man," the headmaster continued, "I spent a year in a Benedictine monastery. I wanted to test the strength of my calling by taking a vow of silence. There were some fifty men there, and the only time we were permitted to speak was on Christmas Day and on Easter Sunday. But it was very hard not being allowed to say a single word. After a month, the pain was almost physical, and once the year was out, I decided to leave the monastery."

He stopped talking, and the buzzing flies could be heard again. Outside the window, in the courtyard at the rear of the college, a man in overalls was examining the engine of a lawnmower.

The headmaster was looking at the figurine of the Virgin of Lourdes. Her robes were more brilliantly white than those of the statue in the grotto. The blue of her girdle was a deeper blue. The yellow of the roses on her feet almost golden.

"What has happened to you here in Beau-Frêne is just dreadful. Would that the Virgin could crush the serpent, all the serpents, but sometimes that just isn't possible. The two that assaulted you here were truly devious. You didn't know how to face down the younger serpent, but you did confront the older one. Am I right?"

Elías lowered his eyes.

The workman in the courtyard started the lawnmower and then let the engine die, repeating the operation several times, apparently testing it out. When the lawnmower fell silent, they heard voices in the corridor. It was a group of students who, grounded for the weekend because of *le ruban*, were making their way to the games room.

"Here's what we thought we would do," said the headmaster, interlacing his fingers. They were pure skin and bones.

"First tell him what we've already done," said Pascal.

"Yes, you're right."

No sooner had he begun his explanation than he was forced to pause again. The lawnmower had been fired up once more and the workman was now testing out the accelerator.

"The older of the serpents is now in the Benedictine monastery," he said presently. "And there he will stay, tending the gardens, among other tasks."

"The monastery is where we usually go for our spiritual exercises," added Pascal. "It is a hard place for serpents."

"I'm tired, and must leave you now," said the headmaster, closing the folder in front of him. "As for you, you will go home tomorrow. You can't stay here. You'll have no peace, and you'll end up fighting with your fellow students. Pascal spoke to your mother this morning."

"I told her you weren't being expelled," said Pascal, "and that half of the fees would be returned to her. As for the reason, I said you'd had a fight with a teacher, and that the shock had left you unable to speak. A temporary upset, so my brother has termed it. He assures me it won't be long before you regain the power of speech."

"Pascal's brother is a psychiatrist in Paris," said the headmaster. "A very good psychiatrist."

Pascal turned to face Elías.

"Anyway, we wanted you to know how things stand. For our part, for now, this is where we'll leave it. Later on, I'll come and visit you, I promised your mother as much, and if further explanations are needed, that's when I'll give them."

"You understand, don't you, young man?" said the headmaster.

Elías nodded. The headmaster stood up.

"You'll be in my prayers."

"It would give me great joy to come and visit your village," added Pascal, picking up his stick and also getting to his feet. "It will be my holiday for the year."

They filed out of the office: first Elías, then Pascal and last of all the headmaster.

3

It was September 10, a Sunday night. Every now and then a gust of southerly wind shook the three pieces of clothing hanging on the washing line: a vanilla-coloured blouse, a white bra and Elías' grey-and-yellow cap. Sitting on the terrace, Marta watched them sway and turn while her husband talked about Munich. The day at the Olympics – the closing day – had once more ended in tragedy.

"Tell me what happened, Julián, but don't let it be sad. I'm feeling good today, and I want to go on feeling good."

Her husband took a drag on his Monterrey.

"What happened with Frank Shorter was definitely sad."

"Tell me anyway, Julián! Go on!"

Marta giggled involuntarily, her eyes fixed on the clothes as they moved in the wind: the blouse, the bra, the cap.

"It's one of those exemplary stories that reveal a lot about the human condition," said Julián. "The American, Shorter, was in the lead in the marathon, and the camera returned to him over and over. The commentators kept saying that, after all these years, an American was finally going to win this great race. Then it cut to a shot of the stadium, everyone in the crowd waiting for the lead runner – Shorter, the American – to appear, but then, rather than him, we see a runner emerge wearing the German strip. All the spectators thought he'd managed to overtake Shorter, meaning one of their compatriots was about to win gold. They went completely wild. But then guess what? It turns out he was an impostor, some guy who'd hidden at the stadium entrance and then run out onto the track at the last moment. A joker! He ruined the marathon for everyone!"

Julián snorted, letting out a puff of smoke from his Monterrey. Marta took her eyes off the washing line and settled back in the wicker chair.

"Dom Pérignon!" she said, laughing.

Julián was briefly unsure whether to go on, but he was warming to the theme:

"One hell of a trick that joker played on Frank Shorter. Put yourself in his shoes: you're in first place, you know you're in first place, and then suddenly you hear the whole stadium going wild. Shorter was on edge after that, that's what they said on the TV, he spent the whole final kilometre in a panic thinking some other runner had overtaken him. He didn't think they could have, but he couldn't be sure, not after he'd just heard all that cheering and so on. And then his own arrival in the stadium was just a bit of a damp squib, because a lot of the spectators were confused and didn't bother to applaud him."

He exhaled his cigar smoke with a sigh. The wind had momentarily died down and the smoke lingered in the air.

"That joker ruined the race of Shorter's life!"

Marta could not share her husband's anger. To her mind, everything was as it should be: Luis, Martín, Elías and their friends were playing in the square, shouting and whistling as usual; the lights were on in people's kitchens and living rooms in the village; the moon up above resembled a huge coin; and the night an endless expanse. Everything called to her, but especially the movement of the clothes on the washing line. The blouse would billow out for a moment; the lacy, flyaway bra fluttered back and forth; the grey-and-yellow cap, still wet, hardly moved, seemingly more modest than the blouse or bra.

"Dom Pérignon!" she exclaimed again. "Dom Pérignon!"

The name escaped from her mouth like a bird, flying up into the vastness of space, into the distance, up to the corner of the sky occupied by the bright moon.

"Bit tipsy, are we?" said Julián.

"I'm just enjoying hearing you talk about the Olympics, Julián," she said. This emerged from her mouth more like a floppy ragdoll bird and barely made it as far as the washing line.

Julián blew out more smoke. He grimaced. He did not enjoy smoking when it was windy.

"After the Palestinian attack, the Olympics deserved to end on a good note," he said. "It seemed like we might get that today. The 5,000-metre final was incredible."

"Who won?" said Marta. Another ragdoll bird.

"Lasse Virén, Finland," Julián said quickly.

"And who came second?"

"Mohammed Gammoudi, Tunisia."

"Third?"

"Ian Stewart, Great Britain."

"How many people died in the Palestinian attack?"

"Fourteen: eight Israeli athletes, five Palestinians and a policeman."

"And who won in the marathon?"

Marta's questions were now like olive stones being spat out one after the other.

"The marathon? I told you already. Shorter!"

He stubbed out his cigar, even though he had not yet smoked it all. The wind was picking up. Sometimes the bra flipped right over and looked like it was about to break free from the clothes pegs. The blouse flapped and strained. Only the grey-and-yellow cap stayed just where it was.

"I mean second; who came second?" Marta said.

"Karel Lismont. And Mamo Wolde was third – the Ethiopian who's won the Cross de San Sebastián a few times."

The shouts and whistles from the children in the square were now joined by the sound of accordion music.

"The Gitane Blonde!" exclaimed Marta. This, again, rose from her mouth like a real bird, flying off into the vast night, towards the moon. "It's the Gitane Blonde, it must be. After the Dom Pérignon, he said he felt like playing his accordion, and that he was going to come later on to get everybody in the bars dancing.

Did you know that Dom Pérignon is the best champagne in the world?"

"And the most expensive!" said Julián.

He sat and waited, watching his wife out of the corner of his eye. Marta lifted her hand, fingers splayed.

"Five! That blind teacher from France brought *five* bottles of Dom Pérignon," she said. "He wanted to give them to Elías' family as a gift. We drank three at lunch, maybe four. I can't remember exactly."

She laughed. A brief chuckle.

The accordion could be heard more clearly now. It was playing a march, and Marta felt an urge to hurry to the front of the house and see whether Martín, Luis and Elías were joining in, but, instead, she stayed where she was – she felt good, wonderfully good and comfortable there in the wicker chair. The wind tousled her hair, and the clothes on the line, the bra in particular, seemed to have a life of their own, to be dancing; even Elías' grey-and-yellow cap, starting to dry, had begun to move a little now. As for the moon, there it still was, so far off, thousands and thousands of kilometres away, glowing a dark, pinkish yellow . . . The only thing missing were the stars, those little silvery dots in the vastness of space; but even without the stars it was all very wonderful, as was being able to hear the accordion music from the terrace, as though the music were coming over the roof or from the alleyway between their house and their neighbour's.

Looking down at the ashtray, Julián reached for his cigar, but the tip had broken, and he got up to fetch another from the kitchen.

"I'll have one of my L&Ms," said Marta.

"And a glass of rum?"

"Do you want to get me drunk, or what?"

Martha's mind was racing; she felt as though she would start talking at any moment and her thoughts would come rushing out, even those that would be best kept to herself.

Julián came back to the terrace.

"Who won the most medals at this Olympics, the Russians or the Americans?" she asked, fumbling when she took the glass from him, spilling a little of the rum. She licked her wet hand.

"The Russians," said Julián, sitting back down.

He put a cigarette between her lips and held out his lighter to her, before lighting his Monterrey.

"It seemed like the Americans were going to beat them this time, especially with Mark Spitz and all his swimming medals. But the Russians got ahead in the end, thanks to the gymnasts."

"What about Kato? How did he do?"

"He won. Japan did well too."

"It seems like everyone won something in these Olympics. Like a tombola. A prize for the young lady over there!"

"And the party at the bakery today, how was it?" asked Julián.

"Negrita rum!" cried Marta, raising her glass. "It's nice, this rum, but that champagne . . . Now I've forgotten the name."

"Dom Pérignon."

"That's it! I've never tasted anything so delicious in all my life. That blind teacher . . . Pascal, yes, he was called Pascal . . . presumably that's French for Pascual, but anyway, he's called Pascal. Well, Pascal brought the champagne with him in his car, a beautiful car, cream-coloured, with leather seats . . . Miguel told me it was a Peugeot 504. And since this Pascal is blind, he had a chauffeur, a very serious fellow, who came in carrying a crate and started saying to me: '*Frigorifik? Frigorifik? Frigorifik?*'" She burst out laughing, before going on: "I finally managed to work out what he was saying, and when I took him into the kitchen he opened the crate and took out the bottles of Dom . . ."

"Dom Pérignon!"

". . . the five bottles of that champagne. I made space in the refrigerator and he, very slowly and carefully, put them in, and then he starts saying, '*Temperatir? Temperatir?*' I had no idea what he was talking about, so he just turned the dial himself, putting it at 8°C. And Pascal . . . yes, it must be Pascual really . . . when he got out of the car, tapping the ground with his white stick,

Elías went running over to Pascal and gave him such an enormous hug that his cap fell off, the cap he put on today, trying to look stylish I think – it's the one drying right there. Then they both burst into tears. Did I mention that Pascal was blind?"

Julián raised his eyebrows. The wind had died down, and the smoke from his small cigar hung in the air. The smoke from Marta's cigarette, perhaps because the tobacco was lighter, rose and vanished quickly.

"Well, Pascal's tears ran down from under his dark glasses, and he was sobbing. Tears of joy – I know they were tears of joy – because Elías had been cured of whatever it was that was stopping him from speaking. Because Pascal knew all about it – that was why he came. But, I don't know, when I saw that blind man there, with that elegant car, and he himself so elegant in a lovely green jacket, crying like that, and Elías' cap lying on the ground . . . it shook something inside me, and even though I knew they were tears of joy it made me feel sad. And even now, with this rum . . ."

She tilted back her head and gazed up at the sky. The moon was shining brightly. A shudder ran through her, and she came out in goosebumps all over.

"No, no, no . . ." she said, taking a deep breath.

She raised the cigarette to her lips and took two quick puffs. A memory from that morning had just come back to her. Miguel and her together in the pantry, her looking for a vase for the roses she had just picked in the garden, Miguel calling to her in a whisper, "Marta, Marta . . ." When she turned, Miguel had grabbed her round the waist and pulled her close, and then, as he bent down to kiss her, she said, "No, no, no . . ."

"I'm not sure I follow," said Julián.

"And if I go on drinking this rum, I'll make even less sense. Don't mind me, I'm babbling."

The accordion could be heard once more in the street. Julián stubbed out his cigar in the ashtray. The southerly wind was getting on his nerves again.

"Luis and Martín are staying at Miguel's tonight," he said. "To keep that friend of theirs, Elías, company. They asked my permission, and I said they could. Okay with you?"

She nodded, but said: "No, no, no . . ."

She could not get the image of that morning out of her mind. She had thought Miguel only wanted to kiss her, but he then enfolded her in such a strong embrace that she had to put the vase down on a shelf so as not to drop it.

"So?" said Julián. "Is it okay if the boys stay over at Miguel's?"

Marta sat bolt upright in the wicker chair, like somebody suddenly waking up.

"Of course it's okay with me! What do you think, that they're going to go down to the canal in the night and have a run in with that boar? Besides, what's so bad about the boar? It was thanks to the boar that Elías got better! If it hadn't been for the boar, he'd probably still be mute, no two ways about it. And he isn't! He talks a lot, in case you hadn't noticed!"

Her head was starting to spin. She was still holding her cigarette, but it had gone out. Julián took it from her and put it in the ashtray.

"It's been such a lovely day," said Marta, closing her eyes. "First, they all went up to the bakery, and then to the canal, and it seems Pascal and that very serious chauffeur of his were quite moved when the boys told them all about what had happened with the boar. They really liked the place. When they got back, the chauffeur just kept saying, '*se-bó, se-bó,*' which apparently means 'very pretty' in French."

The memory of Miguel came back to her. The two of them alone in the kitchen, after lunch, Miguel putting his arms around her, but not as he had in the pantry; this time reaching inside her blouse and licking her bra like some oversized dog.

"Luis played one of his tricks on me," she said. "I was clearing the table, after Pascal and the driver had gone, and just as I picked up the bowl of custard, he crept up behind and pushed me . . . I was holding the bowl like this . . ." She held her arms up for a few seconds, before going on: "I got some down my front, between my boobs, and some of it dropped on Elías' head. He was so upset that his cap had got dirty! But it's fine. I washed it straight away, and I washed it again when I got back here. The blouse is all right too. The bra . . . I don't know, that had a bigger stain. The custard went right down between my boobs!"

She tried to laugh, but that particular bird failed to make it as far as her mouth.

The moon was growing more and more intensely yellow, almost like a spotlight. And the wind was blowing steadily now. The cap, almost dry, flapped about even more. The blouse too. The bra had wound itself round the washing line. But there were no stars, or at least not that she could see, and she could not repeat the game she and Lucía had tried so many times in the days when they used to go dancing, when they would count nine stars and ask to be given the boy of their choice, because the stars had the power to make wishes come true if you asked them like that, counting nine stars one by one, nine different stars . . .

"One, two, three, four, five, six, seven, eight, nine!"

She scrutinised the sky as she counted, and she found she could see some stars, but only a few, and those were obscured by the light of the moon.

Among the shifting images in her mind, Lucía stood out, and she began talking to her inside her head, barely moving her lips: "All the things you missed out on, Lucía, dying at thirty-six. Look at me now, drinking the best champagne in the world, Dom Pérignon! And look at what else has happened. Miguel and I slept together, and, wow . . . How silly you were, Lucía, and forgive me for calling you silly with you being dead and all, but what you did still hurts. You didn't need to kill yourself, Lucía. Dear God, dear God! How could you have done that, Lucía . . .!"

"I need another cigarette," she said out loud.

Julián passed her the L&Ms.

"What are you thinking about? Your lips are trembling. Are you going to cry?"

Marta fumbled as she took a cigarette out of the packet and lit it.

"I'm not planning on crying. Why would I cry? I've no reason to. The party at Miguel's today was just wonderful. As it should have been. It isn't every day that a child gets better the way Elías did; mental problems don't usually just go away like that. Clearly the boar helped too. Nobody can argue with that. Really, it was the boar that sorted everything out."

Julián crossed his arms.

"You said that already. You're repeating yourself, Marta."

"So what if I am? Certain things need repeating, because certain things are very important. And what happened with Elías is just that. Even that Pascal said it was like a miracle, and that all the prayers they said in France must have had something to do with it . . ." She could not stop talking. It was as if she had an engine running inside her head. "When we were having coffee, Pascal played us some lovely songs on the Gitane Blonde's accordion. In the end, he got Elías to go and sit next to him and they started singing that song, *'peti-navi, peti-navi'*, first, just the two of them, then with everyone joining in. God, I'm going on, aren't I?"

Julián laughed and put an arm around her shoulder:

"I think it's the Dom Pérignon."

Initially, while everyone was singing *"peti-navi, peti-navi"* in the kitchen, Marta had felt out of place, alone, the music on one side and her on another, just her and the chauffeur, because the chauffeur did not join in either; but then she had immediately started to feel better, because Miguel, as he sang, was looking at her, was singing *for her*, and what a wonderful voice he had. That, surely, was when it had all been decided, and not with the embrace in the pantry; it was when everyone was singing *"peti-navi, peti-navi"* that it had been agreed between them, and why, once the songs and the conversation had died down, and once she had tidied up in the kitchen with Elías' mother helping her, and everyone had gone their separate ways, Pascal to France with his chauffeur, Elías' mother back to her restaurant, the children into the village to play . . . yes, that's why what happened happened. Miguel had returned to the kitchen after seeing everybody off and had said to her: "Can I close the door?" And she had said, "If you want to", and it was strange to think that a few minutes later the two of them were naked together in the room above the kitchen.

The moon continued to cast its light from one corner of the sky. The shouts and whistles of the children playing in the square had died down.

"What time is it?" said Marta.

Julián showed her his watch:

"Twenty past eleven."

"I thought it was later than that."

Tears came to her eyes.

"What is it now, Marta?"

"I suddenly remembered Lucía, and it made me sad."

Julián grasped her hands and helped her out of the chair.

"Where are you taking me?"

"To bed."

"Good."

Marta wanted to laugh, but somehow just didn't have the energy.

Four friends

1970

1

The truck driver who had given Eliseo a lift all the way from Madrid had dropped him on the outskirts of his home village of Santa María, and it was already very late at night by the time Eliseo set off for the cabins in the woods high up in Valdesalce. As soon as he reached the first hill, he heard some almost imperceptible noises and was tempted to stop and listen. Knowing the Castilian countryside as he did, he immediately identified where those sounds were coming from: mad, late-summer hares capering about excitedly among the brambles. They would be so easy to pick off, even two at a time, with just a single stone. He reined in his hunting instincts, however, and carried on walking.

Had anyone seen him in that guise – soldier's kit bag over his shoulder, bag and body forming a single shape in the darkness – they might have taken him for some kind of animal or else a hunchback, but Santa María was a small village and Valdesalce was a very solitary place, so there was no real danger of him meeting anyone. Yet still he felt uneasy. Mad hares attracted poachers, and poachers attracted the police, and were he to meet the police in that place and at that hour, they would be sure to question him, and that would only delay him.

When he reached Valdesalce, Eliseo left the road and continued across country. There was no moon, and the night was as dark as a windowless cell. Having walked the terrain so often before, however, he didn't need to see in order to find his way. The scrubland of sage and rosemary would soon give way to sparsely growing ash trees and willows, which, down by the stream, began to grow densely enough to form a small wood, which is where the shepherds' huts and the sheep pens were to be found.

He tripped over a tree root and, in trying to regain his balance, dropped his kit bag. He cursed the army boots, the soles of which were so thick that he couldn't feel the ground beneath his feet. He half sat up, opened the kit bag and took out the metal box in which he kept the bird.

"Are you OK?" he asked.

His eyes already having adjusted to the dark, he could easily make out the box. Inside, the bird seemed to be stumbling about, scratching at the metal surface with its talons. All seemed to be well.

"Now stop that!" he said, tapping the lid of the box. "We've arrived."

His mind, like his eyes, was adapting to his surroundings, so different from the barracks he had left only hours before. He heard a sheep bleating, and this was followed by a few languid bleats from other drowsy sheep. This was his place, his home, in Valdesalce. He looked at his watch but could not see the time. He reckoned it must be around eleven o'clock. *Sports Round-up* began at ten, and the truck driver who had given him a lift had tuned into the programme as they were approaching Santa María.

"Call yourself a soldier?"

Eliseo remembered the contemptuous frown on the driver's face. The man could not believe that Eliseo was so ignorant about football that he didn't even know that the League had begun that very weekend.

"Don't you know anything? Not even how Real Madrid did? They beat Valencia two-nil."

"We don't have a TV in the barracks. All I know is that Eddy Merckx won the Tour de France."

"Yeah, except Zoetemelk should have won it really."

The truck driver launched into a monologue about cycling, but Eliseo could not really follow. This was yet another sport about which he knew very little. The real expert was Donato, his co-worker in the barracks bakery. Eliseo had picked up the name Eddy Merckx from him.

It occurred to Eliseo that his lack of interest in sports must have annoyed the truck driver, and that was why he dropped him on the outskirts of the village rather than driving him up to Valdesalce, which wouldn't have taken him more than five minutes.

"Bastard!" he muttered.

Then he heard a cry that people well-versed in sport but ignorant of country matters might well have mistaken for someone blowing a whistle. Eliseo, however, knew that cry well. It came from a bird native to those parts, the tawny owl.

Eliseo slung his kit bag over his shoulder once more and set off briskly, and when he reached the stream a few minutes later, he felt that he had finally come home, as sure of his whereabouts now as if it were broad daylight. To his left lay the path flanked by willows that led to Santa María. A hundred yards straight ahead was the cabin belonging to Basilio, the friend who took care of his sheep while he was away doing his military service. His own cabin was a bit further on. The third one, belonging to Paca and Tono, was over to the left, among the ash trees. Behind the cabins were the sheep pens, with room enough for about three hundred sheep.

He again heard the tawny owl hooting and the sheep bleating. He went slowly over to Basilio's cabin. Not a glimmer of light, only the faint smell of woodsmoke. His friend must be asleep.

A dog barked.

"Shh, Lay! Where are you?" The barking grew louder. "Here, Lay!"

The dog, a brown-and-white collie, crept hesitantly towards him, its belly close to the ground.

"It's me, Eliseo! OK, I'm dressed like a soldier, but it's still me!"

Reassured, the dog started licking Eliseo's ear, but its attention was instantly drawn to the kit bag.

"Wait a moment."

He took out the metal tin, and the dog pressed its nose to one of the holes in the lid. Eliseo snatched it away.

"Down, Lay! That's not your supper."

In the bakery at the barracks, on Saturdays and public holidays, they used to make what they called *choripanes*, small white bread rolls filled with chorizo. He had one left and let the dog sniff it.

"Is that nice?"

The dog wagged its tail.

"Stay here, Lay. Don't go waking everyone up."

As he crossed the wooden bridge over the stream in the darkness, he could just make out a still darker shape, his own cabin. He felt for the key in a hole in the wall, went in and lit the lamp hanging from a beam. After taking off his uniform, he started unpacking his kit bag: a box of biscuits he had bought at the petrol station while he was waiting for a lift, the metal box containing the bird, a silk rug a fellow soldier had given him in exchange for a sponge cake, a pheasant feather, a pair of walking boots, various changes of underwear, socks, a military balaclava and a wash bag. He also removed a towel and the folder that he had placed flat down at the bottom of the bag to provide a base.

He deposited the biscuits, the metal tin, the silk rug, the pheasant feather and the folder in one corner of the cabin. Then, on a shelf, he placed the contents of the wash bag: soap, toothpaste, shaving things, a pack of Winston cigarettes, a red lighter and a box of condoms.

Towel and soap in hand, he went outside completely naked and stepped down into a pool in the stream. The water was very cold, no trace of July or August heat, and, snorting and blowing out his cheeks, he began to splash about and scrub his body clean. His penis, which had been stiff and erect ever since he took off his uniform in the cabin, shrank and shrivelled until it resembled a child's.

He soaped himself all over and again lay down in the water. This time, the cold was less of a shock, and he lay there for a while, motionless, eyes closed. When he opened them, he saw Lay – or, rather, Lay's silhouette – on the wooden bridge. The dog gave a muffled bark and ran off in the direction of the third cabin.

Eliseo sprang to his feet. In the distance, through the darkness, he had glimpsed a whitish shape. He climbed out of the water and hurriedly dried himself with the towel. About twenty or fifteen metres away, the whitish shape gradually became a person, and that person only had to draw a little closer for his penis to become erect again.

"Paca, how are you?" he said.

She was a very big woman. At about a metre eighty-five, she must have been nearly ten centimetres taller than him and weighed in at around a hundred and twenty kilos, some fifty kilos heavier. She was wearing a white flannel nightdress that came down below her knees. She approached on tiptoe to avoid the stony ground hurting her feet, then, suddenly, she took a run and hurled herself at him, propelling him back into the water, and roared with laughter to see him floundering about.

"That's what you get for being late!"

The dog had returned to the bridge. Confused by the situation, it was now barking loudly. That was the only sound. Even the sheep in the pen were silent.

"What time did Basilio tell you I'd arrive?" he asked, clambering up the bank. Despite that second drenching in the cold water, his penis was still erect.

"Oh, who cares? Come here and I'll dry you off."

"No fear. I don't trust you."

He stopped about three metres away, then picked up his towel and started drying himself.

"I'm going in," said Paca. "Let's see if you've got what it takes to get into bed."

"I'll tup you like a ewe."

"What? A skinny little guy like you? No chance."

She strode over to the cabin, with the dog getting under her feet.

"In your corner, Lay!"

The dog hesitated, then waited, slowly wagging its tail.

"In your corner!" said Paca.

In the lamplit gloom, the inside of Eliseo's cabin resembled a chapel, like one of the side chapels in the church in Santa María, only without the images. The darkness was at its most intense near the ceiling and in the corners, and all the light was focussed on one particular wall and on the bed. And Paca, naked now, her long hair hanging loose over her breasts, had deliberately chosen to position herself there in that zone of brightness. As soon as she saw Eliseo come in, she put her hands on her hips and leaned forward.

Eliseo ran towards the bed and leapt on her, but, like a catch wrestler, she launched him backwards, sending him as far as the cabin door. Then he tried grabbing her ankle, but again she repelled him, this time with her leg. Without a pause, Eliseo crawled to the other side of the bed and managed to grab her right breast. When she tried to throw him off, he reached his other arm behind her knee, toppling her back onto the mattress.

There they continued their struggle. Eliseo tried to embrace her, aware for a moment of the warmth of her body, but she responded with another hard shove. Yet although she was fifty kilos heavier than him and nearly ten centimetres taller, she was still not as strong and finally had to give in. At one point, Eliseo seized her arms and pinned them down, exposing her breasts, which he then licked. She tried to wriggle away and turned onto her belly, but Eliseo immediately flipped her hundred and twenty kilos over again and slipped his hand between her legs. He was panting now, and she, too, was breathing hard.

"Like I said, I'm going to tup you like a ewe."

When silence returned to the cabin, she covered herself with a sheet and sat up on the mattress, legs crossed. Eliseo brought her the pack of cigarettes and the lighter he had left on the shelf.

"Oh, you're such a sweetheart!" she said.

She kept flicking the lighter on and off. In the glow of the flame, they could see each other's faces. They were both laughing.

"It's so pretty."

She had seen plastic lighters like that before, but never a red one. She lit a cigarette and exhaled the smoke, blowing it gently into Eliseo's face.

"Great cigarettes too!" she said. "Do you still not smoke? God, how can you stand living in barracks without smoking?"

Eliseo didn't answer. He went over to the other side of the cabin and returned with the folder that had been at the bottom of his kit bag.

"This is for you too."

Inside were three celebrity magazines. Paca held one up to the lamp.

"I'm beginning to forget how to read, you know. I never did learn properly, and I'm finding it harder and harder."

On the front cover was the picture of a wedding, with the groom in tails and the bride in a frilly white dress. Paca took her cigarette out of her mouth and with painful slowness read: "The la-vish wed-ding of the son of hair-dress-er A-le-xan-dre in St Tro-pez." She picked up the second magazine: "Ca-ro-li-ne fi-na-lly grows up." The cover of the third magazine showed a large room, all gilt and red carpets, where two men and two women were posed, smiling: "The Prince and Prin-cess Juan Car-los and So-fi-a wel-comed by the Shah of Per-sia and Fa-rah Di-ba."

She put the three magazines back in the folder and blew another cloud of smoke at Eliseo.

"You really are a sweetie. That'll keep me busy for a couple of months."

"I haven't finished yet. There's more," said Eliseo. He went back to the same corner and returned bearing the pheasant feather and the box of biscuits.

Paca burst out laughing and kissed him on the cheek.

They both felt very at ease. Outside, Valdesalce was equally at ease. They ate a couple of the biscuits. Then Eliseo picked up the feather and tickled Paca.

"It came from a pheasant in the woods around El Pardo."

"Who killed the pheasant? You?"

Eliseo gave a sarcastic laugh.

"That guy on the cover of the magazine, the prince, he probably goes hunting for pheasants there. Him and General Franco are the only ones with permission. No other hunter in Spain is allowed in. Not even the ones, like me, doing their military service there. Makes you sick."

Paca had a large head and an oval face. Her fair hair and freckled cheeks gave her a rather Northern European look. She took the feather from Eliseo and placed it between her breasts, like a flower.

"So, the prince gave it to you to give to me," she said, putting the feather behind her ear now. "I'm honoured!"

Eliseo laughed again, this time without a hint of sarcasm.

"Donato found it beside the bunker where we meet to have supper. Donato works with me in the bakery. We get on really well."

"You and me don't get on too badly either, do we?"

Eliseo pulled back the sheet she had covered herself with and lay her down on the mattress. He stroked her breasts.

"What are you going to do, Paca? Are you going back to your cabin now or when it gets light?"

"Nothing's going to make me leave this bed."

"What about Tono? Won't he be angry?"

"Oh, let him be angry! I'll give him a clip round the ear and send him off to live with the sheep."

They were about to fall asleep. They both had their eyes closed.

"There's something else too."

"What's that?"

"You'll find out in the morning."

The soldiers assigned to the bakery started work at five in the morning. Since Eliseo and Donato were responsible for the oven and for the kneading machines, they were always first in.

Eliseo's body had become so accustomed to that timetable that, even on the days when he did not have to work, he woke at a quarter or twenty to five. When he opened his eyes that morning in the cabin, it was still pitch-black, and at first he thought he was back in the room attached to the bakery where he and Donato slept. Gradually, as he became aware of Paca's warm body and her regular breathing, he realised he was in Valdesalce, where the shepherds from Santa María spent most of the year.

The sheep, Lay and the other dogs were all silent. Equally silent were the birds in the woods, as well as the one in the metal box. He thought about Basilio, and how it would probably be best to give him the balaclava that morning, and, at the same time, he wished he had thought to bring one for Tono too. Then, as if it were simply another thought, the image of his father slipped into his mind. His face was a mask; his body a shadow taking shape on the cabin door.

"Go away!" he cried.

His father was dying in his house in Santa María; he could die at any moment, he might even have been dying right then, which is why Eliseo was there, because the army had given him leave to be with his father in his final hours. Not that he had any intention of doing that. He did not want to.

He was falling asleep again, and the images began to follow one on the other in the disconnected way they do in dreams. His father's ghostly face was followed first by those mad hares racing round among the brambles on the hill leading up to Valdesalce, and then by the truck driver's face – "Real Madrid two, Valencia nil!"; then he saw Lay standing on the wooden bridge over the stream, and Basilio and Tono and Paca, all three surrounded by sheep, then he saw the prince and princess in that golden room in Tehran, and the pheasant feather and the pheasants in the woods surrounding El Pardo, and then Paca again.

He put his arms around her very gently, so as not to wake her. The local gossips called Paca the Virgin of Valdesalce because, they said, she could work miracles, sleeping as she did with all the shepherds in the area but never getting pregnant. With him, though, it was different. She never asked him for money. And, as she had told him many times, she reserved those battles in bed for him alone.

Sleep was about to overcome Eliseo, and he felt as if he were falling into a chasm of darkness. Terrified, he tried to stop the fall by tensing his body, and that movement jerked him back to reality. Sitting up in bed, his head was filled by just one thought, the thing he had so far avoided mentioning: he wasn't being honest with Paca; he hadn't said a word to her about leaving Valdesalce for good. He had made up his mind. He had done so months ago. That very morning, he would ask if Basilio could continue to look after his flock, and, as soon as his father died, he would put the house in Santa María up for sale. Then, in a few months, once he had completed his military service, he would go to Ugarte and work in the same bakery as Donato. The gifts he had given Paca were farewell gifts, which was why there were so many. Eliseo shook his head. No, he definitely did not want to think about it.

A ray of light was coming in through the cabin's one small window. Paca woke, turned over and rolled up against him with her full weight. Eliseo tried to withdraw to the edge of the bed, but she grabbed him by one thigh and drew him towards her.

That second bout of sex, just a few hours after the first, was very brief, and so, before day had fully dawned, Eliseo was again walking out of the cabin and down to the stream, where he once more jumped into the pool. The water seemed colder than it had the previous night, and he puffed and panted as he washed.

"What about that other present?" Paca asked when he returned to the cabin.

"Get up and go outside, Paca. I want you to see it in the daylight."

He dried himself on the towel and got dressed, having chosen a pair of jeans and a red polo shirt that he kept in a big chest in the cabin. He did not put on his shoes because his feet were slightly wet, and he never forgot the advice the army doctor had given during one of the first talks he attended: "Always dry between your toes. If you don't, you could get a fungal growth, which is very contagious and can cause painful lesions." When he heard this, Eliseo had raised his hand: "I understand about the fungal growth and how contagious it is, but may I ask, sir, can we get infected with the disease that makes rabbits' eyes swell up?" The doctor had responded: "Ah, you mean myxomatosis. It *is* a highly infectious disease which, as we've all seen, is rife in the woods around El Pardo, but it definitely isn't a virus that can be passed on to humans, although I have to say I certainly wouldn't eat one of those rabbits for supper." The soldiers all laughed. One man sitting behind Eliseo whispered in his ear: "You and your questions. Always sucking up to the officers." A soldier with blue eyes, who was sitting beside Eliseo, had intervened in his defence: "He who asks questions learns, he who doesn't ends up like you." This was the first time Eliseo had heard Donato speak. Later, they would both be assigned to the bakery, quite rightly in the case of Donato, who really knew the trade, but quite wrongly in his own case because he had falsely claimed to have been apprenticed to a baker.

He was about to retrieve the metal tin from the corner of the cabin, when he noticed the silk rug he had not yet given to Paca. He decided, instead, to give it to Basilio and let Tono have the balaclava. Whenever her husband, Tono, got drunk, Paca would kick him out of the cabin, even in the middle of winter, and he would have to spend the night in a shed in the sheep pen. The balaclava would help keep his head warm. Besides, Basilio was always going into the village, and if he really needed a balaclava, he just had to ask the local bus driver to bring him one from town.

"Now it's my turn to wash. I'm going down to the stream," said Paca and set off, nightdress in one hand, sheet in the other. Her buttocks were not what one might expect in a body weighing a hundred and twenty kilos: far from being a formless continuation of her thighs, they were rounded and shapely and moved rhythmically as she walked.

Eliseo sat on a tree trunk beside the cabin, the metal tin on his knees. When he shook it very gently, he heard a faint noise, then a nervous squeak.

"Behave yourself," he said.

Paca returned, drying herself on the sheet. The cold water had turned her nipples purple. She pulled her nightdress over her head, then stood there, hands on hips.

"Is that my present in that old tin box?" she asked.

Eliseo removed the lid, picked up the bird in one hand, then passed it to the other. At first, it appeared to be simply black and white, a very white white on its breast, and a very black black on its head, neck, back, wings and tail; but when you looked more closely, the feathers had a bluish-green iridescent quality. Its tail was long compared to the body, about six or eight centimetres long, and the bird kept twitching it up and down, occasionally depositing a dropping.

"Is it a magpie?" said Paca.

Eliseo stroked the bird's back.

"What's your name? Name!" he said to the bird.

As if the bird had been waiting for that moment, it croaked: "*Paca! Paca! Paca!*"

Paca tried to say something but couldn't. She made as if to smooth her hair, then wiped her hands on her nightdress to dry them.

"Is it for me?"

Eliseo handed her the bird.

"Hold her in your hand, and she'll grip your finger."

The bird changed hands with a light flap of its wings.

"*Paca! Paca! Paca!*"

"Oh, what a pretty little thing! And she knows my name!"

She shivered, goosebumps standing out on her arms.

"She's a very young magpie, and she'll gradually get prettier," said Eliseo.

"Oh, but she's really pretty now. How did you teach her to say my name?"

2

It was August 2, and there was almost no-one in the barracks, because at the weekend most of the officers, NCOs and other soldiers were given leave to go to Madrid. Along with Donato and others on kitchen or guard duty, Eliseo was among the exceptions. He stayed in barracks all that day, and at three o'clock, as soon as he had finished lunch, he headed for the grove of pine trees next to the bakery. It was very hot and the air buzzed with the sound of cicadas.

He chose a shady spot, took off his boots and lay down on an improvised bed hollowed out of the ground. With his left hand, he took a banana from one of the pockets in his fatigues, then reached into another pocket with his right hand and took out the book Warrant Officer Santos had lent him, entitled *Engine Problems*.

He half-peeled the banana, took a bite, then set it down on a small pile of pine needles. With his hands free now, he opened the book at the chapter headed "Stalling. Causes and Solutions". An ant appeared, running up and down the page. Eliseo blew it away and started to read.

The text was accompanied by a diagram showing the various engine parts and components along with their corresponding names and numbers, and Eliseo returned to it again and again while studying the section devoted to the accelerator cable and trying to imagine the noise the engine would make in each case, with each problem, because engines – "like a person's soul", according to Warrant Officer Santos – sounded different depending on the circumstances; however, he couldn't hear any engine noises at all, only the sounds around him. The thousands of cicadas in the wood were furiously rubbing their wings together, as if in competition, and he had the distinct impression that the whirring was getting closer and closer until it was about a metre from his ears or possibly even closer. Soon all other stimuli disappeared. There was no book, no banana, not even any heat. Nothing.

Time also dissolved into nothing, and the minutes that passed while he slept seemed to be over in an instant. He dreamed he was fixing a truck in the repair shop and that a washer had got stuck on the index finger of his right hand. The washer would not move, and it must have had notches on it or sharp edges because it cut into his skin. He had to get it off and kept rummaging vainly around in the toolbox for some pliers. Except that he was not in the repair shop, he was in the wood, lying on the ground. The sound of the cicadas continued to fill the air, though not as loudly as before, as if they had moved elsewhere. To his left lay the half-eaten banana, covered in ants. To his right, the book: *Engine Problems.*

A baby bird was clinging to his index finger with its clawed feet. It was a black ball with white stripes on its sides, a disproportionately large head and a black beak. Its talons, too, were very large, its eyes blue-black. It was observing him with one of those eyes, its head on one side.

Very slowly, Eliseo reached out his free hand and closed his fingers around the bird, whose only response was to open its beak ridiculously wide. After a moment's hesitation, Eliseo set it down on his right knee, although this took more than one attempt, because the bird refused to let go of his finger. Then, once it was on his knee, he tried clapping so as to frighten it off. In vain. The bird hopped onto his belt buckle and again opened its beak very wide and gave a croak.

Eliseo picked up his book and began studying a diagram of an accelerator but found it impossible to concentrate. The bird would not keep quiet. With the mutual understanding that often exists between wild creatures and people who grew up in the countryside, Eliseo soon realised what the bird wanted and offered it the banana. The bird immediately reached forward and ate one of the ants crawling over the banana skin.

A large magpie was hopping about close by. Then Eliseo realised something else. The baby bird pecking at the banana was also a magpie and would grow up to be as large as the adult bird hopping around him.

He scooped up some of the ants on the banana and stuffed them into the bird's beak. Then he offered it some bits of the banana itself. The bird devoured the lot.

The big magpie came closer still, twitching its long tail. With every move, its black wings shimmered blue and green. Its finest feature, though, was its white breast. Eliseo threw the parent bird a piece of banana. The magpie snatched it up and flew straight to the top of a pine tree, for however ungainly in flight, these birds were very strong.

Eliseo got to his feet and started walking back to the bakery along the path created over the years by the soldiers' repeated comings and goings. The baby bird stumbled along after him, falling over and getting up again as it tried to keep up. After a few yards, it tripped on a fallen branch and began shrieking.

Eliseo ignored it and continued on until he reached the room next to the bakery, where he found his friend Donato sitting on the edge of his bed practising the accordion. From a cassette player came the sound of Luis Aguilé's hit song, "Juanita Banana".

"Are you beginning to get the hang of it?" asked Eliseo.

Donato had startlingly blue eyes, and his head was almost shaven.

"Have a listen," he said and started playing. Apart from the occasional fumble, he managed to play the tune, humming along and singing only the words of the chorus: "Juanita Banana . . ."

He stopped playing then and looked at Eliseo. The song continued on the cassette for a few seconds more, then came to an end.

"That's much better than last week, Donato."

Then they heard the magpie squawking, and Eliseo raced out

of the bakery, imagining that some big cat was toying with the bird, pawing it gently so as not to kill it straight away and thus prolonging the cat's enjoyment. He hated cats and would throw things at them if they happened to come into the bakery – indeed, he had killed one that winter, hitting it on the head with a bread paddle – but all he saw when he came out was the baby magpie. It was still there, unable to get over the branch that had got in its way. It had one foot caught in a small root sticking out of the ground and couldn't free itself however hard it struggled. As soon as it saw Eliseo, it made even more noise.

Eliseo picked it up and tried to put it down on a rock, but it escaped and flew straight over to the bakery, where it landed on the stone bench by the door and promptly defecated, squawking all the time.

Eliseo went into the bakery and returned with a crust of bread. He broke some crumbs off and placed them before the bird, which swallowed them one by one. When it had finished, it again shat on the bench and stood looking at him. Its wings and tail were still short and not yet iridescent. They would take another month to grow to full size.

Eliseo set off back into the pine wood in search of an ant's nest, and the baby bird followed, hopping and fluttering along at ground level. Intrigued, Eliseo tried taking five rapid steps to the left. The bird hurried after him, flapping its wings. Eliseo then ran on ahead. Growing ever more agitated, the bird launched itself into the air three times, trying to keep up.

Eliseo caught two cicadas, broke them into pieces and placed them in the palm of his hand. The bird devoured them in an instant.

"What's up?" asked Donato from the door of the bakery. He still had the accordion strapped over his shoulders.

"I've acquired a new dog," said Eliseo, striding over to his friend. The bird hopped after him.

"We could put on a circus."

"A secret circus, so that no-one finds out. Only our real friends."

100

They agreed. Being seen with a baby bird contravened a soldier's first rule: never draw attention to yourself; besides, it would be perceived as a lack of discipline. The sergeants had made it clear on the very first day that a soldier could have only two things with him: his rifle and his kit bag. Nothing else.

They had just four months left to serve. The last thing they needed was to be put on a charge.

The following Saturday, Eliseo and Donato weighed the magpie for a second time on a small pair of scales in the bakery and were unsurprised to find that it had gained twenty grammes in the six days it had spent with them. Its body was more defined now and its squawk even louder. Its progress could also be seen in its droppings, even though it spent most of its time in a shoebox, for whitish stains were beginning to appear on the floor of their room and on their bedding.

Both the bird's loud squawking and its droppings were a problem. The squawking because the soldiers who worked with them in the bakery might hear, thus jeopardising their secret, and the droppings because they were hard to remove even with a scourer, and because Donato hated dirt. The bird really bothered him. He did not want it in their room.

Eliseo suggested leaving it somewhere in the countryside outside the barracks, but Donato rejected the idea. There was no way the bird would survive on its own now, and that was their fault, because they had spoiled it by feeding it bread and bits of banana and boiled egg rather than encouraging it to find its own food. It would only eat ants and cicadas from their hands, otherwise it would ignore the insects, as if it had no idea what they were.

After lunch, Eliseo and Donato went into the pine grove and agreed it would be best to leave the bird at the Communications Unit. This was located outside the barracks, at the top of the first hill in the woods surrounding El Pardo, a very suitable place for a bird; besides, the radio operators, Celso and Raúl, two of their best friends, were very keen on animals, especially Celso. Their secret would be safe there, because the Communications Unit was like a bunker, out of bounds to all the other soldiers.

"Alright," said Eliseo, "but I don't think it will want to stay there. The bird's clearly infatuated with me. It follows me everywhere."

He told Donato what had happened a few days earlier. After baking the usual bread rolls for the troops, he had gone into their room for a moment to put on the overalls he wore at the repair shop and, a few minutes later, just as he was saluting Warrant Officer Santos, he saw the magpie perched on the bumper of a truck. It had escaped and followed him. He managed to slip the bird into a pocket in his overalls and keep it there while he was working.

"Celso will take good care of it, you'll see," said Donato. "He'll make sure it gets everything it needs."

While they were talking, the bird sat perched on a rock, intently watching their every move, exactly like a dog. Around them, in the air, the whirring of the cicadas was even louder than on previous days, as if a thousand more had been born that very noon. It was extremely hot, even in the pinewood, which was the shadiest part of the grounds.

When they heard the bugle call, they headed back to the barracks. The bird followed them nonchalantly, this time successfully scrambling over any branches in its way. Eliseo picked it up and placed it on the stone bench, outside the bakery.

"Best leave it on the ground, otherwise it'll cover everything in crap," said Donato.

The bird squawked and began to protest even more vociferously when it saw them close the bakery door.

Donato filled his kit bag: two bottles of wine, six *choripanes*, four hard-boiled eggs and two bananas. The wine and the *choripanes* were for their friends in the bunker, the eggs and the bananas for the bird, although they would probably prove unnecessary. Celso would take charge of feeding the bird. He had befriended the soldiers who worked in the kitchen, and they were more than happy to give him anything he wanted.

Eliseo took an empty plastic container intended for yeast and made a hole in it. Then he went out to fetch the bird and put it inside.

To get from the bakery to the Communications Unit, they would have to walk through the barracks for about a hundred metres, then another two hundred metres through the woods and up the hill. As soon as they left the pinewood, the two men could feel the heat on their bodies, especially on their leather-booted feet. It grew even more intense as they crossed the concrete surface of the barracks yard where the sun was beating directly down on them. The day was very hot indeed.

The heat and the sun intensified the usual Saturday afternoon silence. There was not a sound to be heard. And that silence altered their perception of time. The bugle call to stand down, given only shortly before, now seemed terribly remote.

They heard a few rifle shots nearby. There were hunters about in the forest. It was Saturday for them too, a holiday. They almost always fired two shots, one after the other.

"Bastards!" said Eliseo, and he spat on the ground.

"The bird isn't frightened at all," said Donato, taking the plastic container out of the rucksack. The magpie apparently had no idea what those noises were and was sitting in the container, eyes open, but otherwise untroubled.

They heard dogs barking and more shots, this time much closer: first, a whole volley, then single shots, as if one hunter were finishing off the creatures felled by the rest of the hunting party. It felt as if those hunters were right there, in the barracks, walking along a road parallel to the one they were on.

"What are they hunting? Wild boar?" asked Donato.

"Pheasant, deer, who knows? They leave the rabbits for us, especially the ones with mixy."

He spat again.

When they had first become workmates and roommates, Eliseo and Donato only spoke when necessary, sharing neither information about family nor ideas, and not even commenting on what they saw around them, inside and outside the barracks. With time, however, they grew closer; they made a good team. During their afternoon break, they would walk up to the Communications Unit together to share their lunch with the two soldiers with whom they had also become friendly. Then, in their sixth month of military service, when they were granted leave to celebrate St John's Eve, Donato invited Eliseo to his village fiesta, and took him to the bakery in Ugarte where he worked. There, something unexpected happened. That same morning, the delivery van had broken down and the owner of the bakery was looking for a mechanic, but, since it was a holiday, there was none to be found.

"We don't need a mechanic, Miguel. We have Eliseo," said Donato.

An hour later, the van had been fixed.

"Can he make bread too?" asked Miguel.

"He's as good a baker as I am. He takes it very seriously too, sometimes too seriously. But that's his only fault."

"If you like, we could do a trial tomorrow," Eliseo said to Miguel.

"Certainly not. It's a public holiday! But if you fancy working here once you've finished your military service, that would be fine by me."

From that moment on, knowing that they would share many things in future, their conversations ranged far wider, and although El Pardo, the site of Franco's palace, was only a couple of kilometres from the barracks and Prince Juan Carlos' palace not much further, the two of them managed to ignore the pall cast by this proximity and to talk about the powers-that-be, about those in charge of the whole of Spain. Eliseo was more trenchant in his views. He couldn't stand the fact that those people were so privileged and kept the woods around El Pardo – fifteen square kilometres of land inhabited by all kinds of game, a paradise for hunters – entirely to themselves, their collaborators and colleagues. How could they be so greedy, so lacking in humanity? For him, though, and for others like him, it was a dangerous place.

If anyone dared to go poaching there, he would immediately be set upon by the gamekeepers or by the Civil Guard.

Another volley of shots.

"The dogs must have found the boar. It's so easy, even a child could hunt boar here," said Eliseo.

Donato nudged him.

"Now don't get all het up, Eliseo. What would we want with a boar anyway? How would we roast it? None of our ovens are big enough. And a boar has to be roasted whole."

Eliseo laughed. That was just like Donato. When they talked together in their room next to the bakery, it seemed to Eliseo that Donato's engine purred softly, like a car driving on the flat or downhill. He, on the other hand, moved in fits and starts. Sometimes, just as he was about to fall asleep, he could hear the sound of his own engine. It was the sound of a truck labouring up a mountain road.

They left the barracks behind them and continued on to the Guard Room. It was on a slight elevation that you could reach either by a flight of stone steps or via an approach road. They chose the steps. The bird started squawking inside its plastic container.

"Two steps, one squawk," Donato said. "Birds have their own rhythm. Probably all animals do."

"Not the ones firing those rifles," retorted Eliseo. The shots fired by the hunters were now completely random.

Before them, at the top of the steps, lay a wide-open space of over five hundred square metres. A wrought-iron gate and the Guard Room interrupted the three-metre perimeter wall, and between them stood two monoliths, one bearing the company insignia and the other a huge thermometer. Just then, at half past five in the afternoon, it was 31°C.

From the esplanade, Eliseo and Donato looked up at the wooded hills, but the hunters appeared to have withdrawn. They could see only trees now, and above them the sky, which was the same colour as the concrete barracks, except that it glowed, as if lined with a red-hot iron sheet.

A soldier whom they nicknamed Caloco, another of their bunker friends, appeared at the door of the Guard Room. He was ready for sentry duty, with his rifle in his hand and his metal helmet attached to his belt. Adopting the firing position, he approached them, shouting:

"Where are you two off to? What have you got in there?"

Then, poking Donato's rucksack with the barrel of his rifle, he said:

"Show me what you've got in there or it's a night in the cells for you!"

Caloco did about ten sentry duties a month, the one or two that fell to him as a matter of course plus those of any soldiers who paid him to take their place – five hundred pesetas on working days and eight hundred at the weekend – money which, once he was discharged, he planned to invest in a few cows. He did not want to carry on working as a cowherd, looking after other people's cattle in the hills above Santander, as he had before he was called up. However, the stress of being on sentry duty so often, the hundreds of hours he had to spend either in the box or dozing intermittently in a bunk bed were beginning to affect his mind. He often became very heated, as if his engine, as Eliseo put it, was idling too fast. You could see it in his eyes. They were blue, but unlike Donato's, they had a glassy, restless quality.

Laughing and beckoning to him to join them, Eliseo and Donato went out onto the road, passing under the barrier at the entrance to the barracks.

"If this is a trap, you'll be sorry!" shouted Caloco as he passed under the barrier too.

Eliseo and Donato crossed the road and took the path leading to the Communications Unit, pausing at a stone bench. Caloco followed them and, before sitting down between his two friends, he raised one hand, fingers spread. He had five minutes until he was on duty again. He put his rifle on the bench.

Donato opened the kit bag and handed him a *choripán* and the uncorked bottle of wine. Caloco put an arm around each of his friends' necks and gave them a fond squeeze. Then he bit off a third of the *choripán* and took a swig of wine.

"Now that's not the prince," he said suddenly. There was the sound of a motorbike approaching the village of El Pardo. "The prince's bike makes almost no noise at all. His engine runs like silk."

Thanks to his many hours on sentry duty, he could identify every vehicle that came along the road, both those travelling from El Pardo to Mingorrubio and those heading in the opposite direction.

"That's a Sanglas 500. It only comes past on Saturdays. The guy must have a girlfriend in Mingorrubio," he said as the bike drove by.

Then he changed the subject.

"You know Celso's been disciplined again, don't you? Another three months confined to barracks. But that's our friend for you."

Celso had the right to go to his parents' house in Madrid at the weekends, because, during the week, he worked all day – morning and afternoon – at the Communications Unit, and not just half the day like his colleague Raúl; however, during the nearly eight months he had spent at the barracks, he had only managed to do so maybe ten times. He was constantly being disciplined, as he had been that very day. He had tried to leave the barracks before the signal to stand down by way of a hole in the wall at the back. This proved to be a mistake, because the soldier guarding that area was not, as he had thought, a veteran who knew him and would turn a blind eye, but rather a new recruit.

"That's such bad luck," said Caloco. "The moment the guy saw him, he started screaming at him to stop."

Eliseo and Donato gave a resigned shrug. They could easily imagine the scene. They had both been in the barracks for some time and were all too aware of how new recruits reacted. They tended to be very much on edge and, standing in a sentry box, armed with a rifle, they could prove dangerous, especially at night. They were quite capable of shooting at a dog or a cat, or at a drunk who had merely stopped by the wall for a pee, or anything that moved.

Nothing that drastic had happened in Celso's case, because his attempt to leave the barracks had taken place in broad daylight, but the newbie – according to Caloco – had reported him, and as luck would have it, the officer in charge was a new lieutenant, Lieutenant Garmendia, who had previously been posted to the Sahara.

"You know the sort: still full of the whole Africa thing, a real stickler for discipline and all that."

"So that's another three months with no leave," said Eliseo glumly.

"There's the newbie now!" cried Caloco, pointing to the soldier occupying the box at the entrance to the barracks. He picked up a stone and threw it hard. "Squealer!"

The stone bounced off the roof of the sentry box.

"We can do better than that!" said Eliseo.

He picked up another stone, threw it hard and there was a metallic clink. He had hit the soldier's helmet.

They sat watching, waiting for some response, Caloco chewing his *choripan*, Eliseo holding another stone in readiness. The soldier merely disappeared inside his box.

"Hey, Caloco, watch this," said Donato.

He was holding the magpie in one hand, then, with a gentle upward movement, he launched the bird into the air. The bird flapped and fluttered in ungainly fashion, before alighting in the middle of the path and racing back to join them.

Eliseo took a few steps, then abruptly changed direction. The bird ran after him, as if being shut up in the container had given it courage, and with that courage renewed energy.

"You know why it follows you like a dog, don't you?" said Caloco.

Eliseo and Donato said they didn't.

"Because the bird's mad," Caloco explained. "It thinks it's a dog; it happens sometimes. I worked on a farm once where there was a goose that used to follow a cow around everywhere, even sleeping with her. It really thought it was a cow."

He glanced at his watch. It was a quarter to six, almost time for his next turn of duty. He put on the helmet that had been dangling from his belt.

They heard a voice. It was the soldier on guard, shouting at them. He kept repeating the same thing, and finally they understood that he was threatening to report them: he was going to tell Lieutenant Garmendia they were hiding a bird in the barracks.

Eliseo still had a stone in his hand, and he threw it. It landed inside the sentry box, narrowly missing the soldier.

"Easy, Eliseo," said Donato. "What does it matter? If they ask any questions, we have a perfectly good excuse. We say we found it in the barracks and came into the woods to set it free."

There was movement inside the Guard Room. The soldiers on the next turn of duty were already lined up, ready to relieve the other guards. Caloco whistled so that they could see he was there. He took another swig of wine, then returned the bottle to his friends.

"Take it to the bunker and drink a toast to me." He pointed to the magpie. "And give the bird to Celso. He loves dogs, and it might be some consolation to him."

Perched on a rock, the bird was observing them, its head on one side as usual.

Eliseo and Donato set off up the hill to the Communications Unit. As they got higher, the woods gradually spread out beneath them. There were no rifle shots, no barking now. For as far as they could see, the trees appeared to be sleeping. In the distance, the sky was no longer the colour of concrete and no longer seemed to be lined with a red-hot iron plate, but, rather, with a layer of honey; further off still, towards the Guadarrama mountains, it was turning blue.

The Communications Unit, or bunker, was a building spread over an area of about forty square metres, with a vaulted roof, two very small windows and a narrow door. To the left, fixed to the wall, were two radio transmitters, which connected the barracks with the whole of Spain's military network. The second and third walls were occupied end to end with desks and shelves crammed with tools, replacement parts and apparatus in need of repair, especially the URC-77s used in jeeps, and which were always going wrong; there was also a record-player connected to two small loudspeakers, as well as a few records. The final piece of furniture was a bunkbed placed against the fourth wall with a locker on either side, a low table, two wicker chairs, a wooden bench and the two stools that Raúl and Celso used when they were working. The overall impression was one of utter chaos.

"You must see this," said Raúl.

He pressed the button on a slide projector on the desk, and on the screen he'd hooked to the frame of the bunkbed there appeared a strange image: a wall adorned with six stuffed animal heads, all of the same type, three above and three below.

"I've checked in an encyclopaedia, and they're definitely antelopes, but I don't know what sort. They're obviously not gazelles, and certainly not gnus. Gnus have huge heads and look rather like bulls."

Eliseo, Donato and Celso were also in the bunker. Caloco had gone back on sentry duty. It was Tuesday, August 11.

Raúl pressed the button again. This time what appeared on the screen was a close-up of one of the stuffed heads.

"Look at those horns! They must be at least a metre long," he said.

They were very long and rose in a spiral like flame-bladed swords.

"Apart from the horns, they're like the fallow deer we get around here. Well, the head is anyway," Eliseo said, and Donato agreed.

"Keep it down, please. Poki is asleep in my cap," said Celso.

He had agreed to look after the bird but it was up to Eliseo to give it a name. For the moment, it was called Poki.

Celso was a big lad. He wore black-rimmed glasses and had the flaccid body of someone who used to be fat but had suddenly lost weight. Lolling in one of the wicker chairs, his legs resting on one of the stools, he had the cap containing the sleeping bird resting on his belly.

The next slide showed some cylindrical brown stools.

"What do you think they are?" asked Raúl. He wore glasses too, but his had thin gold frames. He kept taking them on and off, depending on what he was looking at. While he was studying the screen, he had them on.

Another image followed. The same stools as before, but this time upside down. On the base were a few whitish marks like nails.

"What do you think they are?" asked Raúl again. Eliseo and Donato had no idea.

"Elephant feet," said Celso. "Or, rather, baby elephant feet. Look at the size. I just hope the murderer of that little elephant is dead and buried!"

He wrinkled his nose as if some foul odour had just wafted into the room.

"It was shot by a businessman who loved safaris," said Raúl. "And don't worry, Celso. The elephant died years ago."

He held another slide up to the light coming in through the small window, then slotted it into the projector tray. The façade of a large building filled the whole screen. The doors, windows and small crenellated towers were a clear attempt to imitate the style of a medieval castle. It was the country mansion of that same safari-loving businessman, Raúl explained, somewhere up in the Guadarrama mountains. Under orders from the lieutenant who had just joined the barracks, Raúl would be staying there over the next few days to install a sound system.

"The lieutenant's girlfriend inherited the place, and apparently she can't live without music. That's why Garmendia gave me these slides, so that I'd have an idea of what the house was like. His girlfriend's name is Vicky."

Raúl's way of speaking was the exact opposite of Celso's. He

111

had a very monotonous voice and made not the slightest effort to make it more expressive.

"Now you know why that Bedouin, Garmendia, decided to keep me holed up here all weekend," said Celso, looking at Eliseo and Donato. "I'm stuck here while Raúl is happily ensconced in the murderer's mountain retreat installing that sound system. It couldn't be clearer, could it? Me here on guard and Raúl up there, playing butler to Garmendia and his girlfriend, that Vicky woman."

He got up from the wicker chair, carefully lifted the magpie out of his cap and went over to the door, holding the bird cupped in both hands.

"It's your own fault, Celso," said Raúl, who looked annoyed. "You're always coming and going out of hours. In the months you've been here, you've spent more days confined to barracks than not."

"This time, I don't mind so much, not now that I'm uncle to this little magpie. Eliseo is her father, and I'm the uncle. I'll give her a few ants, then take her for a walk up the hill. She needs to get plenty of exercise if she's to grow up strong and healthy."

And he gave the bird a kiss.

"Come along with your uncle, Poki," he said, then turned to his friends. "Eliseo, until you've decided on a name for her, I'm going to carry on calling her Poki. Not Vicky, Poki."

"Call her Paca!" said Eliseo.

"Oh, yes, much better! That's a lovely name." And Celso gave the bird another kiss. "Come on then, Paca!"

The Communications Unit was left in near darkness when Celso closed the door. Eliseo and Donato sat down on either side of Raúl. They wanted to see more images of the house in the mountains and the interior with its stuffed animals.

Raúl put another slide in the projector. A lion appeared on the screen.

"The king of the jungle," said Raúl.

It was in the same room as the stools made from elephant

feet and was standing in front of a sofa. Donato laughed. It was the first time he had seen a photo of a real lion. Up until then, he had only seen drawings of them in the school encyclopaedia. What most surprised him were the eyes. They looked as if they were made of gold.

The following slide showed the same lion, only in close-up.

"I think a lion's eyes are usually more amber-coloured," said Raúl, "but this one was stuffed a long time ago. His skin's a bit threadbare too and rather brown, whereas in reality it would have a reddish tone."

"It's still a magnificent beast, though," said Eliseo.

They remained silent for a while. Then, on the following slide, they saw two shotguns displayed on a wall, both with telescopic sights.

"A bit different from our CETME rifles," said Raúl.

Eliseo pulled a scornful face.

"They're weapons for rich guys. I prefer ours. They're decent enough, it's just a shame we only get to use them for shooting practice."

Raúl showed them another three slides. The first was a picture of a corridor in which three suits of armour stood with their backs to the wall, each complete with helmet, coat of mail and sword; the second showed a kind of storeroom full of medieval weapons, swords and arrows, spears and cudgels, bows and hatchets. The third provided a closer view of those same weapons.

"What's that on the left, Raúl?" asked Donato.

It was similar to a traditional long bow, but the bow part was mounted horizontally on a stock not so very different from that of their CETME rifles.

"It's a crossbow," answered Raúl.

"I've never seen anything like it."

Eliseo went closer to the screen for a better look.

"I wonder how accurate it is."

"Oh, very, I bet," said Raúl. "You put the arrow in that groove at the base and it comes flying out."

The screen then filled up with more commonplace animals: an eagle, an owl, a pheasant, a boar.

"He didn't kill that boar in Africa," said Eliseo.

Raúl turned off the projector.

"He probably shot it right here. Lieutenant Garmendia told me that Vicky's father often used to come to these woods. Sometimes with General Franco himself."

Donato helped Raúl put away the slides.

"How long's it going to take you to install that sound system? I'm only asking because of Celso."

"I don't know, but quite a long time, I imagine. Not that it'll make any difference to Celso. He's been confined to barracks for three months. He'll have to be here all the time anyway."

Eliseo and Donato did not agree. It *would* make a difference how long Raúl was away, because when Raúl was in barracks, he could take charge of the transmissions in the mornings and on some afternoons too, which would mean that Celso could go for a stroll around or drop in for a chat with Caloco, or with them in the bakery or in the kitchen at lunchtime. He wouldn't be able to do any of that if he was left entirely alone in the bunker on guard, waiting for the next telegram.

However, Raúl was in no mood for arguing and, without saying a word, went and sat down in front of one of the radio sets.

The images of those stuffed animals remained engraved on Eliseo's memory, and he thought and felt how wonderful it would be to actually see a lion, just like the one on the slide, in Africa, in the flesh, with its mane and its golden eyes, and to come face to face with it, armed not with a shotgun fitted with a telescopic sight, but with a CETME rifle or, at an even greater disadvantage, with a crossbow and at short range. At night, lying in bed in the room next to the bakery after lights out, he would so immerse himself in these thoughts that the image would take on life, as if the lion had leapt out of the slide and into a cinema screen. He would imagine himself crouched in the undergrowth, armed with the

114

crossbow, just fifty metres from the lion, when, suddenly, the wild beast – which, despite weighing more than two hundred kilos, was extraordinarily agile – would start loping towards him. He would get the shivers when he saw those golden eyes fixed on him, but still he would wait until the lion was just ten or fifteen metres away, and finally, without missing a beat, he would fire the arrow straight at the lion's chest. Only when he saw that the lion was mortally wounded would he begin to tremble, as if the fear he had kept under control until then had spread throughout his body, and he could feel the presence of Paca, his Valdesalce lover, as if she were actually there in bed with him. He would embrace her then and fuck her until he came.

At first, this fantasy lasted for only the ten or fifteen minutes he lay awake after his nightly chat with Donato, but if he found it hard to bring the fantasy to a close, if the lion appeared not alone but with other lions, and he was unsure how to act, how to lure the beast closer, how to avoid the other lions turning on him once he had shot the arrow, then his head would keep going over and over the scene during the day, while he was making bread or repairing an engine. The extreme regularity of life in the barracks required no thought on his part, and he found it very easy having his head filled with images of Africa while his eyes, ears, hands and legs continued doing whatever they had to do on autopilot.

As the days passed, he found being in two places at once, both inside and outside the barracks, ever more pleasurable, and his only regret was that he could not spend more time with his fantasy, with those African images and the sex that accompanied them. He began to resent interruptions and, in particular, the visits of other soldiers wanting to see the baby magpie. The recruit who had spotted the bird from the sentry box had spread the news, and men kept coming into the bakery asking to see "the bird you've been teaching tricks to", and asking if it was true that, once he and Donato had completed their military service, they were going to work in a circus, with Donato playing the accordion and Eliseo putting the bird through its paces. "Yes, that's why Donato's learning to play 'Juanita Banana', which is perfect for Paca," he would say jokingly to shut them up. This proved to be a mistake, especially mentioning the bird's name. From then on, from one end of the barracks to the other, from one company to another, over lunch or while they were waiting for the nightly roll call, Paca became the main topic of conversation. The rumours morphed as they travelled, even changing the bird from magpie to parrot.

In an attempt to clear the matter up, Eliseo hung a notice on the door of the bakery stating that the bird, which was a magpie and not a parrot, was flying freely about in the woods around El Pardo, because they had released it into the wild. However, the wind – the little breeze that is there in everyone's head – only reinforced the idea of Paca's existence, adapting it and adding details.

A week after the rumour had begun to gather strength – August 20, a Thursday, and 30°C on the Guard Room thermometer – Eliseo, Donato and Caloco went up to the Communications Unit to have supper, and Celso gave them the latest news from Radio Rumour: the barracks parrot, Paca, had indeed been born in El Pardo, not in the woods, but in General Franco's palace. It had escaped from there and ended up in the hands of Eliseo, who had hidden it away. The people in the palace were desperate because the parrot was a birthday present for one of Franco's granddaughters.

"Radio Rumour talks of little else," said Celso, placing the potato omelette he had been given by the kitchen staff on the low table, where it sat along with half a cheese, two tins of tuna, two bottles of wine and a thermos full of coffee. They had not yet started eating, but already one of the bottles was empty.

"They were discussing it in the Guard Room yesterday," said Caloco. "It seems the military police are investigating the matter. Just you wait, they'll soon be hot on Eliseo's trail. He'll probably be shot."

"I'm afraid the military police are going to have to find someone else to interrogate," said Celso. "Eliseo doesn't even know where Paca is. Where is your little one now, Eliseo?"

116

Celso was standing next to one of the lockers, and his cap kept moving about on his head. Caloco and Donato both laughed.

"I really have no idea, my friend," answered Eliseo.

"Well, you're an extremely irresponsible father. When Paca grows up, she'll demand an explanation."

"He's not listening, Celso. He's got his mind on other things," said Caloco.

Donato agreed:

"Yes, lately, he's always got his mind on something else."

They were both right. Eliseo wasn't interested in anything now. He made the bread, repaired engines, but otherwise lived shut up inside himself, obsessed with just one idea. It had nothing to do with the rumours about the baby magpie; such inventions, and even wilder ones, were commonplace in the barracks. What pre-occupied him was the way his night-time fantasies were evolving. Their effect was gradually waning. When he turned out the lights in the room and allowed himself to drift off to sleep, the lion no longer loped towards him to attack him, giving him goose-bumps and arousing him sexually. Now, the lion seemed entirely indifferent: it would look at him, bored, and start yawning or else turn its back on him. This had a depressing effect on both Eliseo's mind and on his sexual appetite, and, given the lack of stimulus, he would simply fall asleep. Then, during the day, in the bakery or in the repair shop with Warrant Officer Santos, or at the Communications Unit with his friends, that lowness of spirits continued, as if the failure of his fantasy had affected every organ in his body. Before, even when walking uphill, he had always thought of himself as a powerful truck capable of coping with any load, however heavy; now, though, he almost crept along, as if the valves in his engine had stopped working properly.

"Paca!" said, Celso, taking off his cap and revealing the bird. Even though it was still quite small, it was now recognisably a magpie, with its very white breast. "Paca!" Celso said again, more loudly this time.

The bird uttered a squawk that sounded very like "Paca".

"She'll soon learn to talk. I play her the recording every day."

The tape recorder was on top of one of the lockers, connected to the loudspeakers for the record player. He pressed the on button, and the name "Paca" was repeated over and over. After only a few seconds, however, they all began to protest, and Celso turned the machine off.

"With your permission, I'm going to give her some bread soaked in wine," said Caloco. "Where I live, we give the cows a bit of wine now and then. What's good for the cows must be good for this dog of yours."

He looked at his watch and saw that it was eight o'clock.

"Why don't we have supper outside? It will be cooler there. I'll be in charge of the wine bottles."

The Communications Unit was fairly well lit, thanks to the two small windows and the two fluorescent lights, but when they went out through the metal door, it felt as if they were emerging from a dark cave. At that time of day, the sun's rays were almost horizontal, and so dazzling that the four men squinted in the light as they made their way up to the top of the hill.

Vapour trails striped the sky, some still very clear, others already blurred, with orange, red and yellow stripes in among the more subtly coloured clouds, which were pinkish, greyish, greenish. Down below, the first lights were coming on in the barracks and in the houses nearby, and beyond that, the dimmer, drabber lights of Madrid shone in the distance.

In comparison with the sky, the earth seemed a very dull place. The woods around El Pardo turned hazy where they met the Guadarrama mountains; closer to, just a few miles from the Communications Centre, the trees formed a dark green fringe. All was peaceful. The animals in the woods, the soldiers in the barracks, the people living in the houses round about, the inhabitants of the city: all would doubtless have their worries and concerns, but there was not a trace of that anxiety on the earth or in the air.

A stork flew by, very high up, alone in that colourful sky. One of the four friends sitting on the rocks at the top of the hill could have turned to the others and said: "Isn't this a beautiful moment, with the night gently approaching?" but though all felt this, none could put it into words and so they said nothing.

The silence – their own and that of their surroundings – was cut short by the barking of a few dogs.

"That'll be the gamekeepers' mastiffs. You know, those dogs with the massive heads. The prince's friends must be around," said Eliseo. The baby bird was sitting on his knee.

They continued talking about dogs. The hunters who frequented those woods used hounds and mastiffs, forty or more in a pack, and the prince had the same type, albeit more refined, a special breed: one hundred per cent Spanish, huge with very white fur. Eliseo knew this from reading about it in celebrity magazines. Now and then, Warrant Officer Santos would bring him copies of *Hello* that his wife had finished with for him to pass on to Paca.

"Aren't you jealous, Eliseo? White dogs and one hundred per cent Spanish too," said Caloco, and everyone laughed.

Eliseo pulled a scornful face. He disapproved of those dogs and, even more, of that kind of hunting. It wasn't right to set forty dogs on a single boar. That was like shooting a lion from a mile away with a shotgun fitted with a telescopic sight. Only cowards hunted like that.

Then the barking stopped, and peace returned to the woods, the barracks and everything around them. Celso lit a cigarette. Seconds later, Caloco did the same. Donato opened the thermos flask and poured the coffee into plastic cups.

Perched on Eliseo's knee, the magpie chick tucked its head into its back feathers and fell asleep.

The dominant colours in the sky were now violet and maroon; on the horizon, where the sun had just set, the clouds were an intense red. In the woods, on the other hand, it was so dark you could not even make out the trees. The Guadarrama mountains had vanished.

Eliseo lay down in the pine woods in his usual improvised bed and opened the book Warrant Officer Santos had lent him, this time at the chapter about hydraulic cylinders. It was half past four on Thursday, August 27. As always happened when it was very hot, the cicadas maintained their ceaseless whirring.

He tried to concentrate on his studies, focussing on each diagram, each explanation, trying to fill the void that had followed the decline in his night-time fantasies. This wasn't a new experience; at other periods in his life, his dreams or certain thoughts and desires had taken up too much space in his mind, but he had never experienced anything as abrupt as that recent change in mood, going from a feeling of health, vigour and plenitude to a state of fatigue and listlessness.

When he changed position slightly and glanced up, he saw Celso leaving the bakery. He was walking unsteadily, stumbling every now and then. Eliseo whistled to him to join him. Celso was carrying a bottle of wine in one hand.

"I took it from the locker. I deserve it after what's just happened. That Bedouin, Omar Sharif, came to see me in the bunker."

He meant Lieutenant Garmendia. The lieutenant had turned up at the Communications Unit on the excuse that he had come to fetch a record Raúl had recommended, "No Milk Today" by Herman's Hermits, but Celso saw immediately that this was not all that he had come for, since even once he had the record in his hand, he continued snooping about among the URC-77s piled up on the shelves.

"He was looking for the bird, Eliseo! He was looking for Paca!"

He was very upset. He took another swig from the bottle.

Donato arrived then, and Celso repeated what he had just told Eliseo, only in more detail. At the end of the visit, the lieutenant had asked him openly if it was true what the other men were saying, that they kept a little talking parrot there. He told him no, that had all been a while ago. The shots fired by the hunters in El Pardo had frightened it and it had escaped.

"The Bedouin had to leave without a special little present for Vicky. It was just lucky he didn't see Paca. That would have meant another three months confined to barracks."

Donato laughed.

"I don't know where you were hiding her during the lieutenant's visit," he said, "but I know where she is now. I like your new cap by the way."

The caps worn by veterans or by those most averse to discipline usually had a very battered peak, or else had the Bakelite stiffener removed, and the one Celso usually wore was famous throughout the barracks because of its particularly tatty state. Just then, though, he was wearing a cap as pristine and impeccable as that of a new recruit, except that it was far too big for him. He took it off, and the magpie – now almost fully grown – flew from his head onto a branch, and from there straight to Eliseo's book, then, with awkward steps, ventured into the wood, as if exploring the territory. With each step, its wings and tail gleamed iridescent blue.

"Where did you get the cap? Or rather, whose company did you steal it from?" asked Donato.

"Well, yes, I did steal it actually. I can't deny it. The quartermaster will be going mad counting and re-counting the caps, wondering where the missing one's gone. But I had to have it. Paca's tail is getting longer and longer, and it really stuck out from beneath my old cap – I looked like an American Indian. And I'm not an Indian. I'm a Celt from Galicia."

"And did you have Paca underneath that cap all the time the lieutenant was looking for her?"

Donato found this quite incredible, but he knew Celso was capable of that and much more.

"Yes, but I take no credit for it. The Bedouin is very unobservant. He's in *lurve*, you see."

They had decided not to meet up at the Communications Unit that day, since Raúl was still working at the "castle", rewiring the whole place now that he had installed the sound system, and Caloco was on sentry duty for the nth time. Instead, they would have supper in the barracks dining room along with the other soldiers.

They sat down in the shadiest part of the pine wood, around the bottle of wine. The bird was perched on a fallen branch. Celso lit a cigarette with a red lighter.

"I wish I could do a swap with Lieutenant Garmendia," said Eliseo. "I was thinking of giving the bird to my friend Paca, but the other day, seeing those slides of the castle, I couldn't help noticing the crossbows. Think of the fun we could have with one of those. We'd just need a target in the bunker, some place where no-one would see it, and then we could hold competitions."

"Sounds like a great idea. Like shooting practice, only with a crossbow," said Donato.

"Oh, shut up, the lot of you!"

Celso had leapt to his feet. He took a drag on his cigarette, then, turning his back on them, stalked off to join the magpie; contrary to their expectations, though, he did not stop there, but continued in a straight line to the far end of the wood. As he moved off, the whirring of the cicadas seemed to increase in intensity.

Eliseo and Donato found him sitting, smoking, next to a pine tree, his gaze fixed on the three-metre wall around the barracks.

"You see this?" he said, showing them the red lighter. "It belonged to the Bedouin. He put it down on the record player, then forgot about it, and I stuck it under my cap. I put everything under my cap."

"Don't be angry, Celso," said Donato, sitting down beside him.

Eliseo crouched next to them.

"I just really want that crossbow, Celso. More than I do the bird really."

He had the bottle of wine with him. Celso grabbed it and took a drink.

"You made me cry, Eliseo. I thought you really cared about Paca," he said, taking off his glasses and wiping them on his shirt tail.

During the minutes that followed, they talked quietly and confidingly as if they were in the bakery with the door closed.

Eliseo and Donato asked Celso to show some common sense. Looking after animals was all very well, but you mustn't take it too seriously, otherwise you end up getting everything back to front and going mad. Donato mentioned the case of Antoine, a French engineer who ran the mine in Ugarte. He was an educated man, and rich too, who lived in the swankiest part of the village with a maid and a manservant to do his bidding. And yet his days and nights were sheer misery. His only friends were his dogs, and he was always falling out with people over them. For his part, Eliseo talked about Basilio, his fellow shepherd in Valdesalce. Basilio was a good man, who took proper care of his dog, Lay, but every time March came around, he had the grim business of slaughtering the lambs. At first, when he, Eliseo, was fourteen, and his father had left him alone in Valdesalce with the sheep, he had found that unbearable. Gradually, though, he came to accept it and now he wielded the knife as skilfully as Basilio.

"I'm sure that's all true," said Celso. "But in the case of Paca, giving her to the Bedouin would be unforgivable. Raúl can carry on lending him records and buttering him up, but we mustn't do that."

Donato shook his head disapprovingly.

"Raúl has no alternative but to do what the lieutenant tells him," he said.

"Raúl is a snitch, and that's why the Bedouin has given him the longest leave of absence in the history of this barracks. For a Celt like me, such people are beyond the pale."

"Don't talk like that," said Donato.

Celso stood up, looking around him.

"Where's Paca?"

Eliseo and Donato stood up too. In the wood, at that moment, there were three magpies. Two on the ground and a third one on the branch of a tree. They all looked very similar.

"Paca!" called Celso.

"*Paca! Paca! Paca!*" called the bird on the branch and flew down to join them, then stood looking at them in its usual pose, head on one side.

Celso picked it up and planted a kiss on its head.

"Paca!" he called again.

"*Paca! Paca!*" answered the bird.

"You see, Eliseo. We couldn't give her to the Bedouin even if we wanted too. She's learned how to say 'Paca' instead of 'Vicky'."

"A very clever bird!" said Donato, applauding.

Eliseo smiled at Celso and clapped him on the back.

"She's had a good teacher."

They set off to the bakery again, heads bowed, not saying a word – as if they had suddenly taken stock of their situation and realised how painful it was. They had spent nearly eight months imprisoned within the walls of the barracks, to which should be added the three months at training camp, eleven months in all. And they would have to endure another three or three and a half months, until December. This was the mood in which they walked through the woods, occasionally passing each other the bottle of wine.

The magpie flew over to the bakery and alighted on the stone bench. Celso looked at his watch.

"Five past six. I'd better go and send the six o'clock telegram. I'll tell them I was delayed, but that nothing terribly serious has happened. The Commies still haven't stormed the palace."

He took out a cigarette and lit it with the red lighter, then said:

"Oh, by the way, Eliseo, I forgot to ask. How many crossbows do you want?"

Eliseo and Donato stared at him. For a moment, Celso held their gaze, then he started blowing smoke rings, which took some seconds to dissolve into the air.

He explained his plan to them as if he were reading about it in those smoke rings. There was a problem with the electrics in the Guadarrama castle, and Raúl couldn't sort it out because, despite his university studies, he was still only an apprentice. Celso, on the other hand, was a qualified electrician, which is why he'd had the nerve to suggest to the Bedouin that what they needed in the castle was a Celt. And the Bedouin had thought it a good idea.

As he left the Communications Unit, fanning himself with the Herman's Hermits record, he had said: "A soldier will drive you up to the Guadarrama house tomorrow. A new recruit will be put in charge of sending the telegrams in your absence."

"The Bedouin said all that and more, but not a word about reducing my punishment. So . . . how many crossbows do you want, my friend?"

"One will do," said Eliseo, adding: "But I'm not sure you should take the risk. That would be stealing."

Celso threw down his half-smoked cigarette and stubbed it out with his foot.

"The only risk I run is if Raúl were to see me. I don't trust him. For all I know he could be from military intelligence, or the CIA."

He sat down on the stone bench and gave the magpie a kiss.

"I should be back tomorrow night. Meantime, keep Paca in your bedroom." He handed Eliseo the red lighter. "And keep this for me too, booty snatched from the enemy."

When Celso spoke, it was hard not to pay attention, his anger and his agitation finding an echo in the minds of those listening. Even more so on that occasion. Eliseo and Donato silently went over every word their friend had said, fearing that, otherwise, they would not be able to order their thoughts.

It was still very hot. There was no let-up in the noise made by the cicadas. Donato pointed at the stone bench. The magpie had left two lots of droppings.

"She may have learned how to talk, but not how to poo in the right place."

It was August 29, and Eliseo and Donato had gone to their room next to the bakery after meeting with their friends from the bunker. As on other occasions, supper had consisted of a cheese and potato omelette, but accompanied this time by a special drink, the *zurracapote* or fruit punch that Celso had got from the kitchen staff. A whole saucepanful, about four litres.

With the light still on, Eliseo was describing to Donato the cartoons in the celebrity magazine he was reading. In the first, two hippopotamuses were sitting near a swamp and one of them was looking at some passing zebras and saying: "I really envy them. Stripes are so slimming." In the second, a spider was studying its rather clumsy web, and saying to its companion: "However hard I try, I always get in a tangle." In the third, two tortoises were walking along together, one of them with a periscope sticking up from its shell, while the other one, with its head out, was saying: "Come on out, don't be such a wimp."

He put the magazine down on the bedside table and removed his boots, pushing the left one off with his right foot and the right one off with his left. Then he fell back on his bed and lay there with his eyes open.

"I find those jokes about as funny as staring at the ceiling."

"Well, I'm really enjoying my new toy."

Donato was holding a large harmonica, about fifteen centimetres long, with a silvery outer casing and a stock made of reddish wood. It was one of the objects that Celso had snaffled from the house in Guadarrama, along with two crossbows, three bolts and a torch. He had hidden them in his kit bag underneath his electrician's overalls, and no-one had spotted them, not Lieutenant Garmendia, Raúl, the military police, or the soldiers in the Guard Room.

While Celso was unpacking his kit bag in the Communications Unit, Eliseo had said:

"The only thing missing is the lion."

"It wouldn't fit," Celso said, "but I did move it. It's now behind the piano, with its big head peeking over one end of the keyboard. I hope Vicky gets a nasty fright when she starts playing 'Für Elise'."

Holding the harmonica in both hands, Donato was trying to play the "Last Post", which blared out at any hour from the tannoy system, not the military version, but the one played by trumpeter Rudy Ventura.

"I've never known anyone quite like Celso. He's as mad as he is generous," said Donato, examining every part of the harmonica as if it had only just been given to him.

Still gazing up at the ceiling, Eliseo was struggling to piece together the events of the last few days, but the ceiling kept bouncing those cartoon punchlines back at him: "I really envy them. Stripes are so slimming"; "However hard I try, I always get in a tangle"; "Come on out, don't be such a wimp".

He felt his forehead. It was quite cool, so he didn't have a fever. He wanted to break free from all those stupid jokes, and so he tried to focus on the melody Donato was playing. Donato was very generous too, he thought. He really cared about other people. Thanks to him, as soon as Eliseo was discharged, he would be starting a new job in Ugarte as a baker and a driver, and his life would change for the better; on the other hand, that change would have its downside too, its recoil, like a rifle after it had been fired. He would have to say goodbye to his friend Paca and to his lifelong pal, Basilio.

One of the punchlines reappeared in his head, the one about the spiders: "However hard I try, I always get in a tangle". He looked at Donato, who had now put the harmonica back in its white case and was stowing it away under his pillow. It was time to go to sleep. Almost eleven o'clock.

"Caloco isn't a bad shot with the crossbow, but he's not as good as us," Eliseo said. "That's perfectly understandable, of course. Anyone who does ten sentry duties a month isn't likely to have a very steady shooting hand."

Donato agreed and continued putting on his pyjamas.

"It's the same with eyesight," Eliseo went on, trying to untangle himself from the web the spider seemed to be weaving around his brain. "If you don't get enough sleep, that's going to affect your sight as well."

He then turned to the subject of the crossbows and told Donato what was worrying him. The game they were having was such fun and so enjoyable, but it could have its negative side. Caloco wanted to place bets, and that simply wasn't a good idea. The probability of him winning was nil, and it wasn't right to take money from a person like Caloco, who had earned it by doing endless guard duties. But what could they do? They couldn't pretend to lose.

Lying on his bed, Donato was laughing. He covered himself with a blanket even though it was still quite hot.

"If he ever twigged that we were letting him win, Caloco would kill us," he said. "Mind you, he'd feel just the same if we didn't let him win. He's not going to be at all pleased to lose the money he's been saving up for his cows."

Caloco wasn't the only problem, Eliseo went on. There was Celso too. He was a terrible shot and was certainly no hunter. He was sorry to say this because Celso was a really good friend and incredibly generous, bringing them fruit punch and other things from the kitchen and giving them presents for no reason: caps, lighters, harmonicas. What's more, he did this without asking for anything in return, like when he agreed to look after the magpie. It was difficult to help Celso though. He went through life like a dodgem car and probably always would.

Eliseo was feeling slightly dizzy and found it hard to talk.

"You can say what you like, Eliseo, it won't help," said Donato, his eyes closed. "I'm going to beat you all."

Eliseo turned out the light, stripped down to his underwear and got into bed.

It was Saturday night, and they could hear the cars driving along the Mingorrubio road, tooting their horns. Young drivers heading out to enjoy themselves at discotheques always did this as they passed the barracks. It was their way of poking fun at the soldiers on the other side of the three-metre wall, a performance that was repeated every weekend.

Eliseo sighed, then lay staring into the darkness.

"Do you remember what Caloco once said? That if one of those weekend despicables ever pipped his hooter as he passed the sentry box, he'd fire at him. Well, he shouldn't have said that. If anything like that actually happened, he'd get the blame."

"Caloco would never do such a thing," said Donato, adjusting his voice to the darkness. He was slowly falling asleep. "He isn't completely nuts, not like Celso. He'll go home with some money in his pocket and become a cattle farmer. He'll have a herd of a hundred cows before he's forty, you'll see."

"Oh, he's a reliable enough vehicle," said Eliseo. "His only problem is that he turns over a bit too fast when he's idling."

He closed his eyes and immediately felt as if the bed were swaying back and forth like a swing. He opened his eyes and the swaying stopped. A slight pain in his stomach made him change position.

"Santos told me a sad thing today," he said.

"What was that?"

Donato also changed position. He wanted to go to sleep.

"I was helping him repair the engine of a Dodge truck and, out of nowhere, he started talking about his daughter. I didn't even know he had a daughter. Do you know what I mean, Donato? I knew absolutely nothing about her, and so I started asking him questions, how old she was, her name, what she was doing, and he told me that her name's Maribel and that she's nineteen and goes to a special school. So then I asked: 'What's she studying, then, something unusual?' And he says: 'No, not at all. My daughter's nineteen, but she has the mental age of a seven or eight-year-old.' He showed me a photo, and what I saw wasn't Maribel's mental age, but her nineteen-year-old body . . ."

"What are you jabbering on about, Eliseo? You're making no sense at all!" said Donato, unable to control his laughter. "You know what's happened, don't you? You ate all the fruit in the fruit punch, and you're completely pissed!"

The people in the kitchen had prepared the fruit punch. They mixed the wine with some brandy and added chunks of peaches, lemons, oranges, cherries and any other fruit they had to hand, then cooked the whole lot in a big saucepan, along with some sugar and cinnamon. The fruit absorbed the alcohol and could make you drunker than the drink itself.

"Yes, the peaches did have a strong taste of brandy," said Eliseo.

One of those cartoons came into his head again, not the spiders this time, but the hippopotamuses watching the zebras: "I really envy them. Stripes are so slimming". He felt annoyed with himself for not having realised earlier what had happened. He *was* drunk. That was why he couldn't stop thinking about those idiotic cartoons, and why his bed was swaying back and forth. It also explained his tetchiness. And the pain in his stomach.

"Go to sleep, Eliseo. You'll have a bit of a headache in the morning, but it'll soon pass," said Donato.

Eliseo duly fell asleep and, as soon as he did, he heard the baying of a pack of hounds, then the ever more excited barking of a hundred or so dogs fanning out across the terrain like soldiers. To the left, a group of some thirty dogs was advancing in formation, they had huge heads, and in their veins flowed the blood of bulldogs, mastiffs and Dobermanns; in line with them, but on the right, came another group, another thirty bull-headed dogs; a third group, the most numerous, was made up of forty or more dogs, and they occupied the centre ground and were driven on by their handlers. Eliseo was down on all fours among the dogs, and their breath on his face, their drool on his neck, their smell, it was all utterly repugnant, so different from the smell of the sheep in Valdesalce, and then there was the constant barking and howling from those disgusting bull-headed dogs who kept getting in his way, as well as their handlers' endless shouting. Suddenly, three wild boar emerged from the undergrowth and headed for a river bed, and all the dogs, from left, right and centre, raced after them. He tried to stay where he was, but that was impossible. The bull-headed dogs were too strong and carried him along with them. The burning sensation on his skin as he was being dragged over the ground was excruciating.

He sat bolt upright in bed. He was drenched in sweat, thick drops which ran down his cheeks and neck. As soon as he was properly awake, an image came into his head, the saucepan containing the fruit punch, with a slice of peach inside it, and the aftertaste of that fruit in his mouth made him retch. He ran to the latrines located between the bakery and the repair shop, where he vomited up some brownish-grey puke. He pulled the chain, then rinsed out his mouth with water from a tap in the wall.

A dimly lit road separated the bakery from the repair shop. Barefoot and in his underwear, he started walking up and down, stopping now and then to stretch his arms and take deep breaths. Clouds of nocturnal insects whirled about the streetlamps, obscuring the light; bats swooped and dodged, and sometimes flew right over his head without making the slightest noise, as if propelled by a silent engine rather than by their wings.

Then he heard something that made him look up. A patrol was approaching. He stood, waiting.

An order was given, and the soldiers stopped where they were, in a line. The light was too poor for Eliseo to be able to make out any faces. He felt sure that the sergeant in charge would demand an explanation. "I had to rush out and be sick, that's why I'm only half-dressed," he would tell him.

"What's up, Eliseo?" he heard a voice say. It was Caloco, who broke ranks and came over to him, grabbing his arm. "You're all right, aren't you?"

The sergeant took a few steps towards them but remained at a distance.

"I was feeling really sick, but I'm fine now," said Eliseo. Then he addressed the sergeant: "That's why I'm in my underwear. I had to leap out of bed and run straight to the latrines."

The sergeant ordered him back to his room.

"Take care, my friend," said Caloco, giving him a hug.

"See you tomorrow for the championship," said Eliseo.

"Yes, and which I will, of course, win."

"Come on," said the sergeant. "The guards will be getting impatient."

Eliseo went and sat on the stone bench outside the bakery and, for the first time in ages, he felt like smoking a cigarette. No cars passed along the Mingorrubio road. The barracks lay in silence.

He looked at his watch. It was 1.50 a.m. He thought of the wild boar in the woods around El Pardo. Now that they had finally been left in peace, they would be concentrating on looking for food and water without having to worry about those bull-headed dogs from the hunting parties. He felt peaceful too, and relieved, as if, along with the remains of the fruit punch he had vomited up, he had also rid himself of all the rubbish in his head, the cartoons and his concerns about Celso, about the magpie, about having to leave Valdesalce and go off to live in Ugarte. His head was clear again, and he was no longer sweating.

He thought of Warrant Officer Santos' daughter, Maribel. Her body, her nineteen-year-old body, had made such an impression on him when he saw her in the photo that he had almost made an entirely inappropriate comment. She was wearing a very short skirt and bore a close resemblance to a starlet whose photo he had seen in one of those celebrity magazines, a young woman from Las Vegas, who, according to the caption, was the secret daughter of Marilyn Monroe. Maribel was sturdier and had bigger thighs, but the two women were still very alike. When Santos had told him what her mental age was, he had been expecting to see a girl with slanting, almond-shaped eyes and an ungainly body. He had been very surprised when he saw what she actually looked like.

He went back to his room, where Donato was sleeping peacefully. Donato had a slightly childish quality about him, but he was nevertheless sharp as a tack. Maribel, on the other hand, would understand almost nothing. When she felt attracted to a boy, she would behave like a child of seven or eight. Not like Paca, his friend in Valdesalce. When it came to sex, Paca was in a league of her own. She liked to hit him and unleashed some truly ferocious blows. In Santa María it was said that she had once broken her husband's arm with a stick and, on another occasion, had flattened a shepherd's nose. With Eliseo, though, it was different. He faced up to her, forcing her to fight until she began to flag, and then he would push her down onto the bed. Even then, she would continue to resist, or, rather, pretend to resist, because the truth was, she enjoyed having sex with him, which was why she didn't ask for any money.

For the third or fourth time he thought of the cartoon about the hippopotamus who envied the zebras because their stripes made them look slimmer. This time, it made him laugh. Paca was a hippopotamus, but she didn't envy zebras at all.

Eliseo got into bed and, gazing into the darkness, he made another effort to imagine himself lying in the African bush, armed with his crossbow, waiting for one of the lions to leave the pride and make a move towards him, but the lion didn't stir, not even in order to turn its back on him, and so he decided to try and sleep. Shortly afterwards, as he was drifting off, a new fantasy began to take shape in his mind, one that had its roots in the previous one: he was watching and waiting, armed with his crossbow, not in Africa, but in the woods around El Pardo.

He felt a shock run through his body. A wounded boar, bitten by one of those bull-headed dogs, was running towards him, mad with pain. He saw the creature's tusks close by, less than ten metres away, and he stopped breathing. The crossbow wasn't ready. Then, at the last moment, he managed to ready the bow and squeeze the trigger. The arrow pierced the boar's chest, staining it red.

All his tension became concentrated in his penis, and as he turned over in bed, he felt the presence, first, of Paca, then of Maribel, and finally he came, still unclear if, in his fantasy, he was doing so over Paca or over Maribel.

On Wednesday evening, September 2, Eliseo made his way alone into the woods. Heading away from the barracks, it took him a quarter of an hour to get down to the river. He had made his calculations. After the entire month of August with almost no rain, the boar were likely to visit the river more often. Sheep didn't need to drink water, because grass contained enough liquid; pigs on the other hand drank, on average, five litres a day. In that respect, as in everything else, wild boar must be more like pigs than sheep.

133

He found a stone bridge and crossed to the other side. The woods were denser there, thick with brambles and closely grown trees and bushes. However, as soon as he set off, he saw a rabbit stumbling along ahead of him, its eyes all puffy, and he decided to turn back. The doctor at the barracks had assured him that myxomatosis could not be transmitted to humans, but he found the sight of those ailing creatures hard to take.

Back on the stone bridge, he heard rifle shots further up the river, about two or three kilometres away, and he headed in that direction, sometimes leaving the riverbank and going further into the woods. The sandy ground was ideal for spotting animal tracks, but he saw none at all. Besides, even if he had, he wouldn't have found them easy to identify. He could recognise the tracks left by a wild boar, because he had seen them around Valdesalce, but he had heard Caloco say that deer tracks were very similar.

He came to a kind of hollow and saw a log cabin with two small flags on the roof, one was the national flag and the other a grubby white one. He went to take a closer look. The Spanish flag was frayed and worn, the other was, in fact, yellow not white, and decorated with a fleur-de-lys and a small cross; to judge from the few legible letters, it belonged to a Catholic school. He peered inside the cabin. It smelled musty, yet another sign that it had been abandoned. The serious hunters apparently preferred the inner depths of the woods, more suited to the use of hounds and beaters. This was about as far as he could go. He was not allowed to leave the barracks until five o'clock and had to be back by ten, before the "Last Post" sounded, but those five hours were of little use to him because wild boar never left their hiding places during the day. They would probably start to appear towards sunset, around eight o'clock.

He sat down outside the cabin, leaning back against the wooden wall. He listened hard: nothing. He continued to listen intently: he heard the piercing cry of a coot on the river. Then nothing. In the minutes that followed he heard only the occasional chirruping of some small bird. Animals were strange. So cautious, so secret. On the day that he and the others from the new intake had arrived at the barracks, the colonel, in his welcome speech, had mentioned the fauna that inhabited what he called the "neighbouring woods": three thousand fallow deer, five hundred wild cats, hundreds of foxes and hundreds of badgers, no less than thirty thousand rabbits, about ten thousand hares and more than a thousand wild boar. So many inhabitants, and yet the woods seemed deserted. There was no way of knowing where they were hiding. Only the dogs knew that, by scent. But he would have to manage without a dog. He was assailed then by a doubt: if he could not find any tracks, he would have to abandon his plan. His one hope was the knowledge that wild boar liked being close to human habitations. Caloco had told him that while on sentry duty in early summer, he had once seen a whole herd of wild boar crossing the Mingorrubio road.

The birds kept flying back and forth to a small cranny about ten yards from the cabin. When he went to look, he found a spring, a mere thread of water flowing from a cavity surrounded by stones and moss. Eliseo cupped his hands and drank from it. The water was deliciously cool.

He looked at his watch, it was nearly seven o'clock. His friends would already be gathering at the Communications Unit for supper. He headed off briskly, going back down to the riverbank and past the stone bridge. He stopped short. Coming towards him at top speed were two, possibly three motorbikes. He recognised them at once by the sound of their engines. They were Montesas, the off-road motorbikes used by the gamekeepers on their patrols.

He dived in among the trees, but, in his haste, stepped back into a dip he had failed to notice. He was slender and light enough to be able to spring to his feet again, but immediately had to crouch down so as not to be seen. The bikes sped past, very close to where he was hiding. They were probably young gamekeepers out for a joyride, or perhaps some of the civil guards who patrolled the area around the two palaces in El Pardo.

The hollow was about a metre and a half deep. Eliseo looked

around him and realised that he was sitting in the dried-up bed of a stream. The ground immediately ahead of him was covered by a smooth rock, a big slab about two metres wide, topped by a bank of sediment, which formed a natural barrier; from that point on, the streambed continued straight on into the woods, its sandy walls becoming narrower and narrower. In certain places, beneath the roof formed by fallen branches and a tangle of brambles, it resembled a mine shaft.

He shuddered. A row of posts lined the right-hand bank, as though someone had started reinforcing it, and the base of those posts appeared to have been sanded down. This was better than any footprint. Wild boar had clearly been using them as scratching posts. He listened intently, as he had outside the cabin. Not a sound. But perhaps the boar was right there, only a few steps away, listening as intently, as intensely, as he was – except that an animal's ability to concentrate was ten times greater than that of any human. Despite its large body, the boar was as good at hiding as a mouse. Then, if a dog or a hunter came too close, it would flee, using its tusks to batter its way past any obstacle. He shuddered again. If he met a wild boar in that dried-up streambed, it would be as dangerous as confronting a lion.

He continued on his way. Joy made his steps lighter. That streambed formed a natural trench, perfect for anyone lying there armed with a crossbow and hoping to confront a wild boar.

As Eliseo emerged from the trees, he was met by the double sky of evening, pale blue on the upper part – the first sky – and below that, nearer the earth, the second sky, a succession of yellowish, pinkish clouds. The sun had already disappeared, and the light was very soft. The hill on which the Communications Unit stood appeared to have been painted with gold varnish.

He started running up the hill, as if the evening light had lifted his mood still more. He felt no aches, no stiffness anywhere in his body. He hadn't stopped since five o'clock in the morning, working first in the bakery, then in the repair shop, and yet he was brimming with energy.

When he reached the top of the hill, he saw that, to one side of the bunker, they had built a parapet out of wooden fruit crates. This was their secret hiding place for the target they used for crossbow practice. Like the boar, they, too, had to act with caution.

He glanced at his watch. Gone half past eight. Very late to be joining his friends. When he finally opened the door, Caloco lobbed an olive at him, expecting him to catch it with one hand, like a ball.

"There's your supper for the evening. We've eaten everything else," he said.

Celso went over to a box resting on one of the lockers. It was made of wood, like the crates forming the parapet. The magpie was inside.

"Go on, tell that bad father of yours, that neglectful father, tell him your name."

"*Paca!*" said the magpie very clearly.

"Now she'll start to repeat it," said Caloco.

"*Paca! Paca! Paca! Paca!*" the bird said on cue.

Celso gave the magpie a hard-boiled egg in a little cup.

The box showed the bird off to best advantage. In the faint light coming in through the small windows, its body seemed divided into two parts, one very white and the other very black. Its eyes were very black too. Head on one side, it kept one eye trained on what was going on in the Communications Unit.

The two radio transmitters were surrounded by piles of old telegrams, and the shelves were cluttered with portable AN/PRC-77 transceivers, cables and tools, while on the floor there were more transceivers, mostly of the URC-77 type. Two caps and a pair of trousers had been dumped unceremoniously on one of the wicker chairs. On the turntable of the record player was the LP from the film *Lawrence of Arabia*, and, beside it, the sleeve bearing the images of Peter O'Toole and Omar Sharif.

The low table was laden with food: tinned anchovies, tinned tuna with onions, a bowl of olives, another bowl containing lumps of cheese, as well as slices of ham arranged on a piece of brown paper, and a loaf of bread. To drink, a jug of sangria.

"You don't deserve it, but we waited for you anyway. Where have you been, if you don't mind my asking?" Caloco said, then pointing at himself, added: "You can tell me, I'm with military intelligence."

Eliseo sat down on the wooden bench next to Donato.

"The only member of military intelligence here is the Bedouin's servant," said Celso, and he stared over at the image of Peter O'Toole and Omar Sharif on the record sleeve. "Now don't look at me like that, Omar. This has nothing to do with your war."

"Raúl was in the barracks today," Caloco told Eliseo. "They've given him leave for another whole month. Apparently, the work at the Guadarrama house is taking him much longer than he thought."

"He didn't see Paca, though," said Celso. "So no need to worry."

Donato was trying to play a tune on the harmonica.

"*Lawrence of Arabia*. The beginning of the theme tune's fairly easy," he said, stopping, then immediately starting again.

Celso went over to the table and started filling the glasses, telling Eliseo he could drink as much as he liked without worrying about the after-effects. Sangria wouldn't upset his stomach the way the fruit punch had. Then, still talking, he explained how he had come by the *Lawrence of Arabia* LP. He had gone to ask the chaplain for some advice and, who would have thought it, the record was there in his office. The chaplain's advice went in one ear and out the other, but Celso left with the record. No, he hadn't stolen it; the chaplain, obliged as he was to practise Christian charity, had lent it to him.

He raised his glass of sangria and took a sip.

Eliseo was not listening. His mind was still full of what he had just seen in the woods: the dried-up streambed; the slab of rock and the bank of sediment, ideal for a marksman; as well as those posts that looked as if they had been sandpapered. A small object struck his face, an olive stone.

"Oh, good, so you *are* awake," said Caloco before launching another stone.

"Stop it!" said Eliseo, shielding his face with his hands.

"If you don't sharpen up, you won't hit the target and you'll lose the bet."

"I don't want to bet with money."

Caloco flicked another olive stone at him.

"There's no point in betting without money."

"He only wants to bet one peseta, Eliseo, that's all," said Donato.

"In that case, fine."

Eliseo's mind was still focussed on the dried-up stream. He would find it as easy to hit the target with the crossbow as he would with his rifle. If the boar visited those scratching posts, it was only about ten metres from there to the sediment barrier, and, at that distance, it would be hard to miss. The images began to connect like the stills from a film. The boar was running down the streambed, not to scratch itself on the posts, but mad with the pain inflicted on it by the dogs. Suddenly, it saw him there with the crossbow, safe behind the barrier, and hurled itself at him with all the furious impetus of a wild beast. He waited three seconds, hesitating, afraid the string might break when he pulled it taut, but it remained intact, and, a second later, the arrow was piercing the creature's chest. Nothing happened at first, then blood began spurting from the wound, and the boar let out a grunt before collapsing. When it hit the ground, it threw up a small cloud of pebbles, one of which struck his face.

Except that it was not a pebble, it was another olive stone.

"You're really getting on my nerves today, Eliseo," Caloco said. "We know you bakers have to get up early, but the other baker deserves a little respect. There he is delighting us with the *Lawrence of Arabia* theme tune, and you drop off."

"That fruit punch the other day really took it out of me," Eliseo said by way of an excuse.

On the table was a fairly large metal box with two holes in the lid. Celso put the magpie inside the box and closed it.

"We're going outside. Just in case, I always carry Paca in this box now, not under here." Celso indicated his cap. The cap was brand-new, but the bakelite stiffener in the peak was already bent out of shape.

He put the box under his arm and headed outside, followed by Caloco carrying the jug of sangria and the plastic cups, and by Donato, still playing the theme tune from *Lawrence of Arabia* on his harmonica. Eliseo was the last to leave.

"Ah, Panavision! A giant screen!" Celso exclaimed.

He meant the sky, which was still a double sky, two skies in one. Up above, it was a sheet of lilac, while down below it became bright red with wispy clouds that looked as if they were made of curly lamb's wool. Towards the west these formed a kind of cave, inside which sat the last of the day's sun, an ingot of red-hot iron.

Celso opened the box to let the magpie out.

"Go for a little stroll, Paca."

"*Paca! Paca! Paca!*" cried the bird, scampering and hopping down the hill, as if it were doing its daily exercises.

Eliseo reached under a rock and removed, first, one of the crossbows, then the three bolts and the second crossbow. He looked at Caloco.

"Prepare the target, please. Now you're going to see what true marksmanship is."

Caloco waved his hand, indicating that he did not have the energy to get up. He was sitting on a rock and did seem genuinely tired.

"I'll do it," said Donato, picking up the one-metre-diameter target hidden behind the parapet and putting it in position.

Eliseo won four points with his first shot, and five on each of the following two. Then Celso had a go: one zero and only five points in total. Then it was Donato's turn: twelve points. Caloco chose not to take part.

"I thought you said this sangria wasn't very strong, Celso?" he said. "You're clearly not from military intelligence at all. If you were, you'd be much better informed. It's turned me into a frog."

He poured himself more sangria.

"I want to turn into a real frog," he added. "So as not to be outdone by all those fairy-tale princes."

"Same here," said Eliseo.

"The fact is, Eliseo, you do seem a bit strange," said Caloco, and he stared at him hard, as if trying to put his finger on precisely what he found strange.

The sky was changing fast now. What had been lilac only shortly before was now dark grey; the red of the clouds resembling curly wool had changed to an intense purple. The spot where the sun had set was ablaze with light, as if the ingot of red-hot iron had exploded into hundreds of glowing fragments.

The brick-built bread oven in the barracks had a five-metre rotating rack, on which Eliseo and Donato would place the dough rolls that their colleagues had prepared the night before. It took only a few rotations for the rolls to be ready, and they would then scoop them out with a paddle, three or four rolls at a time, and pile them into large baskets. By half past seven in the morning, breakfast time in the barracks, they would have about three hundred, just enough, because those who had been on the night shift would already have had their breakfast. Eliseo and Donato would then take a short break in order to eat something, before going back to work once they had calculated how much bread would be needed for lunch and supper. At around eleven o'clock, with all the work done, Eliseo would head off to the repair shop to help Warrant Officer Santos, whereas Donato, who was in charge of the bakery, would stay behind to supervise the preparation of the dough for the next day. He was particularly fussy about cleanliness, because he always remembered what Miguel in Ugarte had taught him, that in a bakery "hygiene is more important than salt". Finally, at the end of the morning, he would discard all the fly papers, now covered in dead flies, and hang some new ones from the ceiling.

Once they had finished their respective jobs, they would meet up again at lunchtime.

"Eliseo, why are you always late for supper these days? Where do you get to in the evenings?" Donato asked when they sat down opposite each other at the table, each with his tray of food.

It was September 9, and he was referring to the fact that, for a while now, Eliseo had been turning up late every evening.

"You've got us all scratching our heads, especially Caloco. You arrive late and then barely open your mouth."

The food on their two trays was the same: paella, three sausages, mashed potato and an apple.

Eliseo stopped eating and adopted a studious pose, elbows on the table, his head resting on his hands.

"I've developed an obsession, the obsession of a shepherd from Valdesalce," he said at last. "I want to shoot a wild boar with the crossbow."

Donato fixed his blue eyes on him. Eliseo resumed his normal posture.

"I know, Donato. I know you're not much interested in hunting, and I'm not asking you to come with me."

There was a lot of noise in the canteen. Some two hundred soldiers were seated at the tables, eating, and another hundred were waiting in the queue or standing with their trays already full, looking for a place to sit. Some, as they passed, would aim some quip at Donato, often the same one: "I found a fly in my roll this morning." It got to the point where it was hard for them to continue their conversation.

"But where *do* you get to in the evenings?"

"I found some boar tracks in the woods, quite close to the bunker, and I've taken to going for a walk around there to see if there are any fresh ones. And there are, Donato, there are. I've found some boar droppings too, as well as the scratch marks they've left on some wooden posts."

He told him excitedly about the log cabin, the two flags and the little spring nearby; then about the rabbits with myxomatosis, the gamekeepers he'd heard driving past on their motorbikes and about the bull-headed dogs they took with them on their hunting expeditions, before he returned once more to the subject of wild boar.

Donato wasn't much interested in Eliseo's explanations, what worried him was his obsessive behaviour. Miguel, the owner of the bakery, had been the one to invite Eliseo to work with them in Ugarte after they had both visited the village, but Donato had acted as intermediary. Miguel always liked to say that good workers were all you needed to run a good business, and Donato had no qualms about Eliseo in that respect, for he had proved to be an excellent baker, and was so skilled at mending engines that Santos had tried to persuade him to stay on in the army, so that he could study to be a qualified mechanic. However, given his friend's silences, Donato was beginning to have his doubts and to wonder if Eliseo's obsession with hunting might conceal other impulses.

"Not that I mind going boar-hunting on my own," Eliseo said, concluding his descriptions of the tracks he had found in the dried-up stream.

Donato said nothing. He had finished his sausages and was now biting into his apple. Eliseo was still talking:

"Celso is such a terrible shot that I'd prefer it if he didn't come really, but I'll invite him anyway, just out of respect. The same with Caloco. I'll tell him today when we have our crossbow contest."

Donato looked very serious.

"Perhaps you should just give it up, Eliseo. It doesn't seem like a good idea to me," he said.

"It's something deep inside me, Donato."

They suddenly felt rather distant from each other, as if the table separating them had grown wider, and they both realised that if they didn't change the subject, the conversation would end badly. They stood up, left the trays where they were, and, on their way back to the bakery, discussed, half-joking, how Celso should adopt one of the stray dogs that hung about near the barracks, looking for scraps; a nice young dog on which Celso could lavish care just as he did on the magpie, and that would keep him company during his long hours confined to base. However, it wouldn't be at all easy to hide a dog in the bunker. Besides, even a very small dog would eat more than the magpie and would cause much more of a ruckus.

In the afternoon, large, fluffy clouds began to form, gradually covering the sky. By the time the friends had gone up to the parapet behind the bunker and begun the crossbow contest, the sun's rays had pierced the clouds and were so intense that they had to reposition the target twice, as well as changing the angle they were shooting from. It wasn't hot though. 17°C, according to the Guard Room thermometer.

Immersed in their competition, they didn't even mention what Eliseo had told them earlier about his plan to hunt a wild boar, which was pretty much what he had told Donato over lunch, but when they went back into the bunker, they opened the beers Celso had brought from the kitchen and returned to the subject. The dark yellow fluorescent lighting and the light coming in through the windows made the room seem gloomy.

Donato immediately gave voice to his doubts.

"I'm not going down to that dried-up stream. As far as I'm concerned, the boar can stay where they are."

"I agree," said Caloco.

"For my part, I'm going to consult Paca," said Celso, a bottle of beer in one hand. The bird alighted on his shoulder, as if she really were a parrot. "Paca, what do you think?"

"*Paca!*" said the bird.

"She says she wants to take on the boar. So count me in, Eliseo."

Donato tried to dissuade him. It wasn't exactly a good idea for someone who was both short-sighted and a bad shot to go hunting for boar. If the boar did turn up in that streambed, Celso would only get in Eliseo's way.

"No, I want to go. I've been stuck in this bunker for ages now, and a little trip out would do me good."

"You can't go, Celso. You're the only radio operator here at the moment."

"Yes, that was a dirty trick played on me by military intelligence. But that shouldn't be a problem, Donato. You can send the telegrams instead. It's very easy. You just press a button a few times, and that's that. The message is always the same: 'The Commies have not yet stormed the palace'."

Eliseo looked at Celso.

"It's Wednesday now. How about Saturday? That's usually a quiet day in the barracks."

Celso nodded.

"Perfect."

Caloco had stood up and begun moving about in the bunker. He stopped in front of the radio transmitters as if he were looking for something among the piles of telegrams. His friends were watching him.

"No-one will be going anywhere on Saturday," he said. "Didn't you receive a special telegram? You probably did but didn't notice. Hardly surprising, given the mess your desk is in."

"You're talking like someone from military intelligence, Caloco. Isn't he, Paca?"

"*Paca!*" declared the magpie.

Caloco told them that, the night before, in the Guard Room, he had overheard an interesting phone conversation. A sergeant had called his girlfriend to tell her that they wouldn't be able to get together that weekend because General Franco and Prince Juan Carlos would be going hunting in the woods around El Pardo, which meant that there would be no overnight passes issued from Friday onward, not even to go for a walk. What there would be, added Caloco, would be general cleaning duties all round, because it was rumoured that the general and the prince would visit the barracks afterwards for refreshments, so everything had to be spick and span. There would be more guards and more patrols to keep watch on the walls of El Pardo too. They would need a lot of soldiers, including some from other barracks.

"It could be a hoax on the part of Radio Rumour," said Eliseo.

"No way," said Caloco. "The sergeant was really upset. He kept apologising to his girlfriend for standing her up at the weekend."

"We could still give it a go, Eliseo, if you wanted to," said Celso. "We can set off down to the stream and wait for the boar while we enjoy a cool drink."

"I just don't understand you, Celso," said Caloco. "Anyone would think you wanted to get shot."

Donato put his harmonica to his lips and played the "Last Post". It was nearly ten o'clock. Time for them to return to their respective companies for roll call.

There were about forty flies stuck to the flypaper hanging from the ceiling; some were still alive, flailing about in a vain attempt to unstick their wings. Lieutenant Garmendia stood for quite some time studying it, as if he were counting the flies.

"Some of those flypapers would have come in very handy in the Sahara," he said.

He was exactly as Celso had described him: dark skin, black moustache and wavy hair, bearing a vague resemblance to Omar Sharif. Eliseo imagined him showing Vicky a photo of the actor in a celebrity magazine and joking: "There's my older brother."

Eliseo, Donato and the other soldiers who worked in the bakery were standing at ease, lined up in front of the oven and following the lieutenant's every move. He was inspecting everything, paying special attention to any metal receptacles. In the largest one, an electric mixer, there was a large white cloth covering the dough.

"Who's the soldier in charge here?" he asked.

"I am, sir." Donato stood to attention.

"I congratulate you. The bakery is spotless."

There were three flypapers hanging from the ceiling, and the lieutenant spent a while studying the other two. They had trapped fewer flies than the first one, about twenty each, as well as the occasional wasp. Eliseo felt as if he could hear what was going on inside the man's head. He was thinking about the Guadarrama house. About how Vicky found the flies there infuriating, and how they really could do with some fly papers like those. And yet they were so disgusting. They might appear to be impregnated with honey, but one touch was enough to realise that it was something else entirely, a very strong glue that wouldn't wash off even with soap and water.

"Put some more up tomorrow but take them down at around ten or eleven. At midday, you might have a very important visit."

"Radio Rumour," thought Eliseo.

The rumours continually surfacing in the barracks were usually fairly short range, about the same range as a fly. Nevertheless, this rumour seemed to go further. Soldiers and officers were all convinced that General Franco and Prince Juan Carlos were going to visit the barracks. It was far more likely, however, that they would become too caught up in their hunting and lose track of time. There would be no refreshments, and no lunch either, even though, according to one version, the rumour assured them that the higher authorities would be eating with the soldiers in the barracks canteen. Sheer nonsense.

"Radio Rumour again!" Eliseo repeated to himself.

The telephone in the bakery began to ring. The lieutenant ignored it and beckoned Donato over.

"Give me a few of those fly papers, will you, the unused ones. Five should be enough," he said.

"Vicky!" thought Eliseo. He couldn't help smiling. He had guessed what the lieutenant was thinking.

The telephone stopped ringing after a few seconds, then immediately started up again.

It was Friday, September 11, shortly after seven o'clock in the morning, and the breakfast rolls were already in the baskets, far more than usual – about eight hundred – because the soldiers who were normally given an overnight pass had spent that night in the barracks. No-one was being let off cleaning duties.

The smell of freshly baked bread was making all the soldiers hungry, including Eliseo and Donato, but the lieutenant showed

147

no sign of leaving. He kept tossing the can containing the flypaper into the air, as if trying to guess its weight. Each can contained a roll of flypaper.

"I won't take it with me just now," he said at last, handing the can back to Donato. "If I need any later on, I'll ask."

He saluted. He was leaving.

"Go back to your duties," he said.

As soon as he had left, the soldiers all immediately grabbed a roll from the basket, as well as some ham, chorizo and cheese from a locker. Then they went outside and sat on the stone bench, talking and joking, elbowing and shoving, as if trying to push each other off. Eliseo and Donato continued on into the woods.

They saw Warrant Officer Santos walking briskly towards them, still in fatigues. Noticing that he was looking straight at him, Eliseo felt a wave of embarrassment. He thought Santos must have found out that, ever since he had shown him that photo of his daughter, Eliseo had spent his nocturnal fantasies with her, especially over the last few nights, now that he and Celso had agreed to go hunting wild boar. But that simply couldn't be true. *He* might be able to guess what someone else was thinking, because he had worked as a shepherd for fourteen years, and shepherds, obliged to spend long hours alone in solitary places like Valdesalce, were always going over and over things in their minds, and often became excessively sensitive and suspicious, as alert as spies to what might lie behind the words of some stranger; but Warrant Officer Santos wasn't like that. He was a kindly, trusting man. Then it occurred to Eliseo that perhaps the lieutenant had found fault with the repair shop, deemed it not quite clean enough, and that Santos had been reprimanded. But, no, that was equally impossible. A repair shop could never be expected to be as clean as a bakery.

"Celso has been trying to phone you, Eliseo, and when he couldn't get through, he asked me to come and tell you," said Santos. "You're expected back home. The village priest sent a telegram. Your father is dying."

Santos was in his fifties but looked older. He wasn't particularly tall, and yet he was already slightly stooped, probably the consequence of all those hours bent over engines. The lines on his cheek looked as if they had been made with a razor. His small, agile hands and fingers were the exception though. You just had to see those hands taking an engine apart. He wasn't a machine, as some soldiers said. He was an artist.

Eliseo began swearing.

"I'm so sorry, Eliseo," said Santos, removing his cap. "Go and pick up the telegram from the Communications Unit and take it to the general command. They'll issue you with a pass immediately."

He looked at Donato.

"And you can help him prepare his kit bag."

"I'd like to bring your daughter something from my village," Eliseo said, "but I don't know what. If it was springtime, I'd bring her a lamb, but right now, I'm not sure."

"Oh, Maribel doesn't need anything," said Santos. "She's happy watching television. Her favourite programme is *Bonanza*. She says she wants to live on a ranch, not in an apartment."

He smiled, and the lines on his face multiplied.

There was a lot of movement in the barracks, more than usual for that time of morning. Engines were turned on, revved, then turned off again. In the courtyard, the non-commissioned officers were occasionally heard barking out orders.

"We can't afford to have any mistakes this weekend," Santos said, putting on his cap and taking his leave. "I'm going to see if I can get some work done. I hope everything goes as well as it can back home, Eliseo."

He repeated his order to Donato:

"And you can help him."

On his way back to the repair shop, Santos passed the bakery, and the soldiers sitting outside, eating their ham or chorizo or cheese roll, stood up and saluted him.

"Anything wrong?" one of them asked when Donato and Eliseo came over.

"Yes, they've just increased our workload," said Donato. Eliseo had asked him not to mention his father. "We've got to make another eight hundred rolls by midday. We'll start in ten minutes."

Once in their room, Eliseo began packing his kit bag: a towel, the three celebrity magazines Santos had kept for him, various changes of clothes, socks, the silk rug a soldier had exchanged for a sponge cake, a military balaclava, a pheasant feather, his wash bag and the boots he wore in Valdesalce. On the way, he would buy a packet of Winstons for Paca at a petrol station. And some biscuits too.

"Give me your boots, and I'll clean them for you," said Donato.

Eliseo took them off and handed them over. Then he took his service uniform out of the locker.

"Do you need any money?" Donato asked.

Eliseo said no. He was planning to get lifts from one petrol station to another. Truck drivers were happy to pick up soldiers who were hitch-hiking, and he had enough money for any other expenses.

"I'm not as rich as Caloco, but I did sell a few lambs before coming here."

They both laughed. In their conversations, they had talked about many things, but never about money, or only after their visit to Ugarte, when they had discussed how much Miguel would pay him to work there. Almost double what he earned as a shepherd.

There was a knock at the door and, a moment later, Celso burst into the room. He was wearing the new cap, which now looked unusually large, as if it had just sprung into life. He was carrying the metal box under one arm and, in his hand, a white card. He started talking very quickly, as if eager to get something off his chest.

"Here's your pass, Eliseo. I took the telegram to the general command and said I'd bring you the pass myself, that you were sobbing inconsolably and were in no state to deal with it. They were quite happy to do that. I impressed them with my extra special cap and these particularly fine spectacles."

Instead of his usual, black-framed glasses, he was wearing a pair with gold frames. Donato continued cleaning Eliseo's boots, and Eliseo went on packing his bag, but it was impossible to ignore Celso for long.

"They're Raúl's glasses. I found them in the bunker. I don't know how he's going to manage without them."

He handed Eliseo the white card. Then, brushing aside Eliseo's words of thanks, he lifted the lid of the metal box. The magpie's head appeared over the top. Celso had provided it with food for the journey: a hard-boiled egg sliced in two and a whole banana without its skin.

"That'll be more than enough." He bent down and planted a kiss on the bird's head. "Goodbye, Paca. You're going away with your father, and a happy life awaits you in the kingdom of sheep."

Eliseo protested.

"No, don't argue, Eliseo. Never argue with a Celt, especially not a Celt wearing a special cap."

When he bowed his head, the new cap fell off, revealing his battered old cap beneath.

"You're completely mad, Celso," said Donato, laughing.

"What's your name? Name!" exclaimed Celso.

"*Paca! Paca! Paca!*" said the bird.

Celso closed the box and set it down beside the kit bag. He had put his new cap on again, and now placed an unlit cigarette between his lips.

"I'll smoke it later, when I'm back in the bunker," he said. He looked at the boots Donato had just finished polishing. "You can see your face in those. You're going to look very elegant, Eliseo. The sheep will be most impressed. What did you say your friend's dog was called?"

"Basilio's dog? Lay."

"She probably won't recognise you. You look more like a prince than a shepherd."

"Oh, she'll recognise me all right. She's a very bright dog."

He was in his trousers and shirt now and was pulling on his boots.

"When are you going to give your lady friend the magpie, before or after?" asked Celso. Donato laughed.

"We're not going to be able to have our boar-hunt now," said Eliseo. "That's what really pisses me off."

Celso put his cigarette back in the packet. He had to go.

"Don't worry, Eliseo. There'll be another time. I very much doubt that tomorrow's hunting party will wipe out the entire wild boar population. Franco, of course, will kill about ten. And the prince seven or eight."

"They say there's more than a thousand of them," said Eliseo.

Celso hugged him twice.

"A hug from me and one from Caloco."

He opened the door.

"I hope all goes well back in your village."

3

The dog, Lay, was following Basilio and Eliseo along the path from Valdesalce to Santa María, wagging her tail whenever Eliseo spoke.

"Don't go thinking she loves you more than she loves me," said Basilio. "She's just remembering that chorizo roll you gave her yesterday and hoping for another one. These dogs are always hungry."

Basilio, Eliseo's friend and colleague, was about thirty. In looks, he was rather like Caloco, stocky and strong, but in his calm way of talking and his gestures, he was more like Donato.

"And how do you know I gave her a chorizo roll?" Eliseo asked.

"Because she only ate the chorizo."

They were walking quietly along past the willow trees. Basilio was wearing light trousers and a cotton shirt, while Eliseo had on the jeans and red polo shirt he'd been wearing the previous night. They had already reached an agreement about money over breakfast. At Basilio's request, they would carry on as they had until now: he would take care of Eliseo's sheep, cabin and pen, and they would go halves on everything. After all, it made no difference to him if Eliseo was in the barracks or in Ugarte. They had also agreed to divvy things up twice a year, on St John's Eve and on Christmas Eve.

Lay had moved off now and was sniffing the ground. Sometimes, she would plunge into the brambles and give a yelp.

"I heard some hares on my way back last night," said Eliseo.

Lay was barking loudly, getting ever more excited. When Basilio whistled to her, though, she immediately came to heel.

"I bet you El Pardo's a good place for hares. Not to mention rabbits," said Basilio.

"The rabbits there are all dying of myxomatosis."

"What about Franco? Tono says there are rumours he's not too well either."

"I've no idea. Today, he was supposed to be joining a hunting party. And there's been a lot of toing and froing at the barracks recently."

The willows were growing sparser now, to be replaced by ash trees in such orderly lines that the path looked like an avenue in a park. Shortly afterwards, when they reached a clearing full of rosemary and sage, they could see the highest part of the church tower in Santa María. In the distance, in the morning mist, it resembled a lighthouse suspended in mid-air.

"What are you going to say to your father?" asked Basilio.

"What *can* I say to the bastard?"

Eliseo kicked a stone. Lay, walking by his side, moved a couple of metres away.

"I wish he'd died in Switzerland! And I wish I hadn't had to come and see him!"

Lay looked at Eliseo, unsure what to do, whether to keep her distance or come closer. She opted to come closer.

"Oh, I agree, you know I do," said Basilio. "Anyway, you'd have had to put in an appearance sooner or later. You've got all the paperwork to look forward to. It took me weeks to sort that out when my father died."

Eliseo was only fourteen when his father, by then a widower, had left him in Valdesalce to look after a flock of forty sheep, then emigrated to Switzerland to work for a company building nuclear bunkers. The three other men from Santa María who had left with him came back for good the following year, but not his father. He stayed on the next year and the next. And his visits in between became more and more infrequent. At first, he used to come four times a year, then twice, once in August and once at Christmas, and, in the end, only in August. He would arrive in the village wearing expensive cream-coloured suits and pointy shoes and would even walk up to Valdesalce dressed like that, like a gentleman out for a stroll. "How are things?" he would ask nonchalantly. Eliseo couldn't stand him. On his very first visit, Eliseo had pelted him with stones, causing an injury to his hand. Another time, he threw his father's present of a Certina watch in the river. The last time, however, he had accepted the gift of an expensive rifle, but then told his father never to come near him again.

Basilio knew all about this and shared Eliseo's feelings. There was no reason why he should come and say goodbye to his father. The priest, though, thought differently. It had been his idea to send a telegram to the barracks.

"Be ready, Eliseo," Basilio said. "I've heard that he wants to make off with your father's estate, which is why he's taken such care of him these last few months. But you're his sole heir and without your signature he can't do anything. Whatever you do, don't give him the house. Actually, I wouldn't mind renting it myself, if that's all right with you, of course."

Eliseo's father had bought the house a couple of years before returning from Switzerland for good when he began to feel ill. It stood opposite the steps leading up to the church, at the top of the main street.

"That's good to know, Basilio."

They continued walking. The morning mist was very fine now and allowed a view over the surrounding countryside, the central plateau of Castile: a fusion of reds and greens and blacks punctuated here and there by ranks of yellowish trees. The village itself, Santa María, was not yet visible, although two sections of the church tower were: the lower part rather like a square table, and the upper part like a lighthouse and topped by a lightning conductor because of the frequent thunderstorms.

Lay had moved away from the path again and was zigzagging through the clumps of rosemary and sage, as if they were the obstacles in a gymkhana.

"She's still in pretty good shape," said Eliseo.

"So are you," Basilio said with a laugh. "Have you told Paca your plan? I don't think she's going to like the idea of you going off to become a baker."

"Well, she's happy enough now. I had no idea she'd take such a liking to the bird. After all, there are plenty of local magpies."

"But they don't call her by name."

Basilio laughed again. Eliseo gave him a playful punch on the arm.

"And you're happy too. You're doing very nicely out of my flock."

"Working hard, my friend, while you idle around in El Pardo. Although I doubt very much that you're the only idle sod there . . ."

Basilio even laughed like Donato.

They reached the road at the point where it began to go downhill. From there, they could see almost the whole of the church tower, all three sections now, each with its respective windows and arches, and, on the lighthouse-like top of the tower, the lightning conductor. The houses were not yet visible. The village was set in a slight hollow.

"That's where I saw the hares yesterday," said Eliseo, indicating the road to the left of the path.

Lay ran in that direction, occasionally looking back at them, waiting for orders. Basilio shouted to her, telling her they had to head back to Valdesalce. Then he spoke to Eliseo:

"How much leave have you got?"

"A week."

"Are you going to spend the night at your father's house?"

Eliseo shrugged.

"If he really is dying, I'll have to, but if not, no way. He has a carer, doesn't he? That's what Paca told me."

"Yes, the priest arranged that too. It's Pilar, who acts as a nurse in the village. You know Pilar, don't you?"

"Not very well. Not that it matters."

When they parted, Eliseo quickened his pace. The village soon came into view below him: ochre-coloured houses nestling in the hollow and, towering above them, as if built on their rooftops, the vast church, two or three times bigger than you would expect in a village of only a thousand inhabitants. He recalled a story his father had told once in the local bar during one of his August visits: that the church was actually the cathedral from an Italian city that some witches had stolen and carried through the air to Santa María. "By which I mean, of course, that it's Italian in style."

His father liked to boast about all he had learned in Switzerland. "Spanish society is so backward in comparison. In Switzerland, they have universities for workers, which provide a really excellent education. Oh, they're very advanced in all sorts of ways. By government order, for example, there has to be what they call an *abri antiatomique* in the basement of every building. If there's ever a nuclear explosion, then the people who live there, people like me, will be saved, while you lot . . . well, *c'est fini*." The other customers in the bar didn't take him too seriously. "Why not shelter in the cellar here, at least there'd be no shortage of wine!" "No, to be safe from a nuclear attack, you need anti-radiation filters, *des filtres contre la radiation*. Besides, do you really imagine the Swiss haven't thought of that? They have enough wine as well as everything else you could possibly need to survive for a whole year. Believe me, I know what I'm talking about. I'm currently the inspector for more than a hundred nuclear shelters."

If it wasn't nuclear shelters, it was something else; his father never tired of singing the praises of Switzerland, even in Valdesalce, to Basilio, Tono and Paca. He would peer inside the cabins or the sheep pens with an inspectorly air and say: "They'd organise this much better in Switzerland." Paca wasn't taken in. On one of his visits, she did not hold back: "You can say what you like about how organised the Swiss are and about those *abris* or whatever they're called, but I reckon you've got a woman there, and that whenever you talk about Switzerland, what you're really talking about is her, and her face and her body." Basilio's loud peal of laughter distracted attention from his father's reaction, but it was a real lightbulb moment for Eliseo. Suddenly all the pieces fitted together. The fact that his father came to Santa María so rarely and never once suggested that Eliseo should visit him in Switzerland. He was just the same: thinking about Valdesalce meant thinking about Paca. He liked Valdesalce because he liked Paca.

The church was not in fact built on the rooftops of the village, but on a natural platform that raised it above the surrounding houses. It really did resemble a cathedral. A flight of some forty or fifty steps led up to the entrance. The lower walls of the tower were adorned with arches and the statues of saints, the upper walls with dogs and lions with their mouths wide open, as if they were vomiting.

As he approached his father's house, the medicinal smell reached him even out in the street. He stood at the door, listening. He was thinking about what Basilio had told him as they were leaving *his* father's funeral: "He died screaming for morphine, but the doctor refused to give it to him. He said he couldn't, that it was banned in Spain. That's not going to happen to me. I'll shoot myself first. Or you can shoot me, Eliseo, with your Verney-Carron."

Eliseo's thoughts leapt to the Verney-Carron. It was the rifle his father had brought him from Switzerland, a very fancy weapon ornamented with embossed silver. The kind of present that a man with a taste for expensive cream-coloured suits and pointy shoes would buy. What if Eliseo took it back with him to the barracks? He would hide it in the bakery and go hunting for wild boar with that rather than with the crossbow. He immediately rejected the idea. Only Celso would come up with something like that.

There was a strong smell of medicine, but no screams. His father was more fortunate than Basilio's.

The priest welcomed him at the door and shook his hand.

"I'm so glad you've come, Eliseo. I'm the new priest, Juan."

The priest was young, more or less the same age as Basilio. He was wearing a pair of round, gold-rimmed spectacles and seemed very pleasant. Perhaps the rumour that he was intending to appropriate his father's house was false.

"It's ten o'clock," he said, looking at his watch. "Cristino has just been given his medication. He'll sleep for a couple of hours now. The lady who looks after him is there, so would you mind coming to the church with me? I need help moving the harmonium."

This was the first time Eliseo had heard his father's name since arriving in the village. Cristino. Neither Basilio nor Paca ever mentioned it in his presence.

They went straight up the steps to the balustrade surrounding the mirador. The mist had lifted, and the sky was bluer than it was in El Pardo. The fields of poppies near the village glowed in the sunlight; further off, they could see the uplands, with their scattering of small woods, among them Valdesalce. Very high up, the swifts were flying.

They went into the church and slowly made their way towards the altar, allowing their eyes to become accustomed to the dark. It was like entering a palace, and, confronted by that lavish display of wealth, it occurred to Eliseo that the bigwigs who went hunting in the woods around El Pardo would happily celebrate a wedding there, as would Lieutenant Garmendia. Vicky, on the other hand, might find it too modest. She was clearly a very demanding girl, and perhaps only a cathedral would do for her. On the other hand, she might prefer somewhere like this. After all, her house-cum-castle in the Guadarrama mountains and that church had a lot in common. The walls of her house and the walls of the church were equally cluttered, the former with stuffed animals, the latter with statues of saints and tapestries. Even more of a coincidence was the lion's head adorning one of the tombs. Perhaps they also had stools made from elephants' feet. Although that was less likely. The artists of the time would never have seen an elephant and so wouldn't have been able to produce a realistic representation of one. The strangest thing, though, was that there were no wild boar, because there was certainly no shortage of them in the surrounding countryside, and the artists would surely have seen them.

The priest, who was still at his side, spoke in a whisper, as if addressing someone who was sleeping:

"Do you see that, Eliseo?"

He was pointing to the reredos. It was all in gold, from top to bottom, and profusely decorated. The columns were so intricately carved they appeared to be full of protuberances, as if made from some diseased material. On the altar, inside a kind of miniature chapel, a Baby Jesus wearing a white tunic had one hand raised in blessing. Above him, the Virgin, the skirts of her blue cloak billowing, was being carried up to heaven by a choir of angels; higher still, St Christopher, with the Christ Child on his shoulders, was crossing a river, leaning on a stick; and at the very top was Jesus dying on the cross.

"Your father keeps mentioning you," said the priest.

"That's good to know," said Eliseo.

The priest did not insist. Like a tourist guide, he made a sweeping gesture with one arm, as if taking in the whole church.

"Everything here is very beautiful," he said, "but there's too much of it really. Artists then had a horror of empty space. Do you see that?"

He was referring to the steps leading up to the presbytery. A lion's head adorned each of the two points where the steps met the iron grille.

"I spotted another lion elsewhere," said Eliseo, "and I wondered if there were any wild boar in the church too, because there are far more boar around here than there are lions."

Ignoring this remark, the priest took his arm and led him to one of the side naves. The harmonium was behind a column. The priest indicated that they needed to move it closer to the altar.

"I much prefer organ music at a funeral," he said. It was proving surprisingly easy to move the harmonium. "The organ's another of the jewels of this church, although it's in a pretty bad state now. It needs to be repaired, but who's going to pay for that? The church is expensive enough to maintain as it is."

Eliseo could hear Basilio's voice saying: "He's starting to talk about money. Keep your guard up!"

They positioned the harmonium next to the presbytery, beside one of the lion heads, and the priest disappeared off into the sacristy. He returned with a chair. Then he disappeared again and returned carrying a folder. The music scores. He placed one on the music stand and began to play. He adjusted his gold-rimmed glasses so that they were halfway down his nose, and behind them, his eyes moved up and down, from the score to the keyboard.

Eliseo read the words beneath the notes: *Mi-se-re-re me-i, De-us.* If called on, Donato could have played that music perfectly, because it did not seem particularly difficult. But Donato disliked sad things, preferring songs like "Juanita Banana".

The priest stopped playing and stood up.

"Hmm, slightly out of tune, but we'll sort that out."

He went over to the pews and sat in the front row, indicating to Eliseo that he should join him.

"Whenever I come to pray, I always sit here, before the Baby Jesus," he said. "He's the least ornate figure on the reredos, but he's the one I like best."

Eliseo could smell candle wax on the priest's cassock, along with a whiff of medicine from his father's house.

"We need to talk, Eliseo."

"Only by talking can we reach an understanding," Eliseo thought, but said nothing. It was as if Donato were inside him and thinking for him.

"Look, Eliseo, I've been visiting Cristino every day for the last few weeks. He's confessed all his sins, and I've forgiven them in the name of the Lord. But he can only die in peace if you forgive him too. He's genuinely sorry."

"What a nerve!" thought Eliseo. "How can someone have the gall to abandon his son, then, years later, years and years later, ask for his forgiveness. How phoney, how cowardly!" But he didn't say a word. The voices of his friends from the barracks were filling his head, first Donato's and now Caloco's. He felt confused, and his confusion only grew when his friends all started talking at once, as sometimes happened when they were gathered at the Communications Unit. Celso was saying: "My father was very good to me. He would bring me old radios so that I could learn about electromechanics by taking them to pieces. My mother, on the other hand, was dreadful. Instead of the dog I wanted, she gave me two tortoises. And yet I still forgave her because we Celts are quick to forgive. But as for what you should do with your father, Eliseo, I really don't know." He couldn't quite hear what Donato was saying, but it sounded as if he was in favour of forgiveness. Caloco, though, was not. Of the three voices in his head, Caloco's was the harshest.

The priest produced a small Bible from underneath his cassock and began telling Eliseo the parable of the prodigal son. A young man had left his father's house in order to go to some far-off land and live the life of a libertine, squandering his inheritance. One day, though, finding himself penniless, he decided to return home.

"I'm going to read it to you, Eliseo," said the priest, hastily adjusting his glasses again so that he could read:

"And he arose and came to his father. But while he was yet at a distance, his father saw him and had compassion, and ran and embraced him and kissed him. And the son said to him, 'Father, I have sinned against heaven and before you; I am no longer worthy to be called your son.' But the father said to his servants, 'Bring quickly the best robe and put it on him; and put a ring on his hand and shoes on his feet; and bring the fatted calf and kill it, and let us eat and make merry; for this my son was dead, and is alive again; he was lost, and is found.' And they began to make merry."

Caloco's raucous laughter echoed around Eliseo's head. So this is how the priest thought the world worked. When that scoundrel of a son returned home, his father ordered a big fat calf to be killed and held a party in his honour! Not a chicken, not a rabbit, but a three hundred kilo calf! Either the priest was very stupid or the writer of that story was describing something that had never actually happened.

"Eliseo!" said the priest, shaking him gently. "Are you listening with your eyes closed or are you asleep?"

162

He was smiling at him with an expression on his face that you normally only see in dreams. Somewhat disconcertingly, the gold from the reredos was reflected in the lenses of his glasses, concealing his eyes.

"I had a very long journey yesterday, all the way from El Pardo. I'm really tired."

The priest still had the Bible open. He closed it slowly.

"It's a very simple parable, I know. Like the figure of the Baby Jesus before us. But the great truths are always simple. And the duty to forgive is one of them. We should forgive others as the father in the parable forgives the prodigal son."

"But in my case, it's the other way round," said Eliseo. "It was the father who went off to a distant land to live the life of a libertine, not the son. The ending should be the other way round too."

"So is there no forgiveness, Eliseo?"

The priest turned to him. The golden reflection in his lenses had gone, and Eliseo could see his eyes now. They were very dark, his gaze steadfast.

Caloco, Celso and the others had fallen silent, and Eliseo heard his own voice saying very clearly:

"First, I need to see him. One thing at a time."

"He won't last much beyond today. You'll have to decide soon," said the priest.

They both stood up.

"The lady who looks after him will sort out the flowers, and Cristino has left more than enough money for the funeral, so you needn't worry about expenses."

"I wasn't going to," thought Eliseo.

They left the church. The blue sky had started to cloud over, and the swifts were flying lower now, in between the houses and over the rooftops. The weather was about to change.

"You'll need to be patient with your father," said the priest. "He's delirious most of the time. To be honest, the only time he makes any sense is when he asks after you."

163

"Those things floating about in the air aren't moths, Pilar. They're radioactive waves," Cristino said from his bed. Weakness had made his voice much gentler. "Whoever built this *abri*, didn't finish the job. They forgot the filters. Isn't anyone going to install them? My leukaemia's just going to get worse if they don't."

Eliseo was standing about a metre from the bed. Cristino, despite having his eyes open, appeared not to see him.

"Your son is here," said the woman, bending over Cristino's pillow. She was middle-aged and had a rather stern face. She turned to Eliseo. "He's delirious, his mind's going."

A blanket covered the open window, and the room was in near darkness.

"We keep the window open day and night because of the smell, and we can't remove the blanket, because the light hurts his eyes," the woman explained. She went over to the door. "I'll bring you a glass of lemonade."

Eliseo remained standing in the at-ease position to which his body had become accustomed at the barracks. Cristino had closed his eyes and was silent. Now and then, Eliseo could hear the swifts outside. Their cries as they flew past were more refined than those of magpies, almost like a whistle.

Eliseo was trying to work out how long it had been since he had spoken to his father. He had given him the Verney-Carron rifle the summer Eliseo turned eighteen, so that would have been four years ago. They hadn't spoken since. Not even when Cristino came back to the village for good, and moved into the house opposite the church, a few months before Eliseo left to do his military service. Any attempt at a reconciliation on Cristino's part had proved futile.

"You didn't have any problem accepting the rifle I gave you!" Cristino's words of reproach rang in Eliseo's head. He was right. But how could he not have accepted it? He showed it to Paca on the same day his father gave it to him. "I've never seen anything so beautiful!" she cried, running her finger over the hare engraved on the silver inlay. The whole thing gleamed. He had never seen anything as beautiful either, and he knew he would never be able to throw it away as he had the Certina watch. Leaving behind the twine he used for laying traps, he had set off with the rifle that very afternoon. He killed three hares before nightfall and handed them over to Paca to prepare. After supper, she took him to bed with her, and that was the first time he had sex with a woman.

Cristino still had his eyes closed, but now he was talking again. It was impossible to understand what he was saying, but Eliseo assumed it was the delirium preventing him from articulating clearly. Then he heard the word *antiatomique* and realised that his father was speaking to someone in French and occasionally laughing. He listened hard. Some words were repeated over and over: *mamuasel, estefani*. You didn't need to know French to understand what this meant. *Estefani* was *Stéphanie*, the same name as Princess Caroline of Monaco's sister. Eliseo knew this from the magazines that Santos passed on to him. So Cristino was talking to some woman, and he was doing so very affectionately, enjoying the conversation.

Pilar, the carer, appeared in the doorway. She was carrying a jug in one hand and a glass in the other.

"Here's your lemonade," she said. She leaned over the bed. "Cristino, your son Eliseo is here!"

The patient reacted and, slightly more loudly, trying to reach out with his arms, he cried: "Estefani! Estefani! Estefani!"

"There are some things the priest can't tell you," said Pilar. "Your father was living in Switzerland with a woman called Estefani, which is perfectly normal really. He was a widower after all, and a good-looking man too, like you."

Eliseo took a sip of lemonade but said nothing.

"On the other hand, leaving you alone in Valdesalce when you were only fourteen, that wasn't normal at all," she went on. "He's sorry for that now and doesn't want to die without your forgiveness. The number of times he's told the priest exactly that. But I don't know if he'll regain consciousness now. One of the medicines we give him sends him to sleep."

165

The medicines were on the bedside table, and she pointed to one of them, a grey box. Beside it was a calendar, with some of the days marked with a circle.

"*Mon, ma, mamuasel, bon, fam, bon, ma, mon . . .*" Cristino's mutterings had become monotonous, a murmur interrupted only by the screaming of the swifts, and Eliseo was beginning to lose interest. He glanced at the calendar. It was September 12. He had agreed with the owner of the bakery in Ugarte that he would start his new job a week before Christmas, because that was one of their busiest times. This meant that, once he had completed his military service, he would have about a week to collect his things from Valdesalce and move. He had liked everything about Ugarte. The fact that Donato worked there, Miguel the owner, Marta the very pretty cook, and also the man they called Greybeard, a hunter like him, who had told him that the mountains near to Ugarte were teeming with wild boar. He suddenly felt very sleepy and closed his eyes.

The church bell rang out for midday dragging him out of his torpor. The bakery, the people of Ugarte, Donato, Miguel, Marta, Greybeard, all vanished from his mind, and he saw Cristino there, still speaking French, "*mon, ma, mamuasel, bon, fam, bon, ma, mon . . .*" but very feebly now. Suddenly he said a new name: "Erika". By the time Eliseo was awake enough to pay attention, his father had already mentioned a third name: "Yovana", followed shortly afterwards by "Maricler", then "Shantal". He seemed to be reciting a list.

"Estefani *would* be pleased!" Eliseo said sarcastically, a response worthy of Caloco. The reason why his father had left him in Valdesalce was clear for all to see. Paca had guessed as much from the start.

He started thinking about Caloco. He needed to persuade him to go with him on his boar hunt. It was great that Celso would be there, because he was the sort who didn't know the meaning of fear, but he was such a bad shot that he might prove to be a handicap. On the other hand, Caloco was reasonably good. He could finish off the boar if Eliseo missed or, worst-case scenario, if he hit it, but only wounded it. The trouble was that Caloco had his mind fixed on his cows and didn't want to join in the hunt. Eliseo had an idea. He would offer him money. Every time Caloco agreed to go, he would pay him what he would normally earn on guard duty. No, on second thoughts, he would pay him what he earned on guard duty, but only if a boar did actually appear and they managed to kill it. If they waited in the streambed and nothing happened, he would only give him a quarter of what he would earn on guard duty.

He poured himself more lemonade. It was lukewarm. He took a sip.

Cristino was still keeping up the same refrain: "*Mon, ma, mamuasel, bon, fam, bon, ma, mon . . .*"

"I'm sick of listening to you and your French!" Eliseo bawled. "Just shut up, will you!"

Cristino opened his eyes.

"Eliseo!" he whispered. "Eliseo, I need your forgiveness."

"Well, you're not going to get it, Cristino," Eliseo said, and flung what remained of the lemonade at his father's face.

A scream emerged from Cristino's mouth. Not like the screaming of the swifts, nor the shriek of someone in pain, but the death rattle of a dying man.

4

Before leaving the woods, they put the two crossbows and the three bolts in the log cabin, as Celso had asked them to do when they first went down to the streambed. Unless Raúl's leave of absence were to continue indefinitely, he would be returning to the barracks at any moment, and then he would be installed in the Communications Unit watching their every move as closely as they were watching the wild boar. A tiny mistake, a foolish slip, and he could easily stumble upon the weapons hidden under the rock on the hill, and he would know at once that they were the same weapons that had gone missing from the house in the mountains.

"We'd better not let that military intelligence hitman see them, because if he does, he'll tell the Bedouin, who'll tell Vicky, who'll tell her father who art in heaven, who'll tell the general, who'll tell the colonel, who'll tell the captain, who'll take the news back to the Bedouin, and the Bedouin will then have me shot."

He was holding the two flags he had taken from the log cabin, the little Spanish flag and the other one bearing the fleur-de-lys and the cross, and he was waving them about to emphasise his words, as if he were sending a message in semaphore. Then, he started leaping around, performing "a Celtic dance to attract wild boar".

"Now I understand why we didn't see any boar today," said Caloco. "You should have performed your magic when we were down at the stream. There's no point now."

"That's where you're wrong, Caloco. Celtic magic isn't instant like Nescafé. Once the ritual is complete, though, its effect will last throughout the whole hunting season."

They were walking along the path by the river, heading for the Communications Unit. Celso continued his dance, still waving the flags, and every now and then bursting into song at the top of his voice.

"If you carry on like that, you'll attract the gamekeepers not the boar," said Eliseo. He was worried. Celso appeared to be growing wilder by the day, as if his engine was idling even faster than Caloco's.

In their room that same night, Sunday, September 20, Eliseo mentioned his concerns to Donato. Donato found Celso's behaviour entirely understandable, given the life he led, all those months confined to barracks, half the time working alone, unable to leave the radio transmitters for a moment. Yes, it was understandable, but worrying too. The longer Raúl's leave of absence went on, the more resentful Celso became, and he could get himself in real trouble if he did one day confront Raúl with his suspicions. That would be disastrous if Raúl was *not* from military intelligence, and even more so if he was.

"The other day he hurled the pair of glasses Raúl had left there against the wall, cracking one of the lenses. You know the ones I mean, the round, gold-rimmed ones."

Eliseo nodded, but a different image came into his mind: not Raúl's glasses, but the glasses worn by the priest in Santa María, which were also round and gold rimmed.

Silence reigned in the barracks, as it always did on Sunday nights. Nothing moved. There was barely any traffic on the road between El Pardo and Mingorrubio. Donato occasionally played a tune on his harmonica.

"What song are you learning now?" asked Eliseo. They had their boots off and were sitting on their respective beds, facing each other.

Donato pointed to the cassette on top of the locker: "*Tombe la neige*" by Salvatore Adamo.

"I think it means 'Snow is falling'. I need to find someone who knows French so he can tell me what the words mean."

"Ask me, Donato! *Mon, ma, mamuasel* . . . That's French too. I've come back from Santa María speaking French!"

He closed his eyes then and, emerging out of the darkness, he saw Cristino in his bedroom in the house in Santa María: "Estefani, Erika, Yovana . . ." He could see it all exactly as it had happened. Cristino, suddenly awake and looking straight at him: "Eliseo, I need your forgiveness." And him responding: "Well, you're not going to get it!" and flinging what remained of the lemonade at his father's face, and then his father's final death rattle.

Donato was still playing "*Tombe la neige*" on his harmonica. Eliseo tried hard to listen. He wanted to drive Cristino from his mind.

"I'm learning it on the accordion too. It'll come in useful at dances. It's nice and slow," said Donato.

He placed the harmonica on the locker and started putting on his pyjamas. Eliseo had got into bed now, wearing just his underpants. It seemed to him even hotter than usual, as if the oven in the bakery next door had been left on.

"Does it snow in Ugarte?" he asked.

"Two or three times a year at most. It's never very cold."

"How many pairs of pyjamas do you wear when it's cold?" Eliseo felt the need to keep talking so as to avoid hearing Cristino in his head.

Donato laughed and turned off the light.

"One pair of pyjamas and three blankets." Then he changed the subject. "You know, you say Celso's not quite right in the head, but you haven't come back from the village in the happiest of moods either. That's my impression anyway. Weren't there many people at your father's funeral?"

"Oh, it was no big deal." Eliseo still had his eyes open. He gave a hollow laugh. "In his sermon, the priest talked about forgiveness. How God really loves us and forgives all our sins."

"The usual funeral stuff, then."

Eliseo could see the priest's head in the darkness, with his round, gold-rimmed glasses. Basilio had been right, the priest was hoping to get his hands on the house, but he did not need Eliseo's signature to do that, it was all there in his father's will. As allowed by law, Cristino had left a third of his assets to the parish, so that part of the ground floor of the house would now become a venue for catechism classes, and a third of the money in his father's bank account would be used to repair the church organ. Not that there was a great deal of money, because Cristino had squandered most of it on Estefani, Erika, Yovana and the others, plus, since his return to Santa María, his only income had been his pension from the company that built those *abris antiatomiques*. The priest, though, wanted more: "Eliseo, I'm going to ask you to consider something. I know you're not coming back to live in Santa María, and that you're not going to use the house, or only very occasionally. If you could let us have the rest of the ground floor, we could turn it into a youth club for the village kids and set it up for ping pong and table football. I'm only thinking of the good of the village, you know. What do you say, Eliseo?"

"Oh, leave me alone!"

Donato sat up in bed.

"Who are you talking to, Eliseo?"

"The priest in Santa María. I was dreaming."

"Ah, I thought the funeral hadn't gone too well."

"I've been to worse."

Eliseo heard Donato turning over in bed.

"The magpie died."

"Well, whatever you do, don't tell Celso!" Donato paused for a few seconds before going on. "After you took it away, he got really down in the dumps and was on the verge of smuggling a dog into the bunker, but we talked him out of it."

Eliseo didn't want to tell him what had actually happened. That Paca's husband, the much-cuckolded Tono, had become incensed at hearing the bird constantly repeating *Paca! Paca! Paca!*, and while they were all at the funeral had smashed the bird's head in with a hammer. When Paca came back to Valdesalce and saw the dead bird, she had tried to do the same to Tono, but he escaped with only a broken collarbone. Eliseo felt really ashamed about the whole business. In Ugarte they would want to know more about his background, where he was born, his family. Cristino's escapades in Switzerland were scandalous enough, without Eliseo describing the brutal goings-on in Valdesalce.

"It was just bad luck," said Eliseo. "The day after I arrived, my friend Basilio was going off hunting for hares very early and he spotted the magpie round the back of his cabin, in the lean-to where he stores his cheeses. Worried that the bird would start pecking holes in them, he shot it dead."

Donato sighed, and the springs on his bed creaked as he turned over.

"Like I say, don't tell Celso," he said.

The springs creaked again. He was looking for a comfortable position to sleep in.

"He didn't ask about the magpie at supper tonight. He seemed more concerned about the crossbows," said Eliseo.

"He's been getting them ready, and he's very proud of them. He's sharpened the bolts so that the points are sharp as needles."

Donato was falling asleep. He found it hard to speak.

Eliseo was once more gazing into the darkness. Given how alike Basilio and Donato were, Basilio would doubtless forgive him for having laid the blame for the magpie's death on him. When they went to see Cristino's house, Eliseo had not wanted to revisit what had been his father's bedroom, and Basilio had said: "Eliseo, what are you afraid of? When the body disappears, everything else disappears too. It's a nice, cool room. If we do come to an agreement and I rent the house from you, I'll have this as my bedroom."

Donato's breathing was now the only thing to be heard, and Eliseo was waiting for what he feared would happen next. And it did. Bursting out of the darkness came Cristino's final death rattle. Eliseo, alas, was not like Basilio or Donato. Or even Caloco. His friends all had good, healthy engines. His, on the other hand, often ran rough and stalled. The days would pass, and he would keep hearing that death rattle, again and again. Even Celso, a truck with very dodgy brakes, always about to collide with something or go careering off the road, even his engine ran more smoothly than Eliseo's.

Eliseo began taking deep breaths, as he had been taught to do in the gym classes at the barracks, until he could smell the bread from the bakery, which he hadn't done for days, and then, finally, he fell asleep.

During what remained of the month, they only went looking for the wild boar one more time, on Monday, September 28. Eliseo had no desire to go more often, and whenever he saw Celso getting edgy, impatient to return to the woods, he would sit down beside him and try to drive the idea from his head: there was no point in making fruitless expeditions and running unnecessary risks with the gamekeepers. It was best to wait until the days grew shorter. The boar only left their lair as it was growing dark, when the sun was low in the sky. Otherwise, they rarely came out.

His reasoning was somewhat weak, since he had been the one to suggest going down to the streambed at the beginning of the month, although, as it turned out, that idea had come to nothing because it coincided both with the hunting party organised for General Franco and Prince Juan Carlos, and with his departure for Santa María; on that occasion, though, he had merely intended to do some reconnaissance. They must be patient. It would be getting dark earlier and earlier, and the skies would grow ever more overcast. The weather was in their favour.

Eliseo had another reason for delaying their excursions. He wanted to avoid having Celso as his sole companion, and that was difficult because Caloco, with his endless guard duties, was almost never available. He could have gone alone, but that was not an option either. He could not exclude Celso, however bad a shot he was. Caloco and Donato would not have wanted that, nor would he.

On their first two outings, they had established a plan of action.

First, they would make their way into the wood as quickly as possible in order to reduce the likelihood of meeting any game-keepers; then they would sit in the cabin for a while, resting and loading the crossbows; after that, at about half past seven in the evening, they would go down to the stream and take up their positions: Eliseo, armed with one of the crossbows, would lie down on the stone slab behind the sediment wall; next to him, also lying down, in his role as assistant, would be Celso holding the spare bolt; outside the streambed, slightly further back, Caloco would be leaning against a tree ready with his crossbow and bolt.

The third time they met at the cabin, on October 4, they were able to communicate with Donato thanks to the portable AN/PRC-77 radio that Celso had brought down from the Communications Unit in order, he said "to faithfully broadcast the events of the day". However, Eliseo and Caloco asked him not to do this again. It was too big a risk. For mere privates like them, removing that kind of radio from the barracks was a far graver misdemeanour than entering the woods around El Pardo.

Celso did not bring the radio on their next foray, on October 8, but he continued playing the part of radio telegraphist as they lay in the streambed.

"A bird has just landed on a rock about five metres away, and we'd better be careful now because he's keeping a very close eye on us."

"Excrement has been spotted on the streambed. Eliseo is sure it comes from a wild boar, but Caloco seems less certain. We await further information before we can confirm its provenance."

"The wind is stirring the leaves of the bushes opposite us, but not the leaves of the trees."

"Stand by. Eliseo is asking me to be quiet. He's getting nervous, which is only to be expected. He's really enjoying waiting for the wild boar, while I, even though I'm a Celt, am bored stiff. Over and out."

Eliseo needed silence. If there was silence, he could be fully aware of the place and feel the presence of all the trees in El

Pardo, of all the fallow deer, the foxes and the wild cats, of the rabbits, hares and boar inhabiting the woods. He remained like that for twenty or thirty or forty minutes, then suddenly, as if all those beings had become concentrated into one, he sensed a huge boar hidden close by, behind a thicket on the bank, watching him with its little eyes. Then, just as happened at night in bed, the boar began running towards him, getting near enough for him to see its tusks. He saw this whole sequence as if it were really happening. When the creature was almost on top of him, a shudder ran through him, but he managed to get a grip on himself in time and withdraw his finger from the trigger before he could fire the bolt into thin air.

They did not usually go hunting on two consecutive days, but on the following evening, Friday, October 9, Eliseo decided it would be a good idea, and so they set off once again. The sky was overcast, covered in grey clouds from Madrid to the Guadarrama mountains. Besides, there had been other hunting parties during the week. Minor ones – particularly when compared with the party that had apparently been organised for General Franco and Prince Juan Carlos, and which, according to the gamekeepers and dog handlers who had lunched that day in the barracks, had involved more than two hundred dogs – but still noisy enough to scare the boar and drive them into other parts of the wood, possibly to the dried-up streambed.

At seven o'clock in the evening, when they reached the cabin, they saw that the conditions really were excellent. A hundred or so metres away, the woods were growing dark, and beyond that, the trunks and the leaves of the trees appeared black; inside the cabin, the crossbows were mere shadows and the bolts virtually invisible. An occasional bird approached the nearby spring, but otherwise, nothing moved.

"The perfect conditions for wild boar," said Eliseo. The three of them were there – Eliseo, Celso and Caloco – sitting on the ground outside the cabin, preparing to go down to the stream. "We must keep our eyes peeled."

He was trying to encourage his friends. After their four previous attempts, he could see that they were neither very hopeful nor very enthusiastic. Caloco did not want to stop earning the money Eliseo was paying him, but it was all too clear that he would rather have stayed in the Communications Unit enjoying a quiet supper with Donato. As for Celso, he was easily distracted, his mind clearly on other things and certainly not on the boar. At that precise moment, he was scattering biscuit crumbs near the spring so that the birds coming there for a drink would have something to eat.

Eliseo stood up and fetched the two crossbows from the cabin, then the three bolts. With a sigh, Caloco stood up too.

"Eliseo, you're just going to have to give up," he said. "There are no new tracks in the streambed. They've obviously gone somewhere else to scratch themselves."

A bird flew over to the spring and started eating the crumbs. It had blue wings and back, a yellow breast and a black stripe over its eyes, like a tiny mask. Celso began calling to it, throwing more crumbs to attract it. The bird picked them up, then immediately flew off.

"A blue tit," said Caloco. "He just wants to do his own thing."

Celso continued throwing down crumbs, even though the bird was no longer to be seen.

"If you give a dog a piece of bread, it will follow you everywhere, wagging its tail. Birds aren't so friendly. With the exception of Paca, of course."

"Celso, I'm now going to tell you the truth about Paca," said Caloco.

"What do you know about Paca?" asked Eliseo.

"That she was completely mad, like the three of us." He held up his three middle fingers. "Yes, like us. Before, I thought it was just Celso and me who were mad, but after this business with the boar, I've realised that you're mad too, Eliseo: the maddest of us all."

"What did you mean when you said 'the truth about Paca'?"

Eliseo asked. He was starting to feel impatient. The light was fading fast. They had to go down to the stream before night fell.

"I asked the army doctor, that's how I know," Caloco said. "A new-born bird will follow the first moving object it sees, assuming that the object is its mother. If it sees a bicycle, then it follows the bicycle, if it's a cow, the same thing, if it's Eliseo, then it follows Eliseo. There have been studies done."

They all laughed.

"I was afraid you'd be disappointed, but obviously not," said Caloco. "Just as well."

They headed off to the streambed. On the way, Caloco told them something else the doctor had happened to mention, and which was of great importance. It wasn't official yet, but it seemed that they were going to be given their discharge papers on December 6. Only two more months and they could wave goodbye to their military service.

They were going down a slope at that point, making their way through the undergrowth. Eliseo signalled to them to speak more softly.

"So, Eliseo, what are *you* going to do when you leave the army," Caloco asked, giving him a hard shove.

Eliseo had to take two long strides to recover his balance.

"I see you've been talking to Donato."

"Well, Donato's not an unsociable shepherd like you. He actually talks to his friends."

Caloco tried to give him another shove, but Eliseo moved out of the way in time.

"He told me too, Eliseo," said Celso. "You're going to abandon your sheep and go and work in the bakery in his village. I'll visit you at Christmas and decorate a pine tree with lights from top to bottom. We electricians like little jobs like that."

"I'll have a word with my cows," said Caloco. "And if they give me leave, I'll visit you too."

Eliseo and Caloco examined some fresh droppings on the streambed but could not be sure whether they came from a fallow deer or a boar. Any doubts were dispelled, though, when they looked at the posts supporting the wall. As well as scuff marks made by scratching, there were marks made by tusks too. Just as they were about to take up their positions, they heard Celso cursing and swearing.

"God, I'm stupid! I was the one who sharpened them, and now I've gone and pricked myself."

He was sitting on the sediment wall, sucking his thumb. He had pricked himself on the point of the bolt as he was loading the crossbow and was now bleeding.

"It's nothing," he said.

Caloco took his hand.

"You're right, it's nothing. Keep sucking."

He then picked up one of the crossbows and went and stood next to a tree. Eliseo lay down flat on the stone slab.

"Don't stay here, Celso. Go and join Caloco up there," he said.

Celso was still sitting on the sediment wall, sucking his thumb.

A noise came from the left, about twenty metres further along the bank. Caloco heard it first, then Eliseo.

"Celso, get back. Lie down!" yelled Caloco.

Eliseo repeated the order with a wave of his hand. Celso stepped back but did not lie down.

The three of them fell silent. Opposite them were a few blurred trees whose actual size was hard to make out in the evening gloom, and beyond the trees was a motley collection of bushes, some with what looked like white flowers; to left and right, the wood was as dark as a cave; above them, the sky was a slate-grey roof. Another sound, a fluttering noise, as if, behind the trees, a bird had taken flight. The third noise was clearer: the crunch and crackle of branches very close to where they were, about fifteen metres away. Something was moving in the streambed, a shadow.

"Over there!" shouted Caloco, raising his crossbow.

"Don't shoot, Caloco!" ordered Eliseo.

A rabbit was limping clumsily along, its eyes puffy with myx-omatosis.

"Over there!" Caloco shouted again, like an echo.

He lowered his crossbow to the ground. Eliseo burst out laughing. Celso crawled forward as if to get closer to the rabbit.

"Don't touch it, Celso. It's disgusting," Eliseo said.

Then the dog appeared. It was following the same path as the rabbit. One of those mastiffs used by the handlers, about fifty or sixty kilos in weight. A big head and fangs like a bulldog's.

"It must have got lost during yesterday's hunt," said Eliseo.

The dog was looking at them. It took a few cautious steps forward and stopped about ten metres away. It started to growl. Then it continued to advance, more and more slowly, as if wanting to avoid making any noise.

"Here, boy," said Celso, clicking his fingers.

The dog growled again, more loudly this time.

"I'm going to shoot!" yelled Eliseo.

"Yes, shoot!" said Caloco.

"No!"

Celso had stood up now and taken a step towards the dog.

"Here, boy. We're your friends."

The dog leapt up at him and knocked him down. Celso raised his legs in an attempt to defend himself and gave an agonising scream. Eliseo fired at the dog, piercing its throat. A muffled yelp and the animal dropped to the ground.

Caloco slithered down into the streambed and began making a tourniquet around Celso's thigh with his belt. The blood would not stop. Caloco started to cry. Eliseo had recovered the crossbow bolt and was plunging it again and again into the dog. He was crying too.

"It's OK, don't worry. I'm a Celt. I'll be fine," said Celso. He raised his hand to his face. It was covered in blood. "Where are my glasses? I've lost them."

His voice was growing fainter.

"I'm thirsty," he said.

"I'll get some water," said Caloco, tears streaming down his face.

Eliseo was crouched beside Celso.

"Don't worry. We'll take you straight to the infirmary."

Caloco went back up the slope to look for some branches to make an improvised stretcher, but it was too dark to see. He returned to the streambed and, in his confusion, stumbled over something and fell flat on his face. He stood up and kicked the obstacle. It was the sick rabbit. He started to scream.

"Caloco, come here," Eliseo said. "Celso's dead."

Antoine

1985–1986

1

They sat on a pair of leather armchairs two metres or so apart. A rug and a lamp occupied the space between them.

"So how are things, Antoine?" the woman asked.

He said he was fine, then lowered his head. The floor lamp projected a circle of light onto the rug, lending its sandy tones a reddish tinge and partially illuminating the various items in the room: the diplomas on the walls, the graduation photograph and other objects. Among these other objects, on the shelf lined with the works of Sigmund Freud, stood a digital clock with green numbers. The time just then was three minutes past five: 17.03.

Antoine turned to look across at the large bay window; in what little light the blinds let in, the desk beneath them appeared to be made of black wood. The day, October 18, 1985, was rainy.

He muttered something about how hard he found it to begin talking. Then he settled back in the armchair like someone getting ready to start a car. He smiled at the woman.

"Today, I took a wrong turn after coming off the motorway and had a hard time working out where I was. I asked at all the red lights I came to, but it was no use, no-one was any help. As soon as I rolled down the window, they'd just walk off. Not that I'm surprised, mind, Bayonne people have always been unfriendly, and it seems nothing's changed on that front. In the end, I found myself outside the station. From there it was easy: Place de la République, Pont Saint-Esprit, Pont Mayou, Place du Théâtre, and then from Avenue Maréchal Leclerc to the botanical gardens. I parked at the Paulmy car park and walked the rest of the way. I had a cup of tea at the bistro on the corner, and now here I am, in your consulting room."

He fell silent. He had enough air in his lungs to go on, or even to launch into a long monologue, but he stopped himself.

"I used to come here with my mother as a child," he said. "We'd take the train from Dax. I remember the area around the station well. But the city's changed a lot. The traffic lights aren't where they used to be. And the trains don't whistle any more. The other day I really missed that sound, and I did today as well."

The rain muffled the noises of the city outside, and the only sound to be heard in the consulting room was that of the woman very slowly turning the pages of her notebook, back and forth.

"You were talking to me about time last week, Antoine. Could we pick up where we left off? You also mentioned a snakeskin."

He nodded but said nothing.

"If you'd rather not talk about that, feel free to choose another topic."

He made himself more comfortable in the armchair and observed the woman. Nadia. Her hair was completely white, even though she couldn't be more than forty. It might be interesting, he thought, to ask about her name, and why she was called Nadia when she might just as well have been called Nadine, the French way. While thinking this, he noticed something he had missed in the previous session: she had Slavic features, and bore a certain resemblance to Raisa Gorbacheva, the wife of Mikhail Gorbachev, the Russian communist leader. He decided, though, that such comments would be inappropriate, and said nothing until he saw the digital clock change. According to the green numbers it was now seven minutes past five: 17.07.

He repeated to himself the words the woman had used: snake, skin, time. With a heavy sigh, he went on: "It was just a chance association of ideas. I was looking at the digital clock, at those green numbers, and it occurred to me to ask why the sessions are half an hour and not forty-five minutes or an hour, and whether, if they were longer, the price would go up proportionately, that is, 300 francs for a forty-five-minute session and 400 for an hour. Then, out of the blue, I remembered a snakeskin I once saw about a kilometre down from the mine in Ugarte, next to a stream, on a large flat rock. I carried on thinking about it when I was driving home on the A63. Shall I go on?"

"Yes, go ahead. Tell me about this snakeskin."

Nadia really did look rather like Raisa Gorbacheva. When she smiled, she revealed her large front teeth, and the happiness that lit up her face seemed genuine.

He waited a few seconds before going on:

"It was the beginning of autumn," he said in a low voice, eyes half-closed. "The flat rock in the stream was covered in moss and lichen, as well as some dead leaves from the trees in the forest. In the middle there was a bare spot, a circle about sixty centimetres in diameter, the same reddish colour you get on stones and rocks around Ugarte from the iron in the water. Anyway, the snakeskin, which was off-white and tightly coiled – like a rolled-up tape measure – was right there as if sitting on an earthenware plate."

He paused. He was speaking to the woman in French, and that mention of dead leaves had reminded him of the end of a Paul Verlaine poem, *"je m'en vais au vent mauvais qui m'emporte deçà, delà, pareil à la feuille morte"*, "And I go my way on the ill wind that carries me hither and yon like a dead leaf", and he saw himself in the assembly hall at his school in Dax, sixteen or seventeen years old, reciting the poem. He kept the memory to himself, though, and said nothing more.

The digital clock showed that another three minutes had elapsed. It was ten past five: 17.10.

"The snakeskin and time," the woman said to prompt him.

He took himself back to the stream in Ugarte again, beside the flat rock with the whitish snakeskin that looked like a rolled-up tape measure. He decided to explain:

"When I remembered that scene, an unpleasant idea came into my head. I thought that I myself was like that snakeskin, a residue, a substance separate from the flow of society, with not a friend in the world – neither at the mine, nor among the people in Ugarte, or in Dax, or in Paris. I *had* a friend in Dax: Pierre,

185

Pierre Irissou, a childhood friend, but he's retreated to a tiny village in Les Landes now. I had some friends in Paris too, well, not friends exactly, but fellow students from the school where I studied Chemical Engineering, and, for a time, I always used to go and spend weekends with them whenever I had a work meeting there. But I found it hard being away from Louise and Troy and ended up cutting my stays short. I'd get the TGV in the morning, go to the managerial meeting in the afternoon, and head back on the first train next morning."

This was not strictly true. Pierre Irissou did live in a village in Les Landes but they were still in touch and he often went to stay with him in his house. His trips to Paris were not as brief as all that either, because on the way back home, he always stopped off in Biarritz to visit La Petite Pagode, a high-class bordello on the outskirts of the city. But he preferred not to tell her about that.

"Louise and Troy. My two dogs," he added in a very low voice, and a tear rolled down his right cheek.

The woman shifted in her chair. She wrote something down in her notebook with her Montblanc pen.

"You talked to me about your dogs in our last session," she said. "Please, go on telling me about time and the snakeskin."

"There really isn't much to tell. It was so lovely sitting there next to that flat rock beside the stream. It's a very beautiful place. The current is faster there, then it flows on down through the forest, between ferns and beech trees, till it reaches a point where the water joins the canal. The water's very clear, although a chemical analysis would show you that it actually contains more iron, magnesium and calcium than the water in Bayonne. There's a bakery at the end of the canal, quite a good one. When the company sent me to head up the prospecting in Ugarte, I'd stop by there after work to buy bread. Lately, though, my maid's been doing that for me."

The woman underlined something in her notebook but made no comment. The green numbers on the digital display now showed that it was fourteen minutes past five: 17.14.

"The pastries in that bakery are also very good. As good as you'd get in any patisserie in Bayonne. I felt very lucky to have found them. I particularly like the ones they do with the little pieces of orange peel in them."

These were round pastries, orange in colour, and when he remembered them he was transported back to the flat rock with its covering of moss, lichen and dead leaves, and the bare patch in the middle. He considered going into more detail about the snakeskin. When he picked it up and uncoiled it, he found it had grey spots and some yellow stripes, the only indications of the reptile's former life. In the end, though, he came out with something entirely unconnected:

"The head of John the Baptist would have fitted perfectly on that bare patch on the rock."

He had in mind a small portrait in various shades of ochre of a young woman standing beside a stone wall and carrying a dish with the head of a bearded man on it.

"That reminds me of the story of Salome," said the woman. Again she wrote something down in her notebook.

He did not want to talk about Salome and so remained silent. He sat looking down at the rug. It, too, was a reddish colour.

"How do you get on with your domestic staff?" asked the woman. She gave him a sidelong glance and again she reminded him of Raisa Gorbacheva.

"When I moved to Ugarte, I employed a married couple from Andalusia to look after things. But only the wife works for me now. I had a problem with the husband, to do with the dogs. Louise and Troy were still puppies, and that man would give them any old thing to eat, leftovers and whatever, but only once a day, all in one go. That's very dangerous. A Dobermann puppy needs to be fed three times a day, 200 grams of high-quality dry food soaked in milk, with the bowl placed at shoulder height. I told him two or three times that he was neglecting the puppies, but it was no good. One afternoon, I came back from the mine earlier than usual and found Louise and Troy practically starving. They hadn't had a thing to eat since the food I'd given them when I left in the morning. I told him that, from then on, I wasn't going to pay him a centime to look after the puppies, I'd get Julián's twins to take care of them instead. Julián is the company administrator, and he'd mentioned that his twins would be willing to take on the job for a little bit of money. We soon came to an agreement. From then on, the two boys started taking care of Louise and Troy, including when I went to Paris on business meetings."

"And the husband just accepted it when you hired the boys to replace him?"

"No, he got very angry and, soon afterwards, returned to southern Spain. Whereas his wife, Rosalía, opted to stay on and work for me. And I did pretty well out of the bargain: Rosalía's very clean and tidy, as well as being an excellent cook. She lives fifty metres from my house, at the entrance to the village. Her only shortcoming is that she hasn't wanted to have anything to do with Louise and Troy since they stopped being puppies. She says they frighten her."

He took a deep breath and again bowed his head.

"Now I'd like to talk about what's really on my mind."

The woman gave him a look as if to say, of course. *Ça va de soi.* Why else would he come to see her if not to talk about the things that were really affecting him?

"Louise is dead, that's what matters. And Troy, well, he's all over the place. He can't get over not having her around. Like I said last time, it's driving me crazy. The situation is truly, truly heart-breaking."

Tears filled his eyes. He took a white handkerchief out of his jacket pocket and wiped them away.

Another image from the stream came back to him. As soon as autumn arrived, the forest floor around the stream would be covered in fallen leaves. They would lie twenty or thirty centimetres deep in places.

"Let me explain what happened to Louise. It was less than a month ago, on September 22, at six thirty in the evening. As I

188

often do on a Sunday, I went for a walk around the laboratory at the mine and then on into the forest, taking Louise and Troy with me. I was feeling good; all the samples we'd analysed that week had contained particles of silver sulphide, which is one of the minerals our company's most interested in."

He could see Louise in his mind's eye, an eight-year-old Dobermann, her ears, her eyes, her head. Another tear rolled down his cheek. He wiped it away with his handkerchief.

For a while, he said nothing, not until the numbers on the digital clock changed to twenty-four minutes past five: 17.24. Then he went on almost in a whisper:

"We encountered two of the bakery staff and one of them, a man named Eliseo, shot her in the head with his shotgun. Just one shot, and Louise lay dead among the fallen leaves. And he would have killed Troy too if I hadn't stood between them. He's a very dangerous man."

He took another deep breath, and decided to explain in more detail:

"We were walking along quite happily, the three of us, as usual. Louise on my left, a metre and a half from me, and Troy on my right, also a metre and a half away. Two well-trained dogs. If I gave the command for them to stop, they'd stop immediately. If I gave the command for them to start walking, the same. Most important of all, they would only ever attack someone if they saw I was in danger, and, unfortunately, that's precisely what happened that day. They thought I was in danger. They misinterpreted the information provided by their senses: the footsteps in the fallen leaves, the sight of two men walking along the riverbank with their two setters. Louise's hearing was better than Troy's, and she was instantly on the alert. I asked her what the matter was. I couldn't see anything, because the two men were still a hundred metres away, in among the beech trees, both dressed in muted colours, and that Eliseo guy was in camouflage gear. I didn't hear anything, but Louise and Troy did, and they went on ahead. Then suddenly I saw Louise take off at a run, and immediately

189

after that, I saw the two men with their setters. I heard their boots stomping through the leaves. When the setters saw Louise coming, they turned and ran. But Eliseo didn't. He had a shotgun, and it all happened really quickly. Louise was heading straight for him, and he dropped down on one knee. I heard a shot. Louise fell to the ground. I reacted immediately and told Troy to stay, which he did. Even then that Eliseo guy didn't lower his shotgun until I had Troy on the lead."

He let out a sob and covered his face with both hands.

"We'll carry on next week, Antoine," said the woman.

The green numbers on the digital display showed that it was now twenty-nine minutes past five: 17.29.

2

As soon as Antoine sat down in the leather chair, he gave the woman across from him a broad smile and exclaimed, "Good afternoon, Nadia!" An opening that, had it come immediately after the previous session's teary goodbye, would have indicated a very strange mood swing; but a week had elapsed since then. It was October 25, 1985, the last Friday of the month. A bright day in Bayonne, with a scattering of clouds and pleasant autumnal sunshine.

"It was like I was sleepwalking when I drove into the city today, and it wasn't until the car behind me beeped its horn that I pulled myself together. It turned out I was sitting outside the entrance to the car park as if it was a red light, and they couldn't get past. The whole journey, in fact, it was almost as if I was sleepwalking. Don't ask me what the traffic was like on the A63, because I wouldn't know."

The woman listened gravely, not returning his smile. She seemed a kindly person, with her white hair and her somewhat prominent front teeth; but her eyes, more almond-shaped, more feline than those of Raisa Gorbacheva, the skin around them unlined, put paid to that initial impression.

The light coming in through the window, brighter than the previous week, transformed the consulting room. The roller blinds were a matte alabaster white; the floor lamp an amber colour; the rug tinged with pink. The photos on the walls, the diplomas, the graduation picture, along with the other objects were all clearly delineated. On the shelf lined with the works of Sigmund Freud, the green numbers on the digital clock showed two minutes past five: 17.02.

Antoine had a briefcase on his lap and, clicking it open, he took out a large photograph, which he passed to the woman.

"That's Louise. I took it on the day she turned two months: May 23, 1977."

The woman held the photograph under the lamplight. It showed a Dobermann puppy lolling on a garden lawn. Its fur was smooth and mostly black, with light brown patches on its muzzle, chest and legs. Its head and paws were large, slightly out of proportion. It had a hazy, sleepy look in its eyes, and its ears were down.

He handed the woman another picture.

"And this is Troy. He's a bit grumpier than Louise, and a bit less intelligent too. But a very loyal dog. Louise was loyal too, of course, but the way a captain is loyal to his general. Troy is more of a foot soldier."

The second puppy was almost identical to the first, only with a shorter snout.

"Louise and Troy were brother and sister, both from the same litter."

He took another photograph out of the briefcase.

"Here's one of them together."

In the picture, the two puppies were playing at trying to knock each other over, one resting its front paws on its rival's back. Next to them were two cherry trees in blossom, and in the background the white exterior of a house lit by the sun.

"Troy's still depressed. He's having trouble getting over Louise's death. I mean, it happened right in front of him."

He could see the snakeskin on the flat rock, then the water from the stream forming miniature waterfalls as it flowed through the forest, shouldering its way through the fallen leaves. As happened the previous week, he immediately connected the image of the fallen leaves with the Verlaine poem – "*je m'en vais au vent mauvais qui m'emporte deçà, delà, pareil à la feuille morte*" – but this time it was followed by the memory of a remark made by Goethe, another of his favourite writers. On coming back from a walk in the forest, Goethe had said to his friend Eckermann: "The peace and quiet was such that it seemed even Pan himself was sleeping". An impression Antoine had often shared while walking in the Ugarte forest with Louise and Troy. Then the afternoon of September 22 arrived, and they had encountered the monster. It was not sleeping. And its name was Eliseo, not Pan. He saw him again in his camouflage gear, kneeling on the ground, squeezing the trigger.

Most of the leaves covering the forest floor were reddish in colour, as though they, too, were impregnated with iron carbonate. But Louise's blood was far redder, and his eye was immediately drawn to where the shot had left it spattered across the leaves and in the stream. The wound, made by a shotgun slug, went from her shoulder to her neck, leaving the bone exposed.

He started waving his hands above his head, as though his thoughts were flies and he wanted to shoo them away. He took a deep breath, filling his lungs, and exhaled through pursed lips. His face gradually began to relax. He put the photographs back in the briefcase and smiled.

"Pleasant thoughts?" asked the woman. She had the notebook open on her lap, the Montblanc pen in her hand.

"Louise and Troy were so adorable as puppies; I was crazy about them. I'd come back from the mine at the end of the day and find them waiting for me at the garden gate. They'd be so excited to see me, they'd actually pee themselves."

A look of happiness crossed his face and he closed his eyes before going on, as if, that way, he could focus more clearly on his memories.

"Nobody has ever loved me the way Louise and Troy loved me, and I haven't loved anybody as I love them. People think that love is something between a man and a woman, or between two men, or between two women, or between parents and their children – that is, an exclusively human feeling; but, what can I say, people use their brains less than parrots do. That's why they think the way they do. They confuse the feeling and the thing it's wrapped up in, the snake and the skin. Look at me. I'm forty years old and, forgive me if I repeat myself, but the being I've loved the most, and who loved me the most, was Louise. And after her, Troy. Louise did not have a human face, she walked on four legs, but she could talk. Better than many parrots can. I could hear her voice with absolute clarity. Just as I do Troy's."

The woman quickly made a note, as if suddenly alert. She never lost her resemblance to Raisa Gorbacheva, but now it was her eyes that dominated her face. She was looking at him sternly:

"When did you start hearing your dogs' voices? Do you remember?"

"Three and a half years ago. April 10, 1982."

"You've got a good memory." She checked something in her notebook. "Last Friday you told me that Louise's death took place on September 22. Now, you tell me you first heard the voices on April 10, 1982. I'm quite struck by how exactly you remember the date of something that happened so long ago."

"That was when I fell ill. How could I forget that?"

"Of course, Antoine. Tell me about that day."

"It got off to a bad start. The staff at the mine had been on strike for a week, and in the morning I had some heated arguments with the union reps. Then, during a midday meeting, the engineers told me they were worried. Some obscure environmentalist group had been distributing threatening pamphlets in Ugarte. I didn't read what they said until I got home that evening. It was a most unpleasant message. Threats against the company and those of us who worked for it. It talked about the prospecting going on in the Ugarte hills and the environmental disaster that would ensue if mining were to go ahead. The stream and the air would be polluted, the paths damaged, that sort of thing. Parrot nonsense. Except that these parrots were very aggressive. When they referred to me, they didn't say 'the engineer' or the 'company rep', it was 'The Frog', or 'The Cripple'. There came a point when I started cursing whoever had written this clandestine rag, because, unlike that monster Eliseo, my heart isn't made of ice.

And then Louise came over to me, followed by Troy. I said to them, 'Can you hear? The wind is spreading these insults being hurled at me. They don't call me "Antoine", they call me "The Frog", "The Cripple".' Louise and Troy came a few steps closer. 'Does it matter to the two of you that I'm French, or that one of my legs is shorter than the other?' And I heard Louise say, 'No, Antoine. We love you. Troy and I would give our lives for you. Tell us who's been insulting you and we'll tear out their throats.' I felt moved by her words, they gave me a real boost. I stood up and made a promise to them: 'They want me to abandon my post, they want me to leave this place. But I won't. He who leaves Rome loses Rome!'"

The woman went on writing after he had finished speaking, making thick strokes with the nib of her Montblanc pen. When she finally stopped writing, she looked at him hard.

"In our first session I asked what it was that had brought you here, as I'm sure you remember. You told me you'd been hearing voices, and that this was a cause of great distress. And yet, hearing you now declaring that he who leaves Rome loses Rome, I have the sense that you don't in fact find that phenomenon particularly worrying."

He tried to think quickly. He began to say something, stopped, then started again:

"Well, I mean, of course, of course it worries me. More than that, I find it deeply distressing. Especially as regards Troy. As I've said, he's been left traumatised by what happened to Louise. He's getting worse and worse, wanting revenge. Plus, unlike Louise, he talks to me at all hours, even during the night. He's going to drive me crazy. There's no let-up with him, not even when I'm asleep. That's why I came to you."

He took a deep breath, his eyes on the digital clock. The green numbers showed that it was now twenty-two minutes past five: 17.22.

In a faint voice, as though only a trickle of air was making its way from his lungs to his throat, he described a recent dream. He saw Louise in the distance, in the forest, and he whistled for her to come, which was most unusual because he never used to call her like that, but always called her by name, just as he did with people, just as he called his housekeeper "Rosalía", the company administrator "Julián", and the twins "Luís" and "Martín". He whistled again, but Louise still didn't come; instead, she plunged deeper into the forest, going further and further away from him. That was how things were. Soon, Louise would vanish from his dreams too.

His eyes were moist with tears.

"That dream was a premonition. It won't be long before Louise disappears completely from my life. She'll be just another image in a photograph."

He said nothing more for a moment. It was 17.25.

"Whereas Troy is becoming a regular feature in my dreams. The last time was the day before yesterday. I was taking his dinner out to the kennel, and a question came to me: why just the one bowl, instead of two? Because Louise is dead, I said to myself. Then I realised that the bowl was heavier than it should have been. When I looked down I found not a stew of vegetables, rice and meat, but a head, the head of Eliseo, bearded, his hair all tangled, like John the Baptist's."

"Which takes us back to the story of Salome again," said the woman.

He chose not to respond to this, and went on with the dream instead:

"I had stopped to look up at the moon, and then I heard a noise, the sound of bones crunching. Troy was taking bites out of the head in the bowl. I told him not to, but, for the first time ever, he refused to obey. I repeated my command, but he said defiantly: 'Are you telling me I ought to forgive Louise's killer?' I woke with a start. Troy was by my bed. He said to me, very quietly, as if he was worried the police would hear him: 'You're dreaming, more's the pity. Eliseo's head is still on his shoulders. But it'd be much better if it wasn't. Don't be such a coward,

Antoine.' So, as you can see, it sometimes feels like he's trying to take charge of me."

He sprang up from the armchair and hobbled over to the window, but when he tripped on the rug, he had to brace himself on the desk to keep from falling. He sighed and stood looking at the blinds.

"Sit down, please," said the woman.

The green numbers on the digital clock read twenty-nine minutes past five: 17.29.

"Time's up," he said.

"All right, we'll return to this next week," said the woman. "I'm going to ask you to do something for our next session. I'd like you to tell me about your parents, Antoine. You haven't talked about them yet."

For a moment, the woman's voice took on hard edge, and she lost Raisa Gorbacheva's affable look, but when she showed him to the door, her smile reappeared.

3

It was a rainy day, the blinds diffused what little light entered from outside. In spite of this, the objects on the walls – the graduation photograph, the other photographs and the diplomas – stood out more clearly than on previous occasions. The floor lamp had a new, brighter bulb in it. The circle it cast on the rug was almost white.

"Last week you asked me to tell you about my parents. That shouldn't be too difficult. I've been thinking about them every week recently, especially on Fridays."

He giggled. He had resolved to begin the session with a touch of humour.

"As you know, Nadia, I usually take the A63 to get here. Well, every time I go past Biarritz, I see those big hoardings with ads for the golf courses. My parents worked at one of them, Golf Le Phare, my father as an instructor and my mother doing administrative tasks."

The woman had the notebook and the Montblanc pen on her lap, her hands resting on top. The green numbers on the digital clock showed three minutes past five; 17.03.

"My father met a young woman in Le Phare, and the two of them ran off to Paris when I was five. Then my mother returned to Dax and took a job as general manager at a big hotel there, Hotel Le Splendid, I don't know if you know it. It's a very attractive art deco building, built at the beginning of the century, and it has a spa too. Pierre Irissou and I often used to play around the thermal pool there. That was where we became friends. His father was the hotel chef. We were both pretty lonely. He didn't have a mother, and I didn't have a father. We lived on site, in apartments on the top floor. Really nice apartments. With views over the river."

He was speaking in short bursts, as though his lungs were only supplying his throat with air in fits and starts.

"Tell me first about your mother, Antoine," said the woman. She now had the notebook in one hand and the Montblanc pen in the other.

"Are you a mother, Nadia?"

The woman's eyes glinted, like those of a cat watching in the darkness. She gave a slight nod.

"Then you'll understand what I'm about to tell you."

He shuffled forward in the leather chair, his gaze settling on the bright circle of light on the rug.

"I've never seen it myself, but from what I understand, the first thing a mother does when her newborn baby is handed to her is to check it has all its fingers and toes, that it doesn't have any blemishes . . . Which must have meant it was very tough for my mother. Poor Chantal!"

He gave a resigned sigh.

"She didn't notice anything at first; everything seemed normal, and she fell happily asleep. But then, a few hours later, the doctor gave her the news. Her baby's little body had a defect, the left leg was slightly shorter than the right. The boy would be lame. I'm sure Chantal didn't find it so easy getting back to sleep then – not at all."

Another Verlaine poem came to him: "*Un grand sommeil noir tombe sur ma vie: dormez, tout espoir, dormez, tout envie!*" "A heavy black sleep descends upon my life: Sleep, all hope, sleep, all desire!" It was another of the poems that he and Pierre Irissou used to recite when they were part of the Dax amateur dramatics society. He suppressed the memory.

"Poor Chantal!"

He gave an even bigger sigh and sat back in the armchair. He wondered if perhaps he was moving about too much.

"Chantal had a good head for figures, and I've always heard

it said that both at Le Phare and Le Splendid she was an impeccable manager. But she couldn't comprehend the number that is fundamental to our existence – the cipher, I mean. The key. In short, the fact that love must be something very deep-rooted. Dogs know this very well. As I told you last week, I once asked Louise and Troy if they minded one of my legs being shorter than the other, or that I was French, and they answered with a resounding 'No'. What we happen to look like means nothing. Why fixate on a layer of dead leaves when there's soil, minerals, even precious metals underneath?"

He began gesticulating, then took two deep breaths. He felt awkward, he was moving about too much. He had to get a grip.

"We were talking about your mother. You told me her love was nothing compared to the love of your dogs."

This was followed by the first smile Nadia had given him that afternoon. It was not like a happy Raisa Gorbacheva smile though; to him, there was something mocking about it, a touch of the Cheshire Cat. But surely not, otherwise Nadia was being most unprofessional. He wasn't paying her 200 francs a session to be made fun of.

He sat up straighter.

"When I was with my mother, I could never forget that I was lame. Going clothes shopping with her was torture. She'd be so . . . so overly friendly, so solicitous: 'His legs aren't exactly the same length, the left one's a little shorter and thinner, that's why he limps a bit, so you'll have bear that in mind.' It was even worse with the shoemaker. She'd spend a quarter of an hour examining the different kinds of soles for the left shoe. So it was a big relief when I went to Paris to study, but then, of course, my father was in Paris."

"Tell me about your father."

He felt tempted to go back to the image of the snakeskin as a metaphor for his father's behaviour, a man who had simply got on with his life, sloughing his son off, leaving him behind like some sort of detritus. But the change in attitude he thought he could sense in Nadia had dented his confidence, and he decided to add something more about his mother instead.

"There's one thing I'd like to be quite clear about. Though I suffered because of my mother, I never hated her. On the contrary. When the company sent me to Ugarte, she had just passed away, and I called my chalet Villa Chantal in memory of her. Rosalía really likes the name. It makes her feel important, working in a house called Villa Chantal."

The green numbers on the digital clock showed eighteen minutes past five: 17.18.

"As for my father, what more can I say? Perhaps my having excelled as a chemical engineer is down to him because he encouraged me to focus on my studies. But I don't know if that's worth going into, Nadia. It's a common enough story."

She said nothing. In a repeat of the position she had assumed at the beginning of the session, she put the notebook and the pen on her lap and placed both hands on top.

"It bores Troy if I start talking about all that. It not only bores him, it makes him angry. He says he didn't know his parents, but he couldn't care less."

Nadia's face remained impassive. Then came that Cheshire Cat grin again. He felt like shouting: "Don't you laugh at me, Nadia!" then storming out of the room. But no. He needed her. He couldn't give up on the sessions.

He took a deep breath and adopted a more relaxed posture. The dull, crepuscular light coming in through the blinds brought out the whiteness of the lamplight.

"My father was a handsome man. One of those golf players with a good tan, going around in short-sleeved Lacoste polo shirts. He had blue eyes too. Have you read any Agatha Christie novels? I have, lots of them, especially in my university days. Well, I've always imagined my father in the refined settings of those novels, surrounded by well-to-do ladies and holding forth on the secrets of golf. It seems he was rather successful when it came to women."

201

"You said before that your having excelled as a chemical engineer was due to your father."

"That's right, Nadia."

He was reminded of a joke made by one of his university professors who was a fan of murder mysteries. He proposed that the students do lab analyses of the poisons Agatha Christie talked about in her novels. "Get a good handle on the subject," he had said, "because you never know when you might find your enemy's poisoned champagne glass before you." But this joke, very popular among the Chemical Engineering students, might well fall flat here in the consulting room, and he decided to keep it to himself. It was not a good idea to try out any previously unrehearsed lines on Nadia.

"There's no mystery about that. I aspired to outdo my father socially, to be someone. That's why I worked so hard at my studies."

The woman underlined something in her notebook.

"You said in the last session that you first heard the dogs' voices three and a half years ago, at the same time as you were having problems with the engineers and the miners. I've got a note of the date: April 10, 1982. Could we talk about what was going on then?"

"Those were two separate problems. It was one thing with the engineers, and something completely different with the miners."

"If it's okay with you, we'll start there next time."

The green numbers on the digital clock read twenty-eight minutes to six: 17.32.

4

He would set off from Ugarte three and a half hours before the start of the session in Bayonne. He could have made it in half that time, but the extra leeway, as he drove at a leisurely pace along the A63 or had a cup of tea at the bistro near the Paulmy car park, meant he could run through the things it would and would not be prudent to share with Nadia.

He did not find this a taxing exercise. As he had in his days as part of the Dax amateur dramatics society, he prepared the script over the course of the week, organising it scene by scene. Some fragments he merely skim-learned, whereas the key phrases he memorised word for word. Before he left Ugarte, he placed the script next to him on the passenger seat, where he could reach it.

His journey on November 8, 1985 began pleasantly enough: outside the car it was icy cold, with occasional sleet showers; inside, the temperature was 21°C. The contrast generated a sense of wellbeing in him, combined with the joy of taking a new car out for the first time – a Volvo 760, which, according to the adverts, had the best air conditioning in the world. The car salesman had laid great emphasis on this while he was trying it out: "How can it not be the best in the world! Bear in mind it was invented by the Swedes. For them, having efficient heating is a matter of life and death." Your usual parrot chatter. Cliché upon cliché.

It was a two-lane road between Ugarte and the border, full of bends and changes in gradient, and the bad weather meant that he had to focus entirely on driving. Then, once he was through the toll barrier at Biriatou, he let the car cruise along and turned his mind to the script. He would take as his starting point the day he first began hearing Louise's and Troy's voices, April 10, 1982, at the time of the Ugarte mining strikes. He had written down that passage, the cornerstone of the story he was constructing in that Bayonne consulting room, and learned it by heart.

"Does it matter to the two of you that I'm French, or that one of my legs is shorter than the other?" And I heard Louise say, "No, Antoine. We truly love you. Troy and I would give our lives for you. Tell us who's been insulting you and we'll tear out their throats."

It was difficult to say whether or not Nadia had been taken in by this. His impression was that she had, but he would not be the first patient to come to her with a confession of this kind, and he would have to embellish it in such a way as to make it believable, explain the context and, above all, the tensions at play in his work at the mine, the principal cause of his alleged madness. What were the voices in his head if not a symptom of schizophrenia, his psyche reacting abnormally?

Suddenly, I saw that my life was in danger. His delivery here had to be firm and somewhat dramatic because it lay at the very core of his story. This was followed by five or so seconds of silence, and the coda: *The terrorists over the border decided to go after the engineer, using environmental concerns as an excuse. They were trying to stop a nuclear power station being built.*

He would then describe the general atmosphere in the Basque Country in the early eighties but would keep that part brief. The topic had been covered on television and in the press – *Le Monde, Libération, Sud Ouest* – meaning that people in France knew about it. The case of José María Ryan in particular would have stayed in the minds of many, given the sadistic cruelty of the terrorists.

I'm sure you'll remember it, Nadia. The murder took place in February, 1981. The terrorists sent a photograph of the engineer to the press, along with an ultimatum: if the work at the nuclear power station wasn't halted within a week, they were going to kill him, and the blame would lie solely with the electricity company. And they did kill him, of course, despite his wife going on television with her five young children and begging for mercy. The photo was in all the papers: a body abandoned in the forest.

204

Running through what he was going to say to Nadia made him nervous, and he turned on the radio in the hope of finding some music. He was in luck. The presenter on Radio Classique was introducing "Passepied", a piece by Claude Debussy, Antoine's favourite composer. He turned the volume up. The rain was battering the windscreen, almost drowning out the piano. He looked at the clock on the dashboard. It was large and round, with a black face. The numbers were white and the hands were orange. It was a quarter past two.

I'll tell you the truth, Nadia. I find the engineer's murder more upsetting now than I did at the time. Really distressing. Don't forget: I saw Louise's body in the forest, right before my eyes, after Eliseo's slug tore through her. I told you about that the other day.

He managed to bring a tear to his left eye. A skill he had acquired in his time as an amateur actor, and which he had not lost. He was the best in the group at summoning up tears. Unlike Pierre Irissou, who had never learned how to cry onstage. Or who had never wanted to learn. Pierre did not like fake tears; he said that, for him, tears were something sacred. The director couldn't understand it: "Pierre," he would say, "you have too many scruples to be a good actor. You know how to move around on stage, but that isn't enough." Antoine, on the other hand, apart from being able to memorise the words, had the ability to turn on the tears whenever he felt like it; but he was not so good at controlling his facial expressions. Or at moving around the stage, unless, of course, he was asked to play a cripple.

Don't forget: I saw Louise's body in the forest, right before my eyes, after Eliseo's slug tore through her.

He shook his head. No, he wouldn't use that line in Nadia's consulting room. Nor would he start shedding tears. Such emotional outbursts might fool a psychiatrist once or even twice, but there was no sense in going overboard. At the end of the day, the story he had in mind was true, something that had really happened, and did not require any dressing up. He would keep to a straightforward account of the events that had followed Ryan's murder.

The presenter introduced another Debussy piece, "Rêverie". Antoine looked at the clock. The orange hands had moved round to twenty-five past two.

I didn't think, Nadia, that the case of that engineer, Ryan, had any bearing on me. At least, not to begin with. However, I went to Paris for the company's AGM not long after it happened, in early March to be exact, and was surprised by their response. As soon as we sat down in the meeting room, the other directors turned to look at me. "What are you going to do, Antoine? The terrorists must surely be emboldened after the publicity they got with the nuclear power station. They're probably considering sabotaging the mine in Ugarte. And since you're the chief engineer . . . Do you want us to find you an apartment in the city? You wouldn't be so exposed there. Plus, we could get you a bodyguard."

My colleagues' proposal caught me unawares. As I said, Nadia, I wasn't feeling particularly worried, I didn't put the Ugarte mine in the same category as a nuclear power station. Louise and Troy came into my thoughts then. If I went to the city, they'd be all alone in Villa Chantal. Rosalía wouldn't want to look after them – as you know, she was frightened of them. Nor could I leave them with the twins – Luis and Martín were at university by then and their free time was limited. On the other hand, I didn't want to take them to the city. It's possible for a dog who was born in the city to live there, but otherwise, it's very tricky. I refused to take my colleagues' advice. I wasn't going to budge from Ugarte. "He who leaves Rome loses Rome," I said to them. "And I don't need a bodyguard either. I've already got two of my own: Louise and Troy. They've been with me since forever and would give their lives for me. Don't you worry; they're Dobermanns, and I've got them well trained. If I set them on a terrorist, he'd be a dead man."

He was so focussed on his script that he failed to notice that he was at the toll booth at La Négresse, pulled up right by the coin basket. The cars behind him were beeping. He muttered a few insults. Parrots left a lot to be desired, but – you had to give it to them – they were a dab hand when it came to pissing off their fellow man.

He carried on along the A63, and it took three or four kilometres before he was able to pick up his train of thought and imagine himself in Nadia's consulting room again. *Mise en scène.* In their last few sessions, she had been quite guarded, scrutinising him like a sceptical Raisa Gorbacheva, or giving him mocking Cheshire Cat grins. He decided that today he would keep his body almost completely still while he spoke, like news presenters on television, apart from throwing in the occasional smile.

He felt a pang of anxiety, and again wondered if he had been gesticulating too much in some of the sessions, especially during his accounts of Louise's death. Perhaps it was this that had put Nadia *en garde.*

He had to slow down. A message was blinking on an illuminated sign over the road: *Bouchon.* Delays. Another kilometre further on, the traffic was at a standstill. The queue snaked ahead into the distance as far as the eye could see. The rain continued unabated, the drops clattering on the windows of his Volvo 760. There were rolls of thunder, and the rain was forming plump bubbles in the puddles by the side of the road. He looked at the clock on the dashboard: twenty-five to three. He was still in plenty of time.

He breathed in the smell of the new car. A very pleasing smell. Again he turned up the radio and it was as though, like the rain, the piano notes were being driven on by the flurries of wind. He switched off the windscreen wipers and almost instantly the water sheeting the glass made it impossible to see out.

He took the script from the passenger seat. Glancing through it, he saw that there was one phrase he needed to eliminate: *If I set them on a terrorist, that terrorist would be a dead man.* That could be used against him in the future. If his intention was to take revenge on Eliseo and blame the attack on Troy, he had to show that he was a man of peace. He pictured himself sitting beside the floor lamp in the consulting room, explaining what had gone on at the Ugarte mine as placidly as a monk from the monastery in Belloc.

In the year that followed the murder of Ryan the engineer, I didn't notice anything unusual at the Ugarte mine. It was as if the workers knew nothing about it. The administrator, Julián, did talk to me about the problems at the nuclear power station, because he read the papers; the sports section mainly, but he still read them. However, firedamp was starting to fill the air. I don't know if you know what firedamp is, Nadia. It's a gas that's produced in coal mines. Its principal component is methane. It builds up gradually over time and when you get a concentration of more than five per cent of it in the air, it becomes very dangerous. It causes explosions, potentially deadly for anyone in the mine at the time. In the old days, when they had no other way of detecting it, they used a canary; they would put the bird in a cage and take the cage down the mineshaft. It's odd but canaries sing in a particular way when they've breathed in methane, and that's how they sound the alarm. The moment they heard that song, the miners would hotfoot it out of the mine as fast as they could.

He noticed movement through the blurred windscreen and turned on the wipers. The queue of cars was advancing, but very slowly, at walking pace. He started laughing.

No, Nadia, no. The canaries don't really sing in a particular way when they breathe in methane. What they do is they die. That's the signal for the miners. Excuse the joke.

He shook his head. He couldn't allow himself to make a joke like that in front of Nadia.

The presenter introduced another piece by Debussy, "Claire de Lune". He passed another road sign. It was another eight kilometres to Bayonne. His thoughts returned to Nadia's consulting room.

Firedamp was building up in Ugarte without me realising. In a way, I had my own personal canary – Julián, the administrator – but he gave me no warning. And then suddenly, there were the explosions.

208

First, the workers started going on strike. They were striking two or three times a week. Then they declared themselves permanently on strike. The union reps insisted I meet with them. I told them to take it up with Julián. That wasn't the outcome they were hoping for, and so they started making a nuisance of themselves. They'd gather outside my office, waiting for me to come in or out. But I found a way to stop them: Louise and Troy took care of that.

Then the second explosion. Some pamphlets appeared, little post-card-sized ones, distributed in the area around the mine. I knew straight away they were bad news. When I took one back to the office, Julián was waiting for me. He was holding one too. He was looking very serious, and so I made a joke: "What's up, Julián, did Athletic Bilbao lose?" He said: "It's unsigned, but these people could be dangerous." He was right. In the pamphlet, they singled out our company as one of their targets, "because of the environmental damage the mine will cause". But I went on trying to make a joke of it: "Relax, Julián. They say Ugarte's one of their targets, not that it's their main target." He asked me if I'd read the last line. It was addressed to the engineers: "The people in charge of the mine should remember what happened to José María Ryan".

I called a meeting with the engineers, five men in all, and gave them instructions: they were to stick together at all times, travelling to and from the mine as a group. One of them asked if I was going to set up night surveillance at the lab and the offices. Louise and Troy were there with me. Pointing to Troy, I said: "My friend here is all the night surveillance we're going to need. With a security guard like this, nobody'll dare come near the place. As you all know, he's a born fighter."

And they were well aware of this. They'd seen him frighten off some of the union members, and attack one in particular who'd thrown a stone at him. "As for Louise," I said, "she will be my faithful companion. She'll be at my side constantly on my way to and from work. Plus, I'll go through the forest, avoiding the roads. Any terrorist who wants to take me out had better be a damn good shot." Julián was at that meeting. I gave him very clear instructions:

209

"Go and get a Land Rover in the village to ferry these men back and forth between work and home. We'll start following this protocol tomorrow." I looked at Troy. *"And you, Troy, you'll be on guard duty starting tonight. Don't worry. I've got food for you in the lab fridge."*

Antoine turned off the A63 and stopped at a crossroads. He had arrived in Bayonne. For a moment, absorbed in his thoughts, he didn't know which way to go, but he soon got his bearings when he saw, through the curtain of rain, the River Adour and, a little further on to the left, the buildings that made up the Camp de Prats medical centre. He was on Avenue Capitaine Resplandy on the southern approach to the city.

The piece playing on the radio was not by Claude Debussy. He began to pay attention, waiting for the presenter to say something, although he did not actually need any help in identifying the music. It was one of Chopin's nocturnes. He did not know which one, only that it formed part of the series.

A traffic light was causing long tailbacks. Not that it mattered, the hands on the car clock showed that it was only a quarter past three. He could still have his cup of tea at the bistro near Paulmy car park and give the script a final once-over.

He started calculating how long it would take him to deliver the lines he had already rehearsed. A quarter of an hour perhaps, half the session. That left him with another quarter of an hour to talk about the failure of the protocol he had put in place after the threats had come to light, and the consequences this had for him. The image of Eliseo came to mind. He had been the engineers' designated driver. Antoine did not know at the time, how could he, that he was the monster who would end up killing Louise. To Antoine, he was just somebody who worked at the bakery. But, looking back, it made him furious. He cursed, clutched his head in both hands and gazed heavenwards. Misinterpreting this gesture, the driver of the Peugeot 504 inching forward alongside him smiled. He, too, was exasperated by the slowness of the traffic lights on the way into Bayonne.

Still the rain fell, and the day was very dark, almost as though night had fallen already. The floor lamp in Nadia's consulting room would not be enough, and she would have to turn on the lamp on the desk as well.

He again picked up the script from the passenger seat. *Suddenly, I saw that my life was in danger.* He would take this phrase as the basis for the second half of the session. The better he was able to explain the tensions that had rocked the mine at the time of the strikes, the more credible his schizophrenia would appear to Nadia.

It could be said that the threats in the pamphlets were to my advantage. The unions condemned the interference by the terrorist group, and without asking for anything in return, they called off the strike, simply dropping their demands. When I went to the next meeting in Paris, my colleagues received me with applause. "He who leaves Rome loses Rome," said the director general when he greeted me. "Not you, though, Antoine." It was a glorious moment.

However, there was bad news when I got back from Paris. Julián was waiting for me outside my house. On a Sunday, at nine in the evening: pretty unusual. His face was lit by the light from the streetlamp at the entrance to the garden. He looked really dejected. I told him I'd already heard about the murder of Ángel Pascual Múgica, the man who'd replaced José María Ryan. I'd known before I left Paris. It seemed those terrorists weren't going to let up, I said. He just stood there, head bowed, shoulders hunched. In the encroaching darkness he resembled a Rodin statue. He opened his mouth and said something else, but I couldn't hear properly because Louise was whining on the other side of the garden fence, eager to welcome me. I told her to be quiet, and she sat completely still, like another Rodin statue. "There's something else, Antoine," said Julián. "We've been sabotaged. Someone got into the lab and smashed the place up." I was speechless. Alarmed. "What did they do? They didn't kill Troy, did they?" "Troy's fine," said Julián. "I left him eating his dinner." "I don't understand. Troy's been trained. If he'd noticed anyone trying to get in, he'd have gone for them." That was all Julián would tell me. I said: "Let's go and take a look at the lab," and he said, "I'll

211

call Eliseo and ask him to come and pick us up in the Land Rover."
Rosalía came to the door of her house. "What's happening?" she
shouted. "Nothing," I said. "Athletic Bilbao lost again."

I opened the garden gate and greeted Louise. She had clearly
picked up on the fact that something was going on, because, just like
when she was a puppy, she got all excited and peed herself. Then,
and this was unusual too, she started sniffing Julián. "She can smell
some product from the lab," he said. "You didn't touch anything,
did you?" I said. He shook his head and pointed to his shoes, which
were, in fact, what most interested Louise. "What did the vandals
do?" I asked. "Throw everything on the floor?" "Yes, they threw
everything on the floor and smashed it all to pieces." "Did you call
the police?" Again he said no: "It happened this morning, and I only
found out at midday when I went up to give Troy his food. But I
thought it would be best to wait for you to get back from Paris." He
clearly felt uncomfortable, and the look on his face grew increasingly
sombre. "You've done exactly as you should, Julián. I should be the
one to call the police. Phone Eliseo and get him to come over with
the Land Rover."

The driver of the Peugeot 504 was signalling to him from the
adjacent lane, trying to say something to him, and so he rolled
down the window. The cars were beeping continuously, all at the
same time, a horrible, jarring noise. There was a traffic jam in
the city, worse than the one on the motorway.

The driver of the Peugeot 504 was a young man with shoulder-length hair who looked like a beatnik. He held up an empty
pack of Gitanes. Antoine shrugged: *Désolé.* He wasn't a smoker
and had no cigarettes.

"Where are we?" asked the beatnik. "Is this Resplandy or
Boufflers?"

"Boufflers. That's the Pont Mayou over there."

The people crossing the bridge in both directions were hurrying along, hunched against the rain. The umbrellas looked
almost exclusively black from that distance.

The clock on the Volvo dashboard read twenty minutes to four.

He was still okay. Once he got past the lights, it would not take long to reach the car park in Paulmy.

The sound of car horns could still be heard inside the car, even with the windows closed. He turned up the volume on the radio. The presenter was introducing another of Chopin's nocturnes. Gently, the piano transported him back to Ugarte, distracting him not only from his immediate surroundings, the Pont Mayou, the traffic lights, the lines of cars, but also from the script beside him on the passenger seat and his intention to continue rehearsing the play he was going to put on for Nadia that day. The memory of the sabotage absorbed him completely.

There was considerable damage inside the laboratory: liquids all over the floor, shattered test tubes everywhere. Once the inspection was over and they had got back into the Land Rover, he said to Troy: "And where the hell were you? Call yourself a security guard." But this was an attempt to make himself appear relaxed in front of Julián and Eliseo. He who left Rome lost Rome. And the Roman emperor must not show any signs of weakness.

He called Charlie the moment he got home.

"What's up with my friend Antoine, then, for him to be calling a policeman at half eleven on a Sunday night?"

Charlie had the attractively gravelly voice of a smoker. And he was a good-looking man. At La Petite Pagode, all the girls' faces lit up when he arrived, and they would immediately run over and link arms with him. Three or four of them offered him their services for free.

He and Antoine had become friends by chance. They had met there in passing for a number of months, and then, one Saturday night, Charlie came over to ask for his help with something. He was trying to tell a dirty joke in French, but failing. They were both in one of La Petite Pagode's private rooms, each with a female companion. "How do you say flute in French?" "*Flûte.* But I'm not sure the young maiden here will understand. She's Filipino, unless I'm much mistaken." The girl was wearing a kimono. She flung it open to reveal her breasts. *"Je suis ouverte à toutes les langues"* "I am open to all tongues". Both men laughed; Charlie, who had been snorting cocaine, positively guffawed. Charlie did his best to translate his joke into French, and again everyone laughed. Then he asked Antoine: "Haven't you got a joke for Van-Van?" "If no-one minds, I'm going to make a highly intellectual observation," he said. "Montaigne says – and this is a point that rings especially true to me – that she who has not fucked a cripple has never really fucked. Certain people at La Petite Pagode ought to bear this in mind and not overcharge such a special customer." Montaigne had, in fact, been referring to crippled women, but this was not the moment for such details. Charlie exploded with laughter. Then, once he had calmed down, he pointed at Van-Van and said: "This guy isn't paying today, *d'accord?*" She protested, and Charlie's voice took on a harsher tone: "Don't make me get angry, Van-Van. I said, this guy isn't paying today, *d'accord?*"

From then on, whenever they were both at La Petite Pagode on a Saturday night, they would sit and chat over a couple of whiskies. The relationship was of particular interest to Antoine. A foreign company with offices in Spain needed contacts like this, and Charlie was the kind of man one could trust; a policeman, and a very professional one.

"Charlie, the lab's been sabotaged. I haven't alerted the authorities yet. I thought I'd call you before I did anything."

"My friend Antoine's done exactly the right thing. What happened? And don't spare me the details – just like when you're telling me about the ladies."

He laughed. This was Charlie's humour to a tee. Antoine started telling him what had happened.

"Just a moment," said Charlie. "I can't find my lighter."

Footsteps were heard at the other end of the line, the sound of something falling on the floor. Then a lighter being struck.

"Right, Antoine, let's have all the gory details."

Charlie listened to the description of the sabotage in silence.

The sound of him exhaling cigarette smoke was the only indication that he was still there.

"That'll do," he said after a minute. "Whoever's paid your mine a visit, it isn't the terrorists who took out the engineers in Bilbao. If it was, there would be no lab. They'd have blown it sky-high with Goma-2, and then put a few explosives in the offices for good measure. So you needn't worry on that account."

"Maybe it was a warning."

At the other end of the line, Charlie laughed, but very briefly, not like when someone told him a joke.

"Maybe you aren't really a cripple. I thought cripples were supposed to be clever. And not only when it comes to the ladies."

"One of these days I'll take up smoking. That, according to you, is what I need to do if I want to be clever."

"Damn right. Nothing better for the brain than nicotine."

"Or alcohol, as you also often say."

Antoine never mentioned cocaine, not even as a joke, because that was Charlie's real problem.

"So what are you saying? You don't think it was a warning?"

"Come on, Antoine! When terrorists want to give a warning, they do it with bombs. Bombs or a bullet in the back of the head. But let's leave it there for now. We can talk in a more relaxed way tomorrow. Is your house in Ugarte easy to find?"

"It's on a hill at the entrance to the village. A big house with a fenced garden. The people here call it Villa Dobermann. But I don't suppose you'll be going around asking questions in the village."

"We ask lots of questions, but not in plain sight." Charlie cleared his throat. "I'll come by your place at midday, and I'll bring a friend. Before that, I'll send some men to the mine. They'll need someone to go with them."

"Tell them to ask for the administrator. His name's Julián."

The first step in the chemical analysis of any substance or material was to isolate the components and make a list of them – A, B,

C, D, E and F – to study how they interacted. Agatha Christie used the same procedure in her novels. She assembled the main characters in a certain setting, and the murderer's name would emerge out of that coming together of all the suspects.

Sitting in his living room, waiting for Charlie to arrive, Antoine was trying to submit the details of the sabotage to the same kind of analysis. Why had Troy not done his job as guard dog? It was strange in a dog like him. Troy's and Louise's trainer worked with elite dogs in the French police forces, and he was very strict. If somebody brought him a puppy without the necessary qualities, he would refuse point-blank to take it on. It was therefore simply impossible that the people who broke into the laboratory could have tricked Troy with food, tempting him with a piece of meat containing some kind of narcotic. If they had so much as tried, Troy would have attacked them. The only possibility was some sexual ploy. The saboteurs must have brought along a bitch in heat to get Troy to abandon his post and go chasing after her. In this, dogs and men were very much alike. He had seen plenty of heads of households arrive at La Petite Pagode half-crazy with lust, with barely enough patience to park their cars properly. But that was equally unlikely. It was the beginning of May, not the right time of year.

There was a knock on the living-room door.

"Come in," he said.

It was Rosalía, the housekeeper. She had brought coffee and some orange pastries. She put the tray down on the glass-topped table in front of his armchair.

She stood there looking at him.

"What is it, Rosalía?"

There were two guests coming, and Rosalía was concerned about what to serve. She was thinking of giving them some hors d'oeuvres: asparagus, artichokes, tomato soup and foie gras.

"And what about some ham, Rosalía? Ham is the best thing Spain has to offer."

"That's just it, Antoine. I was thinking of serving trout for

216

the main course, and I usually cook trout with ham. But I don't know. Ham as a starter *and* in the main course might be a bit too much. Do you still think I should have ham as one of the starters?"

"Yes, I do."

Rosalía again did not move. Antoine poured himself some coffee. He wanted to be alone with his thoughts, to get his ideas in order before Charlie and his friend made an appearance.

"What is it now, Rosalía?"

"Shall I feed the dogs, or would you rather do it? Perhaps it's better that I do it, so that you can concentrate on your guests. I hope I don't get bitten!"

The task of looking after the dogs rarely fell to Rosalía, but there was no reason why she should not feed them this time. Louise and Troy were used to seeing her go in and out of the house, or watering the flowers in the garden, and they knew they could trust her.

"I'm sure they won't bite you, Rosalía. Thank you."

He found it difficult to speak in a neutral voice as he said this, because suddenly, just as in the lab when the composition of a substance suddenly revealed itself to him, or when he picked out the right thread from the tangled skein of an Agatha Christie plot, he had just found the solution to "The Case of the Ugarte Laboratory". Who would Troy never have attacked? Or indeed, who would the dog have gone up to with head meekly bowed and tail wagging?

He reminded himself to breathe. He needed to calm down. He got up from the sofa and went over to the large living-room window, taking his cup of coffee with him.

After Antoine, there were only four people in the world whom Louise and Troy trusted: Rosalía, Julián and the twins Luis and Martín.

"Martín!" he exclaimed.

It had to be Martín. Rosalía and Julián were both absolutely above suspicion. It was unthinkable that they would ever get involved in some extremist ideology. As for the twins, it could be either of them, but Luis took after his father, a young guy who thought only about sport and nothing else. Plus, he and Antoine got on really well, and even exchanged gifts – recently, Luis had given him a record by the Gary Noak Trio, "Thanks", and Antoine had given him a lump of chalcopyrite he had found down the mine – whereas he hardly ever saw Martín now. He never even came by the house.

Antoine drank his coffee and went back to his armchair. Yes, it had been Martín, there was no doubt about it. He was studying Philosophy at university. Luís, Physical Education; Martín, Philosophy – Julián had told him that. "I'm a bit worried. I've been told the Philosophy faculty is full of Communists." Julián had told him that too.

Two other things came to him, both of which backed up his hypothesis. First, Julián's expression when he broke the news of the sabotage to Antoine on his return from Paris. So, so sombre. He clearly suspected his son. Second, the saboteur had chosen to smash up the lab and not the offices. It made complete sense: the boy was hardly going to carry out an attack on his father's workplace.

"Eureka!" he said, laughing at his own joke. It was a real joy to work out who the killer was in an Agatha Christie novel forty pages before the end, just as it was to crack open a stone you'd picked up off the ground and identify its composition at a glance; but this was an even better feeling. Something real was at stake here. He rose and went down to the wine cellar. They would drink a bottle of Burgundy with the meal, and with dessert an excellent champagne: a bottle of Veuve Clicquot.

He emerged from his thoughts as from a dream and found that he had passed the lights on Pont Mayou and the area around the Théâtre de Bayonne. His Volvo was now gliding along by the river. Alarmed, he looked at the clock on the dashboard. It was fine: the orange hands now stood at a quarter past four. He had the better part of an hour to make it to Nadia's.

He abandoned the idea of leaving the car in the Paulmy car park and went instead to the one before that, Charles de Gaulle, some seven hundred metres away from her practice. After the drive, a little exercise would be good for his leg. It had stopped raining.

Exactly 100 metres up from the pier outside the car park, the smaller River Nive flowed into the Adour. The current was always strong at the point where the two rivers met, but on that day, November 8, it was positively violent, and the wintry, brown, turbulent waters seemed a very different thing from the stream that flowed through Ugarte, which, in his mind, was always crystal-clear whether in spring or autumn. But was that really true? Memory functioned, in the first instance, in a vulgar, entirely predictable way, by clinging to what was the norm – like automated machines, or chemical substances, or charlatans. His was no exception. In the images it presented to him, the water in Ugarte was, in effect, crystal-clear, and far more innocent than the angry Adour he could see before him; but if he probed that particular memory, what instantly emerged was the flat rock with its covering of moss, lichen and fallen leaves, and at the centre of the rock that circular bare red patch, and inside the circle the skin left behind by a snake. A memory that was at once joined by another image: that of Eliseo and the other bakery employee with their setters. And another: the two Dobermanns at his side, awaiting his command. Then the command: "Attack, Louise!" And the final image: Louise sprawled on the ground, after Eliseo had felled her with a single shot.

Had it been stupidity to set Louise on Eliseo, giving way to an emotional impulse? He often asked himself that question. Certainly, there was no way he could have known that Eliseo was such a marksman, but ignorance was hardly an excuse. It had been an idiotic thing to do. To get a good result, you needed to plan ahead.

It seemed to him that the muddy waters of the Adour were flowing even faster than before, surging headlong towards the river mouth, with all of the element's characteristic singlemindedness.

Above the ocean, some ten kilometres away, the sky showed yellowish, the colour of sodium peroxide. The lights of the houses in the city, which were just starting to come on, were the off-white colour of potassium. It was a beautiful view: a beautiful city, a beautiful evening. And yet it was not sufficiently distracting to make him forget the truth: Eliseo was better than him. *Un homme supérieur.* He would always defeat him.

Once more, he saw that man's head on a dish, severed at the neck like John the Baptist's. Among all the lies and half-truths he had told Nadia, that image was real. It also came to him in dreams: Troy taking big bites out of the head. Had he told Nadia about that dream? He could not remember.

Leaving the riverside, he crossed a public park and headed in the direction of Allées Paulmy.

As he did every time he went to see Nadia, he regretted not having Pierre Irissou's talents as an actor. Pierre was a special person. Really special. He had been a huge success in this very place, in the Théâtre de Bayonne, and the newspaper *Sud Ouest* had proclaimed a great future for him as a professional actor. However, rather than follow that path, he had opted for a solitary life. He organised spiritual retreats for Christians in Trensacq, the village in Les Landes where he lived. Pierre was a loyal friend. He never forgot the many hours they had shared at the Hôtel Le Splendid or in their theatre group. Antoine would occasionally be invited to spend the weekend, or Christmas, at Pierre's *ostau*, and he always returned to Ugarte from these trips with a jar of *miel de pin*. And yet, there were times when Pierre looked at him rather sternly; he must have suspected that Antoine frequented places like La Petite Pagode. And that displeased him. He was a devout Catholic. He had been on the point of joining the Benedictine community in Belloc, though in the end he married an equally devout woman, Margarita.

Antoine walked along Allées Paulmy using his umbrella as a kind of walking stick, while reviewing the key phrases he would deliver to Nadia.

Suddenly, I saw that my life was in danger. The terrorists over the border decided to go after the engineer, using environmental concerns as an excuse. They were trying to stop a nuclear power station being built.

Next he would move on to the strike and, in particular, the sabotage. To finish, he would again mention the proof of his schizophrenia. He was still hearing Troy's voice, and this was a cause of great distress.

Troy has always been aggressive, but since watching Louise die in front of him a month and a half ago, he's much more so. He's obsessed. I hear his voice every single night, clamouring for revenge. I hear it even if he's outside in the kennel and I'm inside in my bedroom. I'll lose my mind if things go on like this.

He stopped opposite the bistro and checked the time on his watch, a gold Certina with very slender hour and minute hands. It was not yet half past four – exactly three minutes shy of that. He went in and ordered some tea.

"With your usual croissant?" asked the owner. Antoine nodded. "Have a seat, *monsieur*. I'll bring it right over."

He wanted to go on reviewing the script and tried to force himself to concentrate. Impossible. It was tedious going over and over the same phrases when they were nothing like Verlaine's poems, not at all; they were purely pragmatic exercises, elements in a plan. When the bistro owner came over with his tea and croissant, Antoine's mind went back to the sabotage.

The lunch with Charlie and the other policeman at Villa Chantal was extremely pleasant. The moment they sat down at the table, he said: "We're not here today to analyse the sabotage. We're here to celebrate. Gentlemen: I know how it all happened, and I know who did it."

Charlie glanced at him.

"What should we do then? Just eat, drink and listen?"

"Yes, that's all you have to do," said Antoine.

A hint of a smile appeared on the other officer's face.

"Just how we like it," he said.

He was a young man with a gaunt face and insomniac eyes.

During the starters, Antoine explained the conclusion he had come to that morning, laying on the table, like someone showing his cards, the identity of the culprit: Martín Sola, twenty-two years old, philosophy student. One of Julián's twin sons.

This seemed logical to Charlie. It fitted with their information. Not all the agitators in Ugarte were from mainstream unions; there were Maoists in the mix as well. They were dangerous, but not linked to the Basque separatist group ETA. In that regard, Antoine could rest easy. They wouldn't be putting a bullet in the back of his head.

"That's as long as the other lot don't decide to get involved," said the policeman with the insomniac eyes. "Initially, when everything kicked off at the nuclear power station, they had nothing to do with that either."

"It's unlikely," said Charlie. "This Ugarte thing is small beer. They'll doubtless try and get involved later on, but not at this stage. They need things to hot up a bit. *Sois calme,* Antoine," he said, laughing.

Rosalía came into the dining room. She put a white porcelain dish on the table containing three trout encircled by green peppers.

"They're from the stream in Ugarte. I baked them in the oven but left out the ham. Having ham twice in the same meal seemed too much to me."

"Rosalía is free to do whatever she likes," Antoine said.

"As it should be," said Charlie.

From there, the conversation moved on to other things. The trout were followed by an apple tart. At the end, they drank a toast with the Veuve Clicquot.

Rosalía came in to see if they wanted coffee.

"My colleague and I will stick to champagne, Rosalía," said Charlie. "Thank you. The trout was magnificent. The best I've had in a long time."

"No coffee for me either," Antoine said.

"In that case, I'll go home," she said. "I'll come and tidy up once I've had my lunch."

Charlie was gazing at his champagne glass, as though the continuous upward stream of bubbles was an aid to concentration.

"Once we've had a word with that young man, I'll call you. In the meantime, carry on as normal."

The other officer took a notebook and a biro out of his jacket pocket.

"Do you know Martín Sola's address?"

"His parents divorced a few years ago. His mother's moved in with the bakery owner. Julián lives on Calle Mayor, as he always has, along with Martín's twin, Luis. But I don't know about Martín."

Charlie picked up his champagne glass.

"If we apply a bit of pressure, we'll soon get it out of him. But we need to be careful. You know what happened before."

No, he did not.

"What happened with Arregui after the Ryan case," said the other policeman. "They applied rather too much pressure, and then they had another dead body on their hands."

He fell silent for a moment, a look of distaste on his face.

"People know that pressure can sometimes be necessary, they just don't like anyone reminding them of it."

Charlie finished what was left of his champagne, then shook Antoine's hand.

"I'll give you a call," he said as he left.

The call came four days later, at midday on the Friday.

"Martín's got an alibi. He spent almost the entire Sunday at a symposium on Plato. There are photos."

Antoine was dumbstruck.

"Here's what you're going to do, Antoine. Get in that old Volvo of yours and come and meet me. I'm at La Petite Pagode. We need to assess the situation."

This was an order.

"I'm at the mine right now. I need a bit of time to get the dogs home and have a shower."

"No hurry. I get plenty of love and affection here!"

On the drive there, following first the minor roads around Ugarte, then the A63, Antoine went over and over his analysis of the sabotage. He could not be wrong. In Agatha Christie's novels, purely for entertainment, the different threads could become knotted and snarled ad infinitum, but in real life things were never actually that complicated. There was a clear logic, A + B + C + D + E = F, and in this case F was Martín. And yet Charlie had been unequivocal: "He's got an alibi."

Antoine tried to put himself in Martín's shoes, harking back to his time as an amateur actor. Feeling what the character felt, thinking like him – that was the key to the Stanislavski method. He imagined that he had decided to destroy the laboratory. That he had committed himself to carrying out the act with the support of his fellow Maoists and some of the miners who had been involved in the abortive strikes. "I'll smash up the lab, but not the offices – that wouldn't go down well with my Dad."

He then imagined a conversation between the twins. Martín: "Luis, I need you to go to this Plato symposium instead of me." Luis: "What for? I'm planning to go and watch the match." Martín: "I'll explain later on, but you have to do me this favour."

Yes, that was it, that was exactly how it had happened. Martín had convinced his twin brother to stand in for him at the symposium. Everyone would think that the student listening attentively to the lectures on Plato was him, Martín. Rather a clever move. Not that it would do him any good though, because they'd get to him through Luis. "Luis, where were you last Sunday morning? Did you take a little stroll up to the mine by any chance?" He would try to fend them off by saying he'd been at home, in bed, after spending Saturday night out partying. But, while Julián would back him up on this, it would be of little help. When they put him on the spot, he'd go running to his brother for help, and

Martín would have no choice but to confess the truth. "I was the one who carried out the sabotage," he would tell the police. "Leave my brother alone."

At La Petite Pagode, Charlie burst out laughing when he heard this explanation and even applauded. He had been snorting cocaine.

"The same idea occurred to me, Antoine. I went through the same steps and came to the same conclusion. You know what, though? Someone else had *exactly* the same idea."

He pronounced the word "exactly" while simultaneously slamming his hand down on the coffee table, on which stood an ashtray, a tall glass and a bottle of Chivas. The Bakelite ashtray shifted a few centimetres.

They were in a room full of mirrors, and the one opposite them was floor-to-ceiling, reflecting the two of them sitting on a red sofa. Antoine felt very awkward. Compared with Charlie's body, his looked misshapen. His bad leg rested on the floor at an unnatural angle. He asked if they could sit somewhere else.

Charlie poured whisky into the glass, which was full to the brim with ice cubes, and then lit a cigarette. He was smoking American cigarettes, Marlboros.

"No, we're good right where we are. Sure, a twenty-year-old girl with no clothes on would be a prettier sight than two guys like us, but it's the most discreet room in the house. You've been in here before, haven't you? Don't tell me you only use the upstairs rooms."

Antoine shrugged. He did only use the upstairs rooms.

"You don't smoke, Antoine. That's your problem, I've told you before. With a little nicotine in your bloodstream you'd be more switched on, and everything would work out better for you. The world belongs to the smart guys. And those Ugarte folk are very smart – I bet you they're all smokers. Julián definitely is. He loves his Monterrey cigars."

"Will you get on with it and tell me what's happening, Charlie."

"No, seriously, Antoine, you should take up smoking. *And*

get a bit more whisky down you, that too. Look at me, cigarette, whisky: couldn't be happier."

"I don't feel like drinking today."

Charlie then explained why he was in such a good mood. It wasn't only the cigarettes and alcohol. It was, above all, the nature of the case they had on their hands. He had been dealing with common criminals and terrorists for years, and the method was always the same. Lean on the suspects a little, and the accomplices' names would soon follow.

"As you'd put it: A-B-C, A-B-C, A-B-C."

He accompanied the series of letters by again slamming his hand down on the coffee table, so hard this time that the ashtray nearly fell off the edge. Antoine looked at himself in the mirror. He saw his face: that of a confused man. He was struggling to comprehend what was going on.

Charlie was now talking in a low voice, almost to himself. Sometimes, when he thought about his career so far, it got to him. He was a policeman, but not the policeman he would have wanted to be – he was a mere defender. A central defender, left back, or maybe right back – it didn't matter. The hatchet man, that was him, the guy for putting in the dirty tackles. Nonetheless, his dream when he was younger – because deep down he was an idealist – had been to become someone like Colonel Race, the detective in the Agatha Christie novels, working hand in hand with the secret services, moving in aristocratic circles, among women with class, femmes fatales some of them – the kind of women who wore low-cut black dresses and went to cocktail parties. Not easy lays like the women at La Petite Pagode, who were always ready to drop their kimonos, but women who could still, nonetheless, be won over. Not that he had any illusions about that. His dreams were all behind him now. The mirror was all the reminder he needed. His good looks had not deserted him entirely, but his hair was receding, thinning too, with a bald spot beginning to appear on the crown. All of which meant the question of the Ugarte sabotage made him feel particularly good. It was like a case from a detective movie.

"Please," said Antoine. "Tell me what's been going on."

Charlie straightened up and put an arm around his shoulder. Whispering in his ear, like a person sharing a secret, he said:

"Antoine, you've fallen into a trap."

"Look, I don't understand a thing!" Antoine got up and stood to one side of the table. Charlie lit another cigarette.

"I've told you, nicotine in the bloodstream, that's what you need. That's why you can't see what's right under your nose. Don't worry, though. Charlie's going to fill you in."

Martín was indeed behind the sabotage. He had acted alone, because if he had taken anyone else into the lab with him, Troy would have gone mad. The kid was clearly intelligent, not the kind to go rushing in. He had chosen the date carefully too. May 9, a Sunday. All the employees were at home; the area deserted. The chief engineer – "That's you, Antoine" – away in Paris, as Martín could have found out from his father. And to round things off, a Plato symposium being held at the Philosophy Faculty. Bingo! He had asked his brother, who said he would go along with the plan on one condition, that he would hang around at the university until six in the evening, then go home to watch the match. But there was a weak point in his plan. An admirer of Colonel Race would ask Luis: "Where were you on May 9, between nine in the morning and six in the evening? Do you have an alibi?"

"But I already told you all this when I arrived," Antoine said.

"Right, let's move on then. So I went and asked Luis: 'Where were you on May 9, between nine in the morning and six in the evening?' Obviously he couldn't admit to having been at the university, and, doubtless on his brother's instructions, he said: 'I went trout fishing with Eliseo. We caught five trout, and Eliseo put them in a cage he's made at the top of the canal. So nobody can claim we were poaching. We didn't take the trout out of the river, we just moved them somewhere else.'"

Charlie paused to stub out his cigarette and take a sip of whisky. Antoine rather nervously watched him in the mirror. He was about to find out how it all ended.

"Given the circumstances, I went into Colonel Race mode and made the next move. I went to the bakery for a chat with Eliseo. They told me he wasn't there, that he'd gone to the upper part of the canal, where he kept the trout. I headed straight up there. I found him with his wife and two kids. Do you know his wife, Paca? She's got to be at least 120 kilos. A real character."

Antoine said that no, he didn't know her, then immediately corrected himself. Yes, he did know Paca, he'd seen her sometimes working in Rosalía's vegetable patch. A woman who was as brash and uninhibited as she was big, and who, even when she was planting lettuce, would have the radio on full blast. But he didn't know she was Eliseo's wife, or that they farmed trout.

"They've made a wire cage at the point where the river joins the canal. A mini-fish farm. The trout we ate the other day were from there."

Charlie paused for a moment.

"Eliseo's no fool. No nicotine in his bloodstream, but still, no fool. When I asked him about Luis, he didn't so much as blink. 'He's right, he was with me on Sunday morning. But it wasn't five trout we caught, it was four. He got two, and I got two.' See, Antoine? If he'd told me the same thing as Luis, it would have sounded like they'd cooked up the story together."

"So that confirms Luis' alibi . . ."

"Full circle. Nothing to be done."

"Isn't there any way to get the truth out of Martín? Leaning on him a bit would do it, wouldn't it?"

"No, Antoine. Like I said, you've fallen into a trap."

Charlie was standing in front of the mirror now, adjusting his red tie and smoothing his dark suit, as if about to leave the room. Instead, though, he sat back down. The mirror showed a very sombre-looking man.

"A formal complaint has been lodged against you, Antoine. I'll keep this brief."

Antoine had the impression that the mirror was trembling, as if an earthquake had hit La Petite Pagode, and he could barely listen to Charlie's explanation. He caught only the salient points. There was a complaint against him, lodged by Julián, who had reason to believe that he, the chief engineer, had carried out the sabotage, with the clear objective of neutralising the activities of the miners and the unions. There was a witness who claimed to have seen him in the vicinity of the mine on the Sunday morning, without his dogs. Julián could not confirm this for certain but wanted this to go on the record.

"Tell Colonel Race, Antoine. Have you got an alibi? Where were you the morning of May 9?"

He knew exactly where he had been. On his way back from Paris, he usually spent Saturday night at La Petite Pagode, and he had spent that particular Sunday morning – the entire morning – in bed with Van-Van.

He could see Charlie's face in the mirror, his mocking expression. He was one step ahead of him. He knew about his relationship with Van-Van, that the alibi was watertight. But he also knew, and hence the smile, that he could not use it. He could not confess the truth. His fellow directors at the company would not be in the least amused if word of La Petite Pagode got out. And it would not look good for him either. If there was a trial, Van-Van would be called on to testify, and just the thought of her standing up in court brought him out in a cold sweat. There was no way the lawyer would miss the opportunity to publicise the fact, doubtless to the delight of everyone in Ugarte and everyone at the mine as well, who would then start calling him Van-Van. Sometimes The Frog, sometimes The Cripple, sometimes Van-Van. To cap it all, he could not turn to his friend Pierre Irissou for advice. Devout Catholics sympathised with Mary Magdalene, but not with her clients.

He made to leave, but Charlie grabbed him by the arm.

"Just forget all about it, Antoine. From our point of view, it's the best thing you can do. Martín's shown his hand, and for us that's enough. In a year or two, we'll pick him up along with a dozen of his Maoist pals."

Then, turning to the mirror, Charlie said:

"Mirror, mirror on the wall, anyone here want to pursue the case at all?"

He laughed.

"The mirror says no."

They both went over to the door.

"Am I allowed to know who this false witness is, claiming that he saw me near the mine? Did Julián tell you?"

"Take a guess, Antoine."

"Eliseo."

"Bingo. But these Ugarte folk, they work as a team. And they know what they're about, far better than any criminal in an Agatha Christie novel. I wish I could count on people like them in the fight against the terrorists."

Antoine started when he saw the time. It was already four minutes to five. He left the bistro and set off along Márechal Foch, a broad, pleasant avenue of attractive houses, landscaped gardens, and five- and six-storey buildings with shops and cafés at street level. At present, following the downpours, it was deserted, and in the silence, his footsteps echoed on the pavement, making two different, out of kilter sounds. "The music of the cripple!", as a drunk man had once said to him in Ugarte as they passed one another in the street.

It was not an easy thing to face up to, but it was the truth. Eliseo would always be better than him. *Un homme supérieur.* He had humiliated him during the strikes, when the lab was sabotaged, and again when Antoine had tried to set Louise on him. But it would not happen again. Rome would not fall for a third time. Troy would see to that, and Nadia would sign the psychiatric report, his letter of safe-conduct. "He cannot be held responsible for his actions," the judge would conclude, in the worst-case scenario, if the argument did not wash that Troy had slipped the leash despite Antoine's best efforts.

And yet one thing still worried him. Would the judge be

familiar with the case of David Berkowitz? Berkowitz was a serial killer, also known as the Son of Sam. He had killed five or six youngsters in New York for no reason whatsoever, and had gone on to plead not guilty, claiming that he had acted on the bidding of a dog called Harvey, who had goaded him into killing in the name of Lucifer. Antoine had hatched his plan against Eliseo after reading an article about the case in an American magazine. He would blame Troy, just as Berkowitz had blamed Harvey. Naturally, there was a risk. Someone could bring up the case during his own trial, but this was unlikely. Very few people in Spain could read English.

A man standing in the doorway of a café was waving to him. His long hair was now caught back in a ponytail, and it took Antoine a few seconds to recognise him. It was the driver of the Peugeot 504, the beatnik. He had a pack of Gitanes in his hand and was waving it at Antoine by way of a greeting: he had finally managed to get hold of some cigarettes. Antoine responded with a nod but did not stop. He had his sights on the building where Nadia had her practice, a small house without a garden.

The consulting room looked very different. The desk lamp and the spotlights in the ceiling were on, but the floor lamp was not. On the walls, which in previous sessions had been in semi-darkness, a number of paintings now leapt out, all of them abstracts, or so it seemed to him from a quick glance. After a moment's hesitation, he left his umbrella by the door and went over to the armchair where he usually sat, though he did not get as far as sitting down. Nadia was not on that side of the room but standing between the bay window and the desk.

"Sit opposite me, please," she said. She had the Montblanc pen in her hand, and now put it down on the desk.

According to the green numbers on the digital clock, it was two minutes past five: 17.02.

There was a discreet knock on the door and a man came in. It was the beatnik from the Peugeot 504. He still had the pack of Gitanes in his hand. He put it down next to the Montblanc. Nadia moved it to one side.

"I don't allow smoking in the consulting room," she said. For the first time that afternoon, the Raisa Gorbacheva smile appeared on her face. "This is Christian, a friend of mine. I promised him the meeting would be short and that he wouldn't have to wait too long to go out for his nicotine hit."

The man took a seat on Antoine's left. From close up, he looked quite muscular. An athlete. Not yet forty.

"They say nicotine stimulates the brain," Antoine said, echoing Charlie.

At that moment, the blinds were an off-white colour, and Nadia's head was silhouetted clearly against that background, as if she were sitting for a portrait. The beatnik had a small tattoo, a star, between the thumb and wrist of his right hand.

Nadia continued looking straight at him. There was something strange about her.

"Antoine, I'm going to be blunt about this. You frighten me a little. That's why Christian's here."

The beatnik gave him a judo-style salute. Antoine thought he was probably not pretending and really did practise judo. Whereas Nadia was a fraud. There was no fear in those eyes of hers. They were like a cat's.

"It seems we've swapped roles," he said. "You talking, me listening. I'm not sure this is appropriate."

"This isn't a session. You won't have to pay."

"Again, this really isn't appropriate."

Antoine spun round in his chair, as though a build-up of electricity in his body had sent a shock through him.

"In any case, I'm pleased," he said, sitting up straight. "I can spend the 200 francs on a prostitute instead. Van-Van's my favourite."

The beatnik's response was immediate:

"It doesn't surprise me to know that you frequent brothels, sir."

He was calling him a cripple. Men who, like him, suffered

some defect or disability, would die without ever having known the honest love of a woman. The story of the hunchback of Notre Dame was a lie. Quasimodo and Esmeralda had never fallen into one another's arms, not even at the moment of death. All of Quasimodo's Esmeraldas were really Van-Vans.

To respond properly to such derision, he needed Troy in the consulting room with him. The beatnik would not get very far if he thought he could use judo on a well-trained Dobermann.

Nadia was talking. She was explaining something about the basic principles of psychoanalysis. He paid no attention. He had just noticed that she had dyed her hair jet black. That was why he had thought there was something strange about her. He turned and looked behind him at the bookshelf. The numbers on the clock showed that it was eight minutes past five: 17.08.

"This won't take long, Antoine."

"Get to the point, please."

"Don't worry, I'll be brief. You've done nothing but lie since the moment you walked into my consulting room. I didn't suspect a thing at first and, I confess, your reflections regarding the snakeskin had an impact on me. They seemed significant. But then I started having doubts. Your tears seemed rather over the top. Your breathlessness, that business about the air in your lungs increasing or decreasing in accordance with your emotions, struck me as odd. And when you talked about your dogs, Louise and Troy, the words you came out with just sounded as if you were reading from a script. Before we go on, allow me to ask you, Antoine: in chemistry, what does precipitation mean?"

The Raisa Gorbacheva smile appeared on her face. The beatnik sat with arms crossed, stock-still.

He said nothing. The woman leafed through her notebook.

"In the second session, you were talking about the snakeskin, and then you suddenly declared 'The head of John the Baptist would have fitted perfectly on the bare patch on that rock'. This, as I said to you at the time, reminded me of the story of Salome. I only thought of the story in the Bible, but then, in the next session, you came out with another line: 'He who leaves Rome loses Rome'. Something about it appealed to me, and I repeated it to a theatre director friend of mine . . ."

She indicated Christian. She seemed a very happy Raisa Gorbacheva. She was about to reveal her trump card.

The man took a cigarette out of his pack of Gitanes. He held it between his index and middle finger, as if he was about to light it, but then did not.

"Nadia repeated your line to me after, what shall we call it, an intimate scene between us, and I was quite taken aback. I asked where she'd got it from. Had she ever played Salome? What do you mean, she said? I said that quote about he who leaves Rome loses Rome is one of Herod's lines in *Salome* by the great Oscar Wilde . . ."

He moved his fingers very skilfully, making shapes in the air with the cigarette. He was proud to have a woman like Nadia as his lover. Or if not, he was a regular Casanova, a man who did not need to pay girls like Van-Van. A kind of Charlie. But the resemblance ended there. Christian was not a policeman, as Antoine had thought when he came into the consulting room. He knew too much about theatre. Charlie knew Agatha Christie's work, and that was about it.

Nadia had picked up the Montblanc pen from the desk and was twirling it in her fingers.

"Then came the moment of precipitation, Antoine. I saw it all clearly. Every Friday, I was being made a spectator to a piece of theatre. Once I worked that out, all the pieces fitted together. All except one."

"What part did you play in *Salome*?" said Christian, cutting in. Nadia had not lied when she introduced him; he really was a man of the theatre.

In his mind, Antoine retraced the route he had taken there, from Avenue Maréchal Foch to Allées Paulmy, from there across the park, to the banks of the Adour. A hundred steps further on, and there was the Théâtre de Bayonne, where, in his days as part of the Dax amateur dramatics society, they had put on a production of *Salome*. He saw himself with a beard, his hair all dishevelled, dressed in rags, while Pierre Irissou moved about the stage dressed in layered silk tunics, one crimson, one orange.

"I played John the Baptist. Herod was played by my friend, Pierre Irissou."

The theatre also dealt in lies. If Pierre resembled anyone, it was John the Baptist. He was equally stubborn, not weak and indulgent like Herod. And yet, if the performance was good, there was no way of distinguishing what happened onstage from reality. Antoine, however, was not a good actor, not plausible. That was the problem.

He turned his head. The green numbers on the digital clock showed seventeen minutes past five: 17.17.

"Let's get this over with," he said.

Nadia looked at Christian, then at him.

"The only missing piece was the motive. Initially I thought you were coming to Bayonne to do something, something illegal I mean, and that you came to my practice to give yourself an alibi. But that hypothesis went out of the window the first time Christian followed you. We were able to confirm that you came straight here without stopping, and the same when you went home. Apart, that is, from the night you spent in a Biarritz brothel."

Christian held his cigarette so that it was level with his eyes, and spoke as though he was examining it:

"Unless the brothel was the motive . . . but we don't think that can be it either. Nadia and I talked about it, and it just didn't add up. There are brothels all over the place, plus, nowadays, people don't need to be so secretive. Obviously, it suits some people to be able to pay for sex . . ."

He left this last part of the sentence unfinished, the conclusion hanging in the air: "Otherwise they'd never get any sex at all."

"I've got to go," Antoine said, standing up.

Christian put the cigarette in his mouth and the pack of Gitanes in his trouser pocket.

"For my part, I'd like to thank you for giving me this opportunity, Antoine," he said. "It's been a pleasure to get to play a detective in real life. The only tricky bit was today, with the rain. I couldn't see a thing. Not even if the car in front of me was a Volvo 760. It wasn't until I got you to roll down the window, using the cigarettes as my excuse, that I could be sure."

"That's about it from me as well," said Nadia. "I've considered a number of different hypotheses to explain your behaviour, but you've told so many lies that I'm unable to come up with a diagnosis."

She went on talking. She repeated the word "narcissism" several times. When she finished, Antoine felt relieved. She had not mentioned the name he feared most: David Berkowitz. Neither she nor Christian knew about that criminal and Harvey the dog.

Before picking up his umbrella and leaving the consulting room, he glanced at the clock. It was now twenty-three minutes past five: 17.23.

5

Antoine went for a walk in the area around the mine and headed straight for the flat rock where he had seen the snakeskin. The rock was still covered in moss and lichen, but there were no longer any dead leaves; all the leaves were now the green of spring. The reddish bare patch had grown smaller.

Troy was there at his side, whining continuously and looking up at him.

"Calm down!" he said.

Troy drank a little water from the stream and did not move.

Antoine checked the time. His Certina watch showed six forty-five. Too early. He had been observing Eliseo's movements throughout the spring, since the day Rosalía had shown him the first trout of the season, and he knew that Eliseo never went up to that mini-fish farm in the canal before half past seven in the evening. He sometimes went with Paca, his wife; he had also seen him with one of Julián's twins, probably Luis, but on Sundays he always went alone and slightly later than during the rest of the week. This suited Antoine down to the ground. In the shadowy half-light, weaving between the ash trees lining the canal, Troy would be virtually invisible, although he himself would need to get quite close to be sure it was Eliseo. That was only a minor drawback. Troy would also attack in the shadows. He was trained for that.

He saw the trout Rosalía had presented as if it were there before him. It was about twenty centimetres in length and really very beautiful, grey mottled with pink from the tail to the head. It sat, immaculate, on the white porcelain dish, with not a trace of blood on it. Rosalía had explained that Eliseo did not use a hook and line but preferred using a long pole with a net at one end.

Rosalía meant a *salabardo* or dip net. This did not worry Antoine. Looking through the binoculars, he had seen the pole, and it seemed to him to be made of either wood or plastic. As long as it was not metal, there was no danger. Eliseo would usually spend a few minutes on the canal side crouched next to the cage, removing any slime caught up in it and throwing in bits of bread for the trout. That would be the moment to unleash Troy and, after that, what happened would happen. Without his shotgun, there would be little Eliseo could do.

Troy started whining impatiently again, as if he had read his owner's thoughts. He was strong. Just then, he weighed somewhere around 145 kilos, five kilos heavier than his usual weight.

It was April 6, 1986, and almost five months had passed since Antoine's last trip to Bayonne. The unexpected outcome of that final session had left him worried. If Troy did any serious damage to Eliseo, his performances in Nadia's consulting room could come back to haunt him. In court, they would be taken as a clear sign of premeditation. Nevertheless, after five months, he felt fairly confident. Nadia had talked about his case to the beatnik, but not, it would appear, to the police. Besides, it was unlikely that the Spanish justice system would get in touch with a French psychiatrist.

He heard Troy growling. The dog was on its feet, head raised.

"Is somebody coming?" Antoine said, picking up the binoculars.

There were two people, both wearing anoraks, one red and the other blue. Doubtless mountaineers. They were not walking by the stream or through the wood, but higher up, skirting the mountain about two hundred metres above him.

"Sit, Troy!" he said.

He focused the binoculars and followed the two mountaineers. They were coming down a trail, sideways on and sometimes, where it was steepest, steadying themselves by placing one hand on the ground. One of them, the one in blue, kept lagging behind. The one in red would wait, and then they would go on together with hands joined, until they came to another particularly steep part. They were probably friends or a married couple on their way home after a Sunday hike in the hills.

The one in blue was limping. They were moving further and further off and it was hard to tell, but the person in blue was not limping like someone who has just sprained a knee or ankle. Nor did they limp in the way that Antoine did. Rather, it looked like a consequence of polio. With each step, the blue anorak leaned right over as though to pick something up off the ground, but nevertheless they managed to move along at a fair pace.

The mountaineers carried on down towards the streambed, putting even more distance between their retreating backs and the place where Antoine stood watching. Soon they were nothing but a pair of dark smudges, until they disappeared altogether. All he could see through his binoculars now was the green landscape. The fields in Ugarte were thick with grass, and most of the trees were newly in leaf.

He looked at his watch again. Seven o'clock. He still had time. It only took twenty minutes to get down to the fish cage. Like the blue-anoraked mountaineer, he could limp along pretty quickly too.

Stepping onto the flat rock, he crossed to the other side of the river.

"Here, Troy!"

The dog took up a position on his left and they started moving downhill along the water's edge. He missed Louise. Eliseo would have stood no chance with both dogs there. But there was no going back now.

There never was. He had said as much to Pierre Irissou a few months earlier, during his Christmas stay in Trensacq; to Pierre, and to all the others who had gone to the village to share in a spiritual dialogue: "You're all Catholics, and you accept miracles as readily as the monks in Belloc do. If word came that the Virgin Mary had appeared again in Lourdes or La Salette, you would feel inclined to take it as fact. That same inclination leads you to believe in the most difficult of all miracles to accept: the idea that people can forgive. That's not how it is, Pierre. That's simply not how it is, my friends. I will tell you my truth. I cannot forgive the person who accused me of carrying out the sabotage at the mine and then went on to kill Louise."

He did not mention Eliseo by name during the gathering, but he was so present in Antoine's mind as he spoke that he feared his name might appear etched in blood on his forehead.

"Come on, Toinou. Let's go for a walk," Pierre had said to him some days later. Everyone else had left and the two men were alone in Trensacq.

Dusk was coming on when they set out, not around the lake as they usually did, but into a pine forest, following a dirt track that led to a clearing with a number of beehives in it. There were nine in total, all painted different colours: two blue, three pink and three yellow, with a ninth one, standing slightly apart from the rest, made of glass. It was obvious, and would be to any person who went there, that this was a special place. It was, in fact, a cemetery. Margarita's ashes were buried there. Margarita, Pierre's wife, who had died three years earlier at the age of thirty-seven.

Pierre took a white silk ribbon out of a small leather pouch on his belt and replaced the one that was already attached to the glass beehive. That one was white as well, but it had grown faded and crumpled.

He then went and stood in front of Antoine, and it was a few seconds before he spoke:

"Toinou," he said, "do not commit the gravest of all sins. Life is sacred. Do you promise?"

The surroundings suddenly pressed in on Antoine's awareness. The coloured hives, the new white ribbon on the top of the glass hive, the flowers all around, the blackness of the pine forest, the darkness of the day, the night.

"There's no need for me to promise you that."

"I've never seen you so depressed, Toinou."

240

They headed back, and by the time they reached the *ostau* it was night. Halley's Comet was not yet visible, but it felt as if that were the only star missing from the entire firmament. The stars, planets, satellites and asteroids all combined to illuminate the night sky. Pierre, who had not spoken a word the whole way back, pointed up and exclaimed:

"'*Le pointillement des étoiles . . .*' Do you remember the next part? I'm sure you do, Toinou. No-one in the Dax group had a memory like yours. I can remember part of another poem too: '*Au-dessus des étangs, au-dessus des vallées, des montagnes . . .*'"

Antoine did remember that second poem. It called on the mind to overcome all the heavy and unbearable sorrows, the *miasmes morbides*, and to go soaring up into serene, luminous spaces. He suddenly understood what his friend was trying to tell him: Pierre had misconstrued what he had been saying over the course of those days, as well as the dejection evident in everything he said or did. He thought he was intending to commit suicide. That was what he had meant by the gravest of sins. It was inconceivable to Pierre that the idea that had taken root in Antoine's mind was murder.

A battle raged inside Antoine in the months following his trip to Trensacq. He even considered going back on his plan – so that one day, in years to come, he might say to Pierre: "You're a saint, there's no doubt about it. You worked a miracle on me. You drove all my miasmas away, and I was able to abandon any idea of attacking my enemy Eliseo." Those miasmas, however, proved insidious, and in the end they persuaded him that Pierre's concerns might work to his advantage. He would not have a psychiatrist's report, but he would have the testimony of a friend: "He was deeply depressed, and cannot, in my view, be held fully responsible for his actions."

The sound of frenzied barking roused Antoine from his reverie. A little way off the path beside the canal there was an electricity substation, where the guard dogs were pacing back and forth and hurling themselves against the surrounding fence. Troy was primed, his whole body trembling.

"Settle down, Troy!"

He looked through the binoculars. There were three dogs, and one had now managed to escape though a gap in the fence. It was very small, a mongrel, and it had an annoying bark.

He took Troy by the collar, then thrust him forward.

"Attack!"

Troy leapt into action. Antoine raised the binoculars. The mongrel initially carried on yapping; then, suddenly falling quiet, it stood and stared; the next instant, it had dashed back in through the gap. It made it with seconds to spare. Troy then launched himself at the other two dogs. But they, too, were safe on the other side of the fence. It was mayhem: all four dogs barking at once. Had there been anyone living on that stretch of the Ugarte mountain they would have been at their windows looking out, but this place was utterly deserted. The only people who ever went there were the employees of the electricity company and passing mountaineers.

"Here boy!" he shouted. Troy immediately returned to his side.

It was nearly twenty past seven. The water in the stream appeared black; the leaves of the alders on the bank were dark green; the meadows, bushes and rocks on the hillside were blurred as though wrapped in a pall of smoke. The sky was one huge grey cloud with a few blue cracks in it.

He came to where the path and the stream flattened out. Here it was less steeply wooded, and signs of human life began to proliferate. First, he passed a fountain, then a footbridge, and further on a stand of ash trees. The trout cage was a hundred metres lower down, where the stream joined the canal. Eliseo must already be there with his dip net and his bag of bread.

Between the ash trees lay several piles of felled trunks big enough for someone to hide behind. Stealthily picking his way forward, Antoine took cover behind one that was less than fifty metres from the start of the canal. He felt cold. It was very damp here. On the ground, the moss grew more abundantly than the grass.

The dog was sniffing at a mound of slugs covered in a sticky orange substance. Around it, the moss was pearled with drops of water.

"Here, Troy!"

The dog came and stationed itself at his side, but without sitting down, ready for action.

When Antoine looked through the binoculars again, he saw the two mountaineers on the path, the blue anorak and the red one, and, across from them on the other side of the canal, Eliseo. Judging by the way Eliseo was pointing and gesturing, he was giving them directions. Antoine would have to wait a little.

"Lie down, Troy."

He, too, got down on the ground, kneeling near the mound of slugs. Van-Van came to mind. She used to get down on her knees in front of him. A sexual impulse surged through him.

Troy suddenly jumped up. He could hear something. Antoine got to his feet and raised the binoculars to his eyes. Crouching beside the canal, Eliseo was stirring the water with a stick. It was not the handle of a dip net, but something thicker.

Troy began to growl. He had worked out where Eliseo was now. The tension was causing his muscles to spasm and twitch.

"Here!" Antoine hissed. The dog came over to him.

He turned the focusing knob on the binoculars to try and get a better view of the canal side, but his fingers did not do as he wanted and he succeeded only in blurring the image. When he tried again, he just made matters worse: the image became completely unclear and all he could see was a greenish-black smudge. Taking a deep breath, he turned the knob one millimetre at a time. Finally, he located the canal wall. The water there was hidden from sight, but not so higher up in the stream, where it picked up the day's final rays of sunlight and looked as though it was full of tiny sparkling mirrors.

He thought at first that the object Eliseo was holding was a paddle. That was how he wielded it, like a paddle. But no, rather than a paddle for rowing with, it was a bread paddle, the kind they used in the bakery to take the bread out of the ovens. He saw him lay it down on the canal wall.

He grabbed Troy by the collar, then urged him on.

"*Attack!*"

Troy headed off in Eliseo's direction with such speed that by the time Antoine had located the scene in his binoculars, it was completely different, but not as he had expected it to be. The image he was presented with was not that of a person on the ground trying to defend himself, but that of Troy barking at the side of the canal and Eliseo in the water, inside the fish cage, splashing water up at the dog.

He lowered the binoculars. Troy would not dive in after his prey. He had been trained not to do that. A dog could not fight in water.

Again Antoine raised his binoculars. In exasperation, Troy was running back and forth between the ash trees, biting anything that happened to get in his way, while Eliseo went on splashing water at him. However, it was not only water he was scooping out of the canal; a number of silvery shapes glittered in the half-light. They were trout, and the sight of them flailing around on the ground drove Troy into a frenzy. He would not stop until he had gutted the lot of them.

When Antoine managed to locate the cage again through his binoculars, Eliseo was not there. He had climbed over the wire barrier and into the canal. Antoine imagined the following scene: Eliseo now out of the water, fleeing along the path in the direction of the bakery, and Troy fording the river at its shallowest part before chasing him down from behind.

Once more, the binoculars failed to show him what he had hoped to see: Eliseo had waded over to the canal wall, but rather than being on the side of the path, trying to escape, he was on the side closest to Antoine, where the ash trees were. He was reaching for the bread paddle. Troy was still busy tearing into the trout.

244

Antoine left the shelter of the pile of tree trunks and, moving from tree to tree, approached the canal. He was finding it hard to breathe.

Now he could see what was happening without recourse to the binoculars. Eliseo was letting the current carry him along, generating extra momentum by pushing off from the wall every now and then, drifting a couple of metres downstream each time. He was doing something with the bread paddle. Using the binoculars, Antoine could see what that was: holding it back to front, Eliseo kept giving Troy little taps on the snout with the end of the handle.

"Here, boy!" Antoine shouted.

Troy did not obey. Eliseo's paddle was driving him crazy; he was completely at the man's mercy. When Eliseo drifted a little way downstream, the dog followed him on the bank, and when he stopped, the dog did exactly the same.

"Here, boy!"

Utterly beside himself, Troy turned and scampered away from the canal into the forest.

"Here, boy!"

This time Troy obeyed. He came over to Antoine and crouched on the ground. He had blood all around his mouth. Now Antoine grasped what Eliseo had been doing: he had eventually succeeded in making Troy bite down on the end of the paddle handle, and at that moment had rammed it down Troy's throat.

"Let's get out of here, Troy. We've lost again."

The dog coughed, bringing up blood, then got up and started padding unsteadily away.

Antoine searched for Eliseo with the binoculars. He was now swimming down the canal. When he reached the stone steps, he climbed out onto the path. The mountaineers hurried over to him. Eliseo pointed back along the canal to where Antoine was. Then, as though something blocking his ears had suddenly been removed, Antoine began to hear noises: the muffled conversation between the mountaineers and Eliseo, a shout from someone in the bakery, the barking of dogs coming from the electricity substation.

Troy was lapping water from the river. He must have a few broken teeth and some damage to the roof of his mouth, but he could still use his tongue. A dog with an injured tongue would avoid water.

"We're going to Trensacq tonight. We'll get you better there."

Antoine set off uphill. He would go around the bakery and be back at Villa Chantal before nightfall. Troy followed after him.

Luis' accident

2012

It happened on the second Sunday of August 2012, at around six in the evening, just a few metres from a beach on the Basque coast. As the traffic lights were about to change from amber to red, the driver of the van accelerated and knocked down a young woman on a pedestrian crossing ten metres further on. In his panic, the driver swerved, and the van skidded over onto the opposite pavement. A moment later, it crashed into a horse chestnut tree. A handful of leaves fell to the ground.

The driver managed to extricate himself from beneath the surfboard that had fallen on top of him, and, after dragging himself out of the van, he crawled another couple of metres, then stopped, lay down on his side and looked around. There was a raffia bag lying in the middle of the pedestrian crossing, and next to it a turquoise towel. A little further on, the young woman lay motionless. She was dressed for the beach in a thin, blue-and-white-striped dress. Five metres away, beyond the pedestrian crossing, he could see a single flip-flop and, beside it, a black purse gleaming in the sunlight.

He felt his own body, limb by limb, much as a doctor would. He did not appear to be bleeding from his head, although it felt numb at the back, rather as if his scalp had been anaesthetised. He was aware of a stinging sensation on the skin of his legs, especially on his knees, which were badly grazed, but what hurt most was his right side. He probably had a wound there, and that must be where the drops of blood staining his white trainers were coming from. Since he was wearing a maroon polo shirt, though, he could not be sure.

*

The driver, Luis, began to hear noises. It was the radio in his van, which was still working: "And now the boy band, One Direction, and the song you'll be hearing on all our beaches this summer! 'What Makes You Beautiful'."

The presenter repeated that last word – beautiful-beautiful-beautiful-beautiful . . . – gradually fading away like an echo, just as the first few notes of the song were filling the air.

"One Direction!"

The presenter's final shout merged with another voice screaming:

"The girl! The girl!"

Luis continued listening to the words of the song, "You're insecure, don't know what for . . ." Why did Susana like him? They had been together for three months, yes, it was three months exactly since they first went to bed together. When in bed, Susana always made the same joke: "I'm not the nice girl, I'm the naughty one." Susana loved music aimed at an audience twenty years younger than her, and that summer she was crazy about One Direction, although why he had no idea. "You're insecure . . ." Insecure? Susana wasn't anything of the kind.

A feeling that all was not well made him open his eyes, and he reached out to pick up the phone. However, he was not sitting on his sofa at home, he was in the back seat of an unfamiliar car. He did not know the driver either.

"Where's my surfboard? Where are we going?"

The driver glanced over his shoulder at him. He had a large, fleshy face, tiny eyes, and a boxer's flattened nose. He said gruffly:

"Where do you think we're going? To the hospital, of course. The emergency services are overwhelmed at the moment, and so they called me. You need to get with it, mate!"

They left the B-road and joined the motorway. When they passed a Coca-Cola factory, Luis again thought of Susana. Susana liked Coca-Cola. On really hot days, she would drink three or four cans of the stuff.

"You know what you've just done, don't you?"

"Yes, I've had an accident," Luis said.

"You've killed a girl, that's what you've done!"

"And who are you?"

"Me? I'm the owner of this taxi!"

He was speaking very loudly, as if his passenger were travelling in another car, not in the back seat.

They left the motorway and set off along a road flanked by trees, then up a slight incline, where the first thing they saw was a church with a steeple and, five hundred metres further on, a great concrete pile, the hospital.

There was a stain on Luis' white shorts, a kind of red worm creeping down from beneath his waistband. He touched his shirt and his fingertips felt wet. He was bleeding from somewhere on his right side.

The taxi driver drove on to the entrance to A&E and stopped outside. Before switching off the engine and getting out, he kindly turned on the radio.

"I'll go and find a hospital orderly. I'll be right back."

The radio was tuned to a different station. The presenter announced the next song in an almost confiding voice: "Adele and 'Skyfall'."

Luis allowed himself to be swept along by the melody, and the sharp pain in his side seemed to ease slightly; however, when he realised what the singer was saying: "this is the end, hold your breath and count to ten", he felt afraid and again touched the wound in his side. Yes, he was definitely bleeding. He recalled another of Susana's favourite lyrics from a song: "I'm devoured by my all-devouring fear of being devoured". She found these lyrics hilarious. Just then, though, he went cold with fear. Or perhaps it was the other way round: perhaps the cold he could feel in his body was infecting his thoughts.

The taxi driver reappeared at the entrance to the A&E department. He came over to the car and opened the back door.

"I was wrong. The girl's still alive," he said.

The driver's flattened nose blurred his pronunciation. What Luis heard was: "*Girlz till alibe.*" Luis almost burst out laughing, but when he realised the implications of this news, he started crying instead. "God must have been watching over her!" he said. This was a favourite expression of his mother's, and one that he would never have used in Susana's presence, but it was still there in some corner of his memory. He looked at the taxi driver, who bore a marked resemblance to his mother. If you straightened his nose and smoothed his cheeks, the man could be his mother's brother, or she could be his sister.

His thoughts were getting tangled up.

"Are you alright?" asked another man, sticking his head inside the car.

He wore the pale grey uniform of a hospital orderly and was very solidly built. Luis reckoned he was nearly two metres tall and must have weighed around one hundred and five kilos. Were height and weight related? This suddenly seemed a matter of great importance to Luis.

"Are you alright?" the orderly asked again. "Can you move?"

He had a pleasant voice, similar to Adele's, only slightly deeper. Luis nodded and began to get out of the car. However, the pain in his side made him catch his breath.

"Are you sure you're OK to move?"

"Yes, I think so, very slowly."

The orderly put his left arm around Luis' shoulder and his right arm about his waist. Luis winced. The orderly slackened his grip.

"How's that? Where does it hurt?"

"The back of my head's a bit sore and my side's painful too, but let's carry on with Operation Exit."

"Lend me a hand, will you?" the orderly said to the taxi driver.

Together they laid him on a stretcher. The taxi driver had very strong arms and shoulders.

"You could be a boxer," Luis said. "You look like a combination of my mother and that Panamanian boxer Roberto Durán, aka Hands of Stone."

252

The taxi driver smiled and even laughed. He seemed in a better mood now.

Luis went on:

"Did you see the fight between Roberto Durán and Sugar Ray Leonard? The best fight ever, which is not to take anything away from Ali versus Foreman, of course, because that was amazing too."

The taxi driver smiled even more broadly and nodded his agreement. In different circumstances, he would have happily stayed there chatting.

"At least you didn't get blood on the back seat," he said. "*A leas you din get blud on the ba sea.*"

He went over to the driver's side of the car and turned off the radio, interrupting a jazz number.

"Hope it all goes well!" he said. "*Ohpit aw goes well.*"

The orderly set off, pushing the stretcher through the reception area and along a corridor to a curtained bay.

"What's the girl's name, do you know?" Luis asked.

The orderly helped him off the stretcher and onto the bed, then drew the plastic curtain. No, he didn't know.

"I wasn't the one who brought her in, but I'll find out and tell you later. She's in the operating theatre right now."

A nurse appeared, a young woman. She had curly blonde hair. The blondeness was artificial, but the curls seemed natural. She was rather like Susana, especially in the frank, almost impudent way she looked at him. Without so much as a hello, she asked, "So where does it hurt?"

When he was little, his mother used to ask him the same question whenever he was ill: where does it hurt? In a very different tone of voice, though. The nurse was clearly not the most sensitive of creatures. Susana was the same in a way – no, not so much insensitive, just rather thoughtless. A girl straight out of a Coca-Cola advert, but with an experience of life not evident in the Coca-Cola boys and girls, who all appeared to be permanently marooned in childhood. But what could you expect? They were

253

very young, twenty at the most. Susana, on the other hand, would turn forty-two at the end of August.

"Anyone at home?" said the nurse. She held out one hand and snapped her fingers. "Are you going to answer me? Where does it hurt?"

"Here, and a bit here," he responded, placing his hand first on his right side and then on the back of his head.

The nurse then lifted up his shirt from his waist to his neck and started putting pressure on certain bones and organs.

"What about here? Does it hurt you here?"

He gave very brief answers: "a bit", "a bit more", "quite a lot", "no, not there".

"The doctor may take a while to see you. We're chock-a-block today."

"I'll wait."

When the nurse left, the image of the girl's raffia beach bag came into his head, and he could see the turquoise towel as clearly as if it was there before him now. Then the purse, which was so black that, at the time of the accident, he had thought it was a pool of wet tar, but that was impossible, because it was shiny, and tar was only shiny when very hot. He wondered if it was possible to varnish plastics, because the purse looked as if it had been varnished. As a PE teacher, he had no idea about such things, but when he went back to school, he would consult someone in the chemistry department.

The nurse had returned. She brought him a pill.

"You have to take it without water. Just swallow it."

"Have they finished operating on the girl?"

The nurse waited until he had swallowed the pill before answering.

"You mean the girl who was run over this afternoon? Definitely not. A colleague told me it was going to be a long job."

Not a hint of a smile, and that somewhat austere expression only emphasised her resemblance to Susana, although Susana rarely looked stern. Usually, she seemed very cheerful and would

254

laugh at the slightest thing, especially when she had been smoking weed.

The orderly returned then and stood talking to the nurse about a patient who had just been moved to another bay. Then he spoke to Luis.

"The girl's name is Susana."

How extraordinary, Luis thought, and, for a few seconds, he was lost for words. His girlfriend and the girl he had run over had the same name. How was he going to tell them apart? He thought for a moment, then decided that he would call his girl-friend Susana No. 1 and the girl in the accident Susana No. 2.

"That's all I know, but names are important," said the orderly. "It's always good to be able to put a name to someone. Susana."

"Susana No. 2, if you don't mind," Luis said, turning to the nurse, but she had already left, and so he was unable to judge just how closely she resembled Susana No. 1. If he still thought there was a strong likeness, he would call her Susana No. 3.

The orderly was watching him. He really was a very big man. He seemed even taller and burlier than when he had helped him out of the taxi. How tall would he be? Two metres ten? And how much would he weigh? A hundred and twenty kilos?

"The doctor should have been here sooner, but we're really up against it today. It's always the way in August: the hordes arrive, and then you get hordes of accidents. People love the surf here. So, it seems, do you."

The orderly was reading a piece of paper, doubtless Luis' medical notes.

"You can't take the waves away from a surfer," Luis said. "Where would a surfer be without the waves? Like a gunman without a gun. Or something."

"But who would even think of travelling with their surfboard in the back of the van without tying it down first?" the orderly asked out loud, still reading the information on the sheet of paper. "Not a good idea."

There was no getting away from it, his voice sounded just

like Adele's, and he would probably be able to sing like her, or if not Adele, then like Demis Roussos given his bulk. And given his height and weight, he could easily have made a career as a basketball player. Pau Gasol was a bit taller, two metres fourteen, and leaner, not that this meant much. Yes, the orderly had the ideal physique for a basketball champion.

He would have liked to tell the orderly what he was thinking but could not be bothered. Instead, he asked:

"What's your name? We haven't been introduced."

The orderly showed him the gilt bracelet round his wrist and read out his name, syllable by syllable, as if reading to a child:

"Car-me-lo. And you're Luis, right? It says so in your notes."

"That's what they called me when I was a child, now most people call me Lucky. And since I've been going out with Susana No. 1, I'm Tuco as well. Susana No. 1 says I'm nothing like Lucky Luke, but very like Tuco. You know Tuco, don't you, one of the characters out of *The Good, the Bad and the Ugly*. The Ugly to be precise."

The words came tumbling out of his mouth, as they did when he had been smoking weed. He tried to laugh but could not open his mouth wide enough.

"My ex used to call me Luisillo, which drove me mad. That's why I got divorced."

"I see," said the orderly.

The nurse came into the bay, this time accompanied by a doctor who was of a very similar build to Usain Bolt. Identical really, except that he was lighter-skinned and shorter. Perhaps he was an athlete as well as a doctor, although clearly not a 100-metres man. You needed weight to be able to run short distances at top speeds, weight and tremendous strength. Perhaps he would be better suited to middle distances, the 1,500 or the 5,000 metres.

"Did you see the 100-metres final last week?" Luis asked. "Usain Bolt gold, Yohan Blake silver. Both of them Jamaicans. And in third place, the American, Justin Gatlin."

"Yes, I've been following the Olympics too, but I can't remember the names the way you can. Or only Usain Bolt's," said the doctor. He was holding a small torch, which he shone first in one of Luis' eyes, then in the other.

The nurse gave a weary sigh:

"Even I know Usain Bolt's name. He's everywhere. No-one talks about anyone else."

"That's no reason to get annoyed," Luis said.

He would like to have explained that, as a PE teacher, knowing about sport was part of his job, which is why he followed not only the 100 metres and other big events, but sports that no-one was much interested in, like volleyball or, more specifically, beach volleyball. At the London Olympics, Germany had won gold in that event, which, when you thought about it, was a complete anomaly, or perhaps a paradox, because who could have imagined that the team from a country with such desolate beaches could ever beat Brazil?

However, he was finding it hard to put all these ideas into any sort of order, and so he summed them up in just two words:

"Brazil, silver."

The doctor had turned off his torch now and put it away in one of the pockets in his white coat. But he still would not leave him in peace: move your arm this way, now that way, now raise it up, now touch the tip of your nose with your index finger, now bend your knees. When he had finished this litany of instructions, he started examining Luis' head. Then he vanished, followed by the nurse, and the orderly reappeared.

"We're going downstairs, Lucky," he said, releasing the brake on the bed.

The bed slid forwards, but also rocked up and down like a longboat at the mercy of the waves.

"Tuco, not Lucky. Best call me Tuco. That's what Susana No. 1 would want."

"Fine by me," said the orderly, still pushing the bed. "But I don't know what I would think if my girlfriend landed me with the same name as the Ugly in the film. I'd rather be the Bad. He's better-looking."

"Yes, you're right. Lee Van Cleef is definitely better-looking."

They had reached the doors of the lift, and the orderly waited for them to open. At that moment, he looked just like Demis Roussos, although he still had Adele's voice.

"And what about the Good, Demis?" he asked. "Now Clint Eastwood really is good-looking. And the way he handles a gun . . ."

The orderly whistled the theme tune from *The Good, the Bad and the Ugly*: *Fufifufifuuu-waahwaahwaah, fufifufifuuu-waah-waahwaah.*

"You do that better than the guy in the film, Demis!" cried Luis and was about to emphasise his words by raising one fore-finger, except that he could not get his arm out from beneath the sheet.

"My father was a shepherd. He taught me to whistle."

The orderly pushed the bed into the lift, which jolted into action, traca-traca, traca-traca, as if they were inside the carriage of an old-fashioned train. Luis waited a moment before going on.

"The Good reminds me of my father. Those Monterrey cigars."

He meant to explain that it was his father, not the Good, who used to smoke Monterrey cigars, at least as far as he knew. The cigars the Good smoked seemed shorter to him, given that they only stuck out about two or three centimetres from between his teeth, but just then he was in no state to enter into such details.

"As for me, I only ever smoke dope, just once a week, mind," he went on. "Never more than that. A PE teacher has to take good care of himself. Otherwise, even a game of volleyball with the students could finish you off."

A memory surfaced in his mind.

"A little while ago, I went to get a few things from the house I grew up in, along with Martín, he's my twin brother. Because I have a twin brother, you see. Always have had."

He paused for a moment. That "always have had" hardly seemed necessary. Twins did not become brothers when they were five years old. They were brothers from birth.

"You're not going to believe this," he went on. "We took a book off one of the shelves and it still smelled of Monterrey cigars. And no-one's lived there in more than ten years. Imagine that!"

The lift doors slid open, and the orderly pushed the bed out into a corridor.

"What was the title of the book?"

"*The Gunman Who Should Have Died*. Set in the Wild West. My father really enjoyed novels about hired guns. I do too actually. My twin brother, on the other hand, doesn't approve of them at all. He's always been very political, you see, and says that novels like that gloss over the massacres perpetrated against the Indians by the Whites. I'm sure he's right, but that doesn't stop me reading them. I watch Westerns too."

"They're not all as good as *The Good, the Bad and the Ugly* though," said the orderly. "I loved that film."

The orderly again whistled the theme tune: *Fufifufifuuu-waahwaahwaah, fufifufifuuu-waahwaahwaah* ... Luis tried to imitate him but could not manage to purse his lips.

Coming towards him he saw a rather lean figure, who reminded him of the Bad One. He was carrying a long metal object. Luis looked harder. Yes, there could be no doubt: it was the barrel of a Colt revolver.

"Come any closer and I'll shoot you. Don't you know who I am?"

"Who are you?" asked the orderly.

Luis heard the voice but could not see the orderly's face.

"Tuco!" he said

Luis placed one hand on his hip, but his gun was not there. And it hurt to touch that side of his body.

The lean man came closer.

"Go on, shoot," Luis said. "Finish me off if you can. If you don't, I won't give up until I've put a bullet through your head. And I'll find you even if you hide away in the farthest-flung corner of the world."

"It's all right, you're at the barber's," said the invisible orderly, making him lie back down again. "This guy's just trying to cut your hair, and that's not a gun in his hand, it's an electric razor."

"You can't fool me," said Luis. "A gunman doesn't just become a barber overnight, not even once he's been in prison. Prison doesn't change anyone. It certainly didn't change my brother Martín. He came out with exactly the same ideas as when he went in."

"Well, this one came out transformed into a real barber. Now keep your head still and let him do his work," said the voice of the orderly.

"I'll have the full service then. Haircut and shave. I could do with a bath too. The Good left me to die in the desert, and I've spent days walking under a blazing sun. I've even got sand in my underpants."

"He wouldn't have done that if you hadn't played a nasty trick on him first," said the orderly's voice.

"Careful what you say," Luis said.

A muffled sound coming from outside made him glance over at the window. He saw horses and soldiers. A column from the Confederate Army was passing down the main street of the village with their cannon and their rifles, beating a retreat after having lost Mississippi to the Yankees. There were thousands of them, thousands of soldiers in filthy uniforms and boots caked with desert sand, their grey-and-yellow caps stained with sweat. They were so pretty those caps! He had found one in his parents' house; it had belonged to Elías, a childhood friend who now lived in the United States. How would Elías be faring among the Confederates and the Yankees? Would he have lost the power of speech again? If he had, the best cure would be to go to the upper reaches of the canal in Ugarte and wait for a wild boar to appear. He should tell Elías that, but he did not have his address, he only knew that he taught at the university and lived in Austin, Texas. But where, in which street exactly? His brother would probably know, because the two of them had stayed in touch. But what was the point of all these questions? They just hung there in the air and left him feeling slightly dizzy.

260

The muffled sound made by the horses and soldiers of the Confederate Army suddenly stopped and was replaced by that of people talking. He found himself surrounded by three men, three masked men. One of them shone a bright light in his eyes. Fugitives from Carson City?

A colonel from the Unionist Army started shouting at the masked men. Luis was lying on a camp bed, apparently unable to move.

"Those of us who fight for President Lincoln respect the enemy! We don't torture them! Your behaviour is entirely unacceptable and a dishonourable stain on the blue of our uniform. I will write to General Grant and ask him to take action!"

When he turned to look at the fugitives, he saw that their leader was Lee Van Cleef, the Bad. He wore his usual sneering smile.

"Oh, you can laugh at me now because I have gangrene in one leg and can't fight, but General Grant will make sure you get your just deserts. Torturers!"

Beside Lee Van Cleef stood a very burly fellow who, like the orderly, resembled Demis Roussos. He turned to Luis and stuck something in his arm. It really hurt.

"You'd better tell us the names of your friends. We know who you are. We know everything."

"If you know everything, then why keep me lying on this table? Why make me suffer?"

It was odd. The conversation was a replica of one he had once had in a police cell. The torturer then had also kept his face covered, not with a scarf like those fugitives from Carson City, but with a black balaclava.

"You'd better tell us the names of your friends, Carlitos," the man had said. "Or do you prefer to be called Marty? That's your name, isn't it? All right, not that either. Your real name is Martín."

As soon as Luis heard that name, the penny dropped. His torturer thought he was his twin brother. Being Martín's twin brother was a real drag. It always had been, ever since they were small. And this was the second time the police had arrested him and interrogated him, thinking he was Martín. The first time was during the strikes in Ugarte, when Martín had destroyed the laboratory, although that had not really affected Luis very much; this time, though, he had wound up in a police cell. Feeling angry, furious in fact, he was about to blurt out the truth: "Look, you've made a mistake, the person you're looking for is my brother." But he was suddenly filled with an overwhelming feeling of love for Martín, as if a bag of water had burst, letting a warm liquid spread throughout his body. They had their problems, their disagreements, and had often fallen out, but the bond with the man who had always been his very serious-minded twin brother could not be broken. And that "always" was absolutely spot on in their case, because only twins are siblings from the very first moment of their existence.

Under the influence of that wave of love, he decided to keep his secret. The longer he held out in the cell without giving any information, the easier it would be for Martín to hide from the police. He looked at his torturer:

"Carlitos is a dreadful name. In fact, diminutives in general give me a headache. Carlitos, Paquito, Josecho, Luisillo . . ."

He had to resist the desire to say more about diminutives, because he knew he would end up talking about his wife. Many of their domestic disputes had been provoked by her calling him "Luisillo". But if he started telling them about his life, the police would soon realise that he was not Martín.

There were now two torturers. Luis was lying on a table to which he was attached by straps around his ankles, so that while the lower half of his body was supported, his head and trunk were left hanging. By making a huge effort, he managed to keep himself horizontal or, at least, to allow his head to fall back slowly.

"He's in good shape," said the second torturer to the first one, going over to the table. He was wearing a balaclava too, but his was green. Emerald green.

Luis again felt tempted to tell the truth. That he went to the gym, surfed and played volleyball, which was why he was in such good shape. That he could do any number of press-ups and bench-presses.

"The lad's lucky," said the man in the black balaclava to the man in the emerald-green balaclava. It was as if they were standing at a bar chatting. "The ones who aren't in good shape can't hold themselves up and so they fall backwards and often bang their head really hard."

"It's even worse when the spine breaks, I wouldn't wish that on anyone," said the man in the emerald-green balaclava.

"Yeah, that's happened a couple of times," said his colleague. "They fall back and you hear a crack. I've got a recording of it. After that, it's straight to a wheelchair."

Luis wondered how long he had been there but could not work it out. He looked round at the ceiling and the walls for some sign of daylight, but in vain. He appeared to be in the basement of a police station. He could feel his head filling with blood and was finding it harder and harder to remain horizontal.

"Give us three names, Carlitos, and we'll take a coffee break," said Mr Emerald Green.

"Three isn't enough. Make it five," said Mr Black.

"Look, don't call me Carlitos. I don't like diminutives," Luis said. His head was almost touching the floor now, and it was hard to speak.

Mr Emerald Green slapped him on the stomach. His hand was so cold that it burned Luis's skin.

"All right, I'll call you Marty instead. Anyway, give us some names and then we can have a cup of coffee."

"Five names," insisted Mr Black.

"Four," said Mr Emerald Green.

"OK, four. I'm beginning to get bored."

Mr Black hit him in the stomach too, but this time with his fist and hard. Luis felt the pain, although not in his belly, in his side. Someone was saying into his ear:

"*A leas you din get blud on the ba sea.*"

He turned and saw the taxi driver's face. He really did look incredibly like Roberto Durán, and like Luis' mother too, although his mother was, of course, much prettier.

"What?" he asked.

"*A leas you din get blud on the ba sea*," the man said again, and pointed to the upholstery on the back seat. No red stains.

Then the orderly appeared with a stretcher and helped him to lie down on it, having first asked the taxi driver for a helping hand.

"*Girlz till alibe*," said the taxi driver from behind.

"So am I," Luis said, observing the various things scattered on the ground.

There was a raffia bag in the middle of the pedestrian crossing, and beside it a turquoise towel. A little further off, the young woman lay motionless. She was dressed for the beach, in a thin blue-and-white-striped dress. About five metres beyond the crossing was a flip-flop and a black purse that gleamed in the sun.

"What happened?" he tried to say, but his mouth was hanging open and he could not close it. It hurt. So did his neck. And his back. And his waist.

The flip-flop had now been replaced by a leather boot like the sort worn by cowboys in the Wild West, but without a spur. The leather boot suddenly moved, and then the other one on the other foot moved too. After that, another two shoes appeared, black and round-toed, and they began to move too.

"I have a certain sympathy for Maoists, and I'd really rather not hurt you, but I'm getting a little tired and I'd like to go home with some names in my pocket," said the man with the black, round-toed shoes.

Luis wanted to see the man's face and, by tensing his neck, he managed to raise his head. A waste of effort. The man was, of course, wearing a black balaclava.

"Yes, we have real sympathy for Maoists, it's just that we don't like what some of them have been writing lately. All that talk about bombs and other equally dangerous stuff. We'd like to discuss that with you, Marty."

Luis looked at him. It was Mr Emerald Green. He wore the

bottoms of his jeans tucked into his cowboy boots and a belt with a heavy metal buckle; instead of a shirt, he was wearing a sleeveless black vest, the kind Neil Young used to wear; and his face was covered by that emerald-green balaclava.

"We like Chinese things, but only in moderation. Certainly not bombs," said Mr Black.

The pain was not localised now, no longer limited to certain parts of his body. It surrounded him like an aura. Mr Black kept saying that he was fed up and wanted to go home, which implied that Luis must have been there, at the very least, for five or six hours: four hours before they took him to the basement, one hour to prepare the interrogation in theory, another hour to put it into practice. His wife would be counting the hours. She had her faults, the worst being that mania of hers for addressing him with diminutives like Luisillo, but she was a maths teacher and, as such, had impeccable logic. She knew his brother Martín well, had put up with his speeches about the revolution at family celebrations, Mao Tse-tung this and Mao Tse-tung that, and so, using her impeccable logic, two plus two equals four, she would immediately know what was going on – the police had mistaken him for Martín – and dismiss nonsensical thoughts about him leaving her because she kept calling him Luisillo or because he had found true love with a female basketball player who went to the same gym. His wife knew he loved her, so her logical mind stood her in good stead there, which is why she would immediately take action and phone Martín, saying: "You'd better hide. I think I'm right in saying that the police are looking for you. Luisillo didn't come home for our usual pre-supper walk." The problem was that he could not remember what time in the evening he had been picked up, which meant that he had no way of knowing whether night had now fallen.

He felt another rush of love for his brother. He decided to hang on in there.

"There's an idea of Mao Tse-tung's that I really like," he said. "But if you want me to tell you, you'll have to let me sit up. It's really difficult talking in this position."

Mr Emerald Green grabbed his right arm, Mr Black his left, and between them they pulled Luis upright. The table moved, traca-traca, traca-traca, just like the carriage on an old-fashioned train. He took three deep breaths, as he used to do at the gym before doing his bench exercises.

"Do you know how Mao Tse-tung set about climbing Everest? Well, not him personally, but China. Instead of sending a group of five or six mountaineers, he sent three hundred, the longest rope-climb ever seen on Everest. And they made it to the top easily. I'm not sure, of course, how many of them actually reached the summit, but possibly more than a hundred. Mao Tse-tung wanted to show the world that working collectively is more likely to lead to success than working individually."

Half of his body was once again hanging off the table, his head very close to the floor. Out of the corner of his eye he saw the leather cowboy boot, then he felt a kick close to his ear.

His body rose at least three metres up to the ceiling, and from there he could observe the two men, one on either side of the table. He noticed Mr Emerald Green's boots. He had seen them before somewhere. Of course! They were just like Lee Van Cleef's boots. The two men hurriedly left the basement.

Gradually, like an astronaut in zero gravity, his body began to descend. There were moments when his descent slowed and he remained suspended in mid-air, but finally, he landed back on the table as lightly as a feather. He was suddenly very sleepy.

When he closed his eyes, he felt as if he were advancing along a tunnel in a mine, probably the mine in Ugarte, where Antoine had taken him one day, but this time he was alone and terrified, without a guide. A moment later, having emerged from the tunnel, he found himself in a room, sitting on a white plastic chair. Before him was a table, also white, also plastic. On it stood a coffee pot, two sky-blue china cups, some coffee spoons, a bowl full of sugar lumps, and a small intensely red book. Opposite him sat a thin man in his fifties; he had blue eyes, a receding hairline and a mane of fair hair; he was wearing a white shirt and a flowered waistcoat. He looked exactly like the guitarist in the Mamas & the Papas. He had no wristwatch on, and again there were no windows in the room, so Luis still had no way of knowing how long he had been in the basement.

"Don't worry. It's over now. What did they do to you? The operating table?" asked the man while he poured him some coffee. He spoke very softly. "Milk? A little sugar?"

Luis had a record by the Mamas & the Papas at home and tried to visualise the cover, where the name of the guitarist appeared, but he felt a great pressure on his forehead, as if his head were being squeezed by one of those clamps cabinetmakers use to hold pieces of wood together, and it was hard to get his memory moving.

"The operating table is bad, but waterboarding's worse. Did they waterboard you as well?" the man asked, then poured himself some coffee.

It was odd. Luis could not smell the coffee.

The man sighed.

"It's very cruel what they did to you. I don't agree with it myself. To be honest, I think the police should use different methods."

He took out a pack of Winston cigarettes from one of his waistcoat pockets, removed a lighter from another pocket, and lit a cigarette.

"The American kind," he said. "I got hooked on them when I lived in California and haven't been able to smoke the Spanish sort since."

At last, the name of the Mamas & the Papas' guitarist came into Luis' head: John Phillips, Papa John. Luis had spent time in California too, teaching surfing in San Diego, where he had been lucky enough to attend a concert by Papa John after the group broke up, and a Beach Boys concert too. However, he kept these facts to himself. The police would know that Martín had never been to California, and at that moment, he was Martín, not Lucky or Tuco.

The cigarette smoke drifted over the table into his face. Even then he could not smell the tobacco. Why? He would have liked to ponder this fact, but the Papa John lookalike kept prattling on, preventing Luis from thinking. The man did not stop talking. His words were like small black dots that mingled with the smoke, and because of all those words, the walls and ceiling seemed to be speckled with soot. Papa John handed him a cup.

"Drink your coffee before it gets cold."

The coffee left a medicinal taste in his mouth. A second sip made him choke and cough.

Papa John, entirely indifferent to all this, continued his endless logorrhoea. The words and smoke merged with his lips.

"Do you know why I went to California?" Papa John asked, with just the suggestion of a smile. "To get laid. The hippie years were just fantastic. You got to fuck one or even two women every night. I really liked the hippie mantra: Make love not war. I still do. That's how it should be. Life is short, and there's no point spending it waging war."

I knew that era better than you did, but I'm not going to say anything, Luis thought.

Papa John picked up the small red book from the table and held it out to him. There were Chinese characters on the red cover.

"Mao's *Little Red Book*. A girl I met in San Francisco gave it to me. She was a great admirer of Mao Tse-tung. Like you."

Luis ran his hand over the smooth cover. Not a trace of dust.

"What do you think of Mao's four theses, Marty? I don't find them that interesting to be honest. He gives them high-sounding titles like 'On practice' and 'On contradiction' to explain ideas that seem to have been taken from fables. I know what you're going to say: Mao ruled over six hundred million Chinese people, most of them illiterate, so it's perfectly understandable that he chose to write like that. Fine, I agree. And he does make some good points. The one about the broom, for example. It must be in here somewhere."

He took the book from Luis' hands and opened it. It seemed

to Luis that the Chinese characters on the pages were scurrying about like ants.

"I can't remember his exact words," Papa John went on, "but basically what Mao's saying is that we must destroy all reactionary forces. That if we don't, they'll simply never go away. Like dust. If the broom doesn't sweep away the dust, it won't just vanish of its own accord."

He stubbed out his cigarette in his coffee cup, and pointing behind him with his thumb, said:

"The people in the other room didn't burn you, did they? They just gave you the operating table treatment?"

Luis felt as if he were rising into the air, but not as he had minutes before, like an astronaut in zero gravity, but as if he were levitating, him and the chair, remaining suspended a metre and a half above the floor. From that height, he could see that Papa John was balder than he had first thought. His hair was fairly thick at the back, but very thin on top. He tried to establish whether the man was wearing Lee Van Cleef-style cowboy boots, because it was just possible that Papa John and Mr Emerald Green were one and the same person; however, his feet were hidden underneath the white plastic table.

Papa John was brandishing a typed sheet of paper. A pamphlet.

"Marty, I'm going to keep it short and to the point. I'm tired and I want to go home and watch the match. I'm not a revolutionary like you."

Papa John was looking straight ahead, not up, oblivious to the fact that Luis was a metre and a half above him. The man's face, chin slightly twisted to the left, like someone feeling for a tooth with his tongue, was halfway between a smile and a grimace.

Still looking straight ahead, he reached out both hands. In one he held *The Little Red Book*, and in the other, the pamphlet.

"You copied a phrase from here," he said. He picked up first *The Little Red Book* and then the pamphlet, before reading out: "'All Communists must understand this truth, power grows out of the barrel of a gun.' That's nonsense, Marty. I can't speak for

China, but here in Spain? I read somewhere that the Chinese Communist Party has ten million militants. How many of you are there in the Basque Country? Perhaps a hundred young people in the whole area? Up until now, most of you were idealistic, generous types. We know that. We know, for example, that you gave part of the money you inherited from your mother to a group of strikers. But what's changed? Are you going to start planting bombs, like the terrorists?"

This information was new to Luis. He had no idea that his brother had donated part of his inheritance to a strike fund. Not that it surprised him. Martín's share of the inheritance had been a lot bigger than his! He very nearly made some resentful comment but stopped himself in time. Despite all the family tensions, he loved Martín. They had been brothers from minute zero.

Papa John again waved the pamphlet at him. Now Luis felt as if his chair was moving like a miniature helicopter. After a few seconds, he rose into the air and headed off into one corner of the room.

"I want to help you, Marty," Papa John said, this time looking up at him in his corner. "If you start planting bombs, you could get thirty years in prison, and I wouldn't wish that on anyone. Just give me a couple of names, Marty, and we can both go and watch the Italy-Germany match. I've heard it's being screened live."

"Italy will win the World Cup final," Luis announced from his place high up in the room. "There isn't a team today that can beat the *squadra azzurra*. Germany's on top form physically, but they're going to need more than just muscle."

While he was speaking, a fact elbowed its way into the hubbub of his thoughts: the final was supposed to be played at eight o'clock on Sunday evening at the Santiago Bernabéu stadium. Given Papa John's impatience to go and watch the game, it seemed logical to think that he had been in the hands of the police for at least twenty-four hours. He was pretty sure he had been detained before the match for third and fourth place between Poland and France. Therefore, his wife would have had enough time to warn his brother, who would immediately have gone into hiding.

Papa John got clumsily to his feet, accidentally kicking one leg of the plastic table and almost knocking the coffee pot onto the floor.

"Well, if I miss the final because of you . . ."

He left the sentence unfinished.

"I mean what kind of Maoist are you?" he declared, spreading his arms wide. "Some poisonous terrorist has clearly infiltrated your ranks. Mao's third thesis makes it absolutely clear that the workers' struggle and the national struggle are two completely different things. Didn't you know that?"

"I'm afraid there's been a misunderstanding. I don't know anything about Mao's four theses," Luis said, greatly relieved that he could now speak the truth. He got out of his chair but remained hanging in mid-air, as if there were no gravity in the room.

Looking puzzled, Papa John followed him with his eyes.

"You've mistaken me for my brother," said Luis.

For the second time, he thought and, for a moment, he saw himself sitting in on a symposium on Plato, taking Martín's place among the other students, while a professor lectured them about episteme and doxa. But he said nothing. That had happened years ago, and all that business about the strike would long since have been filed away. Although, who knows. He had heard people say that you should not put too much faith in the Spanish justice system. Some of his colleagues at school said that the government could always, at the drop of a hat, pass a new law that would allow them to impose whatever sentence they wanted.

"My brother knows a lot about politics, and he's always been very hardworking. Me too, but my speciality is sport. Ask me anything you like. Do you want to know Italy's line-up for today's match? Dino Zoff, Baresi, Bergomi, Cabrini, Bruno Conti, Altobelli, Rossi . . ."

Papa John was staring at him hard.

"Who are you, then? Aren't you Marty, Carlitos?"

He was pacing up and down the room now. He was wearing moccasins, not boots, so he wasn't Mr Emerald Green, the one

271

who had given Luis the operating table treatment, with a bala-clava covering his face. Or perhaps he was. It was easy enough to change your shoes.

"No," Luis said. "I'm Luis, alias Lucky, alias Tuco."

As soon as he pronounced that third name, he heard the whistling: *Fufifufifuuu-waahwaahwaah, fufifufifuuu-waahwaah-waah* . . .

"Tuco?" Papa John was frowning now.

"Yes, Tuco, the Ugly."

Papa John stormed out of the room, and Luis sat studying the scene from up above. The white plastic table was still there in the middle, with two equally white, equally plastic chairs on either side. On the table sat the metal coffee pot, the two sky-blue china cups, one of which now contained two cigarette ends, as well as the spoons, the bowl of sugar lumps, Mao's *Little Red Book* and the pack of Winstons.

Papa John came back into the room, followed by a burly bearded individual. The two men went over to the table and started talking. Papa John picked up the pack of Winstons and took one out.

"He says Carlitos is his twin brother. That he isn't Martín, but Luis."

"Alias Lucky, alias Tuco," said Luis. He was once more sitting on the chair, with Papa John to his right and the bearded man to his left.

The bearded man slapped him hard.

"That makes you an accessory! Oh, you're going to pay for this big time!" he roared before slapping him again.

"I know who you are, you're the Bad," Luis said.

He then pointed to Papa John.

"And he's the Good. So here we are, the three of us, the Good, the Bad and the Ugly, and I reckon the best thing we can do is come to some agreement. After all, we share the same objective, which is to recover the money that the deserter Bill Carson stole from the Confederate Army. We're talking two hundred thousand dollars in gold! Two hundred thousand! But it's not going to be easy finding where Bill Carson is holed up. Neither the Confederates nor the Yankees have managed that. I've seen his face on the posters, and he looks like one smart cookie."

He again heard the whistling: *Fufifufifuuu-waahwaahwaah, fufifufifuuu-waahwaahwaah . . .*

The Bad did not take his eyes off Luis for a moment. He seemed annoyed.

"That's it! I'm not having him taking the piss!"

And the man shoved Luis so hard that he slammed face first into the wall. Unable to breathe, Luis raised his head, gasping for air. Then he noticed that his hands felt sticky, as if covered in some viscous substance. Frightened, he opened his eyes. He was standing next to an abandoned carriage in the middle of the desert. The horses' legs were caked in dust. The sun was beating down on his head, and he told himself he should get out of there as soon as possible because he wasn't wearing a hat. It was then that he noticed the blood dripping from the rear door of the carriage. That was why his hands were stained red, not because his nose was bleeding. He heard a voice say:

"Water! Water!"

He opened the carriage door and saw a tangled pile of corpses, ten or more corpses in a six-seater carriage, all of them riddled with bullets, all wearing bloodstained grey army uniforms, all of them dead, with one exception, the man begging for water. He was a good-looking man, with blond hair, blue eyes and an aquiline nose. Luis recognised him at once.

"Bill Carson!"

He was the spitting image of the man on the posters, even though, just then, his face was smeared with blood and dust.

"Water!"

"I'll give you some water, Carson, but, first, you've got to tell me where you've hidden the two hundred thousand dollars in gold."

Again that whistling: *Fufifufifuuu-waahwaahwaah, fufifufifuuu-waahwaahwaah* ... Then, suddenly, the Good appeared from behind some rocks. Not Papa John, but Clint Eastwood.

"Water!"

Bill Carson's blackened tongue was like an old rag, and there was more and more blood on his face, not his own blood, but that of the soldier lying on top of him, with his brains blown out.

"In the cemetery ..."

"What cemetery?"

"Sad Hill!"

"Sad Hill. All right, Bill Carson, but whose grave? Be a good boy now and tell Tuco."

"Water!"

Carson was dying of thirst, and if he didn't drink something soon, he wouldn't ever tell anyone anything again. Half of his body was hanging out of the carriage, and his mouth was almost touching the desert dust.

"Look, don't die, all right. I'm going to get you some water."

He was just coming back with the canteen of water, when he heard that whistling again, *Fufifufifuuu-waahwaahwaah, fufifufifuuu-waahwaahwaah* ... The Good was standing at the rear of the carriage. He struck a match on his thumbnail and held it to his small cigar.

"What are you smoking?" Luis asked.

"A Monterrey," said the Good.

"Wow, just like my father. Be careful though. It was those cigars that took my father to his grave."

"Don't talk rubbish. Your mother didn't smoke cigars, and yet she's dead too." He pointed to Bill Carson. "And so is he."

It was true. The Confederate deserter, the owner of the two hundred thousand dollars in gold who would gladly have handed over his fortune in exchange for a little cool water, was lying now with his lips brushing the desert floor, as if he wanted to kiss the dust.

"What do you know?" Luis asked the Good.

"I know the name of the grave. What about you, Tuco?"

"I know the name of the cemetery."

"That means, Tuco, that we each know half of what we need to know," said the Good. "We have no alternative but to become partners. A hundred each? A hundred thousand for you and a hundred thousand for me?"

"It's a deal," Luis said, indicating the carriage with a bob of his head. "And what are we going to do with that lot? We can't start digging graves in this heat. I'm dying of thirst too. Besides, they stink. I think they've already started rotting."

"Let's leave nature to run its course. It's only right that people should see what happens to deserters."

Together, they picked up Bill Carson and returned him to the tangle of corpses.

"Let's get out of here," said the Good.

They geed up the horses, and the carriage disappeared into the desert in a cloud of dust.

The sheer size of Sad Hill cemetery made Luis laugh out loud, all those thousands and thousands of crosses on the graves. They were so stupid, those Confederate soldiers! They took pride in lining up in front of the enemy in orderly, elegant fashion, as if they were at some sort of gala parade, offering themselves up as targets. And that was exactly how a hundred, two hundred, five hundred young men died each day. In the face of such stupidity, of all those crosses, how could anyone not laugh? Tears were simply not enough.

They were both on horseback. The Good's horse was a chestnut with a white flash; Luis' horse was a pinto, more grey than white.

"What are you laughing at?" asked the Good. For once, he did not have a cigar in the corner of his mouth.

Luis set out his thoughts on the connection between laughter and tears, and while he was doing so, it occurred to him that he was just as bad as the Bad, cut from the exact same cloth. The Bad used to laugh at the sight of dead bodies too. Come to think of it, where had the Bad got to? It had been some time since there had been any sign of him.

Luis heard that whistle again: *Fufifufifuuu-waahwaahwaah, fufifufifuuu-waahwaahwaah* . . .

He looked back and saw the Bad riding towards him. His hat was black, like his horse.

"My thoughts are rather less profound," said the Good. "All I care about are those two hundred thousand dollars in gold. With so many graves, it's not going to be easy to find which one he buried the treasure in."

"Aren't you worried about the guy following us? He likes money as much as we do."

"Not at all. I know how it works in films, and so I know he'll end up losing the duel. The baddies always do. Lee Van Cleef knows that too."

He looked back a second time. The Bad was following them, but further off now, which was logical in a way. The baddies' horses were never as fast. The fate of baddies in films was not exactly enviable, but in real life things were less clear-cut. His brother used to say that, in real life, the baddies – the ones who bleed their fellow man dry at every opportunity – always win. That's why, as Mao Tse-tung said, you have to sweep them up and throw them in the rubbish, as his mother did with the cockroaches that were always invading the bakery.

He wasn't so sure. Perhaps Martín was right when he called such people "scum" and compared them to cockroaches. Then, of course, Martín was a Maoist. A saintly Maoist, who, at least according to Papa John, had given part of the money he inherited from his mother to the cause, and who, again thanks to Papa John, had also spent two years in prison, because Papa John had lied to Luis when he said it was only a few hours until the start of the Italy-Germany match and that he wanted to go home and watch it on TV. The final was, in fact, the following day. Luis had only spent a dozen or so hours under arrest and had been overhasty in confessing that he was not Marty aka Carlitos. Martín had not, therefore, had time to escape and was arrested. There was an upside, though, because his arrest meant that his decision to start planting bombs, assuming he had ever actually made such a decision, came to nothing. This was fortunate because the Maoists were not in the habit of handling explosives and lacked the expertise of other groups. The first one to try had died when the bomb went off in his hands.

Again that whistle: *Fufifufifuuu-waahwaahwaah, fufifufi-fuuu-waahwaahwaah* . . . Luis looked around. He was in Sad Hill cemetery, accompanied by the Good, who, as usual, had a cigar between his lips.

"You go right, Tuco," he said, "and I'll go left. And don't forget that name: Arch Stanton. The two hundred thousand dollars in gold are in his grave. If you find it, fire a shot in the air. I'll do the same."

Luis agreed, but first, he looked around him. All the desert paths were empty. The Bad must be hiding somewhere. Probably right there, behind a grave.

"Are you sure you've memorised the name of the soldier with the two hundred thousand dollars in gold in his belly?" the Good asked.

"Arch Stanton."

"Fine. Let's quit yabbering. And remember: we're going halves. Don't even think of pulling a fast one on me. Try making off with the money, and I'll blow your brains out."

"Oh, not my brains, please. My head really hurts as it is."

Walking along one of the narrow paths between the rows of graves, about fifty metres further on, he came upon a gravestone bearing the name George Harrison. The face of the Beatle surfaced briefly in his mind, along with that instrument he used to play, the one he brought back from India . . . What was it called now? Luis couldn't remember. He felt sad because he had been fond of the shy Beatle, who had died from lung cancer, like Luis' own father. George wrote a song, a song he sang accompanying himself on that Indian instrument, and which talked about a sexy girl, a Susana No. 1 type. But what was he doing thinking about George Harrison? That grave should belong to a Confederate soldier, perhaps one of the four thousand who fell in the Battle of Chickamauga. Right then, though, he was looking for Arch Stanton. Once he found the grave and the two hundred thousand dollars in gold buried there, he and the Good would get the hell out of there. He remembered something Lee Marvin said in *Paint Your Wagon*: "There's two kinds of people: them goin' somewhere and them goin' nowhere." He would go to a place far away from all wars, where there wouldn't be so many bullets and bombs and torturers.

He continued moving from grave to grave. Arch Stanton! Arch Stanton! Arch Stanton! Where did they bury you, Arch Stanton? To one side of the cemetery he noticed a half-hidden area that resembled a garden, the only green spot in that dusty place. Perhaps Arch Stanton was there.

He went through an archway and found a grave decorated with tiny, multi-coloured flowers, as if it had been scattered with a potpourri of seeds. Whose grave could it be? It was not the first time he had seen it. Intrigued, he read the name on the headstone, and immediately burst into tears. It was his mother's grave.

He could not speak for crying.

"What a lovely grave. Martín takes such good care of it, doesn't he, Marta?" he said once he had recovered. But it was not his mother who answered his question, it was Martín himself, who stood like a ghost before the grave and said reproachfully:

"What are you doing here? We don't need you. Go back to California."

During that Californian year, Luis had more than once thought of going home, because he knew his mother was unwell, that she had fallen ill at the worst possible time, just when the ready-meal business she had started with Miguel and his sister was beginning to prosper, with a staff of ten and burgeoning profits, perhaps two hundred thousand dollars in gold a year, possibly more; but he had kept putting it off, merely phoning her now and then, because he was not expecting her to die so suddenly. Nor was anyone else. And so, when they got back from a concert in Palm Springs, him and a girl called Patty, another Susana No. 1 type, and read Martín's telegram, saying "she died today", the shock was enormous, and he even considered jumping on the first plane home.

That night, he and Patty smoked some dope together, and, after a while, probably at around three in the morning – the time great truths tend to enter a person's mind – he made this confession to Patty: "I didn't really love my mother that much, and when she and my father separated, I decided to stay with him and not go to the bakery with Martín. I mean, what was I going to do at the bakery? What do you think, Patty? I would like to have gone on playing at regattas on the canal or heading off into the hills in pursuit of wild boar with Eliseo and Blondie, but what does it matter, Patty? What does it matter to you who Eliseo and Blondie are? They're from over there, from the bakery. Yes, there were loads of wild boar around. One fell into the canal once, but I'll tell you about that another time. Anyway, I chose to stay at home with my father because he was the village sports buff. And in the days when no-one had even heard the word 'surfing', I bought myself a surfboard and went off and did a course in Biarritz. Besides, I enjoyed sitting beside him on the sofa watching football on TV, him with his cigar and me with my lemonade. That's another thing I didn't see eye to eye with my mother about, because she insisted on all three of us – Martín, her and me, I mean – spending Sunday afternoons together, and that was when the football was on . . . Now that I think about it, it seems to me that my mother always had a very bad sense of timing, even in death. Leaving California to go to a funeral just seems absurd to me. Yes, you're quite right, Patty. We should make every effort to attend family funerals, and I did go to my father's and I'd like to go to my mother's too, but I'm twelve thousand kilometres away, and frankly, sweetheart, I'd rather stay here with you."

He heard that whistle again: *Fufifufifuuu-waahwaahwaah, fufifufifuuu-waahwaahwaah . . .* and looked around, afraid he might see the Good among the graves. Instead, he saw Martín. He was standing in the same place, beside the grave decorated with flowers. He was talking to the grave and gesturing like an actor, like Hamlet reciting his soliloquy.

"When you open the phone book and see those long lists of names, don't they all seem much the same? Don't they seem to belong to people who are all much of a muchness? And yet the reality is quite different. If you could turn over those printed names the way you might turn over a stone in a garden and see the lives hidden underneath, you would find that no two beings are the same, that some are like the Good and others like the Bad."

Fufifufifuuu-waahwaahwaah, fufifufifuuu-waahwaahwaah . . . The whistle rang out just as Martín spoke those names, but his brother went on talking, as if he had not heard it.

"That's the thought that came to me, Luis, when the notary read out our mother's will."

Martín did not call him Lucky, and certainly not Tuco. He called him Luis, as he had when they were children. Luis remembered turning up for the reading of the will wearing a half-orange, half-blue shirt that he had bought in the Castro District of San Francisco, hardly the most suitable outfit for an occasion like that.

"There we were in the notary's office," Martín went on. "Twin brothers, two almost identical people, the only difference being that you had more of a tan after all that time spent on San Diego's beaches. But what a gulf lay between us! There I was spending every night with my mother in hospital for the last month and a half of her life, never leaving her side for a single night, and you just making the occasional phone call. I felt I had to lie to her. I told her you couldn't come back to be with her because you had a contract with the surfing club. You're a nasty piece of work, Luis, and always have been!"

That last sentence hit Luis like a bullet, and he realised that he was engaged in a duel, and that his brother was the Good and *he* was the Bad, which was not the most promising of roles, given that, in films, the baddie always lost.

"What are you complaining about, Martín? Most of the money ended up in your pocket, didn't it? You got two thirds of the inheritance. Our mother rewarded you in spades."

His words emerged just like another bullet, but Martín was unfazed. He merely gave a wry smile, the way goodies do in films.

"And what about when the police arrested me thinking I was you? What about that, Martín? I got the operating table treatment. What would have become of me if they'd broken my spine? Bye bye sport, bye bye surf, bye bye California. Even Roberto Durán couldn't have taken the blows I took to keep you safe!"

This time Martín did flinch. Luis continued firing:

"And it's just as well Papa John lied to me and that you got arrested. Otherwise, you'd have ended up planting bombs like that militant . . . What was his name? What was the name of that militant who was about to plant a bomb under some businessman's car when the bomb exploded, killing him instantly? It was just shortly after you went to prison. Ah, yes, Jesús Fernández Miguel!"

Martín ran away, leaving the graveside and hurrying off to the far end of the cemetery. Luis followed him, reading the names of the dead carved on the headstones as he went: Lucía, Miguel, Rosalía . . . But Martín had hidden himself away among the graves, and Luis had to abandon the chase.

Walking more slowly now, he headed along a path that ended in a small stone wall. From there he could see a vast panorama of hills. They were intensely green and arranged in no particular order, each one occupying the space randomly allotted to it thirty-five million years ago, when the surface of the planet fractured. The more distant hills, taller and more rugged, formed an irregular wall, a titanic mass, while the nearer, lower ones formed a kind of barrier of soft, curved slopes, like the hills schoolchildren draw. The scattering of houses on the outskirts of Ugarte, occasionally flanked by groves or copses of trees, were

281

also like childish drawings, white squares topped by red triangles. The prettiest of all, although he could not see it in much detail from the cemetery, was Villa Chantal, the home of Antoine, the chemist who supervised the mines, his father's boss and also, for a time, Martín's friend, until Martín sabotaged the laboratory. He thought: "Remember, Martín, the risks we all ran in providing you with an alibi." This thought, however, was no more than a sigh, and instantly vanished from his mind.

He followed the cemetery path, trampling over dead leaves, which crackled underfoot. When he reached the end, he came across a ladder leaning against a wall, and climbed up to peer over. In the small valley below the mountains and the hills lay the nucleus of the village, about three hundred houses built around a public square and a pelota court. He could see his house, his family's house, then, a little way further along the valley, the bakery and the stream.

He heard that whistle again: *Fufifufifuuu-waahwaahwaah, fufifufifuuu-waahwaahwaah* . . . and got the message: he should leave the cemetery in Ugarte and return to Sad Hill.

He climbed down the ladder and set off, reminding himself of what he was looking for: Arch Stanton. Shortly after that, still within the limits of the Ugarte cemetery, he saw a headstone bearing a photograph of his father. This was hardly unexpected, given that this was the vault of his father's family, the Sola family.

He reached Sad Hill, feeling worried. The Good had not fired a shot into the air. This meant that he, too, had failed to find the two hundred thousand dollars in gold, because it was inconceivable that the Good would have run off with all the money. The Good always kept his word. That is why he was played by Clint Eastwood and not Lee Van Cleef.

"This is ridiculous!" he declared after reading various of the surnames carved on the headstones: Lasa, Flores, Arregi, Mendia, Irazu, Medina, Altuna, Iruretagoiena . . . "These are still people from my village! I'm not in Sad Hill at all!"

The whistle sounded even more urgent now: *Fufifufifuuu-waahwaahwaah, fufifufifuuu-waahwaahwaah fufifufifuuu-waahwaahwaah, fufifufifuuu-waahwaahwaah* ... The Good was somewhere close by, calling to him. Luis could feel the Good's breath on his cheek when he whistled. He opened his eyes. Before him he saw a very large head.

"*Fufifufifuuu-waahwaahwaah, fufifufifuuu-waahwaahwaah* ..." the head whistled. Then it burst out laughing. "I knew the music from the film would bring him back to reality."

The head was talking to a nurse, not to him.

"I'll go and tell the doctor," said the nurse, and left the room.

"It's about time you woke up! You've spent nearly two weeks in the next world," yelled the big head.

Luis was in a room, but it was filled with so much steam that he could barely make out anything.

"Someone must have left the hot tap on. Would you mind turning it off?" he said.

"Do you know who I am?"

Luis was beginning to come round. The man in the grey uniform talking to him was the orderly with a voice like Adele's. And he himself was in a room lying on a bed, with a few wires hanging down above his head which, in the steam, resembled the tendrils of a plant.

"Do you remember what happened?" asked the orderly.

Images began to go round and round in Luis' mind, constantly changing, as if someone had held a kaleidoscope to his eye, and he saw the taxi driver who was the spitting image of Roberto Durán, and then a flip-flop, a black purse gleaming in the sun, a raffia bag in the middle of a pedestrian crossing, with, next to it, a turquoise towel, and, a little further on, the girl he had just knocked over, and her thin blue-and-white-striped beach dress. He immediately asked after her.

"Susana? She's been discharged. It turned out to be just a hip fracture."

The orderly went over to the door. Luis wanted to ask him

283

to turn off the hot tap, but was not quick enough, because at that point, the doctor came in, the one who resembled a shorter, lighter-skinned Usain Bolt. He was accompanied by the nurse.

The orderly, the doctor and the nurse stood in the doorway talking for a while.

"It seems the whistling worked," said the doctor. He was smiling.

He repeated the tests he had carried out on the day Luis was brought in. He turned on a small torch and shone it first in one of Luis' eyes, then in the other. Then he started giving Luis orders: move your arm this way, now that way, now raise it up, now touch the tip of your nose with your index finger, now bend your knees.

"Your eyes are looking good. Much better," he concluded, turning to the nurse and giving her instructions on medication, adding: "He can start drinking water now. And tomorrow, we'll try him on gelatine, then gradually build up to purées."

"Couldn't I have some gazpacho?" Luis asked. "When I was studying Physical Education, a teacher told us that people who had suffered a fracture to the skull were always given gazpacho, because it's a very complete food and as easy to digest as water. Besides, I'd much prefer that to purée."

The nurse's face lit up. The doctor smiled too, but more discreetly than Usain Bolt.

"We'll see."

"When will I be discharged?"

"We don't go in for predictions here," said the doctor and left the room.

"I think you'll probably be let out in a fortnight or so. So you just have to be patient," said the nurse, while she was checking the tubes and drips hanging above the bed.

"One more question: which number room am I in?"

"Number 303."

"Oh, good. A palindrome."

The nurse indicated the television fixed to the wall opposite the bed, although, because of the steam, Luis found it hard to make out the exact shape.

"Do you want to watch some telly? If you do, you'll need a card."

"Yes, I'd like that. There's probably a match of some sort on."

"I'll let the nursing assistant know."

As soon as Luis was alone, he started listening. You would not necessarily hear the sound of running water straight away. It took a while for the ear to pick that up. However, a few seconds passed and the straight line of silence remained unbroken. Apparently no tap had been left running. The steam was still there though.

In Ugarte, when Luis and Martín were children, Marta would take a long bath on Sunday morning. And when they went into the bathroom afterwards to wash their faces, they would find it full of the kind of steam now filling room 303, although the steam then had smelled much more pleasant, impregnated with the smell of the French soaps and shampoos that Julián got Antoine to bring from Paris.

Marta never got dressed immediately after her bath. She would put on a red ankle-length dressing gown and sit on the terrace drinking her second coffee of the day and smoking a cigarette. Then she would walk up and down the terrace, her hands in her pockets, as if checking that everything was in its proper place. Although she might simply have wanted to be out in the open so that the breeze and the sun would dry her hair.

That image reappeared in his memory: Marta pottering about on the terrace, wearing only her red dressing gown. Marta was a pretty woman. Even after having two children. Quite dark, with a somewhat boyish look about her, a slightly flat nose, and a body that ticked all the boxes, and although he could not say quite what those boxes were, she definitely fitted the bill. And then there were her eyes, deep-set and slightly hooded. In the days when she and his father still got on well, his father used to say that one glance from Marta was enough to make any man nervous. He later found out that Miguel, the owner of the bakery, was one of the men she made nervous.

He opened his eyes. The air in room 303 had now cleared completely, not a trace of steam. Opposite his bed, on a shelf, stood a plant. Slowly, he began to make out its shape: there were eight stems in all, each about fifty centimetres long, with twelve or thirteen violet-coloured flowers. With their long bare stems and dark green leaves at the base, the flowers looked as if they were suspended in mid-air.

He was still studying them when the orderly brought him the card he needed for the television.

"I bumped into the nursing assistant and told her I'd deliver it. I wanted to visit you anyway. You've certainly kept us on tenterhooks. How are you enjoying your return to the world?" he asked, adding: "They're orchids," as if Luis had asked him what they were.

"I'm sorry, I can't remember your name."

"Carmelo," said the orderly, showing him the gilt bracelet on his wrist. "I looked after you when you arrived in the taxi. You didn't seem very badly hurt at the time; it was only later that they realised you'd hit the back of your head."

"Now I remember," Luis said. "And I remember the taxi driver too. He looked like a boxer, like Roberto Durán."

"Do you know how you got that blow to the head?"

Luis did not.

"It was the surfboard. You had a surfboard in the back of the van, and apparently it started spinning round when you hit the tree. If it'd hit you in the face, you'd have been badly disfigured. So in a way you were lucky."

He slotted the card into the television and handed Luis the remote control.

"You can pay me when you get discharged. That's the on-off button. Then you just choose a channel and away you go."

"Has anyone ever told you that your voice is just like Adele's?"

Carmelo ignored the remark.

286

"Mind you, there isn't much worth watching," he said. "Not even any sport now that the Olympics is over. Anyway, you'll have to pace yourself. Time passes slowly here."

There was an envelope clipped to one of the plant's stems. Carmelo unclipped it and handed it to him, just as he had the remote control.

He turned round before leaving the room:

"But it does pass. Time I mean."

Luis opened the envelope that had come with the orchids. It contained a message from Susana No. 1, her letter of farewell. She wished him all the best but wanted him to know that she was ending their relationship. She just wasn't prepared to be anyone's carer.

He put the note and the envelope down on the bedside table.

The room, the hospital, everything lay in silence. He closed his eyes and listened. All he could hear was a faint hum coming from the fluorescent light. Nothing else. No voices. Perhaps visiting time was over, or perhaps, quite simply, visitors were not allowed on that floor. He wondered if Martín would have been told about his accident. But how? Through the hospital? Certainly not through Luis' mathematician ex-wife, because she lived about a thousand kilometres away now with another Luisillo, and would know nothing about it. And even if she did, so what? It would be just the same as when the police arrested him, because even then it had not occurred to her to warn Martín. That's what Martín refused to understand, that Luis had really been put through the wringer by Papa John and the other guy, something he could have avoided entirely by telling them as soon as they stopped him in the street: "I'm not the man you're looking for." But he had said nothing, he had kept that fact a secret even when they tortured him, because he and Martín had been brothers from minute zero. Martín, however, chose not to understand this and instead got angry with him. And he got even angrier when Luis visited him in prison and said that Papa John's lie had been for the best because, otherwise, Martín might well have blown himself up like that other Maoist, Jesús Fernández Miguel. Martín was a decent, serious-minded person, but empathy was not his strong point. In that respect he was like the Pink Panther. An innocent. He did not see the problems he created for those around him, for his family and friends, especially for Julián, but for Luis too and for Eliseo, when, for example, he decided to sabotage the laboratory during the strike at the mine. And then, afterwards, everyone had done what they could to help, had to grin and bear it for his sake, just as Luis had when Papa John kept lecturing him about Mao's four theses.

There was no traffic noise outside. He reckoned it must be about four or five in the afternoon. The city was empty in August. Not the beach though. But he could not go to the beach. He imagined Susana No. 1 emerging from the sea in her skimpy emerald-green bikini. How odd. The same emerald green as the balaclava covering the face of Papa John or whatever the real name of his torturer was. Miss Emerald Green and Mr Emerald Green. Was there anything significant about that coincidence? Who knows?

The air in the room was so clean now it was like distilled air. If such a thing existed. Yet another thing he did not know.

He pressed one of the buttons on the remote control. The face of a young woman appeared on the screen. Her eyes were red either with tears or emotion. Then came the image of some scales, followed by that of a trainer in a tracksuit. "Daisy now weighs two hundred and seven kilos, and we have set her the goal of losing a hundred kilos." The woman appeared again, her body encased in the kind of black leotard worn by ballet dancers, and this was followed by the title of the programme: *From Fat to Fit.*

He looked around him. Through the window he could see a wood, and the leaves of the trees looked as if they were made of plastic, as did the clouds in the blue sky, plastic clouds. The tubes of the line inserted into a vein in his hand were plastic too. The walls of the room were just that, walls; the tiles on the floor were tiles; the bed was made of metal; as for the fluorescent light, it was safely attached to the ceiling.

He looked at the orchids then. Their alveoli-shaped petals, violet with white spots, resembled butterflies that had been trapped there, in suspension, unable to leave the room.

Susana was special. And he respected her decision. It had been clear between them from the start: they would stay together just as long as they were having a good time; if things got difficult or boring, then they would both simply call it a day and move on. How long had they been together in total? About ninety days, three months more or less. Had she deliberately chosen the orchid as a symbol of their time together? No, no way. Susana was special, but not that special. Martín, on the other hand, *was* special, very special. Luis had been told that Martín had filled Marta's hospital room with all kinds of flowers, perhaps with orchids too. And then, when she died, he had decorated her grave with masses of flowers. That was why Martín had turned against him, because of the way he had behaved towards Marta, not because of his arrest and all that stuff, for Martín had soon realised that it was not worth risking his life for Mao's four theses. What Martín could never forgive him for was not being there while Marta lay dying in hospital, for not even coming to the funeral, for not having leapt out of the bed he was sharing with Patty and caught the first plane home. Luis felt like crying whenever he thought of it, whenever he remembered that error of judgement, perhaps the fault of the weed or the acid, and even though it was all in the past, even though he had long since drained the glass of time, he could still smell the odour emanating from that glass, and it was a sad odour, very sad. Besides, Martín, if you don't forgive me, what will become of us? Because our relationship is not like my relationship with Susana, no, you and I have been together since minute zero. Does that mean nothing to you? Do you need Mao Tse-tung to come and explain to you what it means to be brothers the way you and I are brothers? Do you need the trade union to come? Eh, Martín?

He heard the whistle: *Fufifufifuuu-waahwaahwaah, fufifufifuuu-waahwaahwaah* . . .

"Stop the film!" he yelled.

When he opened his eyes, he saw Carmelo's beaming face.

"If I don't whistle, you won't wake up! You have a visitor. Look who's here."

"Martín?"

"So you've finally woken up," said a man standing in the doorway. He spoke in a very nasal voice. He bore a close resemblance to Roberto Durán.

It was the taxi driver who had driven him to hospital after the accident.

"Patri has phoned me a few times to ask how you were," said Carmelo, putting his arm around the taxi driver's shoulder. "He was worried because he'd been a bit sharp with you when he drove you to the hospital."

"I thought you'd killed the girl, that's why. Do you forgive me?"

The taxi driver was standing in the middle of the room, uncertain what to do. His tiny eyes disappeared completely when he smiled. The orderly put a chair next to the bed and told him to sit down.

"Talk to him, Patri. Tuco needs to talk."

"The only thing I know about is boxing."

The orderly waved goodbye from the door, first asking:

"Who won the heavyweight gold medal, Patri?"

The taxi driver stood up.

"Anthony Joshua!" he exclaimed. "He's going to be the new king of boxing. He uses his right fist like this, straight up. The most amazing upper cut!"

He positioned himself in the middle of the room and began moving about as if he were in the ring, just like a dancer, but throwing punches.

"He does this, this, this, and then, out of nowhere, the upper cut!"

That tremendous vertical jab would have knocked out any opponent.

The door opened, and Patri interrupted his pugilistic report. A man came into the room. His black-framed glasses gave him an intellectual air.

"Like they say, a bad penny always turns up," he said.

"Martín!"

Daisy on the Television

Daisy pulls her car into a service area, stops at a drive-thru restaurant and orders something from the window. She is a blonde woman who looks to be no older than thirty.

The employee at the window, whom we only glimpse, disappears inside the hut and, for a few seconds, we see shots of the surrounding landscape: huge tracts of arid land under clear blue skies, and a freeway almost entirely empty of traffic. We will later learn that this is a certain county in the state of Texas.

As Daisy waits, we see a close-up of her face: it is plump, oval-shaped and quite pretty. Given the name of the programme, *From Fat to Fit*, we assume she must be very fat, but we cannot be sure until we see a full-length shot of her.

The employee does not, as we might expect, reappear at the window to hand Daisy her order in a paper bag; instead, it's the programme's male presenter we see, a sporty-looking personal trainer tasked with helping this week's contestant in her mission to lose weight. Caught completely off guard, Daisy breaks into nervous laughter, burying her face in her hands. This is a television programme, and yet it appears that not everything has been planned, and Daisy is genuinely disconcerted. She has gone bright red. The trainer laughs along with her. He is outside the drive-thru hut now.

Daisy gets out of the car and runs over to hug the trainer, whooping and laughing like a teenager. She is immense. We will later be told that she is married and has three children. How much does she weigh? 150 kilos?

A title appears on the screen: "Day Two".

We now see a gym which appears very dark, but only in

comparison with the sunny, cloudless Texas sky that has just been filling the screen. The camera lingers on a large set of weighing scales, easily large enough to accommodate a giant Galápagos tortoise. Here comes Daisy: wearing a white dressing gown and looking apprehensive, she says she doesn't know how much she weighs exactly, she can't use the scales at home or the ones at the drugstore. The trainer is holding a monitor. "Go for it!" he says. "Let's find out!" Daisy gets on the scales, and a long silence ensues, one that will last until the numbers appearing on the screen eventually settle. There, finally, is the weight: 456 pounds. "*207 kilos*," says a voice-over. The trainer frowns, and he doesn't appear to be putting it on; he assures us he's never taken on anyone so heavy.

"How long is it since you stopped looking after yourself?" he asks, while Daisy sobs, head bowed.

She talks about her three children, her husband, the effort it takes to look after them while also having to go out to work to bring in some money.

The trainer hugs Daisy, though not, as many would, with sighs of "poor Daisy, poor Daisy", but sternly:

"You've got to lose weight! Your life is at stake! Do it for you!"

Daisy nods, wiping away her tears with her hand.

We see a large box on the ground. The trainer says:

"Pick up those excess pounds and throw them at the wall, Daisy!"

Almost bent double and gritting her teeth, Daisy finally manages to give the box a shove and propel it against the wall. We hear the thud.

The decision to take part in the programme has given Daisy new strength, and we now see her bidding a slightly over-the-top farewell to all the things she usually eats: all those pizzas, French fries and cakes . . . Goodbye to all that forever, *good-by-ee!* As her cries fade away, we see her car driving along the freeway beneath blue Texas skies. At one point, driving past a BBQ restaurant, Daisy tells us that it does the best barbecued meat in the world.

But goodbye, goodbye, goodbye to barbecues too, goodbye forever. The next scene takes place in Daisy's kitchen at home, where we see her alongside the trainer and a dietician. They are preparing the first vegetable purée of the new era.

Day six comes and Daisy is frightened. She has been to the doctor for a scan. There is one quite shocking moment: she has to get inside an enormous metal cylinder while half-dressed, and we are afforded a glimpse of her 207 kilos, roll upon roll of adipose tissue and fat. Seeing her, it is hard not to think of the Willendorf Venus. If the people watching the programme were to include some spiritual double of St Francis of Assisi, that person might conceivably say to her, quite gently: "Dear sister, at 207 kilos you can still be a Venus. To me, that's what you are. If you have to lose weight for health reasons, go ahead, but if not, dear Venus, stay exactly as you are."

Daisy's thoughts, however, are going in another direction. It's there on her face, in her eyes. Overwhelmed by feelings of shame and fear, she would give anything to go back to her time as a teenager, to set her life on a different course; but this is like trying to grasp handfuls of air, mere wishful thinking. There is no going back. She knows this, and the knowledge has her completely floored – if she were really in the ring, facing a flesh-and-blood opponent, the referee would be stopping the fight and sending her back to her corner. The write-up would state: "The weaker fighter lost." But this is not what happens. We are in a hospital, not a boxing ring.

The doctor listens to Daisy's chest with a stethoscope. Her belly is like that of a woman eight months pregnant, but rather than a taut, shapely drum, it's more like a bulging sack empty at the bottom. The kind of abdomen you would see on an insect on the verge of laying thousands of eggs.

We hear the doctor's voice. He's talking about industrially produced pastries, sauces, sugary drinks. The trainer gives Daisy a summary:

"Almost two thirds of your body is fat."

"*138 kilos of fat*," says the voice-over.

"Don't be scared, Daisy," says a female nurse consolingly. "Everything's going to be fine."

Day eight, and a vast array of gym equipment has been brought to Daisy's house. We meet her family: older sister, mother, husband and children.

The sister says:

"You have to learn to love yourself."

She is a stylishly dressed woman, thirty-five or so, with a look of Raquel Welch about her. Her high cheekbones, which commence almost immediately under her eyes, seem to be the result of surgery. The mother says:

"You can do it."

In marked contrast with the sister's appearance, which could hardly be more American, the mother looks positively European. Entirely undemonstrative, and looking most uncomfortable, she clearly has a very low opinion of programmes like *From Fat to Fit*.

The husband says:

"I want to see you live, Daisy."

He does not look well. We are told that, after suffering a stroke, he lost the use of his left arm. Now we can understand Daisy's comment on day two about the effort involved in looking after the family. He isn't going to be much help with the household chores.

The trainer is the last to speak. He explains the objective to Daisy, and the prize she could win if she succeeds:

"You've got three months to lose 45 kilos. If you do it, we'll set you up with a nanny to help look after the kids."

Daisy's eyes fill with tears.

"Having a nanny sure would help," she says.

The next scene comes from day twenty. Squeezed into a black leotard, an out-of-breath Daisy is exercising on one of the pieces of gym equipment installed in her home. Cheeks flushed, sweat dripping from the tips of her blonde hair.

Day sixty-eight. Daisy is doing a workout with her trainer, shadow-boxing the air.

Three months have passed, the moment has come to step on the scales again. The voice-over asks: *"Will Daisy have succeeded in losing 100 pounds, 45 kilos? Is she going to win the prize that will mean she'll have the help of a nanny?"*

For an instant, we see Daisy at the wheel of her car, the freeway, the blue Texas sky, the sun. Then the home gym, the gigantic scales. The trainer reminds us that, at the start of the programme, Daisy weighed 456 pounds. If the scales now show 356, that will be her first test overcome, and she will have a nanny at her disposal. *"She had to lose 100 pounds, 45 kilos, in three months,"* repeats the voice-over.

There are other men besides the trainer in the gym. Daisy, clearly very nervous, approaches the scales alone. She drags her feet, but there's no escape, she has to do it.

A commercial break cuts in: we are presented with various people who have been on the wrong end of botched plastic surgery. On the screen, we see misshapen breasts and monstrous faces, while the voice-over tells us that the people to whom this treatment has been meted out are celebrities or other once-popular figures.

These are heart-rending images, and all the faces, unlike Daisy's face, seem sullen and unfriendly. A question comes up on the screen: "IS THERE ANY WAY TO CORRECT PLASTIC SURGERY GONE WRONG?" Were a young communist watching the programme, he or she would perhaps make some sardonic comment, something like: "Next there's going to be an advert for suicide pills. That's all the capitalist wants: to suck you dry, no matter what. They're vampires, truly dreadful people." But even so, suicide would be only the second port of call. There is a better solution. *"Is there any way to correct plastic surgery gone wrong?"* The voice-over has repeated the question, and, according to what we are being told, there are solutions. A telephone number comes up on the screen. Just pick up the phone.

Next is an advert for a film or a TV series. We see the rooms of a modern, elegant house at night, soft lighting, pale blinds on the windows. A telephone rings. The figure of an apparently young, upper-class woman emerges from the gloom. A man's voice is at the other end of the phoneline: "Something terrible's happened, Charlotte. I've killed Jeff."

Then we're back in the home gym. Gathering all her strength, Daisy steps onto the scales. The numbers go hurtling up on the trainer's monitor. The voice-over repeats: "*If Daisy weighs in at 356 pounds or less, she's passed the test, and the nanny will be hers. Let's see if she succeeds!*" After a few seconds, we see the figure on the screen: 356 pounds, 162 kilos. Daisy shouts for joy and throws her arms around the trainer. In the next scene, she is shown propelling a box against the wall. This time, though, this isn't about something she is hoping to achieve: the box contains the 45 kilos she has actually succeeded in losing.

Blue Texan skies, sun, the city of Houston, a café, plastic, glass, metal. Sitting at one of the tables, Daisy and her mother. They both look dejected. Daisy has gone to meet her mother hoping to be congratulated, to find a friendly echo of her own feelings of satisfaction, but nothing of the kind: no offer of support or companionship on her journey to becoming slim. Not in this café at least. When she tells her mother about her great achievement, the 45 kilos she's lost, and says how wonderful it is having a nanny, her mother's face does not light up, her hands stay just where they are, she does not jump up from the table to embrace her daughter. She looks sad. It could be that she was sad before she came into the café. Perhaps she was sad even before her daughter embarked on her journey to becoming slim. When Daisy was born, she doubtless dreamed of a great future for her; was overjoyed when she spoke her first words, what a clever girl our Daisy is, and the same later on, how pretty our Daisy is . . . But when she started to put on weight, when she exceeded 100 kilos, 120, 140, and when it became clear that she was on track to reach 200 kilos, all the lights that had been turned on in those early years gradually started to go out, like Christmas tree lights once the festivities are over . . . How sad to bring a child into the world and for that child to turn into a walking mass of adipose tissue! Then again, of course, the sadness could have another, more general cause. Old age, for example. When, after a certain age, the past begins to speak and to proclaim its truth – *la verité nue* – all you can do is give up and accept that all happiness is gone. What can be said of Daisy's mother? It is unlikely that young communists watch this kind of programme, but, if they did, they would be sure to put it to her in no uncertain terms: "Why take on the values of a corrupt system? Why be sad? Is that an acceptable reaction?" As everyone knows, that's an easy enough question to ask.

Now a shot of Daisy crying.

"She's never felt proud of me, and since I started putting on weight, even less so." She has been stung by the conversation with her mother. "She doesn't see all the effort I'm putting into trying to save my life."

The St Francis of Assisi double – what a shame he wasn't there with her in the Houston café! – would have said: "Don't cry, Daisy. You're not a walking mass of adipose tissue, you're the Willendorf Venus. I understand, and I know that the ties that bind are not the same for everyone, and that a mother's bond with her daughter ought to be stronger than a daughter's bond with her mother, but, and this is something you just have to accept, that's just how it is sometimes. Dry your eyes, Daisy. Now that you've lost those 45 kilos, your face is even more beautiful than before." Unfortunately, the Francis of Assisi double is talking to her from the other side of the television screen, and she can't hear it from where she is in Houston.

There is the picture-perfect blue sky of Texas, always the same. Daisy is driving along the freeway on her way to work, and as she passes the BBQ place where they serve the world's best barbecued meat, she keeps on going, proudly waving goodbye. She can now control the insatiable appetite to which she always used to succumb. Another obstacle overcome. At home, meanwhile, a slim woman with short hair comes into the kitchen to cook something for the children. She is the nanny, the prize for all Daisy's hard work.

Daisy is now looking through photos from different moments in her life and commenting on them to the trainer. The first one shows a very beefy girl in a pleated skirt and a thick V-neck jumper – the kind of severe uniform worn at Catholic schools. She has a melancholy smile on her face, and her hair, which is black in the photo, is caught back in a thick hairband. In the second photo, she appears with schoolmates on what looks like an excursion, and there once more is her smile – sad now, not just melancholy. A succession of snapshots follows, representing the different stages in Daisy's journey towards obesity: 100 kilos in the first one, 120 in the next, 140 in the next . . .

And yet Daisy has reversed that trajectory and is now on her way to becoming slim. She has already lost 45 kilos, and there she is now, in the room at home where the gym equipment has been installed. Some writing appears over the top of these images, telling us that she works out for four hours a day, while the background music – one of those fast-paced waltzes they play at cowboy weddings in Westerns – underscores how pleased she is with the results of all her efforts. It is hard, though, to imagine Daisy dancing with her husband. Not because of her, but because of him. We see him leaning in the kitchen doorway, watching her work out. The problem is not so much his non-functioning arm as his generally flaccid body. The impression is that his muscles lack the necessary tension to keep him upright. The stroke did not kill him, but it had very grave consequences. A cruel person would say to Daisy: "The reason you got so fat, darling, was because you chose a husband like him. Leave him, and then you'll see how much weight you lose." But Daisy cannot hear this cruel person, if indeed he or she exists.

Another title comes up. Six months have passed, it's time for another weigh-in. Daisy, in a tight black leotard, her hair down, steps onto the scales. Her trainer is next to her holding the monitor. The numbers whirr round and round for almost ten seconds, but finally, just as we're starting to wonder whether the machine is broken, her current weight appears: 288 pounds, 131 kilos.

Another title: "*She has lost 76 kilos in six months.*" The trainer and Daisy hug each other. The trainer says something to Daisy. Daisy is neither crying nor laughing. She closes her eyes and admits:

"It's been very hard, but, thank the Lord, I did it. I've prayed a lot to get this far."

Day 181 marks a new phase in Daisy's journey from 207 to 100 kilos; it's becoming increasingly difficult to continue losing weight, and they have arranged a test for her that will be far more demanding than those gym workouts. We see the place where it's going to take place: a "training tower" used by firefighters in the Texas fire department, a brick construction that would look like something out of medieval times if it wasn't shaped like a chimney stack. The trainer tells us:

"This is where the toughest training sessions happen."

The firefighter accompanying him, a slender black man of about thirty-five, goes into more detail. The temperature inside the tower can reach as high as 55°C. A spiral staircase connects the six sections that make up the construction.

"Daisy will have to climb to the top in a fire-resistant suit weighing twenty kilos," adds the trainer.

With all the gear on, Daisy looks more normal, because anyone looks big in a twenty-kilo fire-resistant suit, even the slender firefighter. They both go inside the tower, and the camera shows us the narrow spiral staircase that would feel claustrophobic to anyone, but more so to someone like Daisy, who, in addition to the heavy suit, is wearing a red helmet, a respirator mask and a pair of enormous goggles. They have gone up the first flight of steps, which Daisy only just manages. She stops to rest for twenty seconds before going on, takes the next two or three steps with the aid of the firefighter and then, suddenly resembling an elephant on its last legs, she staggers and trips, crashing into the wall. Daisy can't go on, Daisy is gasping for air.

When they take her outside and get the suit off her, all the signs are that for the girl with the sad smile, black hair and school uniform, this is the end of the journey. Not the journey that started 181 days ago, the journey from 207 to 100 kilos, but the journey from cradle to grave. She can't breathe, her heart – one of the firefighters says this in a low voice – is about ready to explode. If that St Francis of Assisi double could be there with her, he or she would say: "That's enough, Daisy. At 131 kilos, you're doing great. You look more like those Maltese Venuses than the Willendorf one now. And I'll tell you something: I've seen, not at the Tannhäuser Gate, but right here among us, girls of fifteen shivering in a bus shelter, in miniskirts and thin blazers, when it's three below zero; I've seen men who were once the city's most dashing specimens grown old, with wrinkled hands, bald heads, getting all dressed up with hats and silk scarves as if they were still young things; I've seen men and women who, after repeatedly placing themselves in the hands of rogue plastic surgeons, finally end up like the monsters shown in that advert. And for that reason, because I've seen so many people misled or plain mistaken, I beg you, Daisy, to call it a day – right now. The ancient Greeks, truth-seekers all, only put physical beauty second in their system of values. Think about it, Daisy: physical beauty isn't everything."

But there Daisy still is, outside the training tower in Texas, mouth wide open, gasping for air. Even if that St Francis of Assisi double were there beside her, she wouldn't be able to hear what he or she was saying. The same goes for the cruel individual – which is just as well, for it's far better not to hear his or her joke: "No, Daisy isn't going to die. If she'd died, we wouldn't be seeing her on the programme. If you don't last the course, you don't get your fifteen minutes of fame." "I disagree," the young communist would reply. "Money constitutes the only fixed value in this moribund capitalist society of ours. Broadcasting someone's death live on air would guarantee very good viewing figures, and, consequently, a lot of publicity. This must mean that, so far, no contestant on *From Fat to Fit* has died. Including Daisy."

And indeed, Daisy isn't dead. Normality reasserts itself. We see shots of the blue Texas sky, the freeway, a sign that reads

"Houston, 10 miles". Next, a woman driving a vehicle: it's her, it's Daisy. She's on her way to the hospital. Now that she has made it to 131 kilos, the surgeon has agreed to operate on her. Daisy stands half-naked beside the metal cylinder. She is going to have another scan. The 76 kilos she has lost on her journey towards 100 kilos are noticeable by their absence. It's quite clear she is no longer the Willendorf Venus, she's the Maltese Venus now. In the following scene, we see the surgeon's hands examining Daisy's abdomen while the voice-over reminds us that the operation is a prize. The prize for dropping from 207 to 162 kilos was the nanny; now that she's hit her target of 131 kilos, the prize is this operation.

The programme skips forward: we are told that Daisy has suffered a setback. Various shots ensue of the critical moment, day 209 in the 207–100 kilo journey: chaotic scenes at Daisy's home, the children running wild, not a sign of the nanny or the husband. At the same time, we see her driving along the freeway under the blue Texas sky. She parks outside the BBQ restaurant where they serve the best barbecued meat in the world. The camera lingers over a tray of pork chops, French fries and ketchup and then pans out to show us Daisy, brow knitted, devouring it all with a fury that appears to increase with every fry she ingests. Had the cruel person happened to be in the BBQ restaurant at the same time as her, he or she would have said: "Well, that was a very long journey to nowhere at all." For his or her part, the St Francis of Assisi double would have tried to comfort her: "You're suffering, Daisy, but suffering isn't your enemy, it's your ally." To which the young communist would have replied: "I disagree. Whoever accepts suffering is only endorsing servitude." Daisy, however, is alone at the BBQ restaurant with her pork chops, her ketchup and her French fries, and alone she walks out of the restaurant and drives away under the blue Texas sky.

Nine months have now passed, it's time to be weighed again, and Daisy steps onto those scales that are easily big enough for a giant Galápagos tortoise. She looks worried. She comes resolutely forward, ready to face the music. The trainer looks at the monitor. When the numbers stop changing, he exclaims:

"You've put on two kilos, Daisy!"

The camera doesn't show the end of this scene, but cuts straight to a close-up of the trainer:

"She's gone back to her bad old ways."

It's time for the commercial break. The first advert is for the King of Cakes, a moustachioed Latino man surrounded by the products of his kingdom: chocolate cakes, cream cakes, cups overflowing with Chantilly cream and meringues, custard tarts, more chocolate cakes. Scenes which make it hard to avoid the thought that, much like Daisy, the programme itself is undergoing a crisis – an identity crisis in this case – given how contradictory it is for a programme called *From Fat to Fit* to be encouraging the consumption of such high-calorie morsels. More adverts follow: the next one features a model who seems to have stepped straight out of a calendar, presenting items of jewellery encrusted with rhinestones, fake pearls that look real and colourful crystals. The next, which defends the virtues of plastic surgery, is a variation on the earlier one: close-ups of women who look like replicas of the calendar model but who, unlike the one showing off the jewellery, have wonky chins, balloon lips, one breast pointing off to the side. A voice-over says: "*Sometimes things don't turn out right first time.*" A doctor appears on the screen: "There's a solution to your problem: having repeat surgery can correct earlier mistakes. Call us right now!"

A year has passed since our first sighting of Daisy at a freeway drive-thru. "Day 365," it says on the screen. We are about to witness a reunion. Daisy and her husband are there, along with the Texas firefighters. Everyone looks relaxed and happy. Things have clearly changed in the interim, and for the better. We see a Daisy full of confidence:

"I achieved my goal!"

Daisy is going to be weighed for the fifth time on the same scales as before, though she no longer needs them. A normal set of bathroom scales would now suffice.

The trainer looks at the monitor. The news is better than expected: in this last phase she has lost 19 kilos, one more than planned. Daisy now weighs in at 114 kilos. The trainer is thrilled. "What you've achieved is just incredible!"

We do not see the blue skies of Texas, or Daisy's home, or the gym, but instead a gleaming hotel function room where, seated on wooden, velvet-upholstered chairs, forty or so people await. Daisy's mother, sister and husband are in the front row. After a moment, the camera takes us inside what could well be a green room, skimming along at floor-level until it comes to Daisy's feet, where it stops, slowly moving up her legs as far as her knees; a sight that would be sure to send an Adamov-style fetishist into raptures, such is the daintiness of her black stilettoes. The stilettoes move this way and that, parading past us with practised steps. Daisy is now blessed with nice ankles, nothing like the ankles grown swollen and misshapen from having to support a person weighing 207 kilos.

The camera moves on from the black stilettoes and focusses on some curtains, or to be precise, a theatre curtain. The impatient public awaits. The curtain goes up and the trainer is the first to appear, greeting the audience with a smile. What is Daisy going to look like now? No-one has seen her recently. But here she comes, here she comes at last: she is wearing a pair of very tight black trousers and a sheer, raspberry-pink blouse. She smiles and struts her stuff. She gets up onto a low dais and begins twirling around, showing her body off to the audience. Close-up of mother, sister and husband: their eyes are wide with surprise, but it doesn't look like anyone is about to say "Wow!". Obviously not her mother, who is finding it hard to join in with the celebrations: it seems she can't help but think they're all making fools of themselves. And the sister and the husband are the same. It seems hardly believable that cheerful Daisy hails from this miserable family. She never lacked zest when she weighed 207 kilos, and now, having shed all that adipose tissue, we see her suggestively caressing her thighs and flat tummy, as if she might be about to perform a striptease.

Perhaps this is the moment for the trainer to go over and whisper a piece of advice to her: "Daisy, Daisy, leave this family of yours," he might say. "Get in your car and drive, and don't stop till you hit Mexico!" It's just as well that there are other people in the audience whose clapping and cheering can dispel the atmosphere generated by the family's lack of enthusiasm. The trainer declares that the transformation has been nothing short of astonishing, largely thanks to the courage and bravery shown by Daisy.

The camera, which gives us a 360 degree view around Daisy, confirms the transformation. Before, she was the Willendorf Venus, then she became a Maltese Venus; now she is the spitting image of Anita Wlodarczyk, the women's world record holder in hammer throwing.

Orchids

2017

It was one of the last days of summer, Wednesday, September 5. They gathered up the things scattered around Room 121, put them in the small turquoise suitcase and headed down the corridor from the Paediatric Unit to the hospital exit. His daughter had been discharged that afternoon, ten days after she had been admitted and following an emergency operation for peritonitis.

"Hey, Garazi, we're going home," Martín said.

"About time too," she said, giving him her hand.

She was twelve years old and slightly small for her age, with a very expressive face. In her brown eyes was a mixture of shyness and determination.

On their way to the lifts, they stopped at the nurses' station to say goodbye to Nurse Rosa, only to find she was not on duty. The nurse who was there looked up from the computer and offered them a piece of paper.

"You can write her a note if you like."

Garazi tugged at her father's hand. Martín told the nurse that he would come back later.

He felt his mobile phone buzzing in his shirt pocket. His wife's voice rang out loud and clear, as if she were right next him: "I'm waiting outside with the taxi." Brusque, emotionless. "The nightmare's over, Ana, and I'm so relieved," he said. It was as though he had been cut off mid-sentence, and the reproach with which he might have concluded hung in the air: "You, on the other hand, are in your usual bad mood."

"Are you coming or not?" Ana said.

The hospital lift was enormous, with enough room for fifteen people. At that hour, though, there were barely any visitors, and

311

Garazi and Martín only shared it with an elderly couple. From the few words they exchanged, Martín gathered they had been visiting their son.

Daughters, sons: what exactly was the link between children and their parents? When Garazi ceased being a little girl and began, at the age of eight or nine, to be a person with a voice and personality of her own, he had thought it would be the start of their separation, a new stage in their relationship, when they would begin to grow apart. Garazi would never be someone as alien to him as the elderly couple in the lift, but she would gradually become less connected, as estranged from him as his wife was now. That change – a tiny event compared to the great changes happening in the world – was necessary and inevitable.

However, his prediction had proved wrong. There was Garazi on the threshold of adolescence, and yet she seemed to be more and more a part of him, as if she had been burrowing into his mind; more than that, he found her everywhere. He could not look at photos of the lines of children waiting to board the trains that would take them to Auschwitz; he could not read about the massacres perpetrated on the Lakota and Navajo peoples, during which young girls were raped by cavalry soldiers. He saw Garazi in all of them. Ages ago, Begoña, his colleague and fellow editor at the trade union magazine, had told him: "Since I've been a mother, I simply can't watch films that involve children." At the time, years before Garazi was born, this had struck him as a very odd thing to say. Now, it made perfect sense.

Outside the hospital, in the daylight, Garazi's skin looked as if it were made of cream. He planted a kiss on her forehead just to see if she was still feverish. She wasn't.

"Oh, stop it!" she said, pushing him away.

His over-solicitousness – bordering on surveillance – at the slightest sign of illness annoyed Garazi. It annoyed him too and provoked in him a terrible kind of nervous fatigue. "Tension is far more exhausting than marching along behind a brass band."

312

Another of Begoña's sayings. Garazi was right and so was Begoña, but it was not an easy obsession to shake off.

Ana almost ran up the steps to the hospital entrance.

"The medical report and her discharge letter," he said, handing her an envelope.

Ana took the papers from him and kissed Garazi on the cheek, saying:

"Odín sends his best wishes and wants to know when you'll be paying him a visit."

Ana worked at a riding club, and Odín was Garazi's favourite horse.

Martín went with them to the taxi and handed the driver the turquoise suitcase. Garazi was looking at him from inside the car.

"Aren't you coming back to the house?"

"I have to go to the florist's, remember?"

Garazi and he had agreed that they would buy a white orchid for the nurses who had looked after her. A few families did this as a mark of gratitude, and the plant would remain there on the counter at the nurses' station. That afternoon, the only such offering he had seen was a small, bright green fern.

"Oh, right, I forgot," said Garazi, waving goodbye.

The taxi circled the roundabout outside the hospital and disappeared down one of the exits. Their apartment was just ten minutes' away, in a working-class area of the city.

He could not stop thinking about how pale Garazi looked. The results of the latest tests had been normal, but this still did not reassure him. "Optimism is as contagious as pessimism." That is what Nurse Rosa used to say. She found his attitude annoying too, because she disliked people who were easily discouraged. When Garazi was in the recovery room after her operation, he had asked Rosa: "Is she going to be alright?" Rosa's response had been accompanied by a punch on the arm: "Come on, lighten up! Of course she's going to be all right." The punch had really hurt. She was a strong woman. If she ever had to change Garazi's position in bed, she would do it by herself, with no help from anyone.

The florist's was in the same street as the hospital, about a hundred metres away. As he was heading over there, someone called out his name. Not in the mood to talk to anyone, his first reaction was to pretend he had not heard; then, a little further on, he realised that the voice sounded familiar, and turned to see a man with a broad, beaming face smiling at him. He was waiting on the central reservation for the pedestrian lights to turn green. It was his old schoolfriend Esteban, now the owner of the butcher's in Ugarte. His fourteen-year-old son was in hospital with cancer.

"I'm just going to buy a plant," Martín said, when they met on the pavement.

Esteban shook his hand.

"Pleased to hear it."

He knew what buying a plant meant.

"We haven't reached the plant-buying stage yet," he added. "They're keeping Andoni in. There's no alternative."

He was, by nature, very easy-going and spoke very slowly. At school, Martín and his brother Luis were always getting into fights, Esteban never.

"How is Andoni? I've often seen him in the games room with my daughter. He's a real computer nut."

Given that Martín saw Garazi in every child, Andoni was no exception. Whenever he thought about him, he felt like crying.

Esteban glanced over at the hospital, as if expecting to see his son at one of the windows.

"They've told us we'll have to go to Houston to continue the treatment, and Andoni's trying to improve his English. He's already pretty fluent, but he's been using the computer to get used to the American accent."

"That was a great idea installing computers in the Paediatric Unit, although Garazi hasn't been using it to brush up her English. She's more into video games."

"Oh, Andoni enjoys them too. And he just loves the videos Luitxo sends him."

Esteban always called Martín's brother Luitxo, as if they were

314

still kids. Unlike Martín, Luis often went back to the village, more and more in fact, and he and Esteban saw a lot of each other.

"Didn't he give him that documentary about the Rome Olympics?"

"Yes, and it was in English too. And they talk to each other in English as well. Weird, eh?"

A smile appeared on Esteban's round face, a genuine smile, not put on, as Martín's smile would have been if his son were ill with cancer. Perhaps Esteban was a believer. Believers are better at withstanding life's blows.

The people coming and going from the hospital seemed to be moving as silently as if they were all wearing slippers. The only sound was the high-pitched beep-beep of the pedestrian lights before they turned green for the cars.

"Oh, and Luitxo sent him a link to the national basketball final," Esteban said. "Andoni really loves watching basketball, and now that he's going to Houston, he keeps checking out how the Houston Rockets are doing."

Luis had a real knack for choosing the perfect present. Garazi had loved the kaleidoscope he had brought her the day after her operation. That was the first thing she had put in her suitcase that afternoon, when she was discharged.

It felt to Martín as though the beeps from the lights were getting louder and more irritating. He shook Esteban's hand.

"I'll drop in and see Andoni one of these days."

"Only if you're passing, Martín. If not, we'll catch up in Ugarte. Although you don't go much now, do you? Luitxo tells me the magazine keeps you really busy."

"It's true. I hardly ever leave town."

"Well, I suppose we just have to work with whatever life throws at us, eh?"

Orchids filled almost the whole of the florist's shop window. Martín went in and asked for two with white flowers. The woman who served him questioned this choice:

"Wouldn't you rather have a combination of white and purple? Put them together and you'd have a whole little cluster of colourful butterflies." She was wearing wellingtons and an apron, as if she had just come in from the garden. She had very rosy cheeks too. Not cream-coloured, more like tomato flesh.

"I'm always telling people the petals are like butterflies, but my husband thinks I'm daft. He says I'm too imaginative. But then how would he know – he has no imagination at all!"

She laughed out loud, revealing a gap in her teeth.

The florist's may have been only a hundred metres from the hospital, but on a hypothetical map of happiness, the two would occupy opposite poles. You would never hear a laugh like hers in the Paediatric Unit or any other unit. Not even in the neonatal unit.

"I think I'll just go for two white ones," Martín said. "One is for the hospital and one is for home."

He remembered the orchids he had seen in his brother's room when he went to visit him in hospital after Luis had come out of a coma. That one had been purple, a present from his then girlfriend. Martín did not want them to be the same, because those orchids had meant something else entirely.

"Sure, up to you," said the woman.

She put both the orchids in a paper carrier bag, then scribbled the price on a bit of cardboard: forty euros.

Back home, he sat down at the living-room table and created a new document on his computer: "Garazi's illness. Memorandum." At that moment, half past eight in the evening, Garazi was sitting on the sofa watching television while eating her supper, which consisted of an omelette and a yoghurt. Beside her, Ana was eating a salad straight out of a glass bowl. He heard a voice asking: "How long is it since you stopped looking after yourself?" This was followed by the sound of sobbing. "Oh ages, just ages and ages. The children need me, my husband's disabled and so can't really help, and, as if that wasn't enough, I have to go out to work to bring in some money."

He looked at the television. An extremely obese woman was embracing a man in a tracksuit. They were in a gym. "You have to lose weight! Your life is at stake! Do it for you!" the man said encouragingly, when they emerged from their embrace. Judging by the way he spoke, he was presumably her trainer.

"Well, *I've* always taken good care of myself," said Garazi, "and look where it got me."

"Pick up those excess pounds and throw them at the wall, Daisy!" said the trainer, and the woman took hold of a big box and gave it a shove so that it hit the wall. Martín realised then that this was the exact same programme his brother Luis had been watching when he went to visit him in hospital a few years back.

"Aren't you having any supper? There's salad in the kitchen if you want it," Ana said.

"No, I'm not hungry."

They barely spoke to each other these days but did their best to keep up appearances in front of their daughter.

The white orchid he had bought at the florist's stood beside his computer. The other almost identical one would be where he had left it an hour earlier, at the nurses' station in the Paediatric Unit, next to the green fern. A source of solace for anyone passing by. And for him at home too, a solace for his eyes.

In his mind, the two orchids, on the table at home and in the hospital, became fused into one. He focussed on the computer screen, and, on the first page of the new document, he typed the same title: "Garazi's illness. Memorandum."

During her stay in hospital he had been incapable of writing a single word, on paper or on the computer, out of anxiety that the slightest reference to the illness would set in motion some malign force, some ally of death; an illogical, superstitious fear, utterly alien to the ways of thinking that normally ruled his life, a fear that he had only managed to keep under control by pouring all his energies into work-related blogs. Now, at last, that distressing interlude was over. It was September 6, and they were home again. On the table, next to the white orchid, was the discharge letter signed by the doctors. Death, always on the prowl, would remain close at hand, but had retreated a step or possibly two. It would not be provoked by a murmur, by a few lines.

He thought back to how it had all begun, then started to write:

"*August 26, 2017. On a campsite in the mountains.* It was Saturday, Ana had arranged with some work colleagues to go to the races being held that weekend at the Lasarte racetrack, and so Garazi and I were going to be alone at the campsite. After a quiet afternoon at the swimming pool, we joined some friends at the campsite bar for a simple supper of gazpacho, tinned tuna with onion and roast chicken. And pasta for the kids.

"Garazi was sitting at one corner of the table, and just as we were about to start on the chicken, she came over and said: 'Can we go back to the chalet now? I'm tired.' I responded to this rather brusquely. I assumed she didn't much like the friends she happened to be sitting next to, all of them boys, but I asked her to sit down and at least finish supper, because this was, after all, the last day of the holidays. We would be going home the next day. 'You won't have any problems with wifi there, so you'll be fine,' I said. She had spent the whole holiday complaining about the lack of a decent signal on the campsite. 'I'm not hungry,' she said. 'Well, I am,' I said. The chicken on my plate was getting cold. 'Garazi, go to the chalet and wait for me there.' I held out the key to her, but she did not take it. 'I'll be over by the water slide.' That was the best place for a signal. 'I've got a bit of a stomach-ache,' she added. 'Oh, great, that's all we need!' I said. I felt harassed. With Ana away, I had sole responsibility for Garazi. 'Just give me twenty minutes, and then we'll go back to the chalet to sleep, but, fine, go over to the slide if you want.' I then addressed the friends sitting opposite me. 'That's Garazi for you. She can always be relied on to make life difficult. When she was a baby, and we went out somewhere in the car, within two minutes she would have done a poo, and we'd have to stop at a petrol station to change her nappy.' My friends laughed, but when I looked over at Garazi for her response, she was already walking away from the bar. It was dark by then, and the darkness swallowed her up.

"By the time I met up with Garazi again, the promised twenty minutes had passed, and ten more too. She was sitting hunched beneath the slide. The light from the screen of her mobile lit up her hands and part of her face. She was grimacing. 'My stomach hurts,' she said. I helped her up. When we got back to the chalet and I put her to bed, I asked her where it hurt. She placed one hand on the lower part of her abdomen. 'Don't worry, we'll be heading home tomorrow and, on Monday, we'll go to the doctor.' I went to kiss her, but she turned away. 'Oh, so now you want a kiss, when just a few minutes ago you were telling those imbeciles that I can always be relied on to make life difficult.' 'Yes, you're quite right. I'm sorry.'

"Garazi soon fell asleep. I felt her forehead. No fever. And yet she kept tossing and turning in bed. Towards dawn, she grew increasingly agitated. It occurred to me that there was no need to wait until Monday, there must be a doctor on call in the neighbouring village. 'Do you want some breakfast?' I asked when she woke up. She said no. I said: 'I think we ought to go to a local health centre. What do you reckon?' She agreed and put her mobile on to charge. 'Then I want to phone Mum.' Nothing sadder than seeing a young girl in pain, perched on the edge of a bed in a holiday chalet. I felt that sadness deep inside me."

Martín looked away from the computer and glanced over at Garazi. She was pointing at the television screen with the spoon she had used to eat her yoghurt.

"You mean she's got to climb right up there? She'll never make it!"

Daisy, the competitor on the programme, was in a training camp for firemen in Texas, standing before a brick tower shaped like a chimney. A fireman had just shown her the spiral staircase connecting the six sections of the tower, and warning her that the temperature inside the tower was 55°C. The trainer spoke to camera then, explaining what she was about to do: "She'll have to climb all the way up wearing a fireman's flame-retardant suit, a red helmet, a respirator mask and a huge pair of goggles." The following shots formed an alarming sequence: Daisy going up the spiral staircase, stumbling on every step; Daisy staggering and banging into the chimney wall; Daisy lying on the ground.

"Is she dead?" asked Garazi.

Ana laughed.

"No, she's just fainted."

"Are you glad to be home, Garazi?" Martín asked, turning off the computer. She did not hear him. She was still glued to the television.

He left the room and went over to the kitchen window. There were very few lights to be seen outside, only the lamps lighting the streets of an industrial estate close by. It was not a comforting sight. Several companies had closed, and the abandoned detritus outside some of the warehouses had become overgrown with brambles. The walls were covered in political graffiti and angry posters. Beyond that, in the darkness, he could see the lights of a village, a dozen or so dull, yellowish spots and a red rectangle. The dull lights belonged to the workers' houses, the red rectangle was the sign outside a restaurant. A shrinking population, he thought. Agriculture was in decline too. During his time in jail, the prisoners belonging to different political groups used to make fun of the Maoists: "China, with its 200 million peasants; it's perfectly logical that Mao should consider them ripe for revolution, but here? Really, you Basque Maoists are just a joke." They were right. His political plan had been the fruit of an illusion. *La Cina non era vicina*, as Stefano Ferrante's book about Italian Maoists put it, China was not that close.

Garazi peered round the kitchen door.

"I'm going to sleep with Mum. You can sleep in my bed."

She was still very pale, but her eyes were brighter than they had been in recent days.

"Fine, Garazi. You'll sleep better then."

He was a rather over-zealous nightwatchman. In Room 121

in the Paediatric Unit, he had fought against sleep and spent the hours listening to his daughter's breathing, checking that the saline solution and the antibiotics were still flowing through the IV tubes, putting his hand on her forehead and generally being a nuisance. Yes, she would be better off sleeping with her mother.

He had gone and helped himself to some salad, when, a short time afterwards, Ana appeared. She left Garazi's various medicines on the table.

"I'll give her the antibiotic before I leave to work. Do you have to go anywhere in the morning?"

"How could I when Garazi's still ill?"

"Well, it has been known."

Behind those words lay another reproach: "Up until now, you've left the house whenever you wanted to, on the excuse that you had some union meeting."

"I'll work from home today. Say hello to Odín."

In other words: "You go and look after your horses. I'll take care of our daughter."

He was woken in the morning by Ana making noise in the kitchen. She was opening and closing the door of the china cupboard, then running the tap for a few seconds. What was she doing? A tinkling sound explained everything: she was preparing Garazi's antibiotic by dissolving it in a glass of water and stirring it with a teaspoon. He looked at the time. Ten to seven. The night was over.

He went to check on Garazi once Ana had left. Everything was fine. She was breathing normally. Thirteen times a minute, as it says in Gabriel Celaya's poem, set to music by Paco Ibañez. When he went into the kitchen, he saw the note on the table: "She's had her antibiotic. If she's in any pain, give her a paracetamol." The next line was underscored: "Keep an eye on her dressing, just in case. If there's any leakage from the wound, soak it up with a bit of gauze."

They had performed a "McBurney incision" on Garazi, an incision made a few centimetres below the navel. He knew the name because he had Googled it. He knew other details too: the precautions the surgeon had to take, the path the scalpel had to follow when cutting through the tissue to reach the infected area, and the actual removal of the appendix . . . As he read on, it had seemed to him a complicated process, but apparently it wasn't, not even when the appendix was retrocecal. That's what the paediatrician treating Garazi had told him, a serious, pleasant woman with a very warm manner, adept at dealing with the patient's relatives. He thought that perhaps he should give her an orchid too. He could leave it at the nurses' station in the Paediatric Unit with a message: "For Laura, with our thanks."

It was gradually growing lighter, and from the kitchen window he could see the three hills on the horizon. In the days when he and Ana were getting on well together, they used to look out of that same window with Garazi and tell her: "Those three hills are part of a roller coaster." Now that the lights from the houses and the red restaurant sign had been turned off, the village at the foot of the middle hill was an ochre-yellow blur. There was some movement closer to: a tractor ploughing a field that had already been harvested; the constant coming and going of vehicles on the industrial estate. It was a more cheerful scene than the one last night.

After breakfast, while he checked his emails, he left the living-room door open, as well as the door to the room where Garazi was sleeping. There were two messages, both from Begoña at the office. He opened the one with the most intriguing heading: "The cesspit".

"In an inspired moment, the boss of that private company that manages the care homes has just come up with a lovely name for our trade union: 'The cesspit'. We are dealing here with some very primitive people. Hysterics. See how low they've sunk after just one week of strikes! There's no way they're going to negotiate."

Begoña had studied journalism, but she was fascinated by psychology and always included the personal factor in any analysis. "Primitive people. Hysterics." She was probably right.

As the subject of her other email, she had put "The mud-slinging begins". This was a piece from a newspaper article about the strike at the care homes. Begoña had underlined the quotes from statements made by some high-up government official.

"The strikers are utterly heartless. There have already been several serious incidents. In one home, a diabetic resident was given the wrong food to eat. In another, residents went a whole day without having their incontinence pads changed. Many had to stay sitting or lying in the same position all day because there was no-one to move them. We cannot allow such incidents to be repeated and we therefore call for the minimum service to be 80%."

Begoña added:

"Having Mr Cesspit himself calling the strikers heartless has its funny side. The funniest thing, though, is that another Mr Cesspit has demanded, in the name of the company, that the minimum service offered by the strikers should be 100%. The man's a genius. I'm not surprised they made him a director. He's invented the strike-free strike!"

Martín immediately sent his response:

"We should devote our October issue to the subject. On the cover, in large type, a list of the workers' current conditions and, in the background, a photo of one of the homes. What do you think?"

The cover would lay bare the total cynicism shown by the government and by the private company running the homes where working conditions verged on slavery.

He glanced at the orchid. Its whiteness went well with the silence in the house. It seemed to get prettier and prettier. He got up to look in on Garazi. She was fine, sleeping peacefully.

Back at the computer, he opened the document in which he had started to write an account of Garazi's illness. He did not want to abandon it halfway, as had happened with the diary that he and Ana had decided to keep as a record of their daughter's early years. The hardback notebook they had bought for the purpose was sleeping in a drawer somewhere in the house, with most of its pages blank.

"*August 27, Sunday. First visit to the doctor.* Until my daughter's operation, I knew almost nothing about the appendix, or only what I remembered from a school textbook, that it was like a little worm attached to the large intestine. I know a bit more now, especially about the aspects most relevant to Garazi's case: that the small worm can adopt different positions and be either clearly visible or hidden. If it's hidden behind the large intestine and pointing upwards, it's known as 'retrocecal'.

"When we left the campsite to go to the health centre in the nearest village, I had no idea that Garazi's appendix was retrocecal and therefore difficult to detect using what is known technically as the AIR score. On that scale, as Laura, our friendly paediatrician explained, vomiting is allotted one point; pain in the right iliac fossa another point; serious swelling of the abdomen three points; a body temperature higher than or equal to 38.5°C, one point.

"Garazi only scored one point. Her right iliac fossa hurt, but she wasn't vomiting and had no fever, and she lacked the decisive symptom – namely, abdominal swelling – which would have led to a more exhaustive examination. If her appendix had been normal and not retrocecal, that symptom would have been there.

"'I would say it was just an ordinary stomach-ache,' said the doctor at the health centre. He was a man in his fifties, short and stocky. As it turned out, I had met him before, on a previous consultation, and so I trusted him. A couple of years earlier I had started getting a red rash on my feet, and he had seen me at the local health centre. He took one look at my feet and scribbled a few lines on a piece of paper. 'Go to the pharmacy and tell them to make up this ointment for you. Rub it on the rash before going to bed and it'll have gone by the end of the week.' He added: 'You go jogging, don't you? Well, apply the ointment and buy some proper running shoes.' When I thanked him, he undid a couple of buttons on his white coat and showed me the logo on his sweater: a weightlifting club. 'It was an easy diagnosis to make.

A lot of sportsmen get rashes like that.' I followed his advice and, a week later, my feet were fine.

"When I got back to the campsite with Garazi, the sun – as the poets of old might have put it – was firing its arrows at the trees and making the leaves smile. There was no shade at all in the pool area, and the mountains, swathed in mist, seemed weightless, suspended in the air. Physically, it wasn't the same world as on the previous day, but I did not yet know that its current guise – sunlight, soft green leaves – was retrocecal, and therefore not to be trusted, and I allowed myself to be lulled into a false sense of security by that visit to the health centre. I decided to spend Sunday at the campsite and return to the city in the evening. 'If you like, Garazi, we can have breakfast, then go for a swim in the pool. We ought to make the most of the last day of our holidays.' Garazi seemed unenthusiastic. 'It isn't the last day of *my* holidays. Classes don't start until September 14.'

"She ate very little for breakfast and got out of the pool almost at once, complaining that the water was too cold. I said: 'Is your stomach still hurting?' She said it was. 'Shall we go home, then?' She again said yes. 'Wait for me over by the slide while I get our things together.'

"We left the campsite at around mid-morning. The sun was still firing its arrows at the trees, gilding the rocks on the hillsides and the wheatfields below; however, now and then, Garazi, sitting in the passenger seat, would whimper with pain, and that was enough to cancel out the positive messages I had received from the doctor and from the physical world. Garazi was ill, and that was that. Only one thing kept my negative thoughts under control: my own condition as a hypochondriac. I always assumed that any mild illness was serious, and that any serious illness was terminal. As Ana was always ready to remind me.

"Once we were home, and I had emptied the rucksacks, put the dirty clothes in the washing machine, and made some lunch, it was clear that all my efforts to return us to normality were futile. The forces propelling me in the opposite direction were far too powerful. Garazi lay listlessly on the sofa, sending WhatsApp messages. She barely ate any of the spaghetti I put on her plate. Now and then, she would groan. I asked her: 'Is the pain not getting any better?' 'No, I'm afraid not. It's getting worse. But you know me, I can always be relied on to make life difficult.' 'I'm sorry, Garazi. Don't hate me because of that silly remark I made to our friends at the campsite.' 'I forgive you.' 'I'll get you some paracetamol, I think that might help. You can take it with some yoghurt if you like.' 'I don't want any yoghurt.'

"Ten minutes after taking a painkiller, she fell asleep. I told myself then that, if one paracetamol was enough to relieve the pain, then it couldn't be anything very serious. Reassured, I sat down at the computer and started writing around for contributions to the magazine. Then I wrote to my colleague Begoña: 'Garazi's not well and I might not be able to come into the office tomorrow. We can keep in touch by email, if that's all right with you.' Begoña's reply came back in less than a minute: 'No problem Martín. And give her plenty of cuddles.'

"Garazi slept for nearly two hours. As soon as she woke up, though, she began complaining about the pain, just as she had in the morning. I could not bear it. As Brecht wrote in a poem, the smoke rising from a chimney brings to life what, until then, had seemed lifeless – the small house, the nearby lake; however, it is no less true that hearing a child groan with pain can destroy a whole world, its sun, its blue sky, its wine and its songs.

"I sat down next to my daughter on the sofa. I took her hand. She asked when her mother would be back. I looked at my watch. It was nearly seven o'clock. 'The last race will be starting about now. So she should be home by nine.' I had a moment of doubt. I could call Ana and ask her to come home as soon as possible, but it wasn't worth it. It made no difference if she came home at nine or at ten. On the other hand, Garazi was suffering. She needed her mother by her side. I said to Garazi: 'I'll ask her to hurry right back.' Ana rarely stayed behind to have supper with her friends, and it was unlikely she would be late. Nevertheless,

I decided to phone her, but her phone was off. I returned to the sofa: 'I think we should go and see the doctor again. The hospital's just around the corner. We'll be back by the time your mother arrives.' Garazi nodded. She had her eyes closed.

"I rang the hospital's emergency number. A truly dreadful experience. So dreadful that the desire to put it on record was the main impetus behind writing this memorandum."

He had to stop typing. Garazi was calling him. He went into the bedroom, sat down on the bed and felt for her hand under the duvet.

"How's my little girl?"

"Fine. Where's Mum?"

"She had to go to work. Do you want to give her a call?"

"Later."

Garazi closed her eyes.

"Don't you want to get up? If you sit on the sofa, I'll bring you your breakfast."

"No, not yet."

He plumped up her pillow and put it straight. Garazi suddenly opened her eyes. An idea had just occurred to her.

"Daisy didn't die, did she?"

"Daisy?"

"That woman who weighed 207 kilos, the one who started climbing up the firemen's tower."

He burst out laughing and told her that, no, Daisy was fine. That was just one episode in a whole series.

Garazi still looked very pale and wan after the operation and her stay in hospital, and her eyes stood out in her face like two hazelnuts in a sea of cream. Those eyes then turned to him:

"And what about Andoni? Andoni's not dead either, is he?"

It took him a few seconds to realise that she meant her friend in hospital, the son of Esteban, the village butcher.

"You've been dreaming, Garazi. Andoni's fine. He'll soon be better."

"I'm not so sure."

Garazi was not talking like a little girl. Her gaze turned inwards. She remained silent for a while before going on:

"He speaks perfect English, you know, and he has the most amazing ear for accents. He can say the same words three different ways: how you'd say them in London, in Mexico and even, can you believe it, how an African American would say them."

"Extraordinary. Not what you'd expect of a boy from Ugarte."

Martín suddenly remembered his encounter with Esteban on his way to the florist's. Esteban was an intelligent man and had made sure his son learned English right from when he was small, even, according to Luis, sending him to London on a course.

"Close your eyes, Garazi."

He stood up and raised the window blind. The room was filled with daylight.

"And he's a real whizz at music too," Garazi went on. "The other day, the teacher at the hospital brought a little guitar into the games room, and half an hour later, just by watching some YouTube video, he was already able to play a tune. A *chacarera*."

She smiled when she said *chacarera*. A new word, learned in hospital.

"I feel so sorry for Andoni. He's probably going to die," she said.

This was not a subject Martín wanted to talk about. He went over to the bedroom door, but Garazi had not finished.

"When I left hospital, he said to me: 'I'll be going to Houston after this, but I don't know if they'll be able to cure me there either'."

"He'll be fine. Don't worry. And now, tell me what you'd like for breakfast?"

"Mashed banana with lemon juice."

This was her favourite breakfast. He gave her the thumbs-up and went off to prepare it.

That mention of Andoni, a reminder of the boy's sad plight – the current carrying him off down the canal towards death – had changed Martín's whole mood, and when he looked out of the kitchen window again, everything seemed strange: the three hills; the village at the foot of the middle hill; the red restaurant sign, which was still lit even during the day; the tractor ploughing the field and the warehouses on the industrial estate. Then he gradually calmed down, the way rapid breathing slowly returns to a normal rhythm.

He recalled a poster he saw each time he walked through the industrial estate before his run. "Have you no conscience, traitor?" the headline said in large letters; but all that radical rage was dissipated by the words that followed. The workers mentioned the owner of the company by name and addressed him sadly, saying: "You've left us out in the street when we worked for you loyally for twenty years." That was just pathetic. There was no need for that. If that was the best they could do, the supposed traitor would simply laugh in their faces. They needed to put pressure on all the Mr Cesspits, first, by striking, then, if necessary, by taking certain strategic steps, as Martín had done years before at the Ugarte mine. They needed to put pressure on people too, because people, all people, Ugarte's 1,500 inhabitants, the town's 300,000 inhabitants, the millions of people in Europe and America, were utterly unconcerned about the suffering of others, as unconcerned as those hills, that tractor and those warehouses were about Andoni's illness.

He saw Garazi standing in the doorway. She was still in her pyjamas – flimsy black silk decorated with Chinese motifs – and hugging herself as if she were cold. "Do you want me to bring you your dressing gown?" he asked.

"Yes, the turquoise one."

Garazi liked dressing gowns, and had three of them, one yellow, one white with black stripes and one turquoise.

"Where do you want to eat your banana? On the sofa?"

"No, I'll stay in the kitchen with my phone. I've got loads of messages from my friends."

"I'll go back to the living room then. If you need anything, just give me a shout."

He re-read what he had written in his memorandum on Garazi's illness. He had not yet described the most unpleasant episode, his phone call to the emergency number after coming back from the campsite.

"When Garazi still showed no sign of improvement, I phoned the emergency number. A woman answered and, judging from her voice, she was very young. I explained Garazi's symptoms in detail, adding: 'And she's in real pain. She keeps groaning.' I assumed she would put me straight through to a doctor, but no. She started asking me for all kinds of information, the patient's name, her ID number, her address and so on. And I gave her all the facts. Then, to my amazement, she started giving me advice, as if I were an idiot: 'Take your daughter to your local health centre. It's Monday tomorrow.' My words had clearly gone in one ear and out the other. 'I know tomorrow is Monday. Can you please put me through to a doctor.' She then gave me some gabbled, barely comprehensible spiel, speaking so fast that she swallowed half her words. I rounded on her: 'Unless I'm very much mistaken, this is a service paid for with taxpayers' money. First off, you should at least speak to me in an intelligible manner and secondly, I should have the right to speak to a doctor.' I received another stream of incomprehensible words of which I understood only one: 'No.' She sounded distinctly annoyed, and her voice sometimes quavered. She was clearly even more upset than I was. Suddenly, I understood. Or, rather, I imagined a scene that explained everything: that young woman and others like her had been advised by some technocrat at the service of the system on how best to act as a 'call-stopper'. Everyone knows how easily people panic and end up calling the emergency service for the slightest thing. If the service were to answer every call, they would need double the number of employees, and that was impossible, public finances simply did not stretch that far. The rhetoric of the system. Technocrat crap."

The phone rang in the kitchen. "Fine," Garazi said. "Fine," she said again. And after a silence: "So there's nothing seriously wrong with Odín."

When it seemed to Martín that the call had ended, he went into the kitchen.

"What did your mother have to say? Has something happened?" Daylight was flooding in through the window, making the turquoise colour of Garazi's dressing gown even more intense.

"They found a tick on Odín, but luckily it's not the sort that causes infections," Garazi said. It was so bright in the kitchen that Martín had to screw up his eyes. "Have you ever seen how they remove a tick from a horse?" Garazi asked.

"Yes. I helped your mother remove one once. You have to pull it straight out, no jerking or twisting."

"Or else you can cover the tick with a kind of gel, and then the horrible thing can't breathe and so it lets go."

Garazi's skin was still the colour of cream.

"Do you need anything?"

"No, I'm talking to my friends. They're coming round to visit."

"In that case, I'll carry on working."

He returned to his computer and continued his account:

"The 'call-stopper' who swallowed her words would not budge, and we had to stay at home. Ten hours later, at five in the morning, Garazi was screaming and writhing in agony. We took her to the hospital. Just an hour after that, she was on the operating table. Peritonitis. Ana and I waited for over two hours in the waiting area outside the operating theatre. Finally, the surgeon came out and said: "We were just in time." After ten days in hospital, the antibiotics have done their work, and Garazi is recovering. Now, we're home. Tomorrow, September 8, we go for her first check-up at the health centre."

Neither he nor Ana had ever heard the word "seroma" before, not until September 8, when the paediatrician at the local health centre saw that Garazi's dressing was wet.

"There's a little bit of seroma, but that's to be expected," she said. Whenever she pressed the place where the incision had been made, a brownish liquid oozed out of the wound.

331

The paediatrician explained to Garazi that seroma was an accumulation of fluid or serum in the area that had been operated on, and it usually ended up being absorbed by the body.

"But the nurse will drain it off for you," she said.

Garazi smiled, but only with her lips, not her eyes. She was wearing a navy-blue T-shirt bearing the bright red image of a wild horse, and she pulled it down tight over her jeans so that the image was clearly visible.

The nurse at the health centre was as brisk and energetic as Nurse Rosa. She took Garazi by the hand and led her to the treatment room, where she helped her lie down on the bed.

"It will sting a little bit, but only for the time it takes to inject you," she said, showing her the syringe.

Garazi started lifting up her T-shirt.

"It would be best if you took it off, sweetheart. But watch out. If you're not careful, I might steal it. That horse is just gorgeous. My niece is going to love it."

Garazi failed to get the joke. She looked at Martín.

"Wait outside, Dad."

He left the treatment room and sat on a chair in the waiting area from which he had a view of the whole ground floor. There were a lot of other people, although it was hard to tell exactly how many, because of the constant flow coming and going through the main door, however, there must have been more than forty: about twenty men and women over sixty, ten thirty-somethings, ten adolescents and three children, two girls and a boy. Suddenly, in his head, he heard the voice of the mumbling "call-stopper", and he started cursing her under his breath. What she had done was simply unforgivable. If she had not discouraged him from taking Garazi to hospital, they would not now have this problem with seroma. And the operation would have been a routine appendicitis operation, not a life-and-death affair.

He took a deep breath and tried to calm himself, not entirely successfully, but his insults took another direction. The "call-stopper" was not really to blame. She could certainly do harm, as

332

could any weak-willed person in difficult circumstances, but the real responsibility lay with the instructors who trained those workers and the ideologues from whom those in power took their cue.

The nurse emerged from the treatment room and came over to him.

"Is she OK?" he asked.

"Yes, fine, but there was a lot of fluid. And she's still very pale. I think we need to do a haemogram, a blood test."

Then Garazi and Ana appeared at the door of the treatment room. The navy-blue of Garazi's T-shirt and the bright red of the horse made her look still paler.

"Garazi, you'll need to come back on Monday," said the paediatrician when all three of them sat down in the consulting room. "I agree with the nurse. We'll do a haemogram, just in case."

She seemed very relaxed, as if this were all perfectly normal. She knew they were worried.

"Should we remove a couple of stitches? There's still quite a lot of seroma coming out," the nurse asked.

The paediatrician put her head on one side and closed one eye, as if she were aiming at a target. Then speaking to Garazi, she said:

"We might take out a couple on Monday, but first, the haemogram, OK?"

Garazi nodded and stood up. She could not wait to leave.

Once the consultation was over, they barely spoke as they walked the short way back to their house. In the streets everything was in motion: pedestrians, cars, buses, bicycles, sparrows hunting for crumbs on the terraces outside cafés, children and parents in the parks, the back and forth of the swings. All that movement meant life, animation, the anima mundi, but they, Garazi, Ana and Martín, were on the outside, waiting, motionless, wondering when they would be released from the prison of illness, because that's what Martín's life was at that moment: a prison. Far worse, in many respects, than the steel and concrete one he had known. He had never felt as isolated there as he did now.

When they got home, Garazi sat down in front of the television to watch a cartoon. The protagonists were a raccoon and a friend of his who looked like a bird. Martín and Ana sat in the kitchen and had a cup of coffee.

"Could you stay home on Monday and take her to the doctor's?" Ana asked. "I really need to be at the stables."

"Yes, fine. I can work on the magazine here."

Ana pulled a face.

"These ticks are a bloody nuisance."

"Why don't you go to the stables now. You'd feel better then. I'll take care of Garazi."

"Thanks."

Her eyes had filled with tears and she could not speak. She went into the living room, sat down on the sofa next to Garazi and, with her arm around her, whispered in her ear.

"That's all right. You go and look after Odín," Garazi said, without taking her eyes off the screen. The raccoon and his bird-like friend were fleeing in terror from a meteor that was hurtling towards a park.

Martín accompanied Ana to the front door, and they kissed goodbye.

At midday, five of Garazi's friends came to visit. They all squeezed onto the sofa and started playing with the kaleidoscope Luis had given her. After a while, Garazi said to Martín:

"We're going to my room to watch videos on YouTube. You carry on working." And they all left the living room, all clutching their respective mobile phones.

Garazi seemed more cheerful than she had at the health centre, but there was a big difference between the way she moved and the way her friends moved. They had all sprung up from the sofa, whereas Garazi had got to her feet more slowly.

The white orchid was still next to the computer. The woman at the florist's had seen those flowers as butterflies. For him, though, each flower was a receptacle, its petals collecting up the silence in the room and the light coming in through the window.

There were two new messages in his inbox, the first from Begoña and the second from a fellow ex-prisoner. He opened the second one:

"Tomorrow, September 9, 2017, it will be forty-one years since the death of Mao Tse-tung. Remember, my friend. Don't give up the struggle!"

He responded immediately:

"Yes, indeed, never give up!"

Begoña's email was all about the working conditions in care homes, including statements from two workers.

"Idoia: There are just three of us in charge of getting forty old people out of bed and washed, and even though we start at half past six in the morning, there are always delays – for example, when it comes to giving them their medicines. What's more, the management are timing us, as if we were in a race, recording how long we spend with each person, but not taking into consideration that person's individual needs. To be blunt, they are forcing us to be cruel."

"Florinda: I've spent five years working in care homes for the elderly and I know exactly what I will do when I get to their age: rather than be put in one of those places, I'll simply take a little pill and bye-bye world. Being alive isn't just a matter of being able to breathe. In some homes, they drug the residents so that they don't cause any trouble. Call that a life? I'd rather be dead."

He clicked on the arrow to respond:

"That first statement is very revealing, and I would suggest we use all of it. From the second one, I would just take that bit about how some homes drug the residents."

Begoña responded at once:

"I agree. How's Garazi?"

Martín:

"Better. I might even be able to drop by the office one of these days."

Begoña:

"There's no need, Martín. Email is a wonderful invention."

Begoña had added an emoticon to her message, a beaming sun.

Garazi's condition did not improve. On Saturday afternoon, shortly after getting together with her friends in the local park, she again felt ill, and Ana had to walk her home. When he came back from his run, Martín found them sitting on the sofa with their arms around each other, staring at the screen of Ana's mobile. "Charlot the Kid. Shamahina. Wild King," Ana said. These were the names of horses. "Moonhill. Satine Rouge . . ."

Martín sat down beside Garazi and gave her a kiss, then placed one hand on her forehead, making no attempt now to disguise what he was doing. She did not have a temperature, but she was extremely pale. Her creamy skin seemed an even milkier white than it had twenty-four hours earlier.

"OK, let's watch a video of the race, and you can guess who won," said Ana.

The sound of horses galloping, hooves drumming, grew louder and louder, then faded into nothing.

"Was it Shamahina?"

"Yes, she *was* the winner. Well done, Garazi."

"To be honest, I would have preferred Charlot the Kid to win."

Ana used her fingers to enlarge the image.

"If his jockey had come up on the inside, he could have won, but do you see what happened? He tried to go round the outside to avoid the mud, and that's what lost him the race."

Garazi had sat up on the sofa.

"I need to go to bed."

Her eyes seemed to be focussed on two separate things. In one eye there were the horses, Shamahina, Charlot the Kid, and, in the other, certain less precise images. Perhaps her schoolfriends, to whom she had barely had time to say goodbye in the park. Or the hospital corridor. Or the lights in the operating room. Or Andoni.

"You're bound to feel tired, Garazi, that's to be expected,"

Martín said. "You only got out of hospital a few days ago. It'll take a while to get used to normal life."

He and Ana went with her to the bedroom. When they lay her down on the bed, they checked the dressing. It was slightly damp.

"We have another appointment on Monday, so let's see what the paediatrician has to say then," said Ana, giving her a kiss.

"And see what the haemogram shows," Garazi added. They were all learning new words: seroma, haemogram.

He kissed her too, and together he and Ana left the room.

"What shall we have for supper?" he asked.

Ana's eyes had that same dual focus: the eye pondering the current situation was rather feeble, while the other was sad. She shook her head, she did not want any supper.

"Why do bad things all have to happen at once!" she cried. "On Monday I have to be at the stables. We just can't seem to get rid of this plague of ticks."

"Don't worry, Anita. I'm perfectly happy to take her to the doctor's. I'm up to date on the magazine."

He had unwittingly reverted to that affectionate diminutive "Anita", and they both stood there, not knowing quite how to continue. It was a name from the past. When they met twenty years earlier and started living in another kind of prison – love – oblivious to everything else, the Ana standing before him now, with those sad eyes and the dark circles under them, had been "Anita", a slightly built girl, who wore a red hard hat to go riding.

"I'll make a tomato salad. What do you think? We have to eat something," he said.

Ana shrugged.

The results of the haemogram were good, and when Martín asked if Garazi's haemoglobin levels were normal, the paediatrician turned the computer screen towards him so that he could see the number: 14. Perfectly normal.

"So why am I so pale?" Garazi asked.

Since her stay in hospital, she seemed to be more alert, even when she appeared to be thinking about something else. Her thoughts, like her eyes, were divided, as if they were sensors, with one of them constantly monitoring her body. This was particularly noticeable when it was time for her to take her antibiotics: five minutes before, she was already asking for them.

"There could be several reasons, but what matters now are the haemogram results," said the paediatrician, indicating one by one the most important of these: the red corpuscles, the leukocytes, the platelets. They were all fine. Just then, the nurse came into the room.

"So how's the wound?" the paediatrician asked.

"There's still a bit of seroma."

Her grave expression seemed to suggest she found this more concerning than the paediatrician did, but it was impossible to know if it was Garazi she was concerned about or another patient.

Martín and Garazi were walking back to the house when his mobile rang.

"Ana?" he said, but it was his brother.

"Luis speaking," Luis said in English. "And how's my favourite niece?"

Martín summarised what the doctor had said, then passed the phone to Garazi. Within seconds, she was laughing.

"What did he say?" Martín asked when she rang off.

Garazi shook her head gaily.

"Oh, all kinds of nonsense. My uncle's a real nutcase."

The phone rang again as soon as they reached home. It was Ana. He tried to simply repeat what he had said to Luis but could not conceal his anxiety. Given how pale Garazi was, he just could not understand how the blood test results could be so good.

"I agree, but the facts can't lie," said Ana.

"Yes, you're right."

Garazi took the phone from him and asked about Odín.

"Oh, that's great news," she said after listening to her mother's explanation. "Yeah, I'm doing fine. When will you be home?"

That answer proved fairly long.

"OK," said Garazi, before ending the conversation. She went over to the sofa and studied her mobile.

He sat down at the computer. It was a cloudy day, more like autumn than summer, and the little light entering the living-room window made the orchid flowers seem duller, more vanilla than white. It was the same flower, but in more sombre mood.

He pressed the key to turn on the screen. There was an email message from Begoña: "More than six million a year."

"In recent years, ever since the government privatised care for the elderly, companies in the health sector and all the Mr Cesspits involved have pocketed more than six million euros. You'll find the exact figures in the document attached. How's Garazi? Getting stronger?"

As if to encourage him to answer affirmatively, Garazi got up from the sofa to look out of the window.

"My friends are suggesting we meet in the park, but we can't, it's raining."

"Don't worry, Garazi, there'll be other nice days and then you'll be able to go out as often as you like."

She turned on the television.

"It's the same channel as the other day, you know, the one showing that programme about Daisy, the woman who weighed 207 kilos."

On the screen, in front of a sign covered in Chinese characters, a tiny woman barely one metre twenty tall was speaking in a very shrill voice.

"What's she saying?"

"Something about adopting sick children, I think."

What bad luck to turn on the TV and find a programme about such a grim subject. He was about to say as much but decided not to.

A still tinier man was now talking on the screen. "In China, they can't give them the care they need, and that's why we're going to take them to Chicago. They'll be well looked after there." He pointed to three children lying in one bed. Two were conjoined twins. It was a shocking image.

"Wouldn't you rather watch something else?"

"No, it's really interesting."

The light coming in through the living-room window was growing ever duller. The orchid had turned the colour of sand. He replied to Begoña's message:

"Fine. I'll study the information. We'll have to think about what we want to emphasise. We need to know what these women earn. If most of them earn 600 euros a month, we've got our headline: '600 euros for you, six million for me'. Garazi's getting better. Slowly, but heading in the right direction."

Garazi did not eat much for lunch. Half a bowl of courgette soup and a small slice of chicken. Nevertheless, she was in good spirits and told him how lucky the conjoined twins in the programme had been. In Chicago, they had undergone a seventeen-hour operation to separate them. Fortunately, they had both survived, each with her own heart, liver and lungs . . . As the day wore on, though, Garazi's energy ebbed away. When Ana came home in the evening, and Garazi started telling her about the twins, she suddenly fell silent.

"I'm a bit tired. I think I'll go to bed."

Martín felt briefly annoyed with his daughter: would she never get better?

"I'll take over from your father. I want a chance to look after my little girl too," said Ana, putting on a cheerful face. "Martín, you go for your run."

"Tell Mum about the conjoined twins," Garazi said to her father.

"He'll tell me later," said Ana. "Your father needs some fresh air."

He usually went through the industrial estate, walking the first 200 metres past the warehouses and workshops at an almost normal pace and only starting to run when he reached the back

340

road leading into the village. Then he would gradually speed up until the rhythm and the kind of mental numbness brought on by physical effort either erased all thought or reduced it to a minimum: all he noticed then were the fields of crops, or the stubble yet to be taken up or the marks left by the tractor on the road. That Monday, though, there was no respite, and he continued thinking about the situation they found themselves in, about how their lives had changed in just a couple of weeks, and when he saw the three hills, "the roller coaster", and the memory of when Garazi was little, the stark contrast between past and present took his breath away and he had to stop.

He waited for a couple of minutes and did some breathing exercises, then started running again. When he reached the restaurant with the red sign, he did not head back home, as he usually did, but continued on up, towards the top of one of the hills, until he could run no further and let himself drop to the ground and lie there on his back. Thick clouds were covering the sky. Soon it would start to rain.

He heard the clock in the village chime seven. He got to his feet and started on the homeward stretch. Running downhill, he soon left the restaurant behind and was once again on the back road. A few hundred metres further on, and feeling calmer, he fixed his gaze on what lay before him: the area where they lived, their apartment block, and behind that, other housing blocks and a church steeple. Further off, to the right, the white hospital building.

In the industrial estate, he saw a police car parked outside a warehouse. Two officers were tearing down a poster.

"Why are you doing that? What right have you to tear it down?" he said when he reached them.

All that remained was the top part of the poster: "Have you no consci . . ." One of the policemen planted himself in front of him and put his hand to his waist, close to his gun.

"What right?" Martín said again.

"Look, just carry on with your run, will you?" said the policeman.

"Aren't you ashamed to be working for a thief?"

The second policeman came over.

"Look, go away, unless you want us to take you down to the police station."

He looked round at his colleague.

"Exercise obviously doesn't agree with him."

Martín felt like continuing the argument, but he could not risk being arrested. Garazi was ill.

"And why have you got your hand at your waist like that? Ready to whip out your gun?" he asked the first policeman.

Without waiting for a response, he ran off. Behind him, he heard a voice saying: "Oh, leave him. The guy's mad." The second policeman clearly did not want any trouble.

When Martín went into the house, Ana was speaking on the phone. He could tell at once, from her tone of voice, that she was speaking to a stranger. He listened: she was describing Garazi's condition to a doctor. He went to Garazi's bedroom and sat down beside her on the bed. There was no need to put his hand on her forehead. She was sweating. She had a fever. Garazi made a joke:

"I've been running too. See, that's why I'm sweating."

She smiled. In her eyes, he could still see those two expressions, but the sombre expression was now the more dominant of the two.

Ana came into the room.

"The doctor said we should leave you for an hour without the duvet on, and if your temperature still doesn't come down, then we should take you to the hospital. Don't worry, it'll pass."

Whenever Garazi was asked to do anything, she usually resisted and tried to get her own way, but this time she behaved like a good little girl, lifting up her arms while Ana removed the duvet. She was wearing her black pyjamas. Seen from close to, the Chinese motifs, the flowers, trees and birds, looked very cheerful.

Garazi shivered.

"What's her temperature now?" Martín asked.

"Thirty-eight point seven," said Ana. She pointed to the

bathroom. "Bring me a towel so that I can wipe away the sweat. And take a shower, because we're going to have to go to the hospital."

When he was the only one feeling anxious, he could reassure himself by thinking that this was just the way he was. At that moment, though, there was only one expression in Ana's eyes. She was frightened.

"Yes, we'd better go. Give me ten minutes."

Before showering, he sat down at the computer to write a message to Begoña:

"Garazi has a temperature again and we're going to the hospital. We'll probably have to stay there. I'll take my laptop with me so that we can stay in touch. Send me some more workers' statements if you can. We'll have to add an interview with a union representative. We don't have much time, only two weeks to get it all ready for the printers. October is just around the corner."

It was growing dark, and there was no light on in the room. The fleshy leaves at the base of the orchid looked black, the petals grey. He turned on the light, and the plant was restored to its usual state: green leaves and white petals.

Another email arrived. It was from the friend who had reminded him about the anniversary of Mao's death, a kind of circular. The subject: "Supper for ex-combatants".

"A few of us ex-prisoners thought we might have a get-together over supper later this month. If you'd like to join us, let me know."

He turned off the computer and went for a shower. When he emerged from the bathroom, he saw Garazi's turquoise suitcase next to the front door. Ana was ready to go.

"Hurry up, Martín. The doctor I spoke to told me A&E was pretty busy."

Garazi was sitting on the sofa, wrapped in her dressing gown. Very softly, as if talking to herself, she said:

"A dreadful day to go to the doctor's. But then, I do always like to make things difficult."

Martín cursed himself while hurriedly pulling on his clothes.

343

Why had he made that stupid remark about Garazi at the campsite? He gave himself a slap, as he did sometimes when he felt he deserved to be punished.

Sometimes, if the appendix becomes severely inflamed, it can burst, and the contents of the intestine, its thousands of bacteria, flood the abdominal cavity, infecting the protective membrane or peritoneum, and that's what they call peritonitis. If that unsavoury mixture of blood and pus is not eliminated, the infection can spread throughout the whole body, affecting the kidneys, lungs, liver, and eventually causing death. This happens in a third of cases.

After the first operation, the surgeon had told them he had done his best to clean out the entire abdominal cavity, because all it took was a tiny trace of pus for the bacteria to start reproducing again. Unfortunately, he could not guarantee that he had been successful. If another infection did occur, they would have to control it with a further dose of antibiotics.

"But let's hope that doesn't happen," he had said.

Hoping, alas, was not enough. Garazi's temperature of thirty-eight point seven was proof that the infection had returned.

Back in the emergency bay, Martín could not fend off a wave of negative thoughts: everything that could go wrong was going wrong; everything was turning out to be retrocecal, things weren't working out well for his daughter. He felt overwhelmed and left the bay to get some air and calm down, only to return a minute later.

The paediatrician, Laura, was standing by Garazi's bed alongside Ana. A third expression had installed itself in Garazi's eyes: not the happy expression he had seen when she was following the horse race on her mother's mobile, or the sad expression he knew from when she was lying on the sofa or in bed, feeling ill, but the shifty look of someone who felt ashamed. She thought she was responsible for the situation. Guilt, like the infection, had taken over. And yet he had been the one to inject her with that guilt, by making a stupid remark about how she always liked to make life difficult. Standing behind Ana, he pulled a funny face and winked at Garazi. She smiled, and he had to suppress the urge to cry.

"What's happening to you is not that unusual, sweetheart," Laura said to Garazi. She had chosen to come down to A&E to see Garazi, because they were "old friends". "There's some mucky stuff in your tummy, but we'll get rid of it."

She made a call on her mobile, asking if another doctor, to whom she referred as "the biker", was on duty? It was dark now, and only the night staff were around. It seemed, though, that the answer was Yes. "Good, I'll call his mobile."

Martín's ears pricked up. If they found "the biker" that would be a good sign; if not, it would mean another setback for Garazi.

After just a few seconds, Laura said: "Where are you? Well, that's no distance at all. Climb on your metal horse and come over." She then left the bay, and from what Martín could hear, spent a while explaining the situation.

"He'll be here in a quarter of an hour," she said, coming back into the bay. She then spoke to Garazi: "We're going to take you somewhere else now. Our biker will be in charge of getting rid of the mucky stuff. He's a real whizz, you'll see."

At that moment, Garazi's face seemed to be made of snow. In the midst of that layer of snow sat two bluish hollows, the circles under her eyes.

"Isn't Rosa coming?" she asked.

"You must be telepathic! They told me you were here, and so I slipped away to see you," cried a nurse coming into the bay. It was Rosa.

She went over to Garazi and planted a kiss on her forehead. Shortly afterwards, the orderly arrived to take Garazi to the operating room, and Rosa asked if she could take her instead.

"Would you mind? I haven't seen this friend of mine for ages."

"Five and a half days," said Garazi.

The small operating room set aside for such procedures was on the ground floor. Martín and Ana sat down on two of the plastic chairs in the corridor, next to an open window. A few minutes later, the surgeon arrived. He was young and was carrying a black motorcycle helmet. He strode over to the operating room.

"They'll have to stick a syringe in her belly," said Ana.

She stood up and went over to the window. He followed suit and put an arm around her shoulder.

"Why did this have to happen to us?" she said.

This was a double lament. The first for the illness, the insidious evil that had presented itself in the guise of a simple stomach-ache. The second was for what they happened to see down below, in the inner courtyard, where a van was waiting with its rear doors open to reveal some metal beds. Beside it was a stretcher on which lay a black plastic bag containing what looked like a human body – obviously someone who had just died in the hospital.

Ana clutched her head in her hands and broke down in tears. She and Martín embraced.

Half an hour later, they learned another new word from the "biker": abscess. Most of the accumulated pus in Garazi's abdominal cavity had been removed during the first operation, but a tiny fragment, whose size the biker indicated by holding his index finger and thumb about half a centimetre apart, had got stuck in some cranny that the syringe could not reach. It was what is known in medical terminology as an abscess. They were not to worry though. It would not cause any problems at all. They would tackle the outbreak of bacteria with antibiotics. It would be a matter of a week at most.

"Maximum," he said, before excusing himself to go and change.

The three days following her second stay in hospital, September 12, 13 and 14, Garazi's temperature remained at around 37°C throughout the day, and only in the evening, between seven o'clock and nine, did it rise a little. That was the time Martín would go to the hospital, to take over from Ana and spend the night with Garazi. He could feel how hot she was when he kissed her forehead.

Garazi had again been given Room 121 in the Paediatric Unit, and the three of them would stay there chatting once the auxiliary nurse had taken away the supper tray. Ana usually had most to say. The situation at the stables was getting back to normal, they had managed to control the plague of ticks, and Odín's training was going well. She also had news of Garazi's schoolfriends. They had asked if they could visit her in hospital, but the paediatrician, Laura, had insisted that, during that week, Garazi needed to avoid all stress, and so they had agreed to do as she advised. That was also why she had not brought Garazi's mobile phone with her. Garazi needed complete rest until all trace of fever had gone.

They would talk until ten o'clock at night, and then the nurse would come to check Garazi's temperature and blood pressure, and, at that point, Ana would go home. Martín would then draw an armchair up to the bed and hold Garazi's hand under the sheet. That was enough for them to feel close, and they would stay like that, without speaking.

Thanks to the various substances entering her veins, Garazi's breathing would gradually become deeper, and she would eventually close her eyes and fall asleep. Martín would then turn off the fluorescent light above the bedhead and feel the darkness flooding in through the window, engulfing the walls, floor, ceiling and bed in shadow. When his hand, still holding his daughter's hand, also fell asleep, he would leave her side and turn on his computer.

On the fourth day, September 15, he had an idea. He kept a file containing old photos of the village where he was born, and he started highlighting those that might provide him and Garazi with talking points. He had noticed in the past how intently Garazi always listened to stories about Ugarte. For her, they seemed to belong to a different world. Ugarte was only 120 kilometres away in space, but in time, it was a long way off.

He started clicking on the photos. In the first one, Luis, Elías and he were standing in front of the bakery, each clutching a toy boat. The second showed the three of them again, but this time actually standing in the water. The third showed only the boats, lined up on the edge of the path as if on a quay: a green rowboat, a red barge and a white canoe.

The images brought back a scene for which no photo existed, but which would perhaps be the best one to tell Garazi about: the moment when they saw a wild boar in the canal with its hooves all bloody from its desperate attempts to scramble out of the water. "But it all ended well," he would tell her, "because Eliseo and the Gitane Blonde managed to divert it off down another branch of the canal so that it could escape back into the hills." As soon as Garazi heard the name "Blonde Gypsy", she would want to know who he was. Martín had three photos of him. In one he was with Elías, Luis and himself. In another, it was just him and Eliseo, the "Gypsy" with his accordion strapped over his shoulders, as if he were about to start playing. In the third one, he was with Marta and Miguel.

Garazi knew that Marta was her grandmother's name, but she was slightly confused about her grandfather's name. Sometimes she thought he was called Julián and, at others, Miguel. But she was not yet thirteen, and he did not want to talk to her about certain things until her childhood was properly over.

He enlarged the next photo, and there was Marta. She was posing with a girlfriend of hers in the main street of Ugarte. Two very pretty girls. Her friend, Lucía, was wearing a miniskirt. His mother had told him that Lucía had ruined her life by marrying a good-for-nothing who had then dragged her into a world of gambling and betting, and that she had ended up dying by suicide. "The people in the village covered up what had really happened, because she died a truly dreadful death, and they didn't want her parents to know the truth. They told them she had simply drowned in the river, which was sad enough in itself, but, in fact, she had waded into the river after taking poison. Apparently, the poison brought on a terrible thirst, and that's what drove her into the water. Can you imagine a worse way to die?" His mother would weep for Lucía while she herself lay dying in hospital, not very far from where Garazi was now. "Martín, don't let me talk about these things, they stir up too many sad memories and emotions." He would try to distract her by changing the subject: "Do you want me to phone Luis? It'll be about midday in California now." "Yes, give him a call." Luis would usually pick up the phone and immediately start clowning around. She would pretend to be scandalised: "Have you been smoking marijuana, Luitxo . . .? LSD? No, I don't believe it!" Then, out of the blue, during one such phone call, his mother said: "Martín wants to know when you'll be coming to see me. He wants to know, not me." Needless to say, Luis came up with one of his usual excuses. His mother's tone changed then: "Luitxo, I'm serious. If you don't come and see me, I'll take away part of your inheritance." When she moved in with Miguel and took over the commercial side of the bakery, she had become very much the businesswoman. She never joked about money. The threat was serious.

Martín clicked on another photo. Antoine's two Dobermanns. Both of them good dogs, although on the day of the sabotage, Martín had been rather nervous about going up to the mine. Given how long it had been since he visited Villa Chantal, he was afraid that Troy would not recognise him and so he had armed himself with an iron bar, in case he had to defend himself. However, as soon as the dog heard his voice, he came over to him, head down, rear end wagging, and then, when Martín stroked him, he lay on the floor, just as he used to as a puppy. Then he had remained sitting quietly in a corner while Martín set about smashing everything in sight. Troy had no idea what was going on, but he trusted Martín, the friend who, for years, used to bring him his food on a plate. Dogs know nothing of treachery.

Martín bent over Garazi. She was breathing quietly. He placed one hand on her forehead. It was cool. The IV drip was continuing to do its work.

He returned to his laptop and continued selecting photos from Ugarte. One of them showed a particularly happy moment: all the family gathered on the terrace on a summer night, his father smoking a Monterrey cigar, a glass of whisky in his hand, his mother pretending to offer her glass of rum to the photographer, Martín and Luis laughing.

At that point, he decided he'd had enough of all those images from the past and, instead, checked his emails. There were five messages, the first three from Begoña, the fourth from a friend who had been with him in prison, the fifth from Tuco, his brother Luis, who, ever since his accident and the delirium he experienced while in a coma, signed his emails Tuco, the nickname of one of the characters in *The Good, the Bad and the Ugly.*

The three emails from Begoña contained more statements from carers working in care homes. Martín felt that they should give particular prominence to one from a woman describing what had happened on her night shift:

"The situation gets worse at night. Two carers cannot possibly keep an eye on what's happening on all four floors. A few days ago, an old lady fell out of bed shortly after we'd been to see her, and she lay there for four hours, calling for help. No-one in the neighbouring rooms could help her, and we couldn't hear her because we were on another floor."

Martín wrote back:

"We definitely need to highlight this statement. One incident like that is worth a thousand words."

He then opened the email headed: "Supper for ex-combatants". It was from the organiser, announcing that the supper for ex-prisoners would take place on Saturday, September 23, at around eight o'clock. He read the name and address of the restaurant. It was the one with the red sign he could see from his kitchen window. It was a kind of agritourism hotel, and the plan was that they would all stay the night there after a long after-supper chat "talking over old times".

Martín replied:

"If I happen to be out for my usual run that night, I'll drop in and drink a beer with you, but I won't be able to stay for supper."

Then he opened his brother's message:

"I'll come to the hospital at around eleven and stay with

Garazi until five. Then I'll be sticking around for a while after that too, because some Ugarte folk are planning to visit Andoni: the Gitane Blonde, Eliseo and Paca . . . the whole crew. So tell Ana she doesn't need to go there before five. And last but not least . . . Do you have Elías' email address? Is he still in Austin? I need to talk to him ASAP."

The clock on the computer showed twelve minutes past one: 01:12.

He went over to Garazi again. She was sleeping peacefully, and he did not need to touch her forehead to know that her temperature had gone down. The antibiotics entering her veins along with the saline solution were helping her to rest and, above all, fighting the bacteria in the abscess. He whispered: "Good for you, Garazi!" and kissed one of her hands.

Before trying to sleep, he left the room for a moment to buy a bottle of water from the vending machine next to the lifts. The corridor was empty and silent. The even-numbered rooms were on the right, and the line of odd-numbered rooms on the left was interrupted by the nurses' station, with the white orchid and the green fern still there on the counter.

The silence in the corridor, in the rooms and in the whole hospital was the product of the substances entering the veins of all the patients; it was unnatural, unreal. It might even be deceptive, retrocecal, unclean, but the white orchid neutralised any threat that might be floating in the atmosphere. He continued on to the vending machine, and when he reached the nurses' station and saw the two plants from closer to, he thought of the orchid at home, keeping watch over the dark living room like a lighted candle, and he noticed a warmth in his heart that he had not felt for a long time.

The nurse was checking something on the computer. She turned to him and said:

"I'm just going to look in on Garazi."

"She seems fine, well, at least she hasn't got a temperature."

"That's a good sign. We haven't given her any antipyretics today either."

"Really?"

The nurse pressed a few keys on the computer.

"That's right. No antipyretics."

A tremor ran through him, as if there had been a change in the electric charge in his body. Her words echoed in his head: "We haven't given her any antipyretics today either."

"Great!" he said and waved goodbye. "I'm just going to buy a bottle of water. My throat gets really dry in the hospital."

"I'm not surprised, given how many hours you spend here."

The vending machine, lit from top to bottom, was in marked contrast to the dark brown tiles in the lift area, and to the shadows cast by the fluorescent ceiling lights. It was really only a fridge with a glass door, but it looked like something out of a spaceship.

The blue-tinted bottles glowed inside the machine. When he put his money in and pressed the button, a bottle clattered into the pick-up tray. He took it out and felt the cold plastic in his hand.

He could not imagine why Luis could possibly want Elías's email address. Elías taught at the University of Texas, and visited the Basque Country every summer, but as far as Martín knew, Elías and Luis were not great friends.

He met the nurse coming out of Garazi's room. She was very young, but somehow mature beyond her years.

"Your daughter's sleeping really well. We'll see what the doctor says tomorrow, but I think she'll be able to go home soon."

This was his impression too when he went back in; indeed, if it had not been for the IV drip, he could have mistaken her sleep for a normal placid night's rest after a normal day at school.

He turned the computer on and typed "Elías" in the search window of his email. All the messages from recent years filled the screen. He copied the address, added his brother's and typed a message:

"How are things, Elías? The other day, we watched a reality TV programme filmed in Texas about a woman who weighed 207 kilos. The skies were always blue. I was almost tempted to hop on a plane.

"My brother has asked me for your email. I thought you wouldn't mind, so I'm copying him in here. He's always been a bit crazy as you know, but he's a good guy really. Lately, he's taken to calling himself Tuco."

He still had the file of photos from Ugarte open. He dragged the picture of the three boats into the email and added a PS: "Which one was yours?"

Elías' answer arrived almost instantly:

"The green one. Yours was the white one and Luis' the red one."

He checked on the internet to see what time it was in Austin. Six forty-two in the evening: 18.42. He sent a message back, wishing Elías a nice evening.

Laura the paediatrician appeared in Garazi's room at ten the next morning. She told Martín that she wanted to examine Garazi alone and asked him to wait outside. She would only be about ten minutes. She was accompanied by Nurse Rosa.

By day, the corridor was totally different: knots of visitors hung about outside the rooms, auxiliary nurses in pink uniforms were pushing breakfast trolleys, while blue-uniformed nurses came and went with their trays of medicines . . . Martín needed to stretch his legs and was about to go for a stroll down the corridor, but making his way past all those people proved so awkward that he chose, instead, to wait outside Garazi's room. He folded his arms and suddenly became acutely aware of his heart beating. Ten minutes was a long time. Generally speaking, doctors' visits were fairly brief. A quick examination, a few questions and that was it until the next day.

In the end, he had to wait not ten minutes or even five before Laura, followed by Rosa, came out of the room. She was smiling.

"Garazi's fine. If she remains free of fever today and the blood tests come back normal, then we'll discharge her on Monday."

Rosa took a digital thermometer from her pocket and showed it to him.

"Thirty-six point six, the most normal temperature in the world. I'm going to frame it so that you can take it home with you."

"That's wonderful news," he said, then looked at Laura. "Has the abscess gone?"

"Not entirely, but it's harmless now. It won't cause her any more problems."

"But will it stay there in her abdominal cavity?"

The expression on Laura's face remained unchanged.

"Only for a while, but don't worry, her body will gradually reabsorb it."

"Martín finds it very hard not to worry," said Rosa.

"It's just a matter of will power," said Laura with a smile. She patted him on the arm, and the two women disappeared among the other people filling the corridor.

When he went back into the room, he gave Garazi a kiss.

"Shall we phone your mum?"

"Yes, and tell her to bring my mobile. All my friends have started back at school, and I need to speak to them."

She was sitting up in bed. Her eyes, no longer bright with fever, looked rested. She had a little colour in her face too: peach-pink on her ears, soft grey under her eyes, and a warm white, rather than a creamy white, on her cheeks.

Ana answered immediately, and Garazi spoke before her mother had a chance to say anything. "Don't worry. I'm fine. Look, when will you be going home? I need my phone. OK. And bring the charger too."

From his days as a student of philosophy Martín could still recall the original meaning of the word "euphoria". It did not mean happiness or dynamism, but rather the energy generated by the mind to cope with difficult situations. In his case, it had acted as a dam keeping out a rogue current and had not even broken when the waters were at their height, for example when Garazi was taken into hospital for a second time and he and Ana had witnessed that scene out in the hospital courtyard, one worthy of the underworld: the moment when a corpse, wrapped in black plastic, was being put into a van. Now, September 16, the flood waters appeared to have abated, and that inner energy, that euphoria, no longer knew where to go, in which direction to expend its power. When he phoned Ana again, though, and began explaining that his brother would be staying with Garazi until five o'clock, which meant that she need not turn up until then, he suddenly burst into tears.

At the other end of the phone, Ana said nothing. Then she spoke: "It's alright, Martín." Her voice almost broke too. "If Luis doesn't mind, then I'll stay here. We need to get on top of the backlog of work caused by those wretched ticks."

"Oh, Luis doesn't mind at all, and Garazi will love having him here."

The auxiliary nurse came in with the breakfast tray: chocolate milk, crackers and jam. Garazi immediately tucked in.

"Where's the paycard for the television?" she asked.

It was already in the slot. Garazi picked up the remote and pressed the on button. Images from the cartoon *Dragon Ball* appeared on the screen.

"Do you like *Dragon Ball*?" he asked.

"Not much, but it doesn't matter. You go and have your breakfast in the cafeteria."

Like her skin colour, her normal personality was also beginning to return.

In the cafeteria in the hospital basement, the air was transformed by the comforting smell of coffee: the smell of health not illness. Large piles of pastries, doughnuts and croissants occupied the centre of the counter.

He found an empty table next to a pillar and sat down with his coffee and a croissant.

A small, thin woman with sharp features stopped to speak to him. She was in her forties and wore her hair pinned up on the top of her head. She resembled some kind of bird.

"You're Martín, aren't you?" she said with a smile. He made to get up. "No, you carry on with your breakfast. I just wanted to say hello. I'm Esteban's wife."

It felt wrong to remain seated and so he did finally get up and, rather awkwardly, held out his hand.

"Good to meet you."

"I wasn't born in Ugarte, that's why you don't know me. I recognised you, of course, because you're absolutely identical to Luis," she said. She had lively dark eyes.

Martín then remembered the name of the bird she resembled: a hoopoe.

"How's Andoni?" he asked.

She smiled again, but her smile was more ambiguous than it had been a moment before.

"We're going to take him to Houston. They can't do anything more for him here."

"They do tend to have more advanced treatments in America."

"So they say. And how's Garazi?"

"Much better, thank you."

He noticed a catch in his throat, or, rather, in his mind.

"Andoni's been asking after her," she said. "They've met several times in the games room. They get on really well."

"When are you leaving for Houston?"

"On the twentieth, next Wednesday."

She shook his hand and said goodbye.

Ana always used to say that because horses have their eyes on either side of their head, they have better all-round vision, and are able to see what's happening to the left and to the right. "You have that same ability, Martín," she had said to him once. And it was true. He had always been able to see both sides of a problem, especially during his years of political activism. Now, however, he seemed to have lost that ability. The fact that he had failed to make the connection between his brother Luis' message and Andoni's situation was proof of that. The connection was obvious: Elías lived in Austin, Texas, very close to Houston, and it would

356

be really useful to Andoni and his parents if they could count on the help of someone who had lived there for years. That was why Luis wanted to contact him. Martín had also failed to take on board how serious Andoni's cancer was. That, too, was now clear.

While he was finishing his breakfast, he picked up a newspaper from another table and leafed through it, looking for some mention of the dispute involving care homes. He found it impossible to concentrate though, and a few minutes later, he left the cafeteria and headed up the stairs to Room 121.

There he found Garazi and Luis in fits of laughter. On the TV screen now, *Dragon Ball* had been replaced by a comedy. Charlie Chaplin had just been hit on the head with a frying pan and, stunned by the blow, was staggering down the street, his legs like rubber.

"You carry on watching the film, Garazi. I'll be right back," Luis said as soon as Martín appeared at the door.

"Where are you going?" Garazi asked.

"I need to send your father home to fetch a few things."

"What things?"

"Some DVDs."

"Tell him to bring my mobile too."

"Don't worry, I'll bring it," Martín said.

Garazi burst out laughing again. On the screen, the blows from the frying pan were coming thick and fast now, but, this time, the people on the receiving end were the Nazi police, and they simply dropped to the ground without performing any kind of dance.

"We'll be right back," Martín and Luis said simultaneously, as they used to when they were children.

They sat down on a bench near the lifts, and Luis started talking about Andoni. He was not responding to the chemo as well as the doctors had hoped, and so his parents were taking him to Houston. The hospital had made all the necessary arrangements.

"Yes, I know. I just met his mother in the cafeteria."

Two images came into his head: the mother and her hoopoe-like

357

head and Esteban. Two people who had seemed destined never to leave Ugarte, and who were now having to travel to Texas with their sick son.

"Elías sent me a message, saying he'll do everything he can to help," said Luis, giving a thumbs-up sign, for, despite being almost sixty, he still retained some of his more youthful gestures. He stood up then and added:

"The main thing is, Garazi's better and you'll soon have her home again."

Martín stood up too. They were facing each other now. Luis gave him a hug. Martín suddenly understood what was on his brother's mind. Luis wanted to go to Houston with Andoni and his parents but was still unsure as to whether or not he should. He was wary of his own emotional impulses, of behaving like the old Tuco.

"I think you'd be a real help, Luis. After all, you're used to airports. Besides, it might turn out that next Wednesday, Elías won't, for some reason, be able to come and meet them."

Luis' face lit up and he gave Martín another hug.

"You read my mind, Martín. Twin telepathy!"

And he hugged him again.

"I'm so glad you think it's a good idea, Martín. My big brother's opinion counts for a lot."

"You'll have to buy a plane ticket."

"I reserved one for myself when I bought theirs. Just in case. The new Tuco is not like the old Tuco. He's learned to be more prudent."

Garazi was discharged on Monday, September 18, and that same night, Martín had a dream. Utter chaos reigned in their apartment, as if it had been ransacked by burglars, with drawers emptied of clothes and books strewn all over the floor, the computer smashed to pieces, the white orchid on the table burned to a cinder. This scene of destruction was repeated outside too: the roofs of the warehouses in the industrial park had caved in, and the three roller-coaster hills were all slightly misshapen, as if they had fallen victim to some great natural disaster. When he woke, though, the only thing not in the right place was the orchid, which was no longer on the living-room table, but in Garazi's bedroom. And Garazi was sleeping peacefully. When he touched her forehead, he felt the normal warmth given off by a healthy body.

Dreams were also receptacles of a kind. They did not, like the orchid, collect light and silence, but fear. How many dreams would it take to gather together all his fears and free up his mind? There was no way of knowing, but he knew it would take more than that night's dream. The days passed – the 19th, the 20th, the 21st – and he was still having trouble breathing easily. He was afraid there would be a repeat of what had happened after Garazi was discharged for the first time, that the illness still sat crouched inside her, waiting for the right moment to attack again. Was the abscess really harmless now? On the days when Ana stayed at home, and he went to the union offices, he would jump every time the phone rang; and when he came back from his run late in the evening, he would open the door, straining eyes and ears. However, those days passed and nothing terrible happened. Garazi was improving all the time. The skin on her face had taken on a different tone; she moved nimbly from one room to another; she was constantly on her mobile phone. There was nothing to indicate that these signs were in any way retrocecal.

On Friday, September 22, he got up early to check the PDF of the union magazine. Then he wrote to Begoña:

"It's looking really good. The only thing I would change are some of the photos of the care homes. I'll drop by later, at around four. First, I have to take Garazi to school. Today's the day her life finally gets back to normal."

Begoña replied almost instantly:

"I'm so glad to know Garazi's well again! And that's fine about the PDF. We'll give it another read-through here, and I'll look out some different photos. See you later."

Ana appeared at the living-room door. She was dressed for work, in blue jeans, a red denim jacket and a white T-shirt.

"How do I look?" she asked. She was obviously feeling happy.

"Fantastic."

She didn't look in the least bit anxious. She was far better than him at driving fears from her mind.

"I'm off to work. I've left Garazi's clothes on the bed. Phone me later to tell me what kind of welcome she got at school."

"What time shall I wake her up? Around eleven?"

"Yes, better get her up in good time," Ana said. "She'll want to shower and make herself pretty. And don't forget, I'll pick her up after school. You go off to work."

"Me, forget? No way, José," he said. This was the advertising slogan of a chain of shops, which always made Garazi giggle.

They reached the school shortly before the start of afternoon classes, and a few of her friends, who were waiting in the entrance, escorted Garazi inside, amid much whooping and hugging. After a while, the whooping was repeated, only more loudly, in one of the classrooms. He watched from the corridor: all the students had left their desks and were laughing and shouting while the teacher, hands raised, called for order. He had wanted to remind Garazi that Ana would be waiting for her after school, but it was impossible to get past the friends crowding around her.

He left the school and walked across the park to the union offices. The trees, mostly horse chestnuts, were already wearing their various autumn colours, each with its own particular combination of greens and ochres and oranges. A cheering sight. At one point, a tree released a chestnut in its prickly case, which fell on his head; and he smiled as if nature were making him part of a friendly game. Further on, as he walked through the streets, his thoughts again turned to Garazi. When she was little, and they used to go for walks together, she was obsessed with yellow cars and would shout "yellow car!" every time she spotted one among the traffic. Before he knew it, he had reached the office. In these changed circumstances, time seemed to pass more quickly.

The union offices lined the corridor that led from the entrance to the inner courtyard, rather like the bays in A&E, except that they were separated not by curtains, but by partitions. Fortunately, that was all the two places had in common; the biggest difference was the stink of cigarettes. He never usually noticed this, but, after his brief absence, the smell hit him the moment he went through the door. It was a very persistent smell. Smoking had been banned in the building for ten years now, and yet it was still there. It had been the same in their house in Ugarte. All his father's books, including the Westerns, were still impregnated with the smell of his Monterrey cigars.

The room Martín shared with Begoña was at the far end of the corridor and the only one with a window. Someone had left a page from the local newspaper on the keyboard of his computer, with a Post-it note saying "Read this", and an arrow pointing to a short, ten-line article. It was a report from a news agency: "Boy dies from alleged medical negligence". It was dated September 5. Martín's eyes immediately fixed on the word "peritonitis", and then on "A&E" and "negligence". The incident had taken place in a hospital in Barcelona province.

He immediately searched the internet. A lot of newspapers had picked up the story. A sixteen-year-old boy complaining of stomach pain had repeatedly sought medical advice, four times in the course of ten days. First, at a health centre, where he was diagnosed with constipation. Two days later, the pain had worsened and so he went to A&E. They sent him away, saying it was gastroenteritis. Two days later, he went to A&E again. Gastroenteritis. Three days later, in terrible pain, he went back to the health centre. Gastroenteritis. The following day, he collapsed. The family dialled the emergency number and the boy was rushed to hospital in an ambulance, where he underwent two operations, both of which proved unsuccessful. He died that same night. The newspapers gave his father's comments: "He was taken into hospital with very advanced peritonitis, a perforated intestine and widespread infection. He went into septic shock, which caused multiple organ failure. If they had done a CT scan instead of an ordinary X-ray, our son would still be alive."

Begoña and a young man were standing, smoking, in the courtyard outside, and Martín went to join them, taking with him the page from the newspaper.

"It came out when your daughter was in hospital, and I didn't want to say anything at the time," Begoña said.

She was a fair-haired woman of thirty-seven, always impeccably dressed and beautifully made up. No-one who saw her in the street would have taken her for what she was, a militant who had served time in prison and now worked for a radical trade union.

"Knowing what had happened to your daughter, we were just petrified," said the young man.

For Martín, all children were Garazi, and now she was that Catalan boy. He imagined a child clinging to his mother's skirt and asking: *Mama, per què plores?* Mama, why are you crying? An image that was immediately joined by that of Andoni's mother, with her hoopoe-like head.

"I wrote something about that disastrous emergency call I made. I could perhaps add the facts from this case and turn it into an article," he said, but his mind, still full of the image of Andoni's mother, had already moved on to Houston.

The office window that overlooked the courtyard was open, and they heard three beeps one after the other. Three new emails had arrived.

"That's yours, Martín," said Begoña. "Mine makes a different noise."

He glanced at his watch. It was almost five o'clock. Ten o'clock in the morning in Houston.

"I'll go and check."

Just as he had thought, they were all from his brother, and all three had the same subject heading. "Team Houston". When he opened the first one, he found a photo featuring, from left to right, Esteban, Esteban's wife, Andoni, Elías and Luis. They were posing, smiling, in a beautifully kept but deserted park. Behind them he could see a dozen or so skyscrapers, so bare and empty they did not look quite real. The sky was the same intense blue as in that programme starring Daisy, *From Fat to Fit*.

There was another photo attached to the second email. Elías and Luis arm in arm, with Elías wearing a white hat and Luis in a cowboy outfit.

The photo in the third email showed Luis and Andoni, with Luis wearing a black hat and Andoni wearing the same white one Elías had on in the previous photo.

His brother had added a message:

"Here we are in Houston, Tuco and the Coyote Kid. How are things there? Is Garazi still OK? For our part, we're ready to do battle, with the same winning spirit as the Houston Rockets. Elías is proving to be a brilliant guide. Today he's going to take us to a Thai restaurant."

The sky was immaculately blue, the skyscrapers resolute, the grass green and the orange leaves on the trees joyful. Nothing deceptive about them.

Martín replied:

"Garazi started back at school today. We're fine. How are you all doing over there? Greetings to Elías and everyone else."

The following day, Saturday, Martín returned home from a trade union meeting at seven o'clock in the evening and found the orchid on the draining board in the kitchen.

There was a note from Ana on the table.

"Martín, I watered the orchid and left it there to drain. Put it back in its usual place. We'll be home by nine. Garazi and her friends want to go and see Odín and I'm playing host."

He changed his clothes and went for a run. He had two hours, enough time to go and come back, shower and make supper.

When, as usual, he walked through the industrial estate, he saw a new poster in place of the one the police had removed.

363

The full name of the owner figured in larger letters now, and the workers were warning him that they would not rest until they had received the money he owed them. "You won't get away with it, you bloodsucker!" He thought "bloodsucker" was a much better word than the one they had used before, "traitor", and this was perhaps something else he could write about in the next issue of the magazine.

He emerged from the industrial estate on to the back road and started running. As he ran, his feet rhythmically striking the ground, his mind drifting, he began to associate the dull pad-pad of his shoes with flight, escape. He was escaping from the cave-like period they had just been through, and from the very idea of the cave, of death, like the mountaineer who steps back from the precipice so that the void will not draw him down and swallow him up. Because death had swallowed up so many: Marta had been swallowed up; Julián too; Garazi had almost been swallowed up, as had Luis at the time of his accident, and now Andoni was in danger of being swallowed up as well.

As Martín got nearer to the hills, he could make out their colours more clearly. They were less showy than those of the horse chestnut trees in the city parks, as if autumn was taking longer to reach them. The sky was full of the signs of evening: the sun hidden behind clouds, with occasional clear patches of sky like greenish-blue silk.

He returned to the village, and, as soon as he reached the square, he heard loud laughter and voices, the chatter of people celebrating something. The red neon sign on the restaurant was lit. He remembered then that it was September 23, the date set for the supper for "ex-combatants". The people in the restaurant were his former fellow prisoners. His first impulse was to go and join them, and he even took a few steps in that direction; instead, though, he thought better of it and headed home instead.

An Alphabetical Epilogue

Words are not like distilled water, without substance, untouched by life and the world. It might appear that a simple word like "needle" refers only to a slender, pointed instrument or a polished steel pin, but you just have to think of Sleeping Beauty, or the needles stored in hospitals and clinics or those you occasionally find in the toilets of bars, to realise how far-reaching and profound a word it is. And what about books? All those hundreds of pages, thousands of words, millions of possible combinations . . . They not only suggest a virtual infinity, like the one we imagine when we gaze out over the waves from the sea front, but a real infinity, an exact copy of all possible realities inside and out, both worldly and spiritual.

Given the boundless nature of books, we tend to simplify and reduce their various themes to a single sentence. "It's about war," we say; "it's about a crime of passion", "it's about an expedition to the South Pole"; that, of course, is just a manner of speaking, because, in this sub-lunar world of ours, we have to find *some* way of speaking about it, trusting that there might actually be such a thing as eternal life and that there, in paradise – in the new Byzantium or wherever – we will have more than enough time to hold long, subtle conversations. Until then, let us make do with themes. Among the many themes in this novel, I would put friendship first.

AMICITIA – FRIENDSHIP

Elías and Mateo are friends, so are Eliseo, Caloco, Celso and Donato; ultimately, Martín and Luis, as well as being identical twins, are also friends. And what about the married couples? Marta and Julián? Martín and Ana? Perhaps a close marital bond does not quite fit into the same category, and yet it is clear that at certain stages in life, especially once youth is a thing of the past, the qualities that matter most in a happy marriage are trust, loyalty and *suavitas*, the three virtues which, since Roman times, have always been associated with friendship.

"A happy marriage? A contradiction in terms!" says a malevolent being slipping in among my thoughts and appearing right at the beginning of this alphabet-cum-epilogue. I will ignore him. It is time now to talk about another A: Aldo.

ALDO

The Italian writer Aldo Buzzi and the American-Romanian artist Saul Steinberg wrote to each other regularly for more than fifty years: New York–Milan, Milan–New York. In 2002, Buzzi published a book containing all of Steinberg's letters to him. I first read this correspondence one very cold winter, in a room where someone had lit a wood-burning stove, and that warm atmosphere seemed the perfect match for the feelings provoked in me by those letters.

In one letter, Steinberg mentions a person who, it seems, was his only friend in America, saying: "I can talk to him in the best possible way, that is, I can reason, by which I mean that I invent while I speak." And that is perhaps the great value of friendship: it both transforms and improves conversation.

The Malevolent One might say: "As regards the friendship between Buzzi and Steinberg, I would just like to remind you of the distance separating them: New York–Milan, Milan–New York, almost 6,500 kilometres. A French writer once said that you can live in the same part of town as your enemy, even in the same house, but if you don't want to spoil a friendship, it's best if your friend, male or female, lives in another city or on another continent."

I will ignore that remark too and move on to the letter B for barracks.

BARRACKS

There were only men in the barracks. At least that's how it was when I was there. Of the thousands of memories I have of military service, the one that comes to me now is the morning when, before leaving the barracks for the last time, a dozen or so soldiers who had just been discharged, embraced each other, weeping: "Goodbye, my friend! Let's hope we meet again!" I wanted to include that memory in the second chapter, but other more dramatic ones got in the way and so, in the end, I left it out.

CHACARERA

According to the dictionary, the *chacarera* is a popular Argentinian dance for couples, its rhythm moving between three-four and six-eight time. Accompanying himself on the guitar, Atahualpa Yupanqui sang Cachilo Díaz's last *chacarera*, a beautiful song entitled "La humilde". I listened to it constantly while I was writing this book and one day, the computer, unbidden, made a leap of its own and led me to a performance by Yupanqui, in which he compared life to a river flowing over stones. And because of all the difficulties encountered by Elías, Martín, Luis, Eliseo, Marta, Daisy or Garazi, the book took its title from that image: *Water over Stones*.

DONATO is the fifth letter, ELISEO the sixth,
FRANCO the seventh.

FRANCO

Before *Water over Stones*, this book had another title: *The Soldier who Called Franco a Bastard*. I even wrote part of the text and

369

the introduction: "This novel arose out of a chance observation, or, rather, two chance observations. First, a magpie I saw flying up from a field of potatoes onto an electricity cable. Then, a very odd couple: a mastiff, measuring almost one metre tall and weighing sixty kilos, being followed by a very obedient goose . . ." Both incidents reminded me of an experience I had in the barracks at El Pardo. I was one of the soldiers posted to the Communications Unit, and, together, we had decided to give shelter to a magpie chick, which, true to the theory of zoologist Konrad Lorenz, immediately accepted us as its parents. One of our group wanted to teach it to say "Franco's a bastard!" and would repeat this phrase over and over to the bird. "Once he's learned to say it properly, we can sneak over to the palace one weekend and release him there in the hope that he flies straight up to Franco's window." For various reasons that idea came to nothing. Years later, it occurred to me that the story could take a different direction and I imagined another title: *A Magpie Faces the Firing Squad*. By then, however, I had other geographies in my head, and not just that of the barracks.

GEOGRAPHIES

"Geographies" is a term used by pedants, and yet it has started to gain currency, and many now use it when discussing literary islands invented by the likes of Thomas More, Jonathan Swift and Robert Louis Stevenson. It would be more appropriate to speak of "territories" or "spaces" since, for a writer, an island could just as easily be a barracks, a school or a hospital.

Let us then consider the human mind, for there is no island vaster. When travelling purely inside her mind, the Augustinian nun Anne Catherine Emmerich managed to go as far back as the age and, yes, the geography of the Great Flood, an experience that allowed her to provide precise details on the construction of Noah's ark. Similarly, on several separate occasions, Bernadette Soubirous had the vision described in the first chapter of this book, *uo damo abillado en blan dab'uo cinturo bluo e uo roso iaoumo sus dados pé*, that is, "a lady dressed in white with a blue girdle and with a yellow rose on each foot". So, there's nothing very unusual about that, nothing that should surprise any of us when we think of our own dreams. Proust wrote: "When we have gone to sleep with a maddening toothache, we are conscious of it only as a little girl whom we attempt, time after time, to pull out of the water." Kafka would not have been surprised either; he apparently told the theosophist Rudolf Steiner that *The Metamorphosis* as well as other stories of his, arose out of the images that came to him in that zone between sleeping and waking.

And what can one say of landscapes and characters visible only under the influence of alcohol or drugs? For they are infinite and can help the writer to a deeper understanding of his main theme, which is life itself.

At this point, the Malevolent One might exclaim: "You pedant! You pretentious fool! So much name-dropping!" And he might well be right, but we should take no notice of negative comments made by those who would never speak well of us anyway. And so, with a hop, skip and a jump, I leap into another of the spaces mentioned in the book.

HOSPITAL

On the way to visit one of my daughters in hospital, when she was still very young, for some reason I suddenly remembered a *bertso* – an improvised song – composed in 1926 by Lucasia Teresa Elicegui on the death of her son: *Nun zera gure seme Inazio Mari, Evaren umietan ez zera ageri . . .* "Where are you now, my son, Inazio Mari? Not a sign of you to be found now among Eve's other children . . ." I almost fainted when I found that song in an anthology edited by Antonio Zavala and learned that Elicegui's son had died of peritonitis, the very reason my daughter had been hospitalised.

The whole of I is dedicated to that young boy, INAZIO, Inazio Mari.

Apparently, most of the songs, the *bertsoak*, that his mother wrote for him have been lost. The third one began thus: *Bizitza eta eriyotzan gabiltz zure billa, gure izatia ortan bukatu dedilla* . . . "We search for you in life and in death, and that has become our whole existence . . ." Some people are amazed that spiritual refinement or intelligence can exist in a rural, often illiterate society, but they're just snobs, lacking both spiritual refinement *and* intelligence; they see the world as a pyramid in which they, surprise, surprise, are at the top. Their world is, in fact, the unbearably noisy Island of the Braggarts.

JABALÍ – WILD BOAR

Of the many animals who appear in my books, perhaps the one that appears most frequently is the *jabalí*, the wild boar. It appears in *Obabakoak*, in my children's story *Shola and the Wild Boar* and in two chapters of this novel. Once again, this has its roots in personal experience: growing up in the hills of Gipuzkoa, we children were always terrified we might meet a wild boar on a narrow path or in the middle of a wood. They occupied the place that, in another age and in other places, had been the domain of the wolf. However, as with the word "needle", the significance of the word *jabalí* goes beyond the merely anecdotal. We should remember, for example, that when Ulysses finally returns to Ithaca, his old nursemaid only recognises him when she sees the scar above his knee, from a wound inflicted by a boar when he was out hunting as a youth.

The rural world has many connections with the classical world. The wild boar is a case in point, as are shepherds. Eliseo is a shepherd, like the shepherds in Bethlehem and those whom Virgil knew.

Some writers return over and again to the same subjects and the same themes. I am one such writer. Animals, family life – always in twos: two friends, two brothers, twins – empty landscapes, mines, engineers, political struggles, torture by police, mental labyrinths, songs, gags . . . There is nothing premeditated about this. You only notice these constants when you look back on your work, or when some benevolent person momentarily forgets his benevolent nature and unexpectedly gores us with his malevolent tusks: "Oh, no, not another wild boar! You're obsessed!"

LUCÍA

I was surprised to arrive at my parents' house one day and find Lucía standing outside at the front door. I had not lived in the village for years and had never had much to do with her or with her family. I found out why she was there when I spoke to my father: she was after money, the loan systematically denied her by the banks, who knew the root cause of her financial problems – betting and gambling. "She goes from house to house, but who in his right mind is going to lend her money?" my father said. He simply could not understand such absurd behaviour and, in the face of something apparently so illogical or unreasonable, he merely shrugged.

Less than a year later, I learned that Lucía had been found dead in a river, and that event came back to me when I was writing the chapter about Antoine. I thought I could somehow link her story with that of the chemical engineer. I even wrote the first line of that story: "She was one of those women who looks prettier with short hair." But I could not find a way of telling her story without also appropriating her misfortune and so, not wishing to be a thief, I merely had Marta tell her story.

MOVEMENT

Everything moves, especially the most weightless of things, that is, whatever ends up being transformed inside our head into words, gestures, tones of voice, expressions. We are movement plus a little matter.

NORWICH

On the floor of Norwich Cathedral there is a convex mirror, about one metre square, that reflects the whole interior. If you take your time and look closely, you can even see the decorative bosses in the vaulted ceiling or the angels in the stained-glass windows. This could be a handy metaphor – as it has been traditionally – for what books are aiming to be: mirrors which, on a small scale, gather all the details of a universe. The problem is that universes are never still, and if mirrors are to resemble books, they need to contain moving images too. Another problem, which is actually an advantage, is the shifting light, the iridescence. Like glass – like a magpie's plumage – words can take on different colours, unexpected connotations. When I wrote the third chapter of the book, "Antoine", I suddenly found myself in Agatha Christie territory, and in the fourth chapter, "Luis's accident", in the world of the Western.

OBJECTS

Theory has no need of objects, but fiction does, because objects speak to what we know through our senses. There could be no Sleeping Beauty without a needle, and this novel could not exist without various types of cap, Swiss Army knives, crossbows, cars, televisions, cigarette packets, orchids . . .

POETRY

The reader will find in this novel the poetry of particular poets, Baudelaire for example, but also, or so I hope, the poetry I intended to be an integral part of it. I try to include poetry in everything I write, even in invisible form, like the nutrients in fruit.

And the Q is a Chicano group who called themselves
QUESTION MARK & THE MYSTERIANS.

During my adolescence, I listened over and over to their hit song "96 Tears". I was going to include the song in this book, but, as I got to know Lieutenant Garmendia and his girlfriend Vicky, I decided there was no way they would listen to such a dramatic song: "You're gonna cry ninety-six tears, you're gonna cry, cry, cry . . ." Then I thought of Herman's Hermits, whose pop sound was just right for young ladies who, in the 1970s, strolled about in El Pardo while their fathers went out shooting pheasants, or, in the case of Vicky's father, elephants, lions and antelopes in Africa.

ROMANIAN

I again open the book in which Aldo Buzzi collected Saul Steinberg's letters, and I come upon Steinberg's thoughts concerning his mother tongue. All of them are negative. *New York, April 23, 1991*: "Romanian I've always ignored, even as a twelve-year-old boy: a language of beggars and policemen . . ." But with age comes a problem: his mother tongue has not gone away, it is still there inside him, and sometimes returns to him when he is searching for the right word. *New York, April 23, 1991*: "Certain Romanian words, never used for seventy years or more, leap forth from some corridor of memory." *New York, November 21, 1994*: "I've heard the sad news about Cioran, the Paris-based Romanian who I saw some years ago, one of those who refused to speak

Romanian. Now, at eighty-two, he is afflicted with Alzheimer's, he speaks Romanian only, his childhood tongue (in every sense)." Steinberg takes up the subject again in 1998. *Amagansett, July 7*: "I telephoned one classmate, a doctor who emigrated to Los Angeles twenty years ago. He speaks only Romanian (which I now realise with some alarm, has made a strong comeback in my own mind, perhaps like Cioran, who recalled only Romanian during the last year of his life)."

The first image that comes to me on reading these confessions by Steinberg is that of a man fleeing his own shadow; the second – remembering how much he loved his cat Papoose and the wonderful words he dedicated to her when she died – that of a cat trying to detach herself from her own tail. And yet those metaphors are of no help in understanding his attitude to his mother tongue, perhaps because I was brought up to love my own mother tongue, *Euskera*, the Basque language. Fortunately, I then stumbled across what Steinberg wrote to Buzzi in a letter from 1989. *New York, January 4*: "I have what they call phantom pain, that is, strong and specific pain in the big toe of a leg amputated years before. It's the pain of the Romanian patriot I was until the age of 8 or 10, when the anti-Semitism of the place made me renounce that fucking nation forever, remaining faithful only to the landscape, the smell, the house on Strada Palas."

I finally understand and, as soon as I read those words I saw in my mind's eye the countryside around the village where I was born, the paths, the moss, the Zelatun spring, Mount Hernio. The sound of their names echoes in my head: *bidiak, goroldiyua, Zelatungo iturriya, Hernio mendiya* . . .

I have now reached S, which stands for SEIKILOS, a man who some two thousand years ago erected a tomb for his wife Euterpe. Seikilos leads me to the T of tomb.

TOMB

Near Ephesus, the Scottish archeologist William Ramsay found a marble column bearing an inscription: "I am an image in stone. Seikilos placed me here as a long-lasting token of undying remembrance." The epitaph is followed by a brief song, complete with words and musical notation, lyrics and music: "As long as you live, shine; have no grief at all; life exists but briefly, and Time demands recompense." It is apparently the oldest complete musical composition.

In the rather dark piece I initially wrote as an epilogue to this book ("A lecture on life and death in the cemetery of Ugarte"), one of the speakers, Dr Mortimer – Morty to his friends – tells his audience about a similar case to that of Seikilos, then suddenly declares: "Tell me, all you people listening to me now, where does love come from? From life? Not at all. Life destroys love. On the other hand, death attracts it, strengthens it, even revives it sometimes. The same could be said of songs, poetry and art in general. Death, my friends, reigns supreme!" On hearing this, his assistant Parko – alias Parky – utters a pathetic cry: "And yet, and yet, death gets such a bad rap. Is there no justice in the world!"

On the advice of some friends, I replaced that piece with this alphabet. Where were life's defence lawyers, who could have disproved the theory of that Morty-Parky duo? That text is still on my computer awaiting revision.

UNIVERSE

I did, I think, know the old world, the one that Lucasia Teresa Elicegui knew even more profoundly. It was inhabited by people who, thinking they were being rational and realistic, described – to the anthropologist Julio Caro Baroja, for example, in the mid-twentieth century – the night flight of some deceased relative or the thefts committed by a neighbour after he or she was changed into a cat. However, in rural areas all over the world

– in Asteasu, in Santa María del Campo, in Viandar de la Vera, in Brissac – everything, apart from those seemingly picturesque anecdotes, was radically different. As L.P. Hartley wrote: "The past is a foreign country, they do things differently there." In their vocabulary you would look in vain for words like "depression", "class struggle", "Maoism", "Holy Week in Cancún" or "Black Friday".

In this novel, Ugarte is a place located on the frontier between the old and the new universe, unlike Obaba, which belonged entirely to the former. In Ugarte – and this is a point I want to emphasise – they have television.

No sooner had I written this section on U than I heard someone titter. It was the Malevolent One, who had again slipped into my mind. He waved his hands around a lot like a guest on a TV chat show and said: "Some people believe in witches, others in Mao Tse-tung. What's the difference?" I innocently defended myself, like a child: "You obviously haven't read the book. Witches used brooms to fly on. Maoists, as Mr Emerald Green so rightly says, used them to sweep away reactionaries." The Malevolent One, like all malevolent beings, is entirely subject to his own malevolence and continues to sing the same old song. I, however, turn my back on him and move on to the next letter.

Voyage

All the world's languages allow for absolute statements: this or that; to be or not to be; you're either for me or against me; there are two kinds of people, those who leave and those who stay; there are two kinds of literature, the good and the bad . . . I allow myself to offer my own bold statement: "There are two kinds of literature, the kind that offers you a voyage around the outside of something (Scandi-noir murders, high passions in the Chinese court of the twelfth century, lethal acts of betrayal on an American campus . . .) and the kind that requires the reader to make a further voyage, a voyage inside him or herself."

W

I have read very few books that are as complex as George Perec's *W, or the Memory of Childhood*. When I first read it, it seemed to me merely eccentric, nothing more. It was strange that an author, even an Oulipian, should mechanically alternate, chapter by chapter, an autobiographical text about childhood with an allegorical one in the tradition of the fable.

In the book, W is an island on the other side of the world, near Tierra del Fuego. It is also home to a utopia, an Ideal City devoted to sport, a perpetual Olympic Games, inhabited by men interested only in winning.

As for the childhood described by Perec, it is a ghostly affair, marked by events that memory cannot retrieve: "I have no childhood memories. Up to my twelfth year or thereabouts, my story comes to barely a couple of lines: I lost my father at four and my mother at six; I spent the war in various boarding houses in Villard-de-Lans . . ."

When, some time after that first reading and when I had more experience of life, I picked up the book again, I saw that the autobiographical chapters were inextricably linked with the allegorical ones. Olympia is Auschwitz and Auschwitz is Olympia. The dream turns into a nightmare, or into something even worse, because there is no waking up from this dream-nightmare. I also had the impression that Perec, in perhaps prophetic mode, was thinking that, in some future time, all paradises would become concentration camps. It was, then, a very powerful, far-reaching book. Even better, it was full of the jovial wit that characterised the work of other members of Oulipo.

Many writers try to follow the path of realism, hoping to capture life in all its facets. Many others take a different path and try to make their stories into metaphors of something more general. To judge by *W or the Memory of Childhood*, and by the authors mentioned in the novel – Verne, Flaubert, Leiris, Queneau, Kafka,

Roussel – Perec was trying to follow both paths, to be both realistic and metaphorical at the same time.

A poem by Raúl González Tuñón, later made into a tango by the Cuarteto Cedrón, says this: "All the thieves are in love with Rosita, and so am I." I would change this slightly: "All the writers are in love with Perec, and so am I."

X as in SONNET IN X

I was stationed in a barracks, namely the First Engineer Regiment in Madrid, doing a training course for radio telegraphists. One morning, I picked up a telegram from a desk and noticed that, on it, someone had written out a poem in French. The first line read: "*Sonnet en X, par Stéphane Mallarmé*". As the Rubén Blades song says: "Life is full of surprises, full of surprises is life . . ."

YIDDISH

On December 25, 1911, Kafka wrote a brief note in his diary, in which he talks about plays put on in Yiddish, saying that literatures written in minority languages can prove both strong and fortunate, because they immediately acquire a political value. I cannot comment on the exact meaning of his words, because I do not know the context. On the other hand, I do know something that Kafka could not have known: the fate awaiting those who spoke Yiddish in the Europe of that time.

Z

At the beginning of this alphabet, I said that words are not like distilled water, without substance, untouched by life and the world. I would like to take that simile further: the same applies to individual letters and individual sounds. I am talking about my own experience and about the letter Z. For a long time, I could only pronounce Z as it is pronounced in *Euskera*, as a sibilant S rather than the TH of Castilian Spanish, and so I stood out like a sore thumb at school whenever I had to say out loud any word that included a Z: "*raíz cuadrada*" ("square root") or "*zapatero a tus zapatos*" ("a cobbler should stick to his last"), or even my real name, José Irazu. I became the class *Billage*, and for me the letter Z took on very negative connotations. Then, during the time I lived in Bilbao, things changed. Andone Gaztelu, who, with her sisters, ran the Txoko-Eder restaurant, also noticed the way I pronounced Z, and whenever she saw me come through the door, she would hiss: *zzzzz* or, in my pronunciation, *sssss* . . . Andone – like the Miss Martiartu character who appears in Juan Carlos Eguillor's comic strips – was a larger-than-life figure, as likely to start heaping insults on the ruling classes as she was to burst into a rendition of an old Vizcayan lullaby. You were never bored in her company. I certainly wasn't. Her hissing freed the letter Z from all its negative connotations.

More Zs: those in the word "zigzag". This epilogue, which has now reached its end, this commentary on the novel, may appear to have followed a straight line, like any orderly alphabet, but there is nothing straightforward about it. It has zigzagged all the way from start to finish.

BERNARDO ATXAGA was born in the village of Asteasu in 1951 and still lives in the Basque Country, writing in Basque and Spanish, usually translating his own novels from Basque into Spanish with his wife Asun Garikano. He writes novels, short stories, poetry and songs, and his work has brought him many prizes, including the 2019 Premio Nacional de las Letras Españolas for his complete body of work. Novels such as *Obabakoak* (1992), *The Accordionist's Son* (2007), *Seven Houses in France* (2009) and *Nevada Days* (2013) have won critical acclaim in Spain and abroad. His books have been translated into thirty-two languages.

MARGARET JULL COSTA has translated works by novelists such as Eça de Queiroz, José Saramago, Javier Marías, as well as poets such as Sophia de Mello Breyner Andresen, Ana Luísa Amaral, Mário de Sá-Carneiro and Fernando Pessoa. She has won various prizes, including the 2009 Premio Valle-Inclán for Atxaga's *The Accordionist's Son* and the 2015 Marsh Award for Children's Fiction in Translation for *The Adventures of Shola*. In 2013 she was invited to become a Fellow of the Royal Society of Literature and in 2014 was awarded an Order of the British Empire for services to literature.

THOMAS BUNSTEAD was mentored by Margaret Jull Costa in 2011 as part of a scheme run by the British Centre for Literary Translation. He has gone on to translate novels by writers such as Agustín Fernández Mallo, Maria Gainza and Enrique Vila-Matas, had shorter-form translations appear in publications from *Granta* to The *Guardian* and *VICE*, and twice been a winner of PEN Translates awards. His own writing has appeared in the likes of *Brixton Review of Books*, *LitHub* and *The White Review*, and he is currently a Royal Literary Fellow, teaching at Aberystwyth University (2021/23).

The text of *Water over Stones* is set in Galliard.
Book design and typesetting by CC Book Production.
Manufactured by Versa Press on acid-free,
30 percent postconsumer wastepaper.